THE BATTLE
OF WAGRAM

THE BATTLE
OF WAGRAM

Gilles Lapouge

Translated by John Brownjohn

NEW AMSTERDAM
New York

First published in the United States of America in 1988 by
  NEW AMSTERDAM BOOKS
  171 Madison Avenue
  New York, NY 10016

by arrangement with Century Hutchinson, Ltd., London.

First paperback published by New Amsterdam Books in 1990.

Library of Congress Cataloging-in-Publication Data

Lapouge, Gilles, 1923 –
    [Bataille de Wagram. English]
    The battle of Wagram / Gilles Lapouge : translated by John Brownjohn
        p.   cm.
    Translation of : La battaille de Wagram.
    ISBN 1-56131-013-1 (paper, acid-free paper)
    1. Wagram, Battle of, 1809—Fiction. 2. Napoleonic Wars,
    1800–1814—Fiction I. Title
    PQ2672.A63B3813 1990   90-40444
    843'.914—dc20   CIP

10 9 8 7 6 5 4 3 2 1

This book is printed on acid-free paper.

To Frédérique Garro

'Of the noteworthy incidents to which the battle of Wagram gave rise, I must cite an engagement fought by two regiments of cavalry which, though serving in the opposing armies, belonged to the same colonel proprietor, Prince Albert of Saxe-Teschen. The latter had married the celebrated Archduchess Christina of Austria, Governor of the Netherlands. As one who held the title of prince in both countries, he owned a regiment of hussars in Saxony and another of cuirassiers in Austria. Each bore his name, and, in accordance with the practice common to both countries, he appointed all the officers in either corps. Austria and Saxony having lived in peace together for many years, whenever Prince Albert had an officer to place, he would appoint him at random to whichever of the two regiments had a vacancy, with the consequence that members of the same family could be found serving, some in Prince Albert's Saxon hussars and others in his Austrian cuirassiers. By a lamentable and most extraordinary mischance, both regiments were present on the battlefield at Wagram, where, animated by a sense of duty, they made it a point of honour to charge each other. Strange to relate, the cuirassiers were routed by the hussars.'

'Memoirs of General Baron de Marbot,'
Mercure de France, Vol.I, p.491

1

Professor Schwarzbrod's appearance belied his nature. His nose was on the large side, not to say huge, and his ears were no better. They were crude, convoluted and exceedingly hairy – in fact Schwarzbrod was a hairy professor altogether. The eyes above his beard were grey and lustrous, but cold.

His body did nothing to improve matters. It was lanky and ungainly, with a permanent stoop. When walking, Schwarzbrod seemed to be commanding his shoes to follow him. They jibbed and balked, compelling him to tack in the manner of a ship beating to windward. When autumn came and mist invaded Vienna, he would forge his way through the whiteness waving his arms. Spring suited him better. Once the Prater and the Graben were in flower he would often pause and, very gently, prod shrubs with the ferrule of his stick. If pink and white petals cascaded on to his loden, or a few gnats should take wing, he watched them with his mouth agape, looking vaguely idiotic.

Back home at his house in Donnergasse he would subside into an armchair, sighing, and chew on the long blue china pipe that habitually trembled between his lips. Often he would stir abruptly, as if, unbeknown to him, springs were at work inside his gross carcass. He seemed disheartened, or even incensed, by the incurable twitching of his hands. He would stare reprovingly at his fingers, then lay his pipe on the arm of the chair and give a kind of smile as if to pardon his wayward joints. Schwarzbrod's acquaintances used to say that he had too many teeth and a superabundance of bones. This might have been why his students nicknamed him 'the Triple Kneecap'. He knew this, and it hurt him, since it must be said that, despite his uncouth frame and features, Professor Heinrich Schwarzbrod was a sensitive man. His face and heart were out of tune. His threatening visage concealed a tender, timid soul, but there it was: even when he was serene and happy, his eyes hurled thunderbolts.

Schwarzbrod used to mock himself in the hope that this would help. 'I'm an impostor,' he confided to Countess Pietranera. 'Almighty God – not that he exists – gave me the wrong body. He must have inserted me in someone else's hide.' And, pretending to sympathise with that someone else: 'Somewhere or other, perhaps in South Australia or Calabar, there must be some poor fellow whose mild appearance in fact disguises a black, belligerent soul.' He further accepted responsibility for any misdeeds this unknown associate might commit under cover of his angelic countenance. 'If I were devout I would go and wash away the fellow's sins in the confessional at St Stephan's. The trouble is, I'm a freethinker. If you promise not to tell His Majesty Francis II or his myrmidons, dear lady, I might even admit to membership of a masonic lodge.' He guffawed into his enormous hands. 'So I really can't become a convert simply in order to guarantee eternal life to a blackguard whom I've never set eyes on, and one who has filched my rags and tatters into the bargain. That would be too much of a chore. Imagine having to memorize prayers, plumb the secrets of the Holy Trinity, dip into Origen, make a habit of crossing myself before the shrines of the Virgin and St Anne – no, I'm sorry, I don't have the time.'

Little Countess Pietranera specialized in the defence and glorification of Schwarzbrod. She used to say that one need only dust him down and he shone like crystal. She also said that he should be viewed inside out. 'He's as uncouth as a wild boar with all that beard, I admit,' she simpered, 'but you'd be quite amazed if you could see the inside of him. He's lined with silk, believe me.' She sometimes invoked other fabrics – taffeta, satin, or cashmere – and pouted in her inimitable way. Countess Pietranera was a blithe, kind-hearted, simple soul – a charmer of the first order.

It was in vain, futhermore, that the professor lavished courtesies on people. They were nullified by a hard mouth with drooping, purplish lips, so that his kind words were mistaken for hypocrisy or execration. He was an admirable man. Many appreciated his good faith, candour and sense of fun, but he still inspired fear. Whenever a new batch of students presented themselves at the university, where he held the chair of botany, his introductory address was received in terrified silence. Anyone else would have welcomed such student decorum, but he was dismayed by it. Forlorn and lonely, he gazed down from his desk at the fifty bowed heads, vainly striving to catch someone's eye. He would much have preferred a few surreptitious whispers to this collective catalepsy, and his principal concern for the next few weeks would be to hearten his audience.

The countryside served him well at such times. He organized excursions and took his youngsters off into the gentle hills of the Vienna Woods between the Danube and the Triesting. He enlisted the colours of late autumn on his side, the gurgle of stream and fountain, the placidity of grazing cattle. White clouds bounced helpfully from hill to hill like toy balloons and pine trees formed enchanted forests in miniature. When the wind dropped, shepherds' pipes made elfin music.

Heinrich Schwarzbrod used this landscape as a trap or lure with which to tame his students. He would seat himself on a big rock and tell them fanciful tales. Like everything else on earth, he said, rocks, wind and river water are born, grow old and die. He questioned his pupils on the age of the wind. If a gentle breeze wafted between two hillocks, ruffling the stalks of the ripe grain, he would pronounce it a young wind, a 'green' wind born that morning and fresh as a new-laid egg. On other occasions, by contrast, when a sudden autumn storm blew up, he would claim that it hailed from the time of Attila or Emperor Maximilian . . .

His pupils played their flutes, examined pistils and stamens, picnicked in clearings, unpacked wicker baskets containing black bread and meat pasties, lettuces and apples, immersed pitchers of white wine in springs to cool. If peasant girls came nosing around, there was always some student willing to scrape away at his fiddle and strike up a jig. The professor himself would then dance wildly with terrified shepherdesses. The students enjoyed these

3

outings, which stripped away their master's forbidding exterior until his amiable soul showed through.

Schwarzbrod was renowned for his lectures. His teaching had undoubtedly enhanced the prestige of the Viennese school of natural philosophy, which had flourished from 1750 onwards under Ludwig Kochel. Schwarzbrod had consorted with the finest scholars of his age – men such as Georges de Buffon, Philibert Commerson, Joseph Banks, Captain Cook's naturalist, and even the great Linnaeus. His knowledge was encyclopedic and his reputation extended far beyond the university precincts.

He had given his name to two previously unknown botanical varieties. His thesis, which had found favour when published in 1770, examined the amours of bees and flowers. How had two creatures belonging to different kingdoms overcome their differences sufficiently to share the celebration of their nuptials? By what feat of ingenuity had flowers learned to imitate sexual organs of a conformation so acceptable to bees and butterflies that those insects were deceived? Schwarzbrod appreciated the inexhaustible beauty and universal splendour of the physical world. He did not, however, believe that the marriage between insects and flowers had been divinely instituted. Buffon had already touched on the idea of evolution, and Schwarzbrod contributed a little grist to the same mill.

In the beginning, he explained, it was the wind, and the wind alone – albeit haphazardly and wastefully – that had brought about the fertilization of flowers. Once the fateful insect/plant encounter took place, however, as it one day did, Maia's veil was rent asunder and two disparate species crossed the unreal divide. It was a somewhat daring theory, but Schwarzbrod had buttressed it by citing other, analogous examples from nature. He had read in La Condamine, for example, that the forests of South America contained a fruit, the babassu nut, whose shell was so hard that, once on the ground, it could never have germinated without the aid of a rodent, a kind of squirrel, which gnawed a hole in its integument and thus made germination possible.

His thesis had not proved popular in scientific circles,

4

and Dr Pipermuntel of Vienna described it as crackbrained and ridiculous. But Schwarzbrod's ideas had been seized on by poets. Goethe was reputed to set store by them. Bernardin de Saint-Pierre, director of the Jardin du Roi at Paris, had written Schwarzbrod a nice letter in which he spoke of Providence, and Novalis referred to the Schwarzbrod theory in his notebooks. Schwarzbrod himself had since retreated from it somewhat. But although he poked fun at it, calling it a whimsical 'scientific diversion' similar to his lectures on the age of the wind, his reputation steadily grew. He was now in widespread demand as a lecturer, and learned societies frequently invited him to address their symposia.

These invitations were a torment to him. When confronted by an audience of strangers, Schwarzbrod was stricken with mental paralysis. He would somehow contrive to gabble his way through the text of his paper, grimacing fiercely the while, but question-time was a nightmare. The simplest query flummoxed him completely. His mouth would open, but barely a sound emerged. His hearing was so blurred by fear and embarrassment that all he could detect was a vague murmur, and he would end by blurting out some totally random reply. If questioned about the liliaceous order, for example, he was quite capable of responding with a dissertation on radicular development. His lectures were hugely successful because of their unpredictable outcome.

Functions of this nature exhausted him, and he would return post-haste to his house in Donnergasse, feeling like a regiment in full retreat. His wife Greta, a very gentle creature, sympathized with his distress and respected his subsequent silences. Although he resolved to decline all such invitations as the years went by, a few of his more ill-disposed or simply waggish university colleagues persisted in extending them, simply in order to enjoy his confusion. To the malicious among them, these moments were exquisitely pleasurable. An integral part of the old scholar's legend, they came to follow a ritual pattern. Schwarzbrod would listen politely to the invitation, his head a little on one side, fiddling with the bridge of his spectacles. He puffed at his pipe and was careful to register delight by flaring his nostrils. He accepted as a matter of course – indeed, he looked positively overjoyed and shook his colleague's hand before bounding up the steps of the auditorium maximum, ostensibly on his way to deliver his next lecture, in reality to camouflage himself among his students. But his fellow academics knew that the performance was not yet over. A final act lay in store – the best, so said the experts – and no one would have missed it.

As soon as the class was over, Professor Schwarzbrod would jump to his feet, dash up to the colleague who had invited him, and stammer out an apology. How absurd, how thoughtless of him! It had entirely slipped his mind that he was already bespoken on the day appointed for the lecture: a family reunion, a friend's wedding, a visit to his Aunt Mathilde. It was remiss of him, truly remiss, but what could he do? The colleague would profess to understand and would look indulgent, but by now Schwarzbrod couldn't stop. He would leaf through his diary next, to show that some appointment had indeed been entered on the fateful day. Knowing how hypocritical he looked, Schwarzbrod nevertheless heaped one excuse on another, furnishing details so minute that his lie inevitably took on lurid colours and became grossly overweight.

Dr Ulhue, Schwarzbrod's assistant and former pupil, a mischievous young man with a big white dome of a forehead and a mouth like a pike, made fun of this idiosyncrasy. 'Our worthy professor never tells outright lies, for all that,' he would say. 'Did you know that he forces himself to attend the imaginary functions he records in that famous diary of his? That's how he came to marry Greta Strelhein.'

Ulhue would be pressed for details.

'Well,' he would go on with feigned reluctance, 'the privatdozent at Brünn had asked him to preside over a symposium, and he'd wriggled out of it by pleading a cousin's betrothal. But he became so wretchedly entangled in his own excuses that the other fellow inferred that

Schwarzbrod would in fact be celebrating his *own* engagement on the day in question. This being momentous news, it spread like wildfire and came to the ears of Schwarzbrod himself, who didn't hesitate for an instant. He hurried round to the Strelheins, whose daughter Greta he'd been courting for years – but so discreetly that no one, not even the admirable Greta herself, had noticed the fact. This time, driven by necessity, he formally requested her hand in marriage. The family welcomed him with open arms and made preparations for the betrothal. Schwarzbrod was galvanized. In addition to having overcome his shyness, he even contrived, at very short notice, to get the engagement celebrated on the very day of the famous symposium at Brünn.

'So there it was. For once, he'd acted like the man his face proclaims him to be: with dash and daring. In short, like a hussar who charges the foe, captures a redoubt and wins the Maria Theresa Cross – and all because his squadron commander has booted him in the breeches.'

When in really good form, Dr Ulhue, who prided himself on his wit, would improve on this yarn. Smoothing the furrows from his broad white brow in a way that portended some sarcastic remark, he claimed that Schwarzbrod had only begotten his first-born, Marie-Josèphe, in order to escape a conference at Eisenstadt. At that point Ulhue would pause for effect, stroking his wispy fair hair. 'And do you know what he was due to lecture on? You'll never guess: fertilization in the lamellibranchiate order!'

It was always the same with Dr Ulhue. He was neither stupid nor spiteful, and he respected his old professor, but he often overdid things. In this case his joke was more foolish than cruel. Schwarzbrod's elder daughter, Marie-Josèphe, was a sickly girl and not entirely normal, but Ulhue had no inkling of this because the old man never mentioned his misfortune.

In reality, Schwarzbrod's behaviour was fairly logical. Being a person who brimmed with scruples and abhorred lies, he made it a point of honour to manufacture truth out of falsehood. If he had pleaded a university engagement at

Graz, for example, he really would go there and present himself at the premises of the learned society or local academy, ready to perform, and when he found the place locked up, would then consult the diary in which he recorded his appointments, and, though no one was watching, scowl at himself. Thereafter, purged of guilt, he would seize the opportunity to explore the neighbourhood and collect botanical specimens or go in search of butterflies. By thus harnessing the dreadful results of his shyness to his love of scientific research, he spared himself a wasted journey.

Was it to escape such a commitment that he went in April to Baden bei Wien, south of Vienna on the road to Italy, or was he genuinely planning to botanize there? Whatever the truth, his wife Greta would never have given him away, still less Marie-Josèphe or Ursula, his younger daughter. The month of April being favourable to students of nature, the proprietress of the Three Nails Inn at Baden, who knew Schwarzbrod of old, was not surprised to see him alight from the Vienna mail coach complete with all his naturalist's paraphernalia: the ultravoluminous loden equipped with extra pockets, the big green felt hat, the long Hungarian walking stick with the knob that could be unscrewed to accommodate seed specimens, the magnifying glasses and pincers, the gaudy umbrella in which he collected tiger beetles shaken loose from bushes, the gaiters and gargantuan boots. Schwarzbrod was thoroughly at home at the Three Nails. He repaired to his usual corner room above the fountain, which afforded a view of the Hoher Lingkogel hills in the west and, at right angles to them, the ancient church of St Helena.

He smiled, as he did whenever he entered this room, because the towers of St Helena's were reproduced in a bad painting situated above the fireplace between a crucifix and a picture of St Catherine, as if the landlady were anxious to preserve at least a likeness of the church in the event of its destruction by fire, earthquake, or war with the French. Schwarzbrod sometimes teased the old woman. 'My dear madam,' he would say, 'you're imprudent. You should also adorn the room with a depiction of the room itself, in case it's destroyed, plus a second picture depicting the first . . .'

The room was bare and chilly, with pale blue wash on the walls. The professor stretched out on the red quilted feather bed. It was as plump as an angel's buttocks, if angels could be said to have scarlet buttocks. He experienced a momentary happiness, a modicum of contentment, for despite his infatuation with the human race Schwarzbrod's shyness was such that he tasted true peace of mind only in his moments of solitude. When darkness fell he listened to the sound of the wind competing with that of the fountain. Framed by the window, the branches of the chestnut tree outside were filled with stars.

He awoke early. The mornings at this time of year were cold. Now that the stars had disappeared, the chestnut's branches looked very black and glossy against the green sky. A fat, almost flaxen sun rose, still so feeble that it failed to cast shadows. Far away to the west a supple line scored the sky like a whiplash, defining the mountains' white crests. Then the nearer hills, rust-coloured with an admixture of gold, shed their mists. Dressed and peering through the garden fence a little later, Schwarzbrod discerned the beginnings of the stony path he would soon be ascending to the pine forests in search of flowers and butterflies. By degrees, colours settled timidly all over the slopes. Stealthy as little cats, they sought out their places everywhere save on the dense, dark stain of the pinewoods and, above them, on the grey felt flanks of the mountains with their accumulations of bluish rocks and snow. Down in the meadows, between bulky brownstone farmhouses, red soil showed through the shimmering green of fresh spring grass. Towards nine o'clock the landscape came to a halt. Motionless now, it would await the return of night, yet it was still incomplete. Whole sections of it remained blank, pale and blank, as if someone had run out of paint. The various components of the countryside were ill-knit. It seemed that a wind of moderate strength would have scattered them in all directions.

Schwarzbrod made his way down to the dining-room, where he breakfasted on a bowl of milky coffee and some bread and myrtleberry jam in the company of a corpulent Tirolean merchant with red side-whiskers. The merchant, who was off to sell hobnailed boots in the mountains, betrayed great excitement. The war, as he saw it, was at the very door of the inn. The French were advancing at break-neck pace, so imagine how many hobnailed boots they must be wearing out, the rogues! The fat man was reliably informed that they had already covered a lot of ground since routing Heller at Mantua. That army of madmen marched faster than news could travel, so their vanguard might already be lurking behind the churchyard wall or prowling the banks of the Triesting – who could tell? It was also rumoured that Bonaparte had played a dirty trick on the Austrians: instead of heading straight for Leoben and Baden, he had outflanked the Emperor's forces by way of Vorarlberg.

Schwarzbrod was not much interested in the art of war. He had long since ceased to follow the progress of those exasperating soldiers who had stormed around Europe for so many years, smashing everything in their path. This time, however, the situation seemed critical, so he tried to reassure the merchant. He said that Austria had been in worse straits before now, that the gorges of the Semmering Pass were no joke, and that Bonaparte, if he tried to outflank the Austrians by way of Vorarlberg, would get a drubbing from Archduke Charles. As for the French soldiers, he concluded, he wasn't so very frightened of them. After all, they hailed from the birthplace of the Rights of Man.

The merchant looked appalled. He blocked his ears with his fists, which were covered with sandy hair, stuffed a piece of bread into his mouth, and chewed it vigorously. Then he leant warningly across the table, casting apprehensive glances in every direction, and contrived a thin little trickle of a voice.

'I didn't hear you, Professor. Lips sealed, ears stopped, eyes shut! The three wise monkeys, if you get my meaning.

The district is swarming with police and informers. All the janitors in Vienna submit reports to the police. I don't approve, but I can understand why. We're in grave danger. The common folk of Vienna are demanding that every Jacobin be shot, didn't you know? Suspects are being hunted down, and there are men, be they only freemasons, who are capable of saying anything. Still, they haven't enjoyed the right of assembly since poor Josheph II died. You remember what happened to that Hungarian, Martinovics, the unfrocked monk who was conspiring against the monarchy? Crrrk!'

He drew a finger across his throat with such speed and ferocity that Schwarzbrod looked idly for traces of blood.

'The French guillotined our emperor's sister, don't forget. As for your Bonaparte, did you know that Robespierre was his protector? They even threw him into prison when the Terror ended. Still, as I said, Professor, I don't like trouble. Lips sealed, three wise monkeys, that's me – and in any case, I'm sure you were joking. No one would suspect me, but you, Professor – I advise you to put a bridle on your tongue. Trust no one. Those fellows are lurking everywhere.'

Schwarzbrod, who took fright so readily, was really a most courageous man. He would rather have faced a squadron of cuirassiers than the frills and furbelows of a Viennese drawing-room. The fat merchant's boots would soon be encasing the blistered feet of the soldiers of Napolean's Army of Italy, he reflected. Was there anything to choose between French feet and Austrian?

'I don't see where these spies of yours are operating,' he said. 'There isn't a soul here apart from the two of us, our inoffensive landlady, an equally innocuous-looking young lady whom I saw arriving last night, another two guests, and a yellow dog at least twenty years old and almost stone-deaf. Even if it heard something it wouldn't remember – it's senile.'

The merchant stroked his nose in annoyance. He didn't care for the old man's pleasantries, but he parted from him cordially notwithstanding. Schwarzbrod had an enjoyable day. He went for a long walk in the mountains and caught several butterflies: red admirals like frail wisps of red, black and blue silk, and even, from its perch on an elder twig, an apollo with a bright red corslet and glassy wings. Very early the next morning he saw the merchant again. Someone hammered on the door of his room, he asked what the matter was, and was told that 'they' were coming. He said he didn't understand. 'Soldiers!' he was told. 'French soldiers!' Thinking of hobnailed boots, Schwarzbrod rose at once. He donned his socks, shirt and white gaiters and hurried downstairs to the dining-room. Gathered there, vociferating wildly, were all who had slept at the inn: the proprietress, two maidservants and an ostler, the apparently harmless young woman, the fat Tirolean, and a brace of commercial travellers. Two cats were hiding under the table. The elderly dog was barking at random, but lethargically and without conviction – more from a wish to be a part of things than anything else. The apprehensive boot merchant, too, was giving tongue. It was he who had sighted the soldiers. He spoke of his discovery gloatingly, as if he had come across some precious stone or nugget of gold.

'It's a longstanding habit of mine to rise very early – I like to take a stroll before dipping my bread and butter in my coffee. And so, this morning, I climbed the hill with the ruined castle on its summit. I looked down at the plain – one can see across it for several leagues – I looked, and what did I see? Innumerable figures on the move. And then I realized that they were a large body of mounted men, a column of cavalry, all armed to the teeth. I could see the sunlight glinting on their helmets and breastplates. They were approaching from the direction of Mödling. "Great heavens!" I said to myself.'

Schwarzbrod pointed out that Mödling lay to the north of Baden, half-way to Vienna, whereas Bonaparte's army was approaching from Italy, in other words, from the south. That set the merchant off again.

'He must have outflanked us, Professor, I told you as much yesterday morning. Bonaparte has hoodwinked us once more. He's a three-card trickster. He moves so fast, his ace is never where one expects.'

Then, in a more didactic tone:

'That's strategy for you. We expect him from the south, heading for Leoben and Baden. We guard the Semmering Pass, but no, he goes and catches us in the rear. Perhaps he came by way of Sankt Pölten. He must have occupied Vienna, and now he's swinging round to gather up all the fish he's trapped in his net.'

The young woman looked glum. Through the window, peasants could be seen hurrying past the inn. They were carrying pitchforks on their shoulders as if they had taken it into their heads, several years too late, to join the French Revolution. Everyone in the dining-room trooped after them. The proprietress of the inn, who suffered from dropsical legs, was left behind. The dog sat beside her, gazing into space and emitting a wheezy bark from time to time. The young woman had started to weep. One of the commercial travellers, a tall, scrawny youth, set off at a great rate and was rebuked by the fat Tirolean. Heroics were out of place, he said. They were merely going in search of news. Bonaparte was very easily provoked. This was no time to nip his soldiers in the calf.

2

As one man, Baden's peasants and artisans were converging on the Plague monument in the Hauptplatz. Its middle-class citizens, on the other hand, preferred discretion to valour. After peering out of their windows, they popped back in and barred their doors. A slamming of shutters could be heard. The bourgeoisie of the little town curled up like a plump woodlouse and pretended to go back to sleep, hoping that the war was merely a nightmare. Daybreak itself must have been an illusion, and if all concerned went back to bed and shut their eyes another night would fall at once, dispelling the misapprehension. Meantime, a party of scouts from the hotel, commanded by the dealer in hob-nailed boots, had set up an outpost to the north, on the Mödling road. They were kicking their heels and growing bored when a lookout raised the alarm from his perch in a plane tree.

With a clatter of hoofs, some soldiers came trotting into town preceded by a mounted band. Everyone got ready to be frightened and to feign courage, but the soldiers who debouched into the Hauptplatz were the wrong colour for that. Their dolmans were sky-blue and their pale green shakos bore the two-headed eagle of the Dual Monarchy. There had been a mistake: these cavalrymen appeared to be Austrian, not French. At their head, on a prancing tawny charger, was a distinguished-looking officer adorned with brandenburgs, epaulettes and other embellishments. The dragoons' accoutrements glinted in the sunlight as their horses lolloped along. Clearly victorious, they were never-theless as clean as newly-minted coins, and the townsfolk marvelled that they should look so spruce after such slaugh-ter. Their boldly nonchalant demeanour and the discipline prevailing in their ranks doubled the market value of their victory over those brigands known as the Army of Italy. Cheers rang out and the bells of St Helena's improvised a Te

Deum. Shutters swung back noisily, yellow and black flags sprouted from every window, and women showered the soldiers with armfuls of spring flowers. Reassured, the burghers of Baden peered through their curtains. They were soon milling around the square and venting their spleen on the absent Jacobins.

The Prince of Liechtenstein, as the braid-encrusted officer proved to be, produced a long clay pipe from his cartridge pouch and silenced the band with a peremptory gesture. Then, rather than mince his words, he flatly announced the unwelcome truth: the battle wasn't over; it was yet to come. War was no public festival and bandits weren't to be defeated by blowing fanfares. The prince levelled a ferocious finger at his dragoons. Many of them, he said, were destined to die, others would develop gangrene, and a fair proportion of those sturdy legs would, by tomorrow, be floating in buckets of blood. Eyes, too, would be torn from their sockets. The dragoons received these words impassively, but their effect on the bystanders was immense. Liechtenstein, tossing his pipe portentously from hand to hand, sent for the municipal authorities. They hurried up, their obsequious manner suggesting that they were about to make submission to a conqueror and present him with the keys of the town. Without dismounting, the prince informed them that his men would be quartered at Baden until such time as Bonaparte's intentions became clear. He explained that Baden had been chosen, not only for its strategic position, but because it had once been the cradle of ancient Austria. Roman legionaries had come to treat their rheumatism on the site of the present Kurpark as early as the second century AD. 'It was to this very spot, gentlemen, that Marcus Aurelius's heroes came to recuperate after crushing the Marcomanni on the Marchfeld plain, when Vienna was still called Vindobona!'

Having delivered this harangue, he took the burgomaster aside, together with the senior magistrate, the chief of police, and the parish priest of St Helena's. The military situation, as known to headquarters, was as follows: Bonaparte had occupied Leoben, twenty leagues to the south, and his forward elements were prowling the gorges of the Mur. Archduke Charles's forces were intact, fortunately, and valiant local insurgents were harassing Moreau's armies in the Tirolean highlands. That monster Bonaparte had sent the archduke a preposterous letter in which he had the effrontery to pose as an angel of peace and request an armistice. This Vienna had granted, but the Austrian High Command, scenting a trick on the Corsican's part, had proclaimed universal conscription – a *'levée en masse'* after the fashion of the *'soldats de l'An II'*. The prince stressed these phrases. It clearly amused him to use revolutionary terminology, but his blending of *noblesse oblige* with the common touch rendered it impossible to gauge his true political feelings.

He said that his squadrons of cavalry were only the vanguard of an imposing force that had poured into the capital, as though by magic, at the call of His Majesty Francis II. The entire city had risen in arms against the Usurper, even the workmen – even the students. The first contingents would be entering Baden later that morning. Others would continue to arrive at intervals until nightfall. Officers were to be billeted on the townsfolk, horses stabled in farmers' cowsheds, in coach houses, in warehouses, if need be in schools. Where the rank and file were concerned, Baden would have to manage somehow. The Kurpark was spacious, and cantonments would be erected on its fifty-three hectares. All food and lodging vouchers would be honoured. At this point a plump officer astride a plump horse interrupted in order to emphasize that although the French armies might have dispensed with their commissariat and were living off occupied territory, in other words, picking it clean, Austria's armies observed the rules of war and refrained from despoiling local inhabitants.

More troops presented themselves at the gates of Baden throughout the day. The new arrivals were products of general mobilization, civilians hurriedly tricked out as soldiers. The carpenters' corps – fifteen hundred joiners flourishing the banners of their guilds – cut quite a dash. The students, on the other hand, were a sorry sight.

16

Accoutred in odds and ends and almost entirely ignorant of how to handle a musket, they looked as if their mouths were ill designed to bite the end off a cartridge. The march from Vienna had exhausted them. With their haggard faces and dusty, untidy uniforms, the might have been the survivors of some disastrous engagement. 'Cunning devils, those students,' Schwarzbrod remarked to the weary young woman, hoping to make her laugh. 'They enact a rout before they've even seen the enemy or fired a shot. That way they put defeat behind them. When they go into action in earnest they'll emerge victorious.' The young woman was polite enough to smile.

The professor, who had installed himself in one corner of the Kurpark, saw the boot merchant depart without regret. He was entertained by the colourful commotion around him. He had spotted a sizeable party of students from the Academy of Fine Arts, who were singing patriotic songs. Their commander, a sculptor named Schmutzer, unfurled a yellow and black flag emblazoned in gold with the year 1683 to commemorate the defeat inflicted on the Turks by Count Starhemberg with the aid of John III Sobieski, King of Poland, Duke Charles of Lorraine, and the Blessed Virgin. 'Over a century ago,' Schwarzbrod murmured sadly, as if recalling some childhood memory.

He also spotted several of his own students, and was amazed to see that even Otto Apfelgrun had turned up, looking as unkempt and yet elegant in the army as he did in town. Schwarzbrod was unable to fathom what the young man could be doing in such warlike company – unless, of course, he was observing all this turmoil as he would have studied hawk-moths, red admirals or toads. Schwarzbrod liked Otto for his nonchalance. Everyone liked Otto, yet he was as shy as Schwarzbrod himself. He charmed people as naturally as others turned chair legs or sold vegetables; he charmed young and old, men as well as women and girls, and his friends used to say that he would have captivated a blind man.

Otto was popular at the university. No one could claim to have ever seen him studying, though he always came first in examinations. His classmates held a competition to see who could catch him *in flagrante*, but no one won it. At nights, instead of burning the midnight oil at his desk, Otto went strolling in the Prater with other young people of fashion. He frequented the open-air cafés of Grinzing and Leopoldstadt. He wore his beauty casually, unthinkingly. That was why he set so many romantic hearts aflutter. His shyness, his absent-minded gaucherie, his almost imperceptible stutter, his unaffected laugh, his green, rather wistful eyes – all these attributes entranced the girls. His friends aped him, imitated his mannerisms and repeated his witticisms. When Otto, embarrassed by their mimicry, tried to restyle himself, the others vainly strove to follow suit. In his presence, the most voguish young man-about-town felt bucolic and ill at ease.

He was cheerful by nature but given to fits of melancholy. Once, the previous summer, Schwarzbrod had discovered him seated by himself at a table in the Café Hugelmann, watching the jolly comings and goings of the boats on the Danube. Men were bathing naked in the river while bright, creamy clouds drifted across the August sky. When Schwarzbrod joined him Otto spoke earnestly of Spallanzani, who had refuted Needham's and Buffon's theories of spontaneous generation with the aid of hermetic flasks. He also mentioned that his father, Lawyer Apfelgrun, was in a poor state of health. He could never forget that old men had once been little boys.

Some of Otto's veiled remarks had led Schwarzbrod to suspect that he was indifferent to the Dual Monarchy's claims to greatness and not entirely convinced that Voltaire and Rousseau were villains, but this was no more than a vague impression. In warlike times like these, the Viennese were wary of speaking their minds; they preferred to manoeuvre in no-man's-land. Although the effect of Francis II's censorship and secret police – of all that vile machinery the wheels of which turned in darkness, crushing opposition and excavating a sulphurous, murderous, fetid replica of the capital overhead, with its beauty and gaiety, frills and fripperies – might be to stupefy the stupid, it stimulated the subtle. Schwarzbrod himself was outspoken, to be sure, and did not have to weigh his words. He enjoyed that privilege on account of his fame and eccentricity, but he was careful never to compromise his conversational partners by ramming his views down their throats, so he now refrained from driving Otto into a corner. The young man's equivocal remarks had related to Francis II's system of censorship. 'Did you know,' Otto had said, crumpling his napkin as he sipped a glass of plum brandy, 'that rhetoric was born the day Hieron, the tyrant of Syracuse, resolved to deprive all his subjects of the right of free speech? That was when two of them – we even know their names: Corax and Tisias – invented rhetoric. So you see, Professor, it's possible that literature, art, and even mathematics owe their genesis to tyranny. It may be that man himself originated with the first despot, to wit, Almighty God.' Schwarzbrod laughed but didn't pursue the subject. Besides, Otto had gone on to speak of other things, and his fable might equally have commended censorship or condemned it.

Schwarzbrod was making his way across the Kurpark to Otto when an encounter in the arcade blew him off course. The rector of the university, a professor of medicine named Ouarin, had spotted him and was advancing with outspread arms. Ouarin had exchanged his black frock coat for a colonel's uniform – white breeches and collar, crimson piping – which admirably suited his energetic personality, though the collar, being a trifle tight, had empurpled his naturally congested face. Ouarin adjusted his eyeglasses, threw back his head, and scanned his colleague closely.

'Well, well,' he exclaimed in amazement, 'if it isn't our distinguished naturalist!'

Schwarzbrod emitted a neighing laugh, only to wince with annoyance when the rector seized and embraced him. Imprisoned in crimson piped arms, he felt he was about to be brandished like a sword, or at least like a banner, but the moment soon passed.

The rector's surprise was understandable. Schwarzbrod had an appalling political reputation. Rumour branded him a freemason. It was said that, some years earlier, he had attended a social function sporting the red and gold robe, Turkish slippers and oilcloth cap formerly affected by Joseph II, the imperial philosopher and freemason, the 'crowned revolutionary' who had perpetrated so many blunders with the best of intentions. But the bulk of this tittle-tattle concerning Heinrich Schwarzbrod emanated from that bumblebee Dr Ulhue, and even if the story were true it might have been one of those façades behind which the painfully shy are prone to shelter. The anecdote was an old one, in any case. If teased about the royal encyclopedist, Schwarzbrod would extricate himself with one of his verbal pirouettes. He earnestly contended that Joseph II had not reigned in vain. The monarch had left his mark on history by promulgating an edict for the protection of the nightingales which the music-mad Viennese had made a habit of imprisoning in cages. At this point, Schwarzbrod's equine laugh would ring out. 'Besides, I find it a pretty notion, his idea of burying the dead in shrouds rather than wooden coffins. It preserves the forests, and after all, when you consider what becomes of us in the end . . .'

Thus Schwarzbrod's presence among the April volunteers caused quite a stir. Apparently he had not only enlisted in the patriotic militia; he had also arrived in Baden before everyone else. Ergo, he must be well-informed. There were some who surmised further that his butterfly-catching expedition was a cover for some hazardous secret mission carried out on orders from very high up, possibly from the Ministry of Police, possibly – why not? – from the Hofburg itself.

Could the worthy old gentleman be a cunning impostor? Could his grotesque entomologist's attire be a kind of uniform: the *laissez-passer* of a secret agent? His provocative behaviour, his professions of atheism, his neighing laugh, his outsize nose, his grey beard, his ugly face – all these things might be a snare and delusion, intended to camouflage the fearsome tasks he performed for the preservation of the monarchy. The suspicion grew that he had come to Baden to satisfy himself that his men were doing their duty properly, and, at the same time, to hunt down Jacobin traitors in the pay of France. It was an open secret in Vienna that Bonaparte sent bilingual officers ahead of his armies, disguised as peasants or itinerant merchants, to apprise him of Archduke Charles's movements. Schwarzbrod was doubtless keeping these spies under surveillance. Ten to one he was better informed than the Prince of Liechtenstein himself. His daring and dissimulation became a source of wonder. He spread terror. He was reputed to be merciless. His face was the face of a fiend. If he had cast poor wretches into the monarchy's deepest dungeons, why should he not additionally have supervised their torments through a spy-hole? Anything was possible these days. The man had blood on his hands.

Rector Ouarin towed Schwarzbrod towards the Kurpark's bandstand and invited him to mount it with the other professors, one of them being a historian named Watteroh, who had never made any secret of his Jacobin sympathies. Ouarin embarked on a harangue designed to galvanize students assembled below.

'Others elsewhere have heard the dread words . . .' He broke off, distracted: the Kurpark's broad expanse was alive with noise and movement. The cavalry horses in the background, which had been tethered all day in front of the handsome buildings whose ironwork, acanthus leaves and two-headed eagles they appeared to be munching, were growing restive. They snorted and whinnied at the least excuse, fidgeted and pawed the ground. Dragoons in fatigues were restraining them by main force. Up on the bandstand, Rector Ouarin abandoned his attempt to obtain silence and resolved to cut his speech short. He repeated his preamble in a stentorian voice.

'Others elsewhere have heard the words "The Fatherland is in peril!" Sublime words, but they were uttered in France and in an unworthy cause. Today, although not uttering them, the Dual Monarchy is nevertheless acting on them!'

So saying, Ouarin displayed Professors Watteroh and Schwarzbrod to all, thrusting them against the wrought-iron balustrade like a pair of trial exhibits.

'Masters and pupils, friends! We have all, without exception, heard the call, the plaintive summons of our native soil, the pulsing of our martyrs' blood. In time of trial our differences are effaced, our peculiarities become fused like dissimilar metals uniting in the torrid crucible to form a potent alloy.

'Here is one such metal, namely, Professor Watteroh. I must tell you that this metal was, for a long time, Jacobin. But Dr Watteroh is also, when all's said and done, a historian. He knows full well that our country was chosen by Providence to be a shield and buckler against barbarism of all kinds, from Charles XII to the Prussians and Turks – nor do I forget the threats of Louis XIV. Today, when revolution comes knocking at our gates, when Gallic butchers menace our homeland with fire and sword, when scoundrels usurp the name of soldier, this Austrian historian, rather than write history, has resolved to make it!'

Everyone applauded. Ouarin called for silence. The tumult died away.

'And here we have another metal: Professor Schwarzbrod! Only a few weeks ago, our botanist was craving indulgence for the Land of the Rights of Man, as it is antiphrastically termed, and paying tribute to Messrs Voltaire and Rousseau. Today, Professor Schwarzbrod has exchanged his butterfly nets and herbals for the warrior's sword. I cast you, in your turn, Comrade Schwarzbrod, into the Fatherland's furnace, and already I see you melting on the fiery hearth of our resolve. Dr Schwarzbrod preceded us along the invader's line of advance, the ancient road still flanked by the milestones of that purveyor of civilization, Marcus Aurelius. We shall respect his secret. Defenders of the monarchy must not neglect the virtues of Laconian reticence.'

Schwarzbrod was panic-stricken. Once again he regretted the physique so unkindly bestowed on him by fate: his commanding stature, the lines etched into his sombre countenance, the curling grey moustache – all these were once again betraying him. As usual, his embarrassment only made matters worse by lending him an epic mien. He anxiously drew himself up, looking stiff and stern – every inch a hero -- and failed to stammer out a single word. The crowd mistook his panic for grim determination. If he remained mute it was because he was fulfilling his role as a soldier, and soldiers, whether uniformed or no, preferred deeds to words.

As ever in such cases, Schwarzbrod inwardly sought refuge in self-mockery. 'Here I am, transformed into a metal,' he told himself. 'I'm to be melted down without delay. They're going to appoint me a colonel and a patriot, adorn my head with a crested copper helmet like those of Marcus Aurelius's legionaries. I'll be given a breastplate, too. I wouldn't put it past them to stick a gun in my hand and decorate me.' Somewhat consoled, he embroidered the picture still more. 'They'll end by displaying me at the Arsenal, in the Army Museum's showcases, surrounded by a hundred thousand muskets and cannon. On Sundays, family parties will pay three thalers for a peek at me.'

Towards evening, when the thunder of French cannon had utterly failed to make itself heard, peace descended on the town. The volunteers prepared their supper. Rows of tents were pitched at various points in the Kurpark. Orderlies loaded their officers' field chests on to creaking ox carts and headed for the mansions and patrician residences in the Hauptplatz or Rathausgasse, troopers led their horses off to makeshift stables. Couriers turned up at intervals from Mödling or Vienna, mounts lathered with foam, puce faces seeming to apologize for their belated arrival.

Schwarzbrod had taken leave of Rector Ouarin with a muttered, incoherent excuse, more or less adding up to the one word 'students'. The rector winked discreetly to signify his connivance, his acceptance that Schwarzbrod's official duties required him to go and spy on his flock. It should none the less be said that Ouarin's admiration of his colleague was tempered with a hint of resentment. It rankled with him to have been taken in for so long by a fraud like Schwarzbrod. Worse still, however much of a patriot he was, Ouarin disliked it that the old rogue should trade on his students' affection in order to denounce and betray them.

Camp fires were kindled here and there. Uproar broke out in the bivouac occupied by the students of Romance languages when a spark ignited their flag. The sculptor Schmutzer, who was close at hand, leapt forward to save the square of silk. He had no doubt whatever that one of the 'humanists', as he scornfully characterized them, had chosen this means of advertising his revolutionary sentiments.

Chickens, piglets and rabbits were put on to roast. Big cast-iron cooking pots dangled over the embers. The Kurpark was redolent with horse dung, cabbage and potato soup, leather, dust. Girls in peasant costume, but wearing their best black jerkins and colourful aprons, distributed flowers among the students. Casks of Mur wine were broached. Officers issued a multitude of contradictory orders. The academics' behaviour contrasted sharply with the rigorous discipline of the Liechtenstein dragoons. The professors took their work seriously but were unaccustomed to it. A dozen of them, having swathed themselves in green army greatcoats like a military engraving come to life, were conferring around a large map, though the development of a 'strategy', as they termed this unfamiliar branch of science, was much hampered by the wind's persistent efforts to blow the map away. A student lit the conclave with a lantern unearthed in some stable, while a master from the Academy of Fine Arts sketched the scene for posterity. Fatigue parties tramped to and from the fountains in the square, fetching water in a clangorous assortment of cans and drums. Meanwhile, grim-faced sentries kept watch on the glacis surrounding the town.

Late in the afternoon, one of these sentries raised the alarm, or rather, reported the approach of reinforcements, and another squadron of cavalry came riding down Germergasse. The sun, which was sinking behind the mountains, just had time to light up their breastplates. The cavalrymen gave one concerted flash and then went out. Their mounts advanced at a curious trot, almost on the spot, like horses undergoing dressage at the Spanish Riding School on Sunday mornings, and everyone grasped that this was a sup-remely well-trained body of men. The colonel of the new-comers, who were cuirassiers, gave an order and extended his riding crop at arm's length. His squadron came to a halt so splendidly, with such a clatter of hoofs and jingle of curb chains, that the restless crowd froze. It was as if the colonel's word of command had instantaneously hyp-notized the notaries' clerks, maidservants and shopkeepers who had been milling around beneath the banderoles and multicoloured paper streamers a moment earlier. The horses panted noisily, but the cuirassiers' mounted band reduced even them to silence. Still mesmerized, all Baden looked on as a score of musicians struck up Ludwig van Beethoven's *Song of Farewell to the Citizens of Vienna*, which he had recently composed at Schönbrunn's request.

When the last notes died away, Schwarzbrod – now among the students – leaned over and remarked to Otto that Haydn, too, had been upset by Napoleon's advance through Carinthia. The old composer, who was now said to be at death's door, had written a superb *Missa in tempore belli*. Intrigued by the spectacle confronting him, Otto listened with only half an ear. He was staring at the colonel of cuirassiers. For someone experiencing his first military campaign, he had been fortunate indeed. The battle of Baden was turning out to be a regular bag of tricks. Having begun by finding the world's most peaceable man, his beloved Professor Heinrich Schwarzbrod, amid the fire-eaters of Baden, he had now discovered that the colonel of cuirassiers was, quite simply, a woman! Although he could not discern her face very clearly, her pose conveyed vanity. She sat her horse so erect that her back was arched, and the cuffs and revers of her bright scarlet tunic were trimmed with sable – or otter, he would have to consult Schwarzbrod on that point. Lace frothed at her throat. Her face was almost hidden by the black peak of her shako, but her hair, Otto saw, was as fair as his own. It stirred whenever her charger fidgeted. Now that dusk was falling, torchlight struck sparks from the tracery of aiguillettes and fourra-gères adorning her breast.

Otto gave Schwarzbrod an inquiring glance. The professor stared back at him quizzically and let out an anxious whinny of laughter, which he promptly suppressed as befitted the solemnity of the occasion. He then observed in an offhand tone that women had long played an essential role in war. The armies of Europe had always teemed with women: female sutlers, soldiers' wives and mistresses, and, last but not least, prostitutes. He cited a number of celebrated French *cantinières* such as Pauline Fourès, whom Bonaparte had almost married in Italy the day he learned of Josephine's escapades; Reine, the *vivandière* of the 69th, La Lasajus, Mère Fromageot, and Catherine Béguin of the 14th Light Horse. In Italy Bonaparte had decreed that prostitutes be smeared with soot to deter them, but without success.

'I ask you,' demanded Schwarzbrod rhetorically, 'on what moral grounds should they have been treated so? If men may legitimately murder other men, why should those poor creatures be penalized?' He next pointed out that female captains of war were not unknown – Joan of Arc, for instance, or Penthesilea, queen of the Amazons, or Louise of Mecklenburg, wife of Frederick William of Prussia and colonel proprietor of the Anspach Regiment. The fair Louise liked nothing better than to dress up in uniform and trot down Unter den Linden at the head of her hussars, and could anyone deny that Prussia was a warlike country?

'France is a warlike country too,' said Otto, 'but I don't think Bonaparte has any women colonels.'

'The difference, my dear Otto, is that Bonaparte's army belongs to the nation. In our case, under the monarchies, certain regiments belong to colonels proprietor. There you have one result of the storming of the Bastille: from that day forth, France had no more women officers. With us they still exist. You've just seen one such colonel proprietor. Strange, I'd have wagered you knew her. That was Clémence, Duchess of Saxe-Salza, at the head of her cuirassiers. Everyone in Vienna knows her, so I'd have thought that a fashionable young man like yourself . . .'

Schwarzbrod was still annoyed at having been likened to a metal, at having melted so swiftly, at now being confused with all these patriotic imbeciles. He felt an urge to confide in someone, but in whom? Otto was there, and seemed to be surveying the martial commotion around them with the same sardonic detachment he directed at everything else. Schwarzbrod forgot about the duchess.

'Did you hear poor Ouarin?' he asked rather brusquely. 'I could hardly tell him that I'd really come to Baden to catch a specimen of the Typhoeus that has been eluding me for forty years. Is it possible that Linnaeus invented the creature? I can't believe that. You see, Otto, I'm an old fool. I know the Typhoeus like the back of my hand. It's a dragon with three horns on its head – Typhoeus the dragon, son of Gaia and Tartarus. I know it, but alas, I've never seen it. Sadly for Linnaeus, Typhoeus doesn't exist.'

Otto eyed his mentor more sympathetically.

'Do you know what most surprises me about our *castrum*,' Schwarzbrod pursued, 'apart from my own presence here? Yours, Otto. I had no idea – I saw you in quite a different light.'

The young man declared that he, too, was in Baden on Linnaeus's account. He, too, had had it in mind to categorize, distinguish classes, species and subspecies. So he had amused himself by classifying all these soldiers, or rather their uniforms, according to their primary and secondary characteristics. Didn't they, too, like insects or plants, possess corslets, antennae, carapaces, down or fur, and coloration? Yes, that was it: they were an army of butterflies to be pinned to a big, cork-lined box.

'Linnaeus is a military writer at heart. He forms his beetles into armies, but who copies whom, soldiers or insects?' Otto thought for a moment. 'Almost everyone here could be stuck in a box with the exception of your Duchess Clémence. Unless, of course, she constitutes a species on her own, as I strongly suspect. All else apart, she struck me as uniquely arrogant.'

'You're forgetting Louise of Mecklenburg,' Schwarzbrod said with a gravity ill-suited to the conversation. 'Two specimens are sufficient to constitute a genus, and they're not the only ones. There must surely be some arrogant women generals in China. The Princesse de Condé, sister of the Great Condé, led her troops into battle under the Fronde. Even here in Austria, do you know what they used to call the mother of Francis II? *"Mater castrorum"*, but that wasn't enough for her: she dressed up in general's uniform as well. Throw in Duchess Clémence, and we definitely have the makings of a genus.'

'The genus *Diana rotundiformis*,' Otto suggested. 'Diana carried a bow and arrows, after all.'

'But why *rotundiformis*?'

'Your duchess looked a trifle plump to me.'

'She isn't plump in the least,' said Schwarzbrod. 'She's blue-eyed and very beautiful.'

'Really?'

'I know, I know, my dear Otto – people like to poke fun at Duchess Clémence. They lampoon her: "A cuirassier in petticoats', and so on. It's true she resembles a Christmas present wrapped in silver paper, with ribbons and medals everywhere, but if you tear the paper open . . . She may seem vain, but she's shy really. A shade devout for my taste, I admit, and stiff-necked to the point of absurdity, but a woman of merit. I like her. I helped her to write a sentimental herbal, and she plays the harpsichord delightfully. Shall I tell you something else? Her case is quite different from that of Louise of Prussia. Her association with the regiment we admired just now is really an affair of the heart – a kind of love story.'

Schwarzbrod flapped his arms vigorously to warm himself. Otto said nothing. Knowing Schwarzbrod, he knew it was pointless to hurry him.

'A love story,' the professor repeated. 'Clémence's husband, Prince Ernst, stationed his regiment in Vienna – Saxon hussars, tough customers – and the young woman insisted on owning a regiment too. Prince Ernst is a good fellow. Not as intelligent as Immanuel Kant, but very good-hearted for all that. He presented her with those cuirassiers – Austrians, of course. The trouble is that, ever since then, the couple have engaged in – how shall I put it? – military rivalry.'

'The regiment's a domestic bone of contention, you mean?'

'Not the regiment itself, perhaps, but the two of them may be said to settle their differences by force of arms and through the heroism of third parties – by proxy, so to speak. That's why they get on so well together. Broadly speaking, that's how it works. I'll explain more fully later, dear boy. There go the trumpets again.'

The trumpets were blaring from all directions at once, squabbling over the highest notes. Everyone sprang to life again and the Kurpark's broad acres became a brightly shifting kaleidoscope. Otto learned no more about the duchess that night, not that he cared anyway. He ran to join his battalion, contriving to preserve his natural elegance even with one hand clutching the waistband of his baggy breeches, which were far too big for him.

After supper, which was frequently punctuated by old folksongs, most of them herdsmen's and vine-dressers' ditties, the sentries were assigned their posts. Due on guard at ten o'clock, Otto set off at once across the russet and purple hills for the little village of Pfaffstätten, where he installed himself in front of a dilapidated round-tower and lit a fire of vine prunings. Woodsmoke scented the air. To right and left of him, the glimmer of other sentries' fires could be seen. He filled his long-stemmed pipe, less for the pleasure he derived from the tobacco than to warm his hands on the bowl. He had read that Chinese peasants carried quails around to ward off the cold.

It was a peaceful night. Attenuated clouds, fragile as shreds of silk, streaked the sky overhead. A few isolated cries and farmyard noises drifted up from the valley of the Schwechat, mingled with peasant oaths from the nearby village. In the south, towards the Semmering, the hills melted into the sleek, dark night. A sprinkling of lights signalled the presence of other vine-growers' villages. They was thronged with motionless whirlwinds of them, some yellow, some white. The chill wind fanned them into flame like someone blowing on embers. Even the river Schwechat's sunken bed was indiscernible now. The wind was laden with the scents of soil and lush grass, the pleasant tang of late spring frosts.

Otto felt as if he were on the brink of an abyss. The night was a bottomless pit – it gave him vertigo. After a while, when his eyes had grown accustomed to the gloom, a whole secret topography took shape for him, looming up out of the darkness as reflections rise from the bed of a stream after a storm. The stars were very numerous, and the rocky ridges and gulleys below the old tower were coated with milk. A backcloth of windowpanes and sheets of glass had taken the place of the hills, and Otto found himself looking through them into the bowels of the earth, bright as seams of coal. He fancied that, on the other side of those black lacquer mountains, other soldiers – but French ones, and far more formidable than the Baden volunteers – were keeping watch on him, honing their sabres on farmhouse whetstones, rubbing down their horses, cleaning their muskets and priming them. The darkness was so thin, so threadbare, that he would not have been surprised to discern the pullulating Army of Italy through those oilpaper hills. One shot from a blunderbuss would rend the insubstantial landscape apart, and battalions of French soldiers would trample Austria underfoot, disrupt the orderly countryside, sweep away a river or two, a hill or two, and lay waste the vines so neatly arrayed in squares on the sunward slopes. Otto had been entrusted not so much with watching for the approach of enemy columns as with guarding the wind, stars, and night air; with observing the imminent destruction of an ancient paradise, the displacement of meadows, the migration of swallows, the defeat of the winds, otters frolicking in the pools of the Schwechat. When he shut his eyes for a moment, he could see myriads of stars floating within arm's reach like bubbles winking in a river.

3

When Otto returned from his night on guard the soldiers were at their morning ablutions in the Kurpark, plunging their heads into buckets of icy water with a great deal of splashing. Their greatcoats were hanging up to air on ropes suspended between the lime trees. That was when the war ended. Everyone sensed at once that the orderly officer galloping across the park was the bearer of momentous tidings. He wore lieutenant's uniform, and the little that could be seen of the face beneath his gilt-encrusted black kepi, though pink, looked grim and menacing. He lifted his horse over a field kitchen with a twitch of the knees – he was even arrogant enough, heedless of their protests, to soar over a detachment of carpenters seated on the grass beside their piled muskets. Straight as an arrow, he headed for the emblazoned pavilion that served as the Prince of Liechtenstein's headquarters. Stern, inscrutable, and indifferent to the militiamen's shouts, he was clearly at pains to show himself an instrument of fate – indeed, its strong right arm.

Fate proved kind. Flanked by his two aides-de-camp, Liechtenstein walked up to the messenger, glanced at the proffered communication, refolded it, paced briefly to and fro in ruminative silence, and then gave the order to unpile arms: his men were to strike camp. Some of the volunteers panicked in the erroneous belief that Bonaparte was attacking, and that they were about to be sent to their deaths. Contrary to this dire expectation, their officers amazed them by ordering a wholesale return to Vienna. The volunteers' surprise was extreme. The April warriors, those gallant Viennese for whom Beethoven had already composed a lament, had won the war overnight: Bonaparte, it transpired, had signed a provisional peace treaty at Leoben. The Kurpark dissolved into uproar. Huzzahs and bravos went up like fireworks, lingering complacently on the vowels sounds 'ah' and 'oh'. Impassive in the midst of this

31

pandemonium, officers rode around with their gaze directed southwards as if keeping a wary eye on the Corsican usurper at Leoben. The students exchanged slaps on the back, guffawed, jumped up and down. Rector Ouarin declared that Monsieur Bonaparte, on learning of the militiamen's fortitude, had decided to sheathe his claws and negotiate with the Hofburg after all: 'We have vanquished the Invincible with the effulgence of our arms alone!'

The long march back to Vienna, through vineyard, meadow and copse, was completed within the day. The landscape overflowed with colour. The shrines of the Virgin and St Anne presiding at every crossroads were smothered with yellow pansies and dark blue hyacinths, the villages sported flags, banners and crudely painted placards. Peasant girls decked out in red and green ribbons distributed kisses and patted the dragoons' and cuirassiers' horses as they rode by. Innkeepers had set out barrels of wine and baskets of cakes and rolls on their vine-shaded terraces. The countryside was verdant. Cattle garlanded with flowers grazed in the fields. Cheering peasants waved their pitchforks and rakes aloft in distant farmyards and vegetable gardens.

Victory had revived the students' spirits. Yesterday's dejected-looking youths in dusty greatcoats had been invigorated by a night's sleep and intoxicated by the exemplary bearing of Duchess Clémence's white-uniformed cuirassiers, by Rector Ouarin's erudite enthusiasm – in short, by glory. Dishevelled and exhausted on the eve of battle, they emerged from it in radiant, effervescent mood. Everything had changed.

The war, it was true, had been microscopically small – a puny little dwarf of a war. The only casualty was Friedrich Leppardi, who had been kicked by a horse. His left shoulder was adorned with a bloodstained bandage, but his right supported a musket notwithstanding. Although too good a fellow to show off, Friedrich was a young man of mischievous disposition. The local hens were acclaiming the heroes of Baden, he said, and anyone who listened closely could detect that they were clucking in time to Beethoven's anthem. Tomorrow their nests would be found to contain eggs of black and yellow, Austria's national colours. Otto for his part, claimed to have seen a two-headed cockerel in some humble farmyard, presumably a tribute to Austria's greatness and her double eagle, which Viennese cabbies affectionately called 'the chicken'. Rector Ouarin, who overheard this quip, mustered a sour smile. Friedrich, seizing on Otto's notion, pictured a country in duplicate where every tree had two trunks and the giraffes in the park at Schönbrunn were engaged in growing a second neck.

Otto said that he had seen Duchess Clémence that morning, when her cuirassiers were setting off, and that she had two heads and two gilded black shakos like all the rest. Nineteen-year-old lads being not only flippant but extremely vulgar, the marching column regaled itself with obscene jokes. Ignaz Jungen, a little runt from the Archivists' School, declared that he would have preferred a lovely creature like Duchess Clémence to possess two honeypots rather than two heads, though one, he concluded, was a great deal better than none. Friedrich almost choked with laughter at this. Someone else inquired what would become of Countess Pietranera, who must already possess several honeypots in view of all her amorous activities, if that lovely creature were also multiplied by two. Otto laughed wholeheartedly, wondering in passing if Duchess Clémence was really as beautiful as Schwarzbrod had claimed.

The volunteers reached Vienna at nightfall, so their triumph was celebrated on the morrow. The pomp and ceremony with which the Austrian capital welcomed its valiant children was all the more spectacular because their victory coincided with St Brigit's Day, May 1st, so the returning warriors had the benefit of the streamers, floral arches and paper effigies displayed each year on the Brigittenau. Never had Vienna witnessed a May Day as riotous as this.

Contingents fresh from the front took up their positions in Stephansplatz from mid-morning onwards, occupying the entire square. High clergy were arrayed on the parvis beneath the main portal. The cathedral's massive doors stood open, and clouds of incense drifted forth. Hymns rang out. Banners emblazoned with saints in effigy were held on high by monks attired in white, brown, or black. Just as the bishop stepped forward beneath his purple canopy, the light abruptly dimmed. Everyone gazed up at the sky. Veiling the sun were some little cloudlets reminiscent of the puffs of smoke that drift across a battlefield when the artillery begins to pound. Leaning towards his coadjutor, the bishop observed that God's cannon had opened fire, and that, if a battle was in progress, it must be the mute and unseen skirmish between time and eternity. The coadjutor, looking portentous, gave a silent nod.

It was then that the luminaries of the court, with the exception of Francis II himself, streamed out of the cathedral. The Magyar princes earned a special ovation because of their wolfskin pelisses, which called to mind the valiant army on the Empire's eastern marches, brave guardians of the fortresses of the Banat and defenders of Christendom's outermost bastion against those other henchmen of the Antichrist, the Ottoman hordes.

The crowd emitted an ecstatic sigh when the ancient orders of chivalry emerged from the shadows of the nave. Everyone construed their presence as a subtle retort to the iconoclasts – the deists and atheists who had desecrated the churches of France and guillotined so many priests and Carmelites. Robed figures spangled with gold and silver and adorned with plumes, chains and swords, the Knights Templars and Hospitallers of Malta and the Knights of Santiago and Calatrava glided rather than walked, like ambulant statues, probably to convey that immemorial Austria's response to the alarums and excursions of the regicides was a tranquillity and lentitude, almost a lassitude, against which the tide of events could not but break in vain. Confronted by the soldiers of Bonaparte – of the Devil, in other words – who had been ravaging Europe for fifteen long years, the orders of chivalry bore themselves 'like paralyzed sentinels of eternity'. Such was the precise phrase coined by Rector Ouarin when commenting on this spectacle a little later over a bottle of white wine shared with fellow academics at a tavern in the Augarten.

The day radiated well-being. The clouds had dispersed, and all was blue and gold. The next step was to hand out decorations. Every student received a silver medal. That was the best of a bloodless battle, observed old Schwarz-brod, who was standing in the thick of the crowd with his wife Greta: no one having had a chance to perform an heroic deed, rewards must be bestowed on all concerned, cowards included – indeed, he said, today was a crowds' amnesty. It was Schwarzbrod's misfortune to have an extremely penet-rating voice. His remark was overheard by a lady of quality, to judge by her fine blue-black cloak, which was trimmed with fur and had inset panels of red satin aglitter with sequins and gold tassels. She pursed her mouth into a contemptuous smile, opened a blue parasol, and gathered two little girls to her petticoats, muttering something about university professors and freemasons. Schwarzbrod snorted. His wife frowned at him.

At midday, under a steel-blue sky, the Emperor mounted the glacis at Schönbrunn to review the Liechtenstein Dra-goons, the carpenters drawn up beneath their medieval insignia, the butchers armed with long knives in lieu of daggers and using willow switches to drive Hungarian bulls in black and yellow trappings, their horns wreathed in cowslips, the Fine Arts students beneath a banner captured from Grand Vizier Kara Mustapha during the siege of Vienna a century earlier, and the faculties of literature and law – all, in short, who had survived the battle of Baden. As soon as the cannon had thundered forth, a glittering caval-cade traversed the palace gardens and paraded past the Fountain of Neptune. The Saxe-Salza Cuirassiers were led by Duchess Clémence. The spectators were hugely delight-ed, the more so when they spotted, standing at the Emper-or's side, an exceptionally tall, well-built man with an open, honest face: the Prince of Saxe-Salza, waving to his wife. Otto resolved to question Professor Schwarzbrod further on the subject of Duchess Clémence. Little Leppardi had told him that, whenever she was not making war, she busily flouted the proprieties instead. 'She may look prim,' he'd said, 'but the madam colonel of the Saxe-Salza Cuirassiers is no angel . . .'

Vienna's parks underwent an invasion once the parade was over. The Prater, the Graben, the Augarten, Ferdinandsbrücke Island in the middle of the Danube, even the smallest patch of grass – all teemed with families bearing wicker baskets. Flasks of wine and joints of roast meat, chickens and mountains of pastries were unpacked by mothers and their elder daughters and set out on check cloths. The citizens of Vienna deserted their homes and gorged themselves in honour of Bonaparte's confounding. Fiddlers signalled the start of dancing, and girls cavorted with soldiers while their parents, a trifle ungirt and dishevelled, dozed in the shade.

The students strutted around like roosters. Heads high and legs braced, they amused themselves by making the leather of their new boots squeak. At first they feigned indifference, deliberately ignoring the barefoot flower girls, the goats'-milk vendors who ogled them while filling their glasses, the maidservants in their Sunday best – even the pastel-gowned young ladies who sauntered along with flushed cheeks, disguising their excited giggles for form's sake by tilting their lace parasoles or sniffing their taffeta handkerchiefs. Barouches careered through the crowds at a reckless pace, their drivers playfully skimming past girls without actually touching them. Everyone shouted at once, and good humour reigned.

Otto, smoking a long, thin, very black and noisome cigar, strolled the Prater with a handful of fellow Baden militiamen – 'Otto's copycats', as envious fellow students called his little band of admirers. They paused before a booth in which a puppeteer from Leipzig was exhibiting an automaton wearing a huge cocked hat adorned with a red, white and blue cockade. Propelled by some ingenious mechanism, it fell over backwards, emitted a foolish oath, got to its feet, and fell over again. Elsewhere, Tirolean dancers rotated with piercing cries, the girls' heavy skirts whirling high enough to reveal their legs and draw vociferous applause from the bystanders. A showman paraded a poodle in Jacobin costume. A troupe of midgets had attired themselves as soldiers of the Army of Italy. The smallest and most misshapen of them sported a red dolman *à la* Murat, together with ostrich plumes and enormous fake jewels.

Church bells rang with all their might, but they had pealed so often since early morning that no one knew what they portended. Expert opinions were advanced. Priests who were consulted spoke of vespers, and many ladies set off churchwards. Gowns began to wilt, revellers fell forward into their drinks, cymbals clashed for no good reason. A girl as plump and pink-cheeked as a ripe cherry was lamenting the loss of her scarf, and Otto invited her to join him and the female companion already with him, a pretty, flirtatious creature with violet eyes. The three of them strolled off together, talking of trivia. Otto said little; under the girls' admiring gaze he simply held sway. He couldn't have been born of woman, could never have been a child, they felt, yet he was childhood personified: invulnerable, serene and forgiving – the epitome of gilded youth. Friedrich Leppardi, who had joined the party, suggested crossing the bridge to Leopoldstadt, and by late afternoon or early evening – they had lost all sense of time – Otto and his friends were installed at the Café Hugelmann's open-air tables. The sun was setting.

Hugelmann's was filled to overflowing. Word went round that Werner, Kandinsky and Reich were playing a billiards match inside, but the girls preferred to dance on the terrace, as near to the musicians as possible. Otto partnered them in several galops. His mind went back to the day last summer when he had encountered his professor, dear old Schwarzbrod, in this very same vine arbour, and they had talked about Hieron of Syracuse and the birth of rhetoric. It had been swelteringly hot, he recalled, and Schwarzbrod had polished his spectacles and chuckled wistfully to see the fountains of spray sent up by naked bathers as they dived into the Danube. He had a vision of the old man's freckled, tremulous hands.

Paper flags, Russian, British and Austrian, adorned the

coffee-house tables. Boats with lateen sails circled the island like pollen-laden bees engaged in harvesting the clumps of roses on luminous stretches of greensward sloping down to the water's edge. Other flags, but of cloth, flapped limply above the embankments, and if you focused your gaze on the big river's swiftly moving surface the island seemed to be straining at its anchors. Evening had come, bringing its own special melancholy. The sun had set on the St Brigit's Day girls and the sad, shimmering reflection of last summer. When the girl like a ripe cherry invited Otto to a performance of Törring's *Agnes Bernauerin* at the An der Wien next Wednesday, he told her he had a previous engagement. She pressed him, but Otto, with his feet propped on the back of a vacant chair, gaily retorted that people were always arranging to go somewhere together, so it would be far more original of them *not* to arrange to go to the theatre. Then, as he saw how hurt and crestfallen she looked, he regretted having offended his new acquaintance and cursed his eternal flippancy.

Otto shared Schwarzbrod's frequent inability to remember what he liked and disliked. The old professor would order goulash, for example, and remember too late that goulash was his pet abomination. He was as incapable of recalling who had angered him as he was of recalling who liked him – not, he felt sure, that many people could be fond of an old bear like himself. He had once accosted Dr Sweler in the university's auditorium maximum, treating the man with some deference because he admired him, only to be curtly reminded by Sweler that they weren't on speaking terms. Schwarzbrod used to laugh when he told this story, but his mirth was always tempered with melancholy.

Although Otto would never have mistaken goulash for stuffed carp or Duchess Clémence for the rosy-cheeked lass from the Brigittenau, he readily muddled up days and months. Last year's languid August afternoon in Schwarzbrod's company had become confused in his mind with this year's evening in May. Try as he might to separate them, like a child peeling moistened paper off a transfer, shreds of last summer continued to cling to this pellucid May Day evening. The jugs of white wine continued to accumulate on the tablecloth as St Brigit's chilly night wore on, long after the bathers scrambled ashore and the red and yellow sails returned to their berths – yes, there was no doubt at all that the clear, sparkling wine, combined with the exaltation of battle, the smell of gunpowder, and the charms of the two girls, who were silent now, had scrambled his wits. Numerous jugs of Grüner Veltliner had accompanied their dinner of breadcrumbed collops, potatoes *au gratin*, and currant-garnished turnovers filled with cottage cheese. The girls began to shiver.

Fireworks lit up the sky over Mariahilf and the Hofburg. The Stuwers had excelled themselves: fiery fountains gushed, rockets soared, incandescent rats' tails picked out the Emperor's initials entwined with a huge letter B, and the emblem of Duchess Clémence's white cuirassiers could also be discerned in the sky. The Danube resembled a sheet of black glass. On the far bank, a hurdy-gurdy played the same tune over and over again, but very slowly, as if to match the melancholy that attends the close of every festive occasion. The girls departed for their homes in the suburbs beyond the walls, but not before the ripe cherry had given Otto a languishing glance. His lack of response transformed it a moment later into a furious scowl. He wavered, but the girl was as young and unsophisticated as he himself was shy. Besides, he had genuinely drunk a great deal.

Otto Apfelgrun and three other night-owls headed for the maze of narrow streets in the heart of Vienna. They found themselves in a city at rest, a city of shadows, fountains and flowers. A faint breeze came whispering along the labyrinthine alleyways round St Stephan's Cathedral. From time to time a stronger gust of wind would nudge the iron shop signs into noisy motion, and the squawling of cats could be heard. Broadcast by the same wind were scents of jasmine, geraniums and lilac – fresh scents. Otto drunkenly observed that in certain parts of the world jasmine was known as 'Lady of the Night' because it awaited the advent of dusk before dispensing its fragrance. They skirted the Kapuzinerkirche. When they reached the

Apfelgrun residence in the Bauernmarkt, Otto gave his bell-pull a clumsy tug. Friedrich Leppardi, impressed by all the corbels, balconies and bronze grilles, declared that Otto's home was more elaborately emblazoned than Prince Eugene's coat of arms. The bell set off a host of cavernous echoes, but the big oak door had already been opened by a little bird of a woman rendered almost unidentifiable by several shawls. They made their way across an enormous hall, past a wood store the size of a ballroom, and through a series of spacious reception rooms, sublimely beautiful but dilapidated and almost unfurnished, in which scents of jasmine and geranium fought a losing battle with the combined effluvia of soup, dust and mildew. Rats and mice were going about their business in every corner.

Having gained his companions' attention at the second attempt, Otto declared that ever since his childhood, or for twenty years past, he had been watching and waiting for the sun to infiltrate these dank rooms – and although it had so far failed to do so, he refused to abandon hope. As for the old janitress who had opened the door, there was a strong possibility that she had in fact owned the premises ever since Otto's father, who was the idlest lawyer in Vienna and the most assiduous patron of the Wurstelprater, had rashly striven to maintain an illusion of *grandezza* by running up debts.

'If you searched all these corridors carefully enough,' said Otto, slurring his words, 'you'd unearth something other than rats, mould and spiders. There must be servants here and there, most of them very old because they date from the Apfelgruns' prosperous days – the Renaissance, in other words. You mightn't think it to look at me, but I have a music master who taught harmony to Charles V – even, I suspect, to Marcus Aurelius. We also employ a cook, a butler and a scullery maid. There must be others, though, the house is so big – so big, I've never explored it all. I'm sure I'd find a few more domestics tucked away in corners, so give me a little time, my friends. Only last year I exhumed a footman whose sole function it is to carry my mother's prayerbook when she goes to church . . . I should add that it's a prayerbook with a blue velvet cover and a gold clasp.'

Otto paused in the middle of an almost empty room and raised a portentous finger.

'My mother's becoming less and less devout these days,' he said thickly, 'so the footman has less and less work to do. Another few centuries and he'll be doing none at all. The silly thing is, he's not only irreligious but lazy as a lizard into the bargain, so he does his best to undermine what's left of my beloved mother's faith. Stupid of him. She'll turn into a confirmed atheist, and then he'll be out of a job . . .'

After this final attempt to entertain his friends, Otto gave up. They had to take their leave in any case. He stumbled upstairs and flopped down on his bed without even removing his boots.

Towards mid-morning the next day, May 2nd, four policemen rang the bell and hammered fiercely on the outer door with their sword pommels. Otto's mother was informed of their arrival by the old crone in black. She shut the lid of the harpsichord, which she had just opened, intending to play as she did every day at this hour, straightened the mother-of-pearl brooch on her bodice, and went to meet the unexpected visitors. Her attempt to pooh-pooh their demands failed: the policemen were unmoved. Her next recourse was to sob into a satin handkerchief embroidered with flowers. Then she found a bell-pull in working order and sent for Otto. Still pale but looking rested, he appeared wearing grey breeches and a soft silk shirt. The policemen requested him to accompany them. Otto's two sisters stood weeping beside an araucaria in the corner of the hall. His mother entreated the guardians of law and order to think again. Her son must be the victim of some misunderstanding, some slanderous allegation. Had he not taken part in the battle of Baden? Was his shirt not adorned with the silver medal bestowed on him by Emperor Francis II? The senior policeman gave a condescending, knowing smirk. 'Quite so,' he said sagely. 'Quite so – he took part in the battle of Baden.'

Otto was unceremoniously bundled into a black berlin

with lowered blinds. The big horse harnessed to it set off for the jail of its own volition, without human guidance – almost, thought Otto, who seldom took anything seriously, as if it were the beast itself that had decided to imprison him. The convoy halted briefly at the admissions office. From there, having been issued with prison uniform, Otto was conducted to a cell with cobwebs dangling from its barred windows. Late the same afternoon he was taken out and brought before a magistrate resembling a sheep.

He was informed that, at the Café Hugelmann the previous night, he had uttered politically improper remarks in the presence of a young woman by the name of Anna Lutgren, and that the aforesaid young woman, faithful to the sacred duty imposed on every loyal subject by His Majesty Francis II, had denounced him at the earliest opportunity. The sheep indulged in a touch of eloquence. Jacobins were vermin, he declared, and meet to be crushed. The police were applying themselves to this task. The works of Messrs Goethe and Fichte had been repulsed at the frontier. Austria must preserve her purity and drive out all foreign contagions, notably those emanating from France. Several spies had already been executed, but the magistrate averred that the Dual Monarchy was menaced by an even more pernicious danger: freedom of thought, the spirit of anarchy, and insidious coffee-house propaganda – in short, by that 'coward's weapon', the spoken word. 'You're a student, Herr Apfelgrun,' he added, 'so I shall quote you a well-known Latin proverb, but in reverse: *Scripta volant, verba manent.*'

Otto finally ascertained the details of his offence. Apparently he had vilified and ridiculed the monarchy's noblest emblem, the double-eagle of the house of Habsburg. The lieutenant of police silenced his protests and proceeded, in a monotonous voice, to read out a report drawn up that morning by the clerk of the court. This recounted how a party of students had committed an outrage at the Café Hugelmann on the night of May 1st. The incident had occurred while the proprietor was taking their order. A young woman named Anna Lutgren having suggested that they dine on turkey, one of the students, Otto Apfelgrun (there followed a personal description: tall build, fair hair, green eyes, etc.) had given vent to scandalous remarks. Pointing to a turkey awaiting slaughter in the coffee-house kitchen, the aforesaid Otto Apfelgrun had announced in a voice loud enough to be clearly audible at every neighbouring table that he, for his part, refused to devour a turkey so blind to the perils besetting the monarchy and so contemptuous of the glorious house of Habsburg. He then castigated the fowl for having only one head when, after the victory at Baden, every bird in Austria deemed itself honour-bound to grow a second head in deference to that beloved and sacred emblem, the two-headed eagle.

The report was lengthy, verbose, and solemnly phrased. Evidently this was not the first time Otto had spoken in a similarly sarcastic vein. All along the road from Baden to Vienna, which he had travelled in company with the April volunteers as a member of Rector Ouarin's militia, he had affected to see two-headed sparrows, two-headed crows, two-headed ducks, hens, starlings and cockerels, two-headed ants. He had further insinuated that Austria had been appreciably enriched by this process of multiplication, and that officials at the Department of Agriculture were studying the possibility of breeding two-headed pigs. The listening policemen nodded grimly at this, but far worse was revealed a moment later when they heard that Otto Apfelgrun had consummated his blasphemy by asserting that only two people in the whole of Austria were incapable of duplicating their heads.

The magistrate snatched his clerk's report from the lieutenant of police. Donning a pair of square-lensed spectacles, he read out the document's concluding words himself.

'Those two persons, according to the student Apfelgrun, were Rector Ouarin, colonel of the university's volunteers, and Archduke Ferdinand, heir apparent to the throne. Both of them being notorious, according to Herr Apfelgrun, for their possession of only half a brain, doubling

43

the same would produce no more than a brain of normal size.'

Otto was appalled. The grotesque scene had indeed taken place – he could now recall it in every detail. What a fool he was! Would he never stop playing the lady-killer and saying the first thing that came into his head whenever a petticoat rustled in his vicinity – in this instance to impress a girl who looked like a ripe cherry, and whom he hadn't even taken home with him? He pleaded the day's exertions, the effects of wine and music, the Viennese student's traditional love of quips and buffoonery. The magistrate cut him short.

'Precisely, master student: quips and buffoonery! Our fine city of Vienna revels in gaiety and merriment, does it not? What, then, of the butchers of the Army of Italy? Are *they* fond of jesting? Do the students of the Sorbonne amuse themselves by lampooning "the enemy of the human race"?'

He went on to advise Otto that now was the time, not for quips, but for resolution, fortitude, austerity, self-denial, self-sacrifice and the rest. Austria was defending Christendom against godless revolutionaries just as she had, for a thousand years, formed Europe's bulwark against the multiform and mysterious Orient. Prison would teach the young man to curb to tongue and improve the quality of his jokes, always provided that prompt investigation did not disclose that his utterances at the Café Hugelmann, far from being clumsy quips, were – as certain *evidence* suggested – a profession of the Jacobin faith and an essay in mental contamination. The magistrate's eyes flashed as he uttered the word 'evidence'. Otto inquired the nature of this evidence. 'Certain singular friendships', was the curt response.

Otto was consigned to two policemen who fettered his ankles and conducted him, hobbling, along endless passages flanked by massive doors from behind which came moans, the rattle of chains, and the rasp of clogs on flagstones. He was thrust into a cell slightly more comfortable than his first, in that it contained an iron bedstead, a small table with a Bible on it, a slop pail, a tallow candle, a crucifix and an iron stove. A skylight admitted the after-glow of day.

Otto stretched out on the bed and folded his arms, furious with himself. Nonchalance and charm had been succeeded by folly. But how could the girl have denounced him, and so promptly too? He had hurt her feelings, admittedly. And, even though he had not set out to capti-vate her – he never did anything with captivation in mind – that was a lame excuse because everybody knew he capti-vated without meaning to. He was never sufficiently on guard against his own charm. Well, this was an object lesson. From now on he would hold himself in check. He would be more considerate of others.

Despite everything, Otto refused to mistrust people on principle. That was his fundamental objection to life in Francis II's dominions: that everyone was suspect and all thoughts had to be weighed – and now, he even had to weigh the smiles he directed at girls who resembled ripe cherries! Otto waxed heroic on this point: he might rot in the monarchy's dungeons, but he would never denounce his friends and neighbours any more than he would mis-trust them – never under any circumstances would he debase himself in such a way! The truth was, however, that this fit of heroism had scant effect. Otto trembled on his wretched bed, feeling frightened and forlorn. Sleep eluded him, so he tried to take his mind off his fears. He pictured the magistrate's shoulders surmounted by a pair of sheep's heads. Then he pictured a two-headed turkey. Since that bird lay at the root of his predicament, why shouldn't it make itself useful and serve to distract him? It was a vain attempt. The bicephalous fowl that had so tickled his fellow students last night failed even to make him smile. Poor jokes worked only once, if that. Bemused, he pro-ceeded to conjure up, on the underside of his hot, smart-ing eyelids, Friedrich Leppardi's roguish expression and in his ears Ignaz Jungen's roars of laughter at the mention of Duchess Clémence's 'honeypot' and that of little Countess Pietranera, but all to no avail. The air struck chill.

The moon was shining, fortunately, so a little of its radiance penetrated the skylight. Otto heard the prison chapel's bell strike the hours until daybreak.

4

Frau Apfelgrun's footman – he who specialized in carrying her blue velvet prayerbook – covered a lot of ground that summer. His mistress entrusted him with messages for delivery to all the influential people with whom the family still retained contact in its time of adversity. She harboured few illusions, however: the Austrian police were incorruptible, and only an order from Schönbrunn itself could have revoked the magistrate's open-ended sentence on her son Otto. Vigilance was the order of the day. Although Bonaparte had signed an armistice at Leoben, he continued to prowl the environs of Austria. He was currently installed at Monbello, where a motley court had assembled round him. An unrefined gang of military men and intellectuals – scholars like Monge and warriors like Murat, not to mention Bonaparte's sisters – were camping at the little resort while their lord and master played havoc with the map of Europe.

Constanze Apfelgrun's entreaties bore no fruit. Their recipients treated her in a friendly, gracious manner and promised to help, but they were careful afterwards not to put in a good word for her imprisoned son. They either completely avoided mentioning Otto's name or else laid the blame at his own door. Lawyer Gruhlpraser told his old friend point-blank that the young man had displayed stupidity, if nothing worse. The Jacobin menace was no figment of the imagination. Austria stood on the brink of terrible times. The murderers were at the gate, said Gruhlpraser. Besides, Otto's little ordeal would do him good. He was a charming youngster with a talent for turning girls' heads, but extremely irresponsible. Prison would teach him that life was more than a promenade amid petticoats.

Constanze, who took a pessimistic view of the situation, sighed. 'But what if he remains in that prison for another ten years? What if they send him to Spielberg, or . . .'

She dared not put her direst fears into words. Truth to tell, she felt very much alone. Her husband was no help whatever: overwhelmed by his son's misfortunes, Lawyer Apfelgrun was spending more and more time in coffee-houses. Although this enabled him to improve his game of billiards, he had an equal and regrettable fondness for whist, at which he lost his remaining thalers. His memory was becoming frayed, and he seldom opened the few briefs still entrusted to him. They reposed on his desk, quietly gathering dust. But still Constanze refused to give up. She had gallantly braved the long, hot summer, and now it was winter. One morning, alerted to the passage of time by the hoar-frost in her garden, she decided on a change of tactics.

She rediscovered her faith – or rather, to begin with, its outward forms. The footman, who had laboured so long and insidiously to snuff out religion in his mistress and augment his hours of leisure, saw all his indoctrination undone by Otto's imprisonment. Much to his fury, he now had to carry the blue velvet prayerbook around from morn to night, for Frau Apfelgrun, who had previously lost the habit of attending divine service, began to put in appearances at numerous churches. She attended High Mass at St Stephan's every Sunday, presenting a picture of extreme piety. A black-veiled figure with downcast eyes, she could regularly be seen hurrying from one place of worship to another. She was shrewd enough to demonstrate the sincerity of her faith in ill-attended churches. She knelt very visibly in St Carlo Borromeo's, in the churches of the Order of the Visitation, the Friars Minor, and the Sisters of the Holy Virgin. She also spent hours at St Michael's, which had the advantage of being close to the Hofburg and popular with dignitaries of the court.

She prostrated herself for choice in chapels consecrated to the veneration of the Virgin Mary, peering furtively through her veil to satisfy herself that her penitence had not passed unnoticed. An essentially good and simple soul, she was committing the sin of hypocrisy and believed herself in hell as a result. Her reasoning was childish: Vienna having led the crusade against atheistic revolutionaries since the death of Joseph II, her devout behaviour would not only commend itself to Francis II and his advisers but would also redound to the benefit of her son.

The outcome was surprising. After some months, as a result of going through the motions of piety, of shamming prayer and kneeling on every prie-dieu in sight, she found her way back to genuine religion. Although her reconversion did little to melt the cruel hearts of the mighty of this world, it at least touched the Virgin Mary, whose love of maternal devotion was beyond doubt. By some miracle or act of grace, she began to pray with true sincerity as early as the month of November, when the first hard frosts came. The same could not be said of her uncouth footman. An inordinately sly and slothful individual, he strayed ever farther from religion the more his duties multiplied.

Even before this, however, Constanze had carried her self-abasement, as she secretly termed it, to considerable lengths. For one thing, she revolutionized her wardrobe. Her favourite gowns in the past had erred on the gaudy side. Having packed these away in mothballs, she rigidly conformed to the sartorial code adopted by Vienna since Leopold had been succeeded by Francis II. This development did not escape the authorities. They noted it carefully. It gratified them that this stylish woman – this somewhat frivolous bohemian whom many believed to be a freethinker – had finally bowed to convention by exchanging her eternally springlike garb for clothing of sober appearance. Constanze got her dressmaker to make up some long, dark, straight, flowing gowns which she wore with the sole accompaniment of a grey or silver turban encircling her chestnut hair. She looked more beautiful than ever.

This equipment proved all the more useful when Constanze, at one time aloof and independent, gay and flighty, solely preoccupied with the makeshift running of her large and ramshackle house, with practising the harpsichord or pianoforte and cultivating the company of Vienna's most outrageous bohemians, now took it into her head to re-enter society. Utterly uncalculating prior to her son's imprisonment, she now compelled herself to play the minx and worm her way into as many *salons* as possible. Sorrow had wrought a change in her. She was prepared to risk damnation for her child's sake, especially now that the Blessed Virgin had declared in her favour. If someone had intimated to her that an affair could unlock the door of Otto's cell, she would have resigned herself to committing adultery. She had deceived her lawyer husband in the past, and with great enthusiasm, but only in obedience to her passions, never as a devious means of currying favour or pulling strings. It was strange, her readiness to embrace the worst now that she had rediscovered the faith of her childhood, but she blithely brushed this contradiction aside. Fortunately for her, the Viennese court had espoused such high moral standards since Francis II's accession that she was not obliged to demean herself.

The vicar of St Anne's, Father Thaler, became intrigued by his dutiful, sorrowful parishioner. Thaler was a man of some standing. Though endowed with more distinction than delicacy, more acumen than warmth, he came of an old Carinthian family, fulminated against freemasons, and wore cassocks cut from the finest cloth. When he walked, a white lace hem billowed above his gleaming pumps. On first learning of Otto's plight from Constanze's lips, he crossed himself and muttered, '*Vade retro, Satana.*' Then, moved by the grief-stricken woman's beauty, he relented and mapped out a plan of campaign. In his view, now that young Apfelgrun had spent eight months in prison, Schönbrunn could afford to show clemency. It went without saying, however, that this clemency would be more easily obtainable if the young man decided to abandon his futile study of biology and joined the army instead.

'Do you think, dear lady, that your son would accept a lieutenant's commission? I'm sure I could find him a regiment of quality.'

Constanze was forced to admit that she didn't think so. Father Thaler understood but urged her not to despair. Meanwhile, they would storm a few well-defended positions. The vicar was as good as his word. Thanks to him, Constanze Apfelgrun secured an entrée to some influential

50

establishments. She was received, with Thaler in attendance, by the Constable of the Court, by senior officials at the Department of War, by the Schwarzenbergs and Kauskys, by one of Archduke Charles's aides-de-camp and the general commanding the Second Army. Father Thaler's only setback was a humiliating one: he failed to extract the least little invitation from the Prince of Saxe-Salza and Duchess Clémence.

Prior to this, furthermore, a crisis had occurred. Word of the Café Hugelmann incident had gone the rounds. Although revolutionaries were rare in Vienna and extremely discreet, a spirit of irreverence prevailed in artistic circles and among the student population. The two-headed turkey had amused the city's *jeunesse dorée* and tickled the Jacobin palate. It became the talk of several coffee-houses. A turkey ballad gained currency at the university and at various inns, the patrons of which sang it after drinking, but there was an even more dangerous development. An elderly and rather eccentric draughtsman named Gravitsky saw fit, while carousing one night at the Golden Rose in Nussford, to scrawl on the menu, immediately below the Habsburg coat of arms: it was a representation of a pig with two heads, one of them resembling Rector Ouarin and the other Archduke Ferdinand. This caricature was pocketed by one of Gravitsky's table companions, a red-haired republican from Strasbourg who published the *Squirrel's Courier*, a fortnightly periodical whose confetti-sized pages were crammed with fiery political diatribes.

It so happened that Professor Schwarzbrod got wind of the affair through one of Otto's friends. If the two-headed pig appeared in print, the young man was doomed. His sentence would be increased – he would be transferred to Spielberg Castle and, quite possibly, executed. Schwarzbrod ascertained where the pamphleteer lived from another of his students. He slowly mounted a staircase smelling of cabbage. On reaching the door at the top, he knocked as he had been instructed: three knocks followed by one light tap and another so light as to be almost inaudible. After some delay the door half-opened and a jovial gentleman bade him enter. Schwarzbrod put on his spectacles and scrutinized the plump, youthful face at close range. Then, without comment, he subsided on to a grubby sofa, carefully polished his glasses, and resumed his scrutiny. His young red-haired host declared that he was beginning to feel like a cabbage white or a tortoiseshell caterpillar. Schwarzbrod told him that they had already met. The pamphleteer replied that, although he was acquainted with Schwarzbrod's scholarly reputation, circumstances had never – to his profound regret – brought them face to face before. Schwarzbrod gave an indulgent laugh.

'But my dear Monsieur Charles, I can even describe the circumstances under which I made your acquaintance. I had gone to Baden to catch butterflies, and there was a fellow guest at the Three Nails Inn who sold boots, hobnailed boots, to the mountain folk. Am I right, sir?'

Now it was the other's turn to laugh. His round florid face radiated honest mirth. He simply didn't understand – he'd never set foot in Baden, with or without hobnailed boots, and he certainly wouldn't have forgotten if he'd had the honour of being presented to a man of Schwarzbrod's eminence. Schwarzbrod persisted, but all he got was amiable banter. He gave up. His eyesight wasn't of the best, after all, so he might be mistaken. Besides, he had a more urgent matter to discuss.

'This Apfelgrun business,' said the pamphleteer, 'yes, yes, I know. I have friends at the university – they told me to expect you.'

Schwarzbrod told him that by reproducing the two-headed pig in his *Squirrel's Courier* he would inevitably lop off another two heads: that of the hapless Gravitsky, whose style the Emperor's sleuths would readily identify, and Otto Apfelgrun's. The pamphleteer was unmoved. He spoke of justice and equality, Brutus and Saint-Just, Savonarola and Mucius Scaevola. Schwarzbrod returned to the attack. He rejected these arguments, calling them hot air and sounding brass. This incensed the other man. Being aware that Schwarzbrod, though not a very active Jacobin, was sympathetic to the ferment of the time, he drew him into a dark corner and confided under seal of secrecy that a band of conspirators met weekly at a disused sheepcote in the Vienna Woods, there to dig the pit in which Francis II's despotic regime would ultimately be engulfed. He concluded his eloquent revelation, hooked one fat forefinger in Schwarzbrod's waistcoat, and then, slowly removing his spectacles, regarded the professor with immutable, implacable sincerity.

'Our cause has need of martyrs, Herr Schwarzbrod. It may be that fate has cast Otto Apfelgrun in that role.'

'But my dear fellow, I know the boy well – he's one of my pupils. Otto has as little in common with the Jacobins as with Francis II. His bugs and beetles are all that concern him.'

'Revolutions are cemented by the blood of innocents. The blood shed at Golgotha by Jesus Christ continues to anoint the world and bind the bricks of God's holy temple.'

Schwarzbrod was surprised to discover that the pamphleteer combined Jacobinism with Catholicism, but the need for urgent action dissuaded him from raising this supplementary question. Yet when, instead, he was maladroit enough to utter threats and spoke of denouncing him to the police, the effect was disastrous. The red-headed revolutionary, who found this prospect alluring, declared that a man's life counted for little provided his death helped to blaze a trail into the future.

'Twilight is descending on the monarchies of old. A martyr's death will paint that twilight the colour of blood and enrich the glorious dawn awaiting his comrades on the morrow.'

Dismayed, Schwarzbrod changed his tactics. He said no more about denouncing anyone and represented himself as a Jacobin sympathizer. Sipping wine and nibbling cream pancakes, he battled away, well into the night, until he managed to sway his awkward adversary.

'Bonaparte won't spend the rest of his days at Monbello,' he said. 'The man's an express coach. He has sworn to crush Vienna, which is the living heart of monarchism. It is then, my dear fellow, but only then, that you and your comrades will be able to strike with success.'

The pamphleteer looked mysterious. Lowering his voice, he said that he had some idea of Napoleon's plans, and that Schwarzbrod's argument was not without merit. It might after all be better to refrain from publishing the caricature of the two-headed pig until Austria was ripe for its reception. He and Schwarzbrod embraced.

★　★　★

Otto was unaware of these goings-on. No whisper of the world's doings penetrated his cell. Day succeeded day, and every one was the same. He had several meetings with his mother in a shabby old visiting room, but a spiteful warder was always close at hand in the adjoining guardroom, and he could find little to say.

The change in his mother filled him with remorse. The exuberant, sparkling, impulsive woman of yore had become a grey shadow, and all because of him. She was still beautiful, but sorrow lay on her face like a dusting of rime. She had also grown thinner. The diamond ring which Otto had known since babyhood was now too big for her finger. It was a piece of jewellery that had belonged to her mother. Women, Otto reflected, passed on more to succeeding generations than wedding rings, brooches and lockets of their hair; they also bequeathed their hands, which grew old and, in so doing, inherited the brownish flecks transmitted by the desiccated hands of their mothers. Every family must surely possess, hidden away in some sandalwood coffer at the back of a secretaire, a store of old women's hands with prominent blue veins. Otto heaped reproaches on himself. If he had at least been thrown into prison for espousing the Jacobin cause, this whole affair would possess some meaning, some nobility, but he had merely led a butterfly's existence – he had dreamed his way through life. The fate of Austria was no more a significant item on his agenda than that of the Revolution. He was just a smug, conceited, flippant young man of fashion who had caused his family great distress simply for the pleasure it had given him to crack a joke, and a foolish one at that.

It could not be said that Otto was in torment. His penitence was gentle, almost unreal. He trained himself to enjoy the monotony of the passing hours, the tedium of prison routine. For the first time ever, he became conscious of his own existence. He learned to caress time, run his fingers over it, listen for the silken sound of springwater and birdsong conjured up by hours of darkness and silence. He thought of studying the cockroaches that shared his quarters. Perhaps he would make a scientific discovery like Schwarzbrod, with his theory about the intercourse between insects and flowers, but the days were too short to allow him much time for research. In the evenings, when the prisoners trudged round a bleak courtyard hemmed in by formidable walls, he chatted with his guards. They were nice enough fellows at heart.

Otto took stock of his life. After twenty years spent flitting about the exquisite Austrian countryside, the meadows of the Vienna Woods, he had inadvertently pushed open a hidden door and fallen through into his country's cavernous underworld. He who had so loved Vienna for its glitter and vivacity, its amiable, easy-going ways, its pleasure-loving girls and women, was now discovering the sewer that underlay it. The capital city of music, flowers and love was an illusion, a stage set. All that separated it from horrific reality was a tenuous film through which he had passed like a circus animal jumping through a paper-covered hoop. That genial, languid society, that picture painted in glossy colours, those scents and melodies, those lovely women with lithe, slender figures – all these were merely baubles and bangles, merely a theatre that had closed down years ago, if not centuries, and been replaced by a slum. Vienna was an imaginary city, and the great conflict in progress between the Dual Monarchy and Napoleon's glorious rabble was a duel between dreams and reality. Austria was a compound of darkness and conspiracy, police and cobwebs, stench and brutality, the rattle of chains. Flames were licking at the scenery in the

Habsburg's decrepit opera house. Otto's family home in the Bauernmarkt played a role in his imaginings at such moments. He likened it to the emblem of Austria and thought how apt it was to speak of the *Dual* Monarchy, the *double*-eagle. Austria was a land of make-believe, an aristocratic façade embellished with millennial curlicues and resplendent in beauty and tradition. A wizened old crone had only to open the door to disclose that the rooms within were bare and bereft of life.

Otto made the most of the tiny rectangle of sky framed by the high window of his cell. However minuscule, that scrap of blue belonged to him. He was the owner of that luminous morsel and, thus, of the entire sky, for an entire sky was contained in his poor little share of it. The colours were ever-changing. He discovered an infinite number of blues, for instance. By slowing time down he speeded it up, and one day, because his brain tired quickly now, he speculated that the men of the future would invent a microscope for eternity and telescopes for the hours, just as their forebears had contrived to see the infinitely small and infinitely large through lenses. When that day came, they would discern a whole accumulation of creased and folded millennia in a single minute, a single second. Otto also collected the storms and downpours that buffeted his window and classified the colours of the hoar-frost. He was hypnotized by his bare surroundings and empty days. To a recluse like himself, everything became an event: wind swirling over the roofs of the city, rain and the scent of rain, the wan light seeping into his cell, the coming of day.

If only he had loved, at least! He would still be in prison, true, but preoccupied from dawn to dusk with her from whom the Emperor's myrmidons had parted him. He would feel himself the victim of an unjust fate and pine for his lost love. He would picture her scattering grain for his birds in the morning or plying her needle for hours at the embroidery frame – picture her being both kind to all and at the same time indifferent to them because her thoughts were elsewhere. Her sorrow would be bitter and irremediable . . . But there it was: he had neither loved nor been loved. Though reputed to be a young man besieged by women, he was totally lonely. He had loved everyone – his mother and old Schwarzbrod, his university friends, children at play on the city walls, shepherdesses from the hill farms, the elderly ladies who called on his grandmother, his grandmother herself – he had loved them all equally, and that was no way to get yourself immortalized by one of the tragic poems imported from Germany in recent years, which told how young lovers chose to die by their own hand if love was denied them.

In the evening he would bring his nose up level with the windowsill by mounting a stool. From this observation point he could see a triangle of field some way off, and late one autumn afternoon he noticed a woman standing there. Although he could not distinguish her features at this range, he fancied that the distant figure might be the girl from the Brigittenau. Looking more closely, he recognized her costume: a pleated skirt, a pink and white apron tied around the waist, a low-necked, snow-white blouse with tucks and puffed sleeves, and a laced black bodice. It was the same girl, the one named Anna. He felt no resentment. Circumstances had enforced his repentance. He had inadvertently offended the girl by his shyness, and now in her own way she was sharing his penitence. She did not come every day, either because she worked as a vendor of goats' milk or trinkets in one of the municipal parks, or because she was afraid of being seen by an informer, so weeks went by and the field remained empty – green, girlless and empty. Then, one morning at the beginning of winter, Otto sighted her again. He wondered how he could have likened her to a cherry, but at this distance who could tell? It was a bitterly cold day. Otto had wrapped himself up in every scrap of clothing he possessed, and the field and the prison roofs that encroached on his window were glittering with frost. The girl stood motionless in the dazzling white field. Otto remained transfixed at his window as if afraid that the girl from the Brigittenau, too, would acquire a coating of rime, and that she would prove to be no more than a transient particle of this winter in the year 1797. She never reappeared, so he ceased to look out for her and brooded on her charms instead. He had found a lost love to pine for.

He was told at Christmas of his forthcoming release, so the girl, if she ever came after that, would be waving to an empty cell. Francis II, in his mercy, had decreed an Easter amnesty for prisoners serving short sentences. The prison governor, a kindly man, conveyed this news with satisfaction. Otto was then visited in his cell by the magistrate resembling a sheep, whose curly white hair had grown still longer – so long, thought Otto, that he would soon need shearing. A tiresome flood of moral precepts ensued. Otto was advised to guard his tongue, or rather, to develop a sager awareness of the perils of history. 'Yes,' he replied. The Emperor, being of a clement disposition, said the magistrate, had expressed the wish that special care be taken to ensure that Otto Apfelgrun, whose merits were universally appreciated, did not relapse into evil ways. 'Yes,' Otto repeated. Many of his university classmates, said the magistrate, had decided to postpone their studies and offer their services to the Austrian nation. Young Ignaz Jungen, for example, was at the cadet school in Wiener-Neustadt. Other contemporaries were standing guard in Vorarlberg and even in the fortresses of Hungary, Transylvania and the Banat, on the far-off Military Frontier. The magistrate was infinitely tactful. When danger threatened, he said persuasively, love of peace dictated war.

5

The vicar of St Anne's was determined that Otto should be commissioned in Prince Ernst of Saxe-Salza's regiment. Although he had never yet entered the prince's illustrious house near the Kärntnertor, Vienna's Carinthian Gate, the difficulty of the undertaking redoubled his enthusiasm for it. His talent for subterfuge and gossip worked wonders. He much enjoyed hatching his plot and sharing its preparations with Constanze Apfelgrun. By night he devised the design of his tapestry; by day, once morning Mass was over, he busied himself at the loom. On the pretext of visiting his parishioners he dropped a few casual words here and there in the knowledge that they would travel from *salon* to sacristy, flitting along like the tiny blue flame of a will-o'-the wisp, until a few days' peregrinations brought them to the boudoir he had chosen to ignite.

The little priest had become attached to Otto. He seemed to see, reflected in the young man's limpid gaze, all the emotions that had stirred within himself when wavering as a youth between the call of God, the pleasures of diplomacy, and service in the army. He had opted for the Church, but today, with Europe in such turmoil, he found it natural and even virtuous for others to embrace a military career.

It was true that after the treaty of Campo Formio, which ceded Venice to Austria but restored the left bank of the Rhine to France and recognized the Cisalpine Republic, Mars had transferred his attentions from Vienna and was currently foraging, so everyone believed, in the neighbourhood of England. The Austrians therefore had relit their paper lanterns. The actors had reopened their trunks and unpacked their costumes, the same old measures were being trodden in front of the same old mirrors, and Vienna had yielded to the sensual delights of yore, but Father Thaler knew that this lull was deceptive. The Dual Monarchy had dismantled neither its military panoply nor its police apparatus. The ponderous machinery of repression which Francis II and Baron Thugut had regulated with a watchmaker's care was still intact. It needed only a single cannon-shot or the discovery of some plot to set the cogs grinding again. When that happened, Otto would be crushed unless he had agreed to serve in one of the Emperor's regiments.

Thaler acquainted Otto with his views, lovingly rapping out the martial metaphors. He revered the Austrian army because he had it, so to speak, at his fingertips. He adored all the world's armies, provided their officers were heroic, of good family, and attired in uniforms as elegant as the stoles, albs and chasubles of the army of God. His knowledge of military matters was much admired. He knew all the insignia and the colours of every sabretache to be found in the legions of Archduke Charles and General Mack, of Marshal Suvorov and Prince Eugène, of the Great Condé and Bonaparte himself, of Pitt and Frederick William of Prussia, and he happily paraded his knowledge whenever possible. If he adjudged the Prince of Saxe-Salza's regiments the finest in Europe, it was for their gallantry in the field, to be sure, but still more so because of their officers' appearance.

'Not even Liechtenstein's cuirassiers can compare with those of Duchess Clémence,' he would say to Otto. 'The Liechtensteiners' collars and breeches are immaculately white, I grant you, and their dolmans are sky-blue, but that braid, those black facings and gorgets – no, Otto, *that* colour doesn't figure in the Austrian palette.'

Otto was a tractable, easy-going young man. He listened respectfully to the vicar's rhetoric and his mother's exhortations, but he was bored. Vienna now seemed alien to him. He had celebrated an emotional reunion with the worthy Schwarzbrod, revisited sundry fashionable coffee-houses with his little band of 'copycats' and broken a heart or two, but eight months' solitary confinement formed an impalpable screen, a film of ash on the windowpane, and his pursuit of pleasure lacked zest. Besides, his fundamental recognition that the vicar's arguments were sound made

60

him feel like a man under an only temporary stay of execution. He had no doubt that a cornet's commission awaited him, even if the storm raging over Europe struck him as somewhat unreal – but which cause to espouse? He saw no good reason for these sanguinary squabbles. How could he champion the fortunes of the tottering, worm-eaten, farcical Habsburg dynasty? On the other hand, how could he fraternize with the champions of fraternity when they had sullied the hopes of 1789 with blood in the Place de la Grève?

The vicar's allusion to Duchess Clémence of Saxe-Salza – the beautiful blonde duchess, as he meaningfully called her – revived Otto's memories of Baden. The cavalcade of cuirassiers had ridden across the Kurpark to the thunder of drums, but Otto had watched them in a dream. Although Duchess Clémence was just a fleeting mental impression, he consented to the vicar's scheme. Not being an intimate of the Saxe-Salzas, Father Thaler proposed to introduce Otto to one of Duchess Clémence's aunts, Her Excellency Duchess Gertrud von Mahlberg, in the almost certain expectation of securing an audience with Prinz Ernst of Saxe-Salza. Otto would therefore have to charm the elderly duchess. 'I don't know how kindly you're treated by the girls in the Wienerland taverns,' Thaler said with a smirk, 'but I'll wager that all the more venerable old ladies yearn to gobble you up.'

Duchess Gertrud lived at the Palais Questenberg-Kaunitz, No.5 Johannesgasse, not far from the Gothic spire of St Stephan's. 'The duchess is a trifle Gothic too, so be punctual. She collects clocks, and capricious old ladies are quickly irritated.'

Thaler leant forwards and gave Otto a familiar little tap on the knee.

'This particular old lady is so advanced in years that she may slip through our fingers unless we hurry. Let's try to forestall her death. We have no other duchess on our menu, after all, so don't dilly-dally – don't waste time admiring the chandeliers in her antechambers, the work-manship of her inlaid floors, the musical boxes littering her whatnots. In fact, don't look at them until the interview's over. At her age, every second of life counts.'

Otto, thoroughly disconcerted by the vicar's macabre sense of humour, was then advised to dress with subtlety. He must wear a tightly buttoned frock coat of martial cut to contrast with the silks and satins that would froth at his throat and wrists.

'Another point,' said Father Thaler. 'The duchess is fond of ceremony, but not of convention. In an emergency such as this, one must be irreverent. An almost imperceptible touch of arrogance will go down well with her.'

He accompanied Otto to the door of the Johannesgasse mansion to impart a few last words of advice. Snow was scudding through the streets and turning to yellow dust in the light of lamps at the crossroads. It was evening, and Otto wondered why snow always seemed to him to fall in another country, in centuries dead and gone. The vicar, who had taken his protégé's arm and was striding out briskly, warned him that Duchess Gertrud was exceptionally quick-witted and ferocious into the bargain. 'She's a carnivore – a ferret. She goes for the jugular, and her teeth never release their prey. She sucks for a long time at the wounds she inflicts, so beware! People say she acts the madwoman, but don't believe a word of it. For one thing, she probably *is* mad; for another, madness sets her whimsical mind ablaze. Preposterous she may be, but bear in mind that all she does is done for a reason. Personally, I think she has the devil in her.'

They were now outside the Palais Questenberg-Kaunitz. The lofty entrance was approached by two curving flights of granite steps that converged and met beneath a very ancient, time-worn coat of arms. The vicar deciphered it with relish.

'Sable a spread eagle checky argent and gules, membered and crowned or,' he said reverently. 'Those are the arms of Gerhard Mahlberg, founder of the line. A giant of a man nicknamed "Wolf-jaw", he was grand master of the Teutonic Order at the battle of Tannenberg. In other words, the Mahlbergs are related to Sigismund of Magdeburg and his descendants, likewise to Frederick I of Prussia.'

Thaler embraced the young man, waited until he had been admitted, and hurried off to report to Constanze Apfelgrun. Otto was ushered into an anteroom as spacious as a riding stable. A squad of lackeys, several of them negroes liveried *à la française*, with glossy black shoes, white hose and clubbed hair, steered him up and down carved oak staircases, across rotundas, and along endless passages flanked by immensities of blackness in which crystal chandeliers glittered like frozen fountains. Venetian mirrors on the walls reflected the nocturnal gloom.

The duchess's apartments comprised a series of rooms entirely steeped in shadow. It seemed to Otto, as the lackeys walked ahead and the mansion's twists and turns were unveiled by the glare of their torches, that those torches manufactured everything – passages, oaken tables, marble fireplaces – in their passing. He saw, trembling in the fitful light, twenty full-length portraits that recounted the epic history of the Mahlbergs from 'Wolf-Jaw' of Magdeburg, the medieval warrior monk, to the Barons Mahlberg in the retinue of Sobieski the Pole during the war against the Turks, to the effeminate Mahlbergs at the court of Dresden under Augustus the Strong, and finally, in recent times, to corpulent, gorgeously attired notaries in their offices at the Hofburg.

Whether fat or thin, forbidding or appealing, handsome or pallid, haggard and shifty-looking, all these faces had features in common: the noses were long and thin, the beards fair, sparse and silky, the eyes invariably cruel, the jaws predatory. When the innermost room was lit *a giorno*, Otto realized that all these paintings converged on a single vanishing-point: a high-backed crimson velvet armchair enthroning a body topped by a gaunt face coated with powder and rouge like that of a corpse lying in state. From it jutted the straight nose of the Mahlbergs, and a strong, bony chin reposing on a big ruff of violet faille. Embedded in a monumental silver peruke, the face was gazing eagerly ahead but slightly to the right of Otto, who might have been invisible. It was as if the din of all the battles ever fought on

European soil, and the rivers of spilled blood, and the Mahlbergs' twenty bestial glares, and the sound of bones splintering under the concerted onslaught of Teutonic broadswords, and the mounds of desecrated flesh, and the death-throes in the snow, in fields of rotting grain, in the mire of Prussia, Hungary and Bohemia – yes, as if four whole centuries of entombed history had voided their waste fluids and their foul, stale odours into the body of the last of the line, this indomitable old crone whose flaccid, musty skin and ferocious eyes, Otto reflected, had already been latent in the blood and sperm of the dynasty's founder, Gerhard 'Wolf-Jaw' Mahlberg, the giant monk whose descendants were merely his discoloured, degenerate and decadent copies: echoes that faded a little with each generation but remained as dauntless and implacable as the woman in the crimson armchair.

The duchess was seated at an angle, one hand fondling the neck of a tremulous pug-dog which she periodically kissed on the nose and addressed as 'Herr Feldmarschall'. The other hand, a shrivelled bird's claw shrouded in quivering black lace, reposed on the barrel of a cannon whose date, 1683, suggested that it had been captured from the Turks at Vienna a century before, probably by one of the Mahlbergs serving under Sobieski and Starhemberg. The old lady was cocking an ear at this piece of ordnance, possibly, Otto thought with mingled amusement and horror, in the hope that the cannon ball cast in the arsenals of Constantinople and jammed into the bronze muzzle would at long last erupt and put to flight the gluttonous ancestral ghosts that were flocking around the mortal remains of the last of their line – circling that old and infertile but still throbbing womb as if the collectors of the dead, the washers of corpses, were already ringing their bell in the street outside.

Otto started at the sound of the duchess's voice, which was shrill but very distinct. Having congratulated him on his appearance, she curtly beckoned him closer and ran a finger over the cloth of his frock coat.

'Father Thaler told me you would be wearing grey. Good, excellent. You will also be aware, sir, that the two-headed turkey has predisposed me in your favour. It tickled us to death last summer, Christine and me. I don't know if Thaler mentioned Christine, who acts as my . . . my housekeeper. You shall see her in a moment – I'm always in need of her. She's related to our family, even though she's only a Kinsky, but she cajoles me, she wearies me – we're always bickering. Yes, the turkey amused us greatly. It wasn't worth making such a fuss about, considering how well populated Schönbrunn is with turkeys. You should realize, however, that they seldom have two heads, and so much the better. Between you and me, they talk enough twaddle with one head only. Just imagine poor Emperor Francis with two heads instead of one. Austria would be in a pretty pickle! He's a nice enough fellow, but niceness doesn't make an emperor . . .'

She tugged impatiently at a dark red tassel. A bell awakened echoes in the distant recesses of the house, and a young woman appeared.

'Christine, this is Herr Apfelgrun, son of Lawyer Apfelgrun, whom we used to like so much. I say we liked him, but I trust he isn't dead – we should have learned of it, should we not? Christine, I heard the clock chime its five-thirty minuet. You will be late.'

She gave Herr Feldmarschall a tap on the nose.

'Christine is cousin to Duchess Clémence of Saxe-Salza. Yes, we're all related. Our families are a hotchpotch, a regular mishmash. Christine is kind enough to visit the conservatory every evening and describe the sunset to me.'

The housekeeper withdrew. Otto, who had sat down, crossed and uncrossed his legs. Ten or twelve minutes went by. The crackle of the flambeaux evoked an almost inaudible tinkle from various cut glass ornaments arrayed in cabinets. Otto reflected that he might perhaps form some idea of Duchess Clémence's face, which he had only glimpsed beneath her ridiculous shako, from that of her cousin. The housekeeper was a tall, exceedingly beautiful young woman with copper-coloured hair and dark eyes sprinkled with tiny flecks as black as ink. Her timid manner had been that of a girl who keeps a journal and spends hours poring over old letters, reading *Werther* and *Manon Lescaut*, gazing at lockets and faded miniatures, stitching away at her embroidery. She was a serene and melancholy young lady perfectly attuned to a room in winter, to frosty weather and its attendant scents of vanilla, herb tea and hot milk. Duchess Gertrud was craning forward, listening to the faint music of the chandeliers and epergnes, when Christine returned and proceeded to describe the approach of nightfall.

Otto thought it was a prank at first. Quite straight-faced, she declared that Vienna was bathed in glorious sunlight, whereas Otto knew full well that the city's ice-encrusted roofs were cowering beneath a dark and stormy sky. She further described a vista of fields and hills beyond the city walls, towards Essling, and made the following bizarre announcement: 'This evening, Excellency, the earth is a cornucopia of blossom, fur and greenery.'

The duchess pressed her for more details, fiercely rapping the floor with the tip of her cane. She demanded some clouds. Christine manufactured one in the direction of Enns, but the old lady hissed like a cat, so she obediently erased it and restored the sky to a flawless blue. The duchess sat back in her chair, purring with contentment.

'People are surprised,' she said, 'but you see, Herr Apfelgrun, Christine keeps the world alive for me. I don't care if it's orderly or in turmoil as long as it's alive. I'll wager Father Thaler omitted to tell you that my eyes no longer see a thing – he's as genuine as a Revolutionary banknote, like all priests. I lost my sight ten years ago, but what's so extraordinary about that? Christine deputizes for my eyes; she describes the sky to me every morning, every evening . . .'

She pulled a childish, almost impish face and turned to her niece.

'But this evening, Christine, I do believe you've lied to me yet again. You'll never quite persuade me that the weather is always superb, that it never rains in Austria, that Francis II's police have thrown all the cloudbursts and tornadoes into prison, that autumn and winter don't occur

66

in the Habsburg dominions, or that all the mists and snows have decamped for good and are stored away who knows where. You're a liar, my girl, but I know – I know what you're going to tell me. You tell it me night after night. I employ you to lie – in fact it's your very skill at lying that makes me so satisfied with your services. I shall increase your wages, my dear, because you're a liar of genius. You're a liar born and bred, a true Mahlberg, and I've every right to relish your untruths. Another twenty thalers for you!'

The bewigged head moved jerkily, like that of a disjointed doll, in the direction of Otto, who felt thoroughly ill at ease and darted an apprehensive glance at Christine.

'Why should I care if she doesn't describe the sky as it is today? There are times when she quotes me a twilight from last summer, four or five months old, but why should I complain, Herr Apfelgrun, as long as Fräulein Kinsky's twilight *looks* new, as long as it's fresh as an egg emerging from a hen's bottom – as long as she presents it to me with sufficient artistry to make it credible? My pleasures are meted out to me in the cutthroats' alley which the Good Lord – the Good Lord . . . what a misnomer! – which God has appointed to be his rendezvous with me. No, far be it from me to turn up my nose at a lie, a few days' discrepancy, a mix-up in the seasons.

'Past, present, future . . . I've ceased to reside in any of those. I inhabit the same boundless, trackless territory as all the Mahlbergs, all those faces you see on the walls. I manage to thread my way through the days. And besides, it's a little notion of mine that the sky will end by making a mistake, or by letting itself be intimidated into complying with Christine's fancies. Herr Goethe imagined the Devil, did he not, and wouldn't you agree that the Devil's affairs have prospered since the storming of the Bastille? Thaler tells me you're a very young man. You won't understand, I feel sure, but I'll tell you even so: when people are in utter despair, they snatch at any hope that comes within reach. I gorge myself on hope, Apfelgrun. I hunt the hope of seeing again and Christine acts as my beater, that's the truth of the matter. And yet hope gives me indigestion. I'll believe any lie as long as it agrees with me – doesn't everyone function in much the same way? I sometimes believe, though I don't know for sure, that it might even be possible to convince me, with a little perseverance and persuasion, that Francis II is an emperor, that Father Thaler is a priest, that Christine is a young woman . . . I might even, forgive me, come to believe in my own existence . . .'

She put a hand to her brow. Christine slowly and carefully applied a vesicatory, but without interrupting the old lady's terrible monologue. Duchess Gertrud, whose voice was flagging, beckoned Otto even closer. More and more dismayed, he listened on his knees beside her, with his ear to her lips.

'Some years ago, Apfelgrun, I used to know an Englishman named Lord Misrule. He was a friend of William Beckford, an extremely handsome and disreputable young man of whom I was also very fond. Misrule, for his part, was big, bloated and world-weary, but he used to travel the length and breadth of Europe by stage-coach. The English are insane, as you know. They for ever insist on touring Europe by way of Venice, Zurich, Rome, Paris, Constantinople. Lord Misrule adored this city of ours. He used to stay here in this very house, but I guarantee he never once put his nose out of doors in a score of visits. Shall I tell you what method he adopted? He had a manservant who explored the streets in his place, who strolled through the markets and prayed in the churches. At first this manservant reported on his doings every evening – like Christine, if you will – but later even his reports were waived. It sufficed Misrule simply to know that the man was inspecting our monuments and chapels on his behalf.'

Gertrud's childish laugh rang out once more. She raised a lorgnette to her eyes and studied Otto avidly, or so it seemed.

'Lord Misrule died fifteen years ago, if not sixteen. He ended by becoming more bloated and world-weary than ever. His heart was diseased, and that charlatan Mesmer had terrified him by telling him that the slightest shock might stop it beating. But Mesmer was right for once, I suspect, because the flesh he put on was white and un-wholesome, and his hands shook incessantly. He sat up-stairs in his apartment, his sole form of activity the avoi-dance of all emotion, and do you know what he told me one day?

'One day he said to me, "I love life so much that I'm trying to prolong it beyond the normal span, even if I have to deprive it of all that goes to make up life itself – isn't that odd?" He also said, "There's nothing left between life and me, Gertrud: no partition, no intervening space to keep us apart, no joy, no surprise, no affection, no memory, no enjoyment, no pleasure – nothing at all. I'm in contact with the very skin of life – life reduced to its simplest manifesta-tion, when all that nourishes life has melted away. That's the price one pays for the privilege of hearing life's heart-beat." And again: "Life is life only when" – the phrase eludes me – it was a strange one . . . Ah yes – "only when it becomes indistinguishable from death and finally resembles life itself: in other words, nothingness." He even said, "when life becomes frozen."

'Towards the end, Misrule grew even more eccentric. He'd devised a complete strategy of his own. He allotted his emotions to servants with special functions. When his son William was drowned at sea, he instructed one of his footmen to attend the funeral and another to mourn on his behalf, so that he himself, who had adored his son, was wholly absolved from grief. The servant wept to order, but Misrule was happy as a lark. He used to say that he was rich, whereas the squires of England were hedonists who squan-dered their revenues on game forests and packs of fox-hounds. For his part, he used his wealth to purchase tranquillity and absence of feeling. He was a miser, that is to say, lavish with his money and thrifty with his emotions. In that respect he spent nothing. He even made another servant responsible for joy and happiness. That man, whom I disliked, used to frequent taverns, gaming rooms and women's beds in his master's place, for Misrule consid-ered happiness as debilitating as sorrow. He had a theory that still defies my comprehension. He used to say that happiness cuts you off, irrevocably, from happiness. I ask you, where's the logic in that?'

The duchess fell silent and sank back in her chair. Her hands sought the arms and alighted on them like a pair of birds. Her breathing was laboured. A pointed white tongue flickered over her shrunken lips.

'But imagine, Fräulein Kinsky refuses to believe what I say! She contends that Lord Misrule never existed!'

'I've never said any such thing, Excellency,' Christine protested.

'Just so. You've never disputed Misrule's existence purely to demonstrate that you consider me a liar, a lunatic old crone. I know you, my girl – you're a fraud!'

She picked up her cane, which was propped against the Turkish cannon, and tapped Christine on the head with it.

'You're not only heartless but a fool, my dear. Lord Misrule paid many visits to this house. I've only to shut my eyes and there he is again. He was one of the most elegant men in Vienna, especially when he began to put on weight towards the end and became all bloated. He dressed in the old style, with a curly white peruke *à la* George II, black silk knee-breeches and buckled shoes. You see, I can even describe him! He used to sit just there, in the chair you're occupying now, and he couldn't rise without a footman's assistance.'

The duchess amiably requested Christine to serve tea. Otto mustn't be offended, she said, but tea would be served in ordinary china cups. The Mahlbergs' gold tea service was no more. As one who was eager to enter the Saxe-Salzas' employ, Otto would understand. Francis II had set the fashion by having his gold plate melted down to buy cannon for the purpose of crushing General Bonaparte, whom Gertrud found odious, if not vulgar, but more intelligent than poor Francis and Archduke Charles put together. The whole court, the whole of the Austrian nobility, had followed their sovereign's example. The craftsmen's guilds had offered the treasury their most precious insignia, some of which dated from the Middle Ages.

Christine returned wheeling a silver table on which Otto

70

discerned cups of the finest old gold bearing the same coat of arms as that which adorned the mansion's granite façade. Another eccentricity . . . ? Why should the old woman pretend that her gold plate had been converted into cannon? Otto said nothing, just glanced inquiringly at the housekeeper, who smiled and put a finger to her lips. The 'tea' proved to be coffee. Duchess Gertrud drank hers with much smacking of the lips to convey the pleasure it gave her. According to her, coffee tasted just the same in china as in precious metal. Then she raised her lorgnette and glared at Christine.

'And this young woman would have us believe that Lord Misrule never existed! We're to take it that Francis II exists, but that Lord Misrule is a fiction. While you're about it, Christine, why not deny that I gave my gold tea service to the nation? Go on, don't be bashful. You're employed to lie, so do your duty. These are gold cups, aren't they, so why not say so? My poor Christine, you do everything the wrong way round. You lie when you should tell the truth and tell the truth when you should lie. Just now I increased your wages. Well, now I propose to reduce them. I shall fine you thirty thalers and two groschen.'

The duchess grew calmer, but her withered face was suffused. Red blotches like blisters had appeared beneath the layer of white powder on her cheeks. She tried to smile. Christine dabbed her lips with a handkerchief. She took the girl's hand in hers, stroked and kissed it. Then she spoke of the Saxe-Salzas. Her niece Clémence's regiment of cuirassiers was an affair of the heart, she said, precisely echoing Schwarzbrod's remark of a year before, in the hurly-burly of the battle of Baden. She would be pleased to have a word with Duchess Clémence and the prince, and Otto would be assigned to one regiment or the other. She had taken a liking to him, so the choice would be his: either Dresden and Ernst's blue hussars, or Vienna and Clémence's white cuirassiers. At present, however, the couple were away. Ernst and his wife spent some months of every year at Greinburg, their castle near Linz in Upper Austria, for the sake of the hunting to be had in the region of the Black Lakes. Gertrud confessed herself a trifle weary. She congratulated Otto and exhorted him to sacrifice his pleasures, and if need be his life, to save 'the kingdom of the two-headed turkey'.

Mention of the turkey provoked a paroxysm of laughter, whereupon the duchess instantly dozed off as if prostrated by such an unforeseen convulsion. Otto gazed anxiously at her pink and white face. Despite the violet silk ruff, her mouth sagged open, limp and black within.

★ ★ ★

'She's asleep,' said Christine. 'The duchess sleeps like a child – she hears nothing, believe me.'

Conversation turned to the tea service. The fine gold cups had belonged to Thomas Mahlberg, who had fought the Turks in 1683 as one of Sobieski's lieutenant-colonels. It would have been pointless to sacrifice them to equip half a dozen fat Tirolean soldiers whom Murat's men would in any case have shot like rabbits. So aloof at first, Christine now brimmed with gaiety. Her shyness had evaporated. She had made a pretence of obeying Gertrud's instructions to have the gold cups melted down, but had the old lady been deceived? 'Can one ever tell, with her?' Christine said archly. Otto was to preserve a vivid recollection of the girl and the scent of jasmine that enveloped her. Austria, she declared, was not a country but a disease, an itch, administered by decrepit old men. Every morning, valets dusted them off, rouged their cheeks, propped them up, got them into their uniforms, and ensconced them in their armchairs at the Hofburg. When Bonaparte decided that the time was ripe he would invade this city of the moribund, gallop to Schönbrunn and air it by flinging the palace windows wide, and the only visible memento of the officials who had been strutting around there the previous day would be a cloud of fine dust.

'My aunt will rejoice when that day comes. She has a passion for calamities. Apocalypses are her favourite treat.

Little ones, gigantic ones – she has a whole assortment in stock. She makes bonfires out of disasters. Everything is an illusion, she thinks, and she changes her illusions as often as her clothes. She speeds hell-for-leather through the night, flogging her horses till they drop and maintaining her breakneck pace by demanding a fresh team, a new illusion, at every staging post.'

Christine burst out laughing. Clearly, although she might be an ice maiden, a melancholy girl with a predilection for *Werther*, she was also prone to day-dreams of a different kind.

'She believes in nothing,' Christine went on, 'that's why she strives so hard to believe in everything. For instance, it's true that she adores Austria and Duchess Clémence's white cuirassiers and handsome uniforms and the smell of gunsmoke, just as she considers Bonaparte uncouth. On the other hand, it wouldn't surprise me to learn that she also admires the French Revolution, if only for having severed the neck of Marie-Antoinette, whom she thought a silly goose. These quirks of mood amuse her. They reduce the world to a trifle, and trifles are all she feels at home with. They help her to pass the time and while away the nights . . .'

Christine had a theory: Duchess Gertrud was envious of God and coveted his position, his throne; that was why she talked such nonsense and told so many lies. Her notion of God was a peculiar one. She felt certain that he cherished no beliefs. He believed in nothing, had no ties, and could do as he liked because he was accountable to no one. That was why he contradicted himself so often and acted so arbitrarily. Every one of his compositions was original, whereas mortals were condemned to observe the rules laid down by Bach or Mozart. God knew no rules, had no past, experienced neither youth nor age – hence his personification of absolute freedom. Gertrud had eventually become convinced that by lying whenever possible she would produce something which, instead of merely copying and perpetuating the fruits of inheritance, would constitute an original invention. That would compensate her for the children whom her three husbands had never succeeded in begetting of her.

'She's proud through and through,' said Christine, her voice sounding tiny in the vastness of the drawing-room. 'She's strong and resilient, but she sometimes suffers from attacks of weakness – dizziness, or so it seems. She's sad at such moments because she reckons that God's place is already occupied, that he's clinging to his throne and refuses even to lease it to her. She jokes about this. She loves to profane, besmirch, repudiate, reduce things to absurdity and set them at naught. She's a champion of sacrilege. "He won't let go," she sometimes says, meaning God, but at heart she doesn't care. Her line of retreat is well prepared. She has accepted, once and for all, that superior forces must be bargained with. If need be – if God really declines to "let go", as she puts it in her mirthful moments – she'll content herself with the Devil's place instead. In any case, I'm not so sure she sees much difference between God and the Devil.'

Christine hadn't moved. Very tall and slender in her black satin gown, she was toying with her emerald necklace and leaning forward a little so that the two of them could converse across the duchess's inert form.

'Never fear,' she said. 'Interested though she is in Judgement Day, the last trump wouldn't rouse her once she's set on sleeping. She does precisely as she pleases. By the way, did you gather why she told you that tale about Lord Misrule? She may be eccentric, but nothing she does is fortuitous. Even Father Thaler grasps that.'

Otto hesitated, 'Was she speaking of herself – of herself and you?'

Christine put her head on one side, miming doubt.

'Oh, naturally she was speaking of herself, herself and me, but that gets us nowhere because she never thinks of anyone *but* herself. Of course she chose the Misrule tactic when she went blind. She lives by proxy, at secondhand. Do you know her favourite military rank? That of lieutenant. She dotes on it because the word means "deputy". To her we're all lieutenants. Each of us deputizes for another, for all the others. That's what her Misrule story signifies.

'Don't be misled, Herr Apfelgrun. My aunt has designs on everyone else's property. If she obtains you a commission in the Saxe-Salza Cuirassiers, it will be partly because she has taken a fancy to you, perhaps, but mainly in order to wage war through you. If you took a bullet between the eyes, that would be perfection: you would die for her. Through your mediation, she'd be sampling the delights of death itself. Or suppose you fell in love with some girl or other. I'm sure Aunt Gertrud would do her utmost to smooth your path – yes, but you'd merely be a wraith, merely one of Misrule's lackeys charged with experiencing, on her behalf, the love she has never known. She's very romantic, as the English would say.

'By talking at such length about Lord Misrule, who's one of her favourite puppets, she meant to enlighten you about the Saxe-Salzas. That's the fact of the matter. You're puzzled? I have faith in you. You'll soon understand when you've met my cousin Clémence.'

Otto chose to be jocular. Would he end by dying of love for this duchess whom he'd never yet properly set eyes on? Was it possible to fall in love with an unknown woman? His thoughts strayed to the girl who resembled a cherry, whom he'd seen in the snow from the window of his cell, and who might even now be blowing kisses to another prisoner, mistaking the man for himself, but Christine told him that they hadn't really digressed from the subject of Misrule.

'I'm very attached to my cousin, Duchess Clémence,' she said. 'We were brought up together. I had no friend but her – she knows me inside out. At school they used to call us "the Double-Eagle". I'm also fond of her husband, Prince Ernst, whom you'll meet in due course. He's less of a fool than Gertrud makes out, and he's a kindly man, but the two of them together are another matter – married couples always are . . . Men and women belong to two different species, don't you think? God deposited them on the same planet by mistake and was mischievous enough to compel them to meet for the purpose of producing children. God is a devil, as my aunt would say. He has confined all manner of things in the same cage: giraffes and trout, elephants and semi-colons. When one speaks of men and women, one isn't speaking of antitheses and opposites, reverse and obverse, but of incompatibles and incommensurables. I'm sure you agree?'

Otto said haltingly that he didn't know – he'd never given any thought to such matters – but what had Lord Misrule to do with the Saxe-Salzas?

'You'll see for yourself, Otto, mark my words. After all, if every couple had several thousand wretched soldiers at their disposal, ready to make mincemeat of each other on their behalf – why, married life would be plain sailing. Domestic squabbles and tragedies would still occur, but on another plane. That's roughly what I mean, though there's a great deal more I could say if I cared to put my mind to it.'

Christine had risen. She rang for a footman and told him to take the candles away. Their removal seemed to extinguish the pale form nestling in its silks and shawls. The chandeliers sparkled in the gloom.

6

The hunting season dragged on. Although Prince Ernst and his wife had slaughtered a great many wolves, deer and wild boar in the snows of the Weinsbergerwald, they were apparently insatiable. On learning from Duchess Gertrud that they had decided to prolong their stay at Greinburg Castle, Father Thaler conveyed this news to his protégé in a fine fury. Otto, for his part, congratulated himself. He had won another reprieve, and if the war took advantage of it to end in the interim he might yet escape military service. He remembered former joys, dreaming of a long, serene, peaceful life like a country highroad, and there at its end, bathed in restful light, would be the evening of his days and the consolations of age. The earth was a blessed place, he told himself, and called down blessings on all its creatures.

He had resumed his studies. In a few years' time he would present his thesis on tiger beetles in the university's auditorium maximum. Professor Schwarzbrod would preside over the examiners, bewigged like an English judge and attired in a black robe trimmed with ermine. Very old by then, he would hail his favourite pupil's triumph with an explosive whinny of laughter. The Baden episode was taking on a different complexion. So, even, were Otto's eight months in prison. He had converted them into amusing recollections, a trifle absurd but charming none the less, which he would one day recount to his grandchildren, smoking a long-stemmed china pipe and stroking his grizzled beard. His hands would be sprinkled with little brown freckles . . .

He often pondered on his interview at the Palais Questenberg-Kaunitz. Duchess Gertrud haunted his dreams. He had developed a soft spot for her, but she also inspired dread. Otto was a simple soul, a lover of pleasure, of field and forest. He had made very little of the old lady with the graveyard aroma, of her jeremiads and

imprecations and preposterous dissertations on Lord Misrule. His thoughts turned instead to the housekeeper and her
faint scent of jasmine. She had awakened a recollection of
Duchess Clémence. Although Otto would gladly have dispensed with that, Clémence refused to be banished. Some
evenings, when late winter scents of woodsmoke and rain
rose to his nostrils as he leant on his windowsill, he pictured
her galloping headlong through the Moravian forests,
slaughtering wolves and stags. She had the cruel, inflexible,
stubborn face common to all the crackled and discoloured
portraits in the Mahlbergs' ancestral gallery. Otto credited
her with barbarous, loathsome habits in an attempt to break
her spell, but he still continued to think of her.

Father Thaler, his plans in ruins, fretted and fumed.
Otto's interview at the Palais Questenberg-Kaunitz had
encouraged him to hope that a military career was almost
within his young friend's grasp – that he would soon be
inhaling the scents of gunsmoke and glory – but weeks went
by and the Saxe-Salzas found still more beasts to slay in the
environs of their gloomy lakes. Otto cared more for his
friendships, his games of billiards and colourful cravats,
than for war. The vicar, who would have plunged all
Europe in blood and fire to assuage his martial yearnings,
urged Constanze Apfelgrun to persuade her dreamer of a
son to get to grips with life instead of reading Novalis,
Schlegel or Linnaeus and devoting himself to flirtation and
frivolity. He and Otto resumed the same old argument
every time he called at the Apfelgrun residence. It always
took place beside the big tiled stove in Constanze's music
room, the other furnishings of which comprised her precious harpsichord, some armchairs upholstered in threadbare tapestry, a rather pretty games table, and a black desk
bearing a large collection of goose quills, the latter being a
hobby of Lawyer Apfelgrun's.

Otto sat with his long legs stretched out stovewards while
the vicar constructed sinister castles in the air. War would
break out, Vienna become a fiery furnace, corpses litter the
streets in their thousands. Otto sought refuge in banter.
The vicar, he said, was too well versed in the Bible – he saw

swarms of locusts, the Seventh Seal and the fires of Sodom at every turn. 'Listen, Your Reverence. I know that it saddens you never to have pursued a military career – never to have charged with drawn sabre at the head of a squadron in white and gold – but when all's said and done, why should I be expected to live out your destiny for you? *Can* a person live by proxy, through the medium of someone else? You reproach me for reading Novalis, but it's you who have become infected with the fanciful notions of the German poets: men who cast no shadow, men dogged by their doubles – that sort of nonsense . . .'

On other occasions he would play along with Father Thaler. He told him about Lord Misrule. 'Would you like us to exchange places? If so, buy yourself a handsome, sturdy charger, climb into a uniform and sabre away with all your might while I take up my duties in the house of God. Besides, I suspect you aren't wholly indifferent to Duchess Clémence, whereas I see her merely as a conceited, pretentious, almost faceless creature who dresses up as a carnival colonel and loves to slaughter animals into the bargain. No, I prefer goat girls, believe me. They don't wear fancy dress – they don't even wear shoes.'

The vicar grew heated. Not being quick-witted, he was thrown off balance by Otto's mischievous changes of tack. The young man declared that the Baden era was over. War had fled the scene, and it was no use sending people to look for it: they would return empty-handed. France was being affable toward Austria. Paris had just appointed an ambassador to Vienna, and not just any old ambassador: Bernadotte himself. Didn't this prove that France set store by Austria's friendship? As for Bonaparte, whom the royal courts of Europe described as an ogre, he was a good fellow. 'Yes, yes,' Otto insisted, 'a decent, sensible fellow . . .' He had crushed Italy purely for the sake of international concord, and possibly – why not? – to restore the old monarchies. After that hideous interlude, the French Revolution, Bonaparte was metaphorically joining hands with the late Louis XVI and shutting the sluice-gates on the revolutionary tide. Hadn't he decided to conduct the

Rastadt negotiations in person? Yes, and they would lead to the reestablishment of peace for years to come.

Universal harmony reigned. As though conscious of this, spring blithely embarked on its usual preparations. Little evidence of seasonal change was so far detectable in the crypt of St Anne's, still less in the dank and cavelike atmosphere of Frau Apfelgrun's drawing-room, but in a few weeks' time spring would explode even there. For the present it simply stole across the hills with soft and furtive tread. And it was at night, when men are at rest, that it went about its secret business. Walking in the woods every morning, Otto picked up its trail as he might have spotted the tracks of a squirrel or a bird. As soon as the sun shone, however faintly, the trees became studded with glossy, sticky buds like miniature candles. One fine day, a whole expanse of mountainside turned green. Willow trees emitted a scent of honey, dandelions strewed their mimosa dust across the meadows, and bushes blossomed on river banks, white and round as blobs of foam – so insubstantial-looking that one was tempted to blow them away.

All was as it should be. The ewes had brought forth their lambs. The sun rose precisely when the almanac foretold and dusk was punctual to the minute. Musicians made music, barbers trimmed beards, jasmine smelt of jasmine and not of lilac. Everything had resumed its proper place. Otto gave thanks to the flowers. Invoking Goethe and Paracelsus, he contended that the world was a book, and that the book lay open at the page inscribed happiness. Duchess Gertrud and Father Thaler continued to peddle heroism and disaster, but they were the exceptions. Having rattled his sabre at Baden the previous spring, Emperor Francis II was back in character again. He had suddenly remembered the peaceful tenor of Austria's national motto: *Bella gerant alli, tu, felix Austria, nube.*

Francis could be seen strolling the Prater every morning in commoner's attire, a fat umbrella on his arm, a stovepipe hat surmounting his long, pale, equine face. Austria had retreated a year, and her clocks were going in reverse. Things were progressing, Otto told the vicar, but progressing backwards. All of Austria's historical figures would file past in due course – for instance Emperor Joseph II, who might at that very moment be pulling on his old, patched, lemon-yellow breeches and his green coat with the red collar. One of these days he would turn up in the Graben accompanied by the nightingales he loved so dearly, to be followed by the great Maria Theresa herself. Charles V and Charlemagne, too, were packing up their traps in the depths of the past.

Father Thaler grunted, patting the creases from his cassock. He was unamused by Otto's whimsies. Testily, he drained the small carafe of white wine which Constanze had set out on one of her remaining silver trays, together with some buttered semolina and a compote of cherries. Lawyer Apfelgrun came tiptoeing across the room looking like a big, dishevelled blackbird in his dark coat and yellow nightcap, the latter framed by an aureole of wispy white hair, one finger to his lips to denote that he was disturbing no one. He tried to join in the conversation even so, not that he got very far. With advancing years he wept for no good reason and roared with laughter at trivial pleasures. His thoughts, of which he was no longer in command, for ever overlapped and intermingled. He liked to sit beside his son, wriggling with delight. In deference to Father Thaler he would cup both hands round his left ear and nod, again and again, with an indefatigable smile on his face. Sometimes, when Otto and Thaler called a verbal truce, a different kind of battle would ensue at the chess table. Little though he minded, Otto always lost. On other occasions they would make up a trio with Frau Apfelgrun and dash off a piece of Mozart or Salieri.

Otto was lying, however. He knew in his heart that the peace and quiet wouldn't last – that the book wasn't open at the page entitled happiness. In reality, fire was smouldering in the theatre's wings. One act had ended and the next would resound to the roar of cannon. The scenery would burst into flames and death's supernumeraries invade the stage at any moment. Otto believed in portents, so it didn't surprise him to encounter the house-keeping niece, Christine

Kinsky, one Sunday, after an outing in the hills with some youthful companions of both sexes. They had played bowls at an open-air café in Grinzing where three Tirolean musicians led the dancing in the centre of a circular clearing bright with periwinkles, and they had all whirled and spun on the fresh, fragrant grass. Otto had stolen a kiss from an exceedingly plump young peasant girl. Later he had left the party by himself and walked for several hours in the luminous green depths of the beechwoods. The trees trembled, transfixed by a myriad sunbeams. He would have liked to remain there for ever, strolling on and on through the balmy twilight with only birds for company. Not long afterwards, when he caught sight of Christine in the Augarten, it was therefore as if a time of carefree unconcern had ended – as if the last grain of happiness had dropped into the bulb of the hourglass. Yes, but what hourglass? He pondered the question as he watched the young woman standing there in the blue of the evening, a solitary figure amid the Augarten's good-natured, chattering throng. This was no chance encounter, he decided: Christine had engineered it. Not displeased by the thought, he searched the combined odours of hot dust, sweat and horse dung for a whiff of jasmine.

Christine spoke unguardedly. She trusted Otto, she said. After all, hadn't he been imprisoned for six months or more? He cherished political beliefs and was bold enough to voice them. In self-defence, Otto resorted to sarcasm. His imprisonment had been a misunderstanding, he told her. It was one of the characteristics of an authoritarian régime to penalize innocent blockheads like himself. Christine refused to be deceived. Otto had raised the subject of authoritarian rule, she retorted, and people had ended up in Spielberg Castle for less. Besides, he hadn't turned a hair on learning that the Mahlbergs' gold plate had not been melted down into cannon for His Majesty. That knocked the wind out of Otto's sails. He tried another evasion or two, but Christine, with her scent of jasmine and her ink-flecked eyes, had undeniably won his admiration. That was why he accepted her invitation to attend the following Tuesday's meeting of 'Hope Crowned', a secret society to which she apparently belonged.

Although Christine had given him a sketch-map, finding the rural venue of the meeting proved complicated. Mounted on a borrowed mule, he took innumerable wrong turnings and strayed into some unpleasantly precipitous terrain before he at last glimpsed the dim lights of the charcoal-burners' village which Christine had specified as a landmark. His mule traversed some small terraced vegetable plots, trampling tomato plants and pumpkins on the way, until it came to the gutted, smoke-blackened tower marked on Christine's map. At risk to life and limb, Otto climbed the stairs to an arrow-slit at the top. Once there he had only to face in the direction of the Plough to discover, situated on the edge of an oakwood several hundred yards away, a long, low building with a stone roof and a chimney belching smoke. Otto descended, urged his mule towards this sheepcote, and reached it without further incident. Before entering, he was careful to conceal his face beneath a black handkerchief provided by Christine.

Inside he found himself encircled by more black handkerchiefs of very sinister aspect, most of them encasing beards. Of the two beardless persons present, one was unmistakably Christine and the other a woman dressed in red. The conspirators stood clustered round a log fire blazing on a big flat stone in the middle of the single vaulted chamber, which reeked of greasy wool, mouldering plaster and rat droppings. Otto was welcomed with a largely inaudible rigmarole full of allusions to liberty and equality, popular enlightenment and the abuses of tyranny. He had evidently been recognized by the leader of the group, a short, stout man with a barrel chest tightly constricted by a green silk waistcoat and a beard that glinted red in the firelight. Mention was made of the two-headed turkey. Otto winced, wondering if he would ever shake off his association with that idiotic fowl, but the other man grew eloquent. He informed Otto that it was only thanks to Professor Schwarzbrod's personal intervention that the two-headed turkey, or rather Gravitsky's caricature of the two-headed pig, had narrowly missed being printed in the *Squirrel's Courier*. Otto said he was grateful to the professor, but the red-bearded man lost his temper and said something about Brutus and Mucius Scaevola.

Personages from Roman history were much invoked in this company. Another black handkerchief cited Romulus, Cato, and the mother of the Gracchi. Yet another referred to an operation code-named 'The Rape of the Sabines'. 'No, really!' thought Otto. Being very young, he had an almost irresistible urge to guffaw. He suppressed it by looking at one of the two beardless handkerchiefs. The eyes above it were Christine Kinsky's, but the smile he directed at her evoked no response at all. He began to feel uneasy. Why should Christine, who had enticed him to this sheepcote, be ignoring him? The whole tone of the meeting, too, was changing – losing what little conviviality it had ever possessed and becoming thoroughly grim. The participants were about to swear a dreadful oath to kill or be killed and to seal it by mingling their blood. Their leader set an example by producing a pocket knife from his cloak and gashing his left wrist.

Otto declined to take the oath. Christine promptly claimed the floor in her capacity as his sponsor. In that case, she declared, he must on no account be permitted to leave the sheepcote alive. She spoke in a flat, unemotional voice as though indifferent to what she was saying. Otto was distressed by the prospect of dying. He seemed fated to blunder every time in his relations with women. This girl was a fiend – she smelt of soot and mildew, not jasmine. He braced himself to talk his way out of the trap. But how could he explain to such perfervid conspirators that he had accepted the invitation to them meeting simply because he was susceptible to high-spirited young women – even though this particular specimen had turned out to be anything but sentimental and seemed quite prepared to send her admirer to his death without a moment's regret?

It was the stout man who came to Otto's rescue by ruling out the ultimate sanction.

'Brothers,' he said firmly, 'we are champions of peace

and fraternity, not men of death.' He turned to Otto. 'You need not take the oath, but you must mingle your blood with ours. That will bind you to secrecy, and know this: if you betray our plans, however inadvertently, for instance by chatting to that dirty priest Thaler, we shall strike. Professor Schwarzbrod and Lawyer Apfelgrun will be executed by our number. You I shall dispatch myself, and Brutus, believe me, has a steady hand!'

Having duly gashed his left wrist and deposited a few drops of blood in the hot ashes, Otto undertook not to breathe a word about the meeting, its participants or plans. Happily, those plans had been formulated in language so oblique that no one understood them. Even the identity of the 'Sabines' and the place appointed for their ravishment remained obscure. Furthermore, the proceedings were decidedly fragmentary, since the fat man kept interrupting them with appeals for caution. 'Remember the three wise monkeys,' he exhorted at intervals. 'Lips sealed, ears stopped, eyes shut . . .'

Having exhausted lyricism, the conspirators applied themselves to philosophy. Most of them were educated people. They discussed Kant, Jean-Jacques Rousseau, Goethe, Montesquieu. Otto now felt sufficiently at ease to make a contribution of his own. His remarks on rationalism as a historical trend and objective were favourably received, but he spoke only to anaesthetize himself against the depressing effects of Christine's attitude. He was reminded of Anna Lutgren, the girl like a ripe cherry, whose motive in having him imprisoned had been a kind of love. As for Christine, she had now calmed down, and Otto thought he detected a hint of affection in her eyes, but he couldn't be sure. . . and anyway, he had already been mistaken about her once too often. He was all the more astonished therefore, as he trotted back to Vienna alone hours later, not long before dawn, when she emerged from a coppice on a small chestnut horse, her face unmasked now, and proposed to accompany him for the two leagues that still lay between them and the capital.

They proceeded at a walk, giving their beasts free rein. It

was still dark, and Otto did not recognize the route. He had just begun to suspect that Christine was luring him into an ambush – skirting the edge of a precipice over which her accomplices would hurl him to his death – when she calmly inquired if he had appreciated the reason for her innocent subterfuge at the sheepcote. He must try to understand, she went on: her condemnation of him had simply been a means of saving her own life. Otto was staggered and outraged. She had behaved despicably, he cried. Was she cruel or merely naive? Christine laid a soothing hand on his arm.

'Those people may look as if they'd stepped out of an operetta, with their handkerchiefs and beards,' she said serenely, 'but they're not to be trusted. Their operetta doesn't satisfy them – they like to play Shakespeare now and then. Their leader, the one they call Brutus or Monsieur Charles, is a formidable character – an Alsatian merchant in the service of Napoleon. He's not only strong but fearless.'

She gave a disarming smile.

'He's merciless, too, and doubly so since the others took it into their heads to nickname him Brutus. A name like that puts you under an obligation, he says. What's more, he's much preoccupied with the two-headed turkey affair. Schwarzbrod's approach disarmed him – the professor is 'right-minded', as he puts it – but your mother's friendship with Father Thaler drives him frantic. Father Thaler is a notorious informer who reports all he hears to the imperial police. There's more, though. Brutus himself has informants everywhere. He learned of your interview with Duchess Gertrud and concluded that you were paying for your release by hatching a plot, with my assistance, to destroy his organization.'

Otto's mule had come to a halt. He sat there astride it with his mouth open. The female Mahlbergs were anything but easy to handle.

'So that's why I invited you to the meeting, to kill two birds with one stone. I knew perfectly well that you would refuse to swear the oath, and that Brutus's suspicions would be allayed because a man in the Emperor's pay would have sworn any oath without compunction, secretly cocking his pistol meanwhile. That was the saving of you. As for me, I had to propose your execution, thereby convincing Brutus that we were neither in collusion nor. . . nor sentimentally attached. Do you understand now? Do you forgive me?'

Otto forgave her, forgiveness being his speciality. He claimed no credit for this. It was simply that he couldn't recall ever having borne anyone a grudge. He was somewhat unperceptive, that was all, so he wondered aloud why Christine hadn't warned him of her intention. She said that, after some hesitation, she'd decided a gamble was necessary.

'Brutus is a wary man, and very acute. If we'd rehearsed our scene in advance you'd have been self-conscious. Brutus would have noticed, and that would have been our undoing. In such a quandary, valour seemed the better part of discretion. I was obliged to gamble, Otto – compelled to.'

She gently spurred her horse into a walk.

'Compelled to, yes, and also, if the truth be told . . .' Christine groped uneasily for her words. 'I feel I can tell you this now – it's been such a strange night altogether. During those few seconds when I was waiting to see how you would react, a vile sensation overcame me – a sort of vertigo. I understood why men engage in duels with pistols of which one contains a bullet and the other is unloaded. They know which one they've chosen only when they pull the trigger. In their case the decision between life and death is left to chance – to God, if you prefer. In this case my life or death, your life or death, rested in your hands without your even knowing it. I own I thoroughly enjoyed that dizzy sensation.'

Otto reined in his mule once more.

'For all that,' he said, 'I still fail to see why you joined their society.'

'I share their ideals, that's why. I was born too close to princes, and born of a line too decadent, not to share in the lower orders' aspirations towards freedom. I know that those conspirators are merely courtiers of a different kind, and that they cherish dark ambitions, but I respect them even so, and I quite admire Brutus. Besides, listening to them enables me to refresh my knowledge of Roman history.'

'A Mahlberg,' Otto said softly, not at all amused, ' – a Mahlberg joining forces with those scoundrels to topple the throne . . .'

'Precisely,' Christine retorted, 'a Mahlberg. The Mahlbergs weren't archdukes when God created the world six thousand years ago, they took time to evolve. Well, I've evolved too. Besides, you may have noticed when visiting my aunt that the Mahlberg womenfolk tend to be rebels.'

Dawn was breaking. Otto could now distinguish the girl's face more clearly. Her eyes looked drained and weary.

'Tell me something else. We didn't meet in the Augarten by chance. What made you lure me into that nest of conspiracy?'

She looked him boldly, squarely in the eye and spoke like someone stating the obvious.

'Why, I wanted to see you again, Otto, that goes without saying. I knew I was running a risk, but, as I said just now, I quite enjoyed doing so.'

Otto pointed out that they would have seen each other again in any case, if only at Duchess Gertrud's, once the Saxe-Salzas had finished slaughtering wolves and wild boar.

'My only reason for calling on your aunt was to obtain an audience with your cousin Duchess Clémence, don't you remember?'

'Exactly, my dear Otto. I wanted to see you before you had an interview with my cousin. There! Don't misunderstand me. Clémence is like a sister to me, as I told you. But it's precisely because she's my only friend that I wanted to see you again before you saw her, that's all.'

She hesitated for a moment. Her horse pranced around in the dewy grass, whinnying with delighted anticipation. Suddenly she spurred it into a gallop and disappeared from view behind a rocky outcrop.

Otto plodded on, abstractedly gazing at his mule's ears. He got so thoroughly lost in the fields and orchards that it was mid-morning by the time he entered the outskirts of Vienna. His mule brushed against a peach tree in passing. He captured one of the red petals in his hand, thinking of Christine, or Clémence, or Anna Lutgren – he wasn't sure which. God, he thought, how fickle I am!

7

Otto was destined to see Brutus again two days later, on
April 13th, when a rumour reached the university that the
French were causing ructions in the city. Rector Ouarin,
seething with excitement, stationed himself in the aula and
called for volunteers. The veterans of Baden were overjoyed. Ouarin declared that Austrian scholarship was going
to fly at the Jacobins' throats, so to speak, as it had the year
before. A bevy of students flocked to Wallnerstrasse in the
rector's wake, expecting to see the cobblestones red with
the blood of their fellow patriots. Otto followed them at a
distance, cigar in mouth. Wallnerstrasse was in chaos. A
vociferous mob composed of workmen, coachmen, shop
assistants, chambermaids, innkeepers, carpenters and
middle-class citizens had gathered outside the handsome
town house owned by Banker Geymüller. Those nearest to
it were spitting at an enormous tricolour flag draped across
the mansion's entire frontage and billowing in the spring
breeze.

Banker Geymüller's crime was no crime at all. He had
merely rented his house to General Bernadotte, the Directory's ambassador and Bernadotte had quite reasonably seen
fit to fly the French colours. It was the flag's extravagant
dimensions that had so incensed the crowd. Stones whizzed
through the air. Rector Ouarin scrambled up the steps like a
monkey and clung to the balustrade, crimson in the face.
The tumult increased, the street rang with angry shouts. It
was then that Otto caught sight of a short, stout man with a
bushy red beard in the forefront of the rioters. He was
reminded at once of the leader of 'Hope Crowned', whose
face he had never seen. The man, who possessed an immensely powerful voice, was now inveighing against the
'priest-killers' of France. He invoked the example of the
great Brutus, who had unhesitatingly plunged his dagger
thirty times into the body of a dictator more illustrious than

Napoleon, the 'rat' of Leoben and Rastadt, the 'firebrand' of Mantua.

The chief of police came running up with a squad of gendarmes. He tried to seal off the street, but the rioters would have none of it. Bounding up the steps, he roughly thrust the now orating Ouarin aside in mid-harangue – the rector's mouth remained ajar – and took the floor himself. He explained that the French had signed a treaty at Campo Formio and were negotiating at Rastadt to determine what compensation Germany should receive for the left bank of the Rhine, the intention being to conclude a peace treaty with the Holy Roman-German Empire. Vienna had no present quarrel with Paris. Besides, however inordinate the size of the flag, no diplomatic convention had been infringed.

Brutus gave tongue. 'Austria,' he cried, 'is being smothered, stifled by that flag!'

Otto was dumbfounded. What *was* this man? When was he shamming and when not? Had he really been plotting the Rape of the Sabines in that smoky sheepcote, or did he take his orders from the Hofburg? Was he a subversive pamphleteer or one of Schönbrunn's paid informers? If he *was* in the pay of the police, Otto's goose was cooked: it meant prison again. On the other hand, Christine admired Brutus and had called him a formidable character. No, he must be fanning the flames to supply the French with a pretext for war. Or again, was he one of those born agitators who espoused any cause as long as it made sufficient noise? He bore a strong resemblance to the monarchy he claimed to defend by day and yet undermined by night: he was two-faced. Austria in general was a land of make-believe, a fantastic country populated by invisible, insubstantial men with equivocal faces like Duchess Gertrud's, like animated portraits – a realm of reflections and echoes, a fairy-tale world that combined glitter with dust. And anyway, if Brutus was really a scoundrel, what did that make Christine Kinsky, with all her lying and equivocation?

Bernadotte appeared on the first-floor balcony, half entangled in the breeze-blown folds of his flag. He might have

91

been modelled on a painting by David, with his tall stature and noble bearing, his aquiline nose, his charming, boyish face, his air of vigour and self-confidence. One of the hostile crowd, an elegantly dressed individual with a diamond pin in his cravat, tried to deflate the Frenchman by reminding him of his humble beginnings as clerk to an attorney at the Parliament of Pau. 'Have a care, Sergeant Belle-Jambe,' yelled the man with the diamond pin. The chief of police then requested that the flag be taken down to placate the mob, but Bernadotte eloquently, haughtily rejected this demand. Thereafter the police cordon was jostled by a group of workmen led by Brutus, the first-floor windows disintegrated under a volley of stones, and more uniformed men, this time French soldiers with fixed bayonets, emerged from two side doors.

'You entered this country behind your soldiers' bayonets,' roared Brutus, 'and you'll be driven from it by our peasants' knives!'

This earned the self-appointed tribune of the people an ovation. A skinny, flour-covered young baker, having scaled the front of the building with great agility, seized the flagpole and hurled it to the ground. The French colours were thereupon torn to shreds and burnt.

The baker was carried around in triumph. Demonstrators injured in the affray were also borne shoulder-high. One big fellow shouted that French troops were butchering the inhabitants of Vienna. The word spread like wildfire, and hundreds more townsfolk converged on Wallnerstrasse. The door of the French ambassador's mansion was broken down, and seconds later documents and furniture came flying out of the windows. The house was ransacked. A party of women combed it from cellar to attic in search of Bernadotte, but the ambassador had already taken refuge nearby at the papal nuncio's residence. Rector Ouarin resumed his place on the steps and proclaimed that the citizens of Vienna had won a victory to stand beside that of Baden this year before. He assured the mob that Beethoven would write them another anthem, and then enjoined them to disperse.

Bernadotte, writing from the nuncio's residence, sent Francis II an outraged letter. He demanded the return of his credentials unless the Austrians supplied a replacement for the desecrated French flag and hoisted it over the embassy themselves. In default of such reparation, he added, the offence would be construed as a *casus belli* and Bonaparte would avenge it in an unforgettable manner. The Emperor and his Minister of Police were extremely concerned. They had no wish to start another patriotic riot, but neither did they wish Bonaparte to march on Vienna.

The Emperor's diplomatic advisers counselled a firm stand. According to their secret dispatches, Bonaparte's attentions were directed elsewhere, namely, eastwards. Only last summer Talleyrand had treated the Institut de France to a reading of his *Essai sur les avantages à retirer des colonies nouvelles*, which stressed the rich resources of the Nile Valley. In January of the present year, 1798, the same Talleyrand had presented the Directory with a plan for the dismemberment of the Ottoman Empire. 'That explains one of the mysteries surrounding the negotiations at Leoben,' Foreign Minister Thugut said earnestly. 'Bonaparte was most insistent that France should retain the Ionian Islands, Corfu, Zante and Cephalonia. And why, I ask you, should Poussielgue have visited Malta at Bonaparte's behest, if not to assess the military strength of the Order of St John of Jerusalem – why, tell me that?'

The drawing-rooms of Vienna had acquired enough conversational fuel to last them for weeks. The mood was half jocular, half apprehensive. Armchair warriors ridiculed the Corsican general, accusing him of imagining himself Alexander the Great just because he'd defeated poor old Wurmser at Mantua. Well, they added slyly, they wished him a fair wind for Egypt. By all means let him march his exhausted soldiers through the desert sands, along the Euphrates, or even to the borders of India. The British wouldn't look on idly for ever. They disliked anyone meddling in that area, and Nelson was quite capable of sending the Directory's frigates to the bottom. Dr Ulhue delighted himself while dining at the Schwarzenbergs' one night by coining a splendidly well-turned phrase. Seated at the lower end of the table because of his youth, he da⁻ed not say too much in such exalted company, so he waited for a lull in the conversation and spent the interim polishing his *bon mot*. When the lull came, he jumped in quickly. 'At the close of the Italian campaign,' he blurted out, 'Bonaparte wrote to the Directory that the Austrian army had vanished like a dream. Well, the soldiers of France will melt into the sands of Babel like a mirage.'

Thugut's diplomatic advisers were right. Bonaparte made light of Bernadotte's fury. He had been wearied by the tedious technical niceties of the Rastadt negotiations, and was thirsting for action. An invasion of England being unwise at the moment, he itched to start a conflagration in Egypt instead. This was no time, therefore, to pick a fight with Archduke Charles. Besides, he was not adverse to teaching Bernadotte a lesson. A mediocre general and an inveterate ladies' man, Bernadotte had made eyes at the lovely Désirée Clary, with whom Bonaparte himself had dallied at Marseilles. Cursing, Bernadotte collected his credentials and set off for Rastadt, where he arrived on April 15th.

Vienna experienced the fleeting relief an insomniac feels when he turns over in bed. The Rastadt negotiations were hanging fire, and the French Republic's armies panted and snorted on every side. Quickly the Austrian authorities tightened their grip. It became risky to attend the Burgtheater or the An der Wien. Ears lurked behind every velvet curtain. It was unwise to clap at inopportune moments. Police spies took note of plaudits directed at any actor impersonating a revolutionary, or even a philosopher, and the mountainous archives at the Ministry of Police would be swollen by yet another report.

Professor Schwarzbrod, who sometimes chose effrontery over discretion, asserted that musical notes themselves were under surveillance. Their political import varied. Do, re, mi and so were reputed to be monarchical. The case of fa, a less unequivocal note, was still under investigation. Sharps and flats, on the other hand, were not only revolutionary but probably Jacobin as well, and for obvious reasons. The old naturalist loudly claimed that policemen now underwent courses in the rudiments of musical theory, and any opera-goer caught with a look of ecstasy on his face at the sound of a sharp or a flat risked being clapped in irons.

There was an incongruous side to all this police activity. Although Jacobins and revolutionaries were undeniably at work in Vienna, and although a few masonic lodges went through the motions of dissent, in fact the city's liberals numbered a mere handful. The truth was that Vienna, situated in the heart of a Europe paralyzed with cowardice, remained the bastion of monarchical resistance to the Directory's ravings. Drawing-rooms rang with warlike rhetoric. Viennese writers, painters and musicians, supported by their confrères from Moravia, Hungary, Bohemia and other parts of Europe, notably Germany, sang the praises of Austria's ancient values: tradition, Nature, Providence, the Church, Christianity, royalty, immobility. General Bonaparte was the Antichrist in person. Even the city's numerous French exiles came under suspicion. They were aristocrats to be sure, but Bonaparte, with fiendish skill, had converted several of them into renegades who submitted reports to the Directory.

Father Thaler leapt into the breach. His cheeks glowed, his lips cried out for a dab with a handkerchief, so foam-flecked were they with the vehemence of his incessant denunciations. He expanded his network of social contacts. New *salons* were opening. Taking advantage of the prevailing turmoil, he insinuated himself into one of Vienna's most brilliant social sets, that of Karoline Priecher, who assiduously practised the art of intelligent gossip. The vicar had almost forgotten about the Duchess of Mahlberg and his protégé Otto, but he remembered them as soon as he heard that the Saxe-Salzas, having slain a sufficient number of wolves in the neighbourhood of the Black Lakes, were returning to their Kärntnertor mansion – a sure sign that war was at hand once more. He called on Constanze Apfelgrun in high delight, convinced that her son would at long last shake off his lethargy and enlist in the Saxe-Salza Cuirassiers.

Otto, sad to say, had nothing against lethargy. Anxiety, enthusiasm, ardour, gossip – all these struck him as futile. He was no lover of history, he confided to his 'copycats'. One item of news did, however, rouse him that summer. Professor Schwarzbrod, whom he saw quite often, informed him that Bonaparte's spies had pulled off an unexpected coup. With whose connivance no one knew, they had gained access to one of the central government's most closely guarded departments, the cartographic section. Once there, they wasted no time. One of their teams, headed by a man named Schulmeister, alias Brutus, alias Monsieur Charles, had purloined the copperplates engraved by His Majesty's cartographers, which were about to be sent to the printers'. With unparalleled daring, they had then transported these cumbersome plates to Paris, where the Imprimerie Nationale, having transliterated the place-names and keys into French script, produced some excellent facsimiles. The result was that, whenever Bonaparte chose to go to war, every French officer would be equipped with highly detailed maps covering the whole of Austrian, Moravian and Hungarian territory.

This was momentous news indeed. Heads rolled, tongues wagged, and panic spread. The prowess displayed by Monsieur Charles and his men advertised the skill and impunity of the Directory's secret agents. It became patently obvious that Paris had far from abandoned its invasion plans, and that when the appointed day came the Austrians would have lost one of their few advantages over the French: an intimate knowledge of the terrain, the layout of roads and rivers, the location of villages and, more particularly, the bridges which were Bonaparte's speciality.

The success achieved by Bonaparte's spies made a deep impression on Otto. Clearly Vienna was swarming with these unseen, unidentified agents. They formed a population of invisible beings, of sprites and hobgoblins whose transparent throng mingled imperceptibly with the city's corporeal inhabitants. Otto, always of a fanciful nature, was titillated by the thought. New mirrors glinted in his night-mares: these Austrians, all of whom were multiple persona-lities like Duchess Gertrud, or at least dual personalities like Brutus and Christine Kinsky, had been joined by an indiscernible, innumerable host of diffuse, misty, ethereal, insubstantial beings whose ghostly and non-existent bodies one continually and unknowingly encountered.

At first Otto thought this a new source of amusement, but little by little his defences crumbled. He recalled his night on guard outside Baden in that village whose name he'd forgotten – no, now it came back to him: Pfaffstätten, overlooking the Schwechat. He saw again the lights of the neighbouring villages, the profusion of stars overhead, the hills and mountains, and, lingering like a luminous thread in the gloom below the tower, the river. That night he had pictured French soldiers taking advantage of the hours of darkness to dismantle the Austrian landscape, remove the hills and cows, meadows and apple orchards, load the farmsteads and villages on to their limbers, and trundle the larchwoods back to France. It must surely have been a flight of fancy, a product of fatigue or hallucination; and yet, one evening after the theft of Austria's maps, when he climbed the Leopoldsberg and looked down in the fading light, he was genuinely moved to see the vast panorama of forests, hills and dales which Bonaparte's soldiers, with their stolen maps, had sworn to make off with. Although Otto would never have pulled the trigger on some poor devil of a Frenchman to safeguard the honour and authority of the Habsburgs, he would have flown into a lethal rage had anyone laid hands on those mountains, those outspread fields, those thalwegs stretching away into the gathering darkness.

However, being a young man who soon tired of dramatic pathos, he addressed himself in a carefully waggish under-tone: 'Duchess Clémence of Saxe-Salza may look puppet-like and absurd in that cuirasse of hers, I admit, but the preservation of those cumuli and nimbi drifting past in the moonlight requires me to overcome my prejudices.' Then, rather ashamed of this poetic self-indulgence, he tried to trivialize his case: 'But will I have the gall to tell Duchess Clémence or her husband, when applying for a commission, that my sole reason for wanting a handsome white uniform and a crested helmet is to defend the beetles and butterflies, slugs, larch trees and streams of Austria?'

Although the tricolour flag affair did not become the *casus belli* Bernadotte had hoped it might, tension steadily mounted. In May Bonaparte embarked forty thousand men at Toulon in three hundred ships, destination Egypt. Negotiations with the Holy Roman-German Empire had not precisely been broken off, but the delegates were marking time, and the Austrians, feeling temporarily rid of Bonaparte, stealthily disengaged themselves from Rastadt. Their complacency was greatly encouraged by events in the Eastern Mediterranean, where Nelson struck at the beginning of August. Under the command of Brueys, Bonaparte's fleet went to the bottom in Aboukir Bay with the loss of five thousand French seamen. Sporadic skirmishes then took place on Austrian soil, and Vienna permitted Russian troops, led by the redoubtable Suvorov, to infiltrate Galicia and Moravia. In December the Russians sidled into Austrian territory proper. Mars had returned to the stage by a secret door, and on March 12th 1799 France and Austria were formally declared to be in a state of war. The Directory's representatives at Rastadt packed their bags. On April 28th, two years after the battle of Baden, while setting off for Paris they were attacked by a detachment of Hungarian hussars from Skelzar's corps, and two French envoys were killed. All Europe, from the Rhine to Lombardy, burst into flames.

8

Duchess Clémence of Saxe-Salza held herself like a strung bow. She was always on parade, even in her drawing-room. The receptions she held at her mansion near the Kärntnertor resembled military reviews. The huge first-floor room was decorated with exotic flowers, caged birds, glittering epergnes. The duchess herself presided at its focal point, her face made up in mutedly martial hues, her head tilted slightly backwards in a way that lent her the haughty expression peculiar to certain pedigree cats. She cultivated an air of disdain. Being mindful of her social duties, however, she was courteous and even gracious enough to show off her lovely milk-white shoulders and her gown of white and gold – the colours of her regiment – which was adorned with brandenburgs, aiguillettes and chevrons picked out in diamonds. Her eyes never moved. They absorbed the images that strayed into her vicinity but reflected nothing, not even the flickering light of the flambeaux and candelabra, still less the men and women who made obeisance to her. No object was substantial enough to leave an imprint in the depths of those huge, translucent, empty eyes.

Stern and motionless, her mouth expressive of indifference and unsuited to smiling, Clémence surveyed the courtiers, dignitaries and officers who thronged her reception rooms as though contemplating a desert. She devoted all her skill to making such functions a joyless duty. If she ordained one of these tedious rituals, however, no one could afford to decline. She took pride in them. And since all Vienna, the world's most frivolous, licentious and pleasure-loving city, fought to gain access to these doleful soirées at the Carinthian Gate, didn't that prove how infinitely, awesomely powerful the Saxe-Salzas were?

'There's no doubt about it,' thought Otto, as courtiers jostled him on every side, 'Duchess Clémence is a vain creature. I wasn't mistaken at Baden: she's consumed with pride. Her cousin Christine may be an alarming person, but at least there's some genuine fire in her – *and* she smells of jasmine. . .' Otto was comforted by this thought, first because he had come to the Kärntnertor only out of a sense of duty, at Father Thaler's insistence, and secondly because he knew from his patron that Duchess Clémence had looked contemptuous when told that such a scion of the petty nobility as Otto Apfelgrun dared aspire to an officer's galloon in her renowned white cuirassiers – or even in her husband's blue hussars, less exalted though the latter were. She had even found her aunt's request impertinent, and only a browbeating from Gertrud had induced her to retract her refusal.

'But I'm bound to admit she's very beautiful,' Otto told himself, toying with a bowl of strawberries and cream. 'At Baden I was denied all that beauty by her shako. The fact is, if only her expression were less forbidding, she'd be one of the most enchanting women in Austria . . .' His growing excitement was understandable. Everything this evening was new to him – new and dazzling. On reaching the Kärntnertor he had marvelled at all the carriages bearing the ciphers of Austria-Hungary's noblest houses. Lighting each cabriolet and barouche were haiduks, Hungarian footmen dressed *à la turque* in plumes, flowing sashes and boots with upturned toes, who thrust the onlookers aside with long canes, the gold knobs of which could be unscrewed to accommodate notes addressed by ladies of fashion to their lovers. A platoon of lackeys in scarlet livery was drawn up in two ranks on either side of the marble steps. The women's jewels caught the light, the crowd applauded every new arrival.

At Otto's side Father Thaler was congratulating himself. His lengthy labours had borne fruit. He was at last storming the ramparts of an establishment so illustrious that any man of rank would have risked damnation to set foot in it. His own lowly status as vicar of St Anne's would of course have debarred him from admittance had not Duchess Gertrud insisted that both he and his young protégé be invited to the spring reception. Thanks to Otto, Father Thaler was now entering the holy of holies, and the entire city would soon know that he had been invited to one of the soirées which the Saxe-Salzas gave at each change of season – in this case on March 21st. They adhered to this custom whatever the circumstances and wherever they happened to be, whether at their castles in Hungary or Bohemia, or at Greinburg near Linz, or here at their mansion near the Carinthian Gate. This, so the envious alleged, was to demonstrate that a family hailing from the dawn of European history regulated its pleasures by the moon, sun and stars, not by social chitchat or historical ephemera. To Father Thaler, however, the evening represented a banquet of prestigious delights. He was determined not to waste a morsel of it – to pick the smallest bone clean. It would be something to lick his lips over later in the confessional or at Mass.

With Otto in tow, the vicar fought his way over to the princely couple. Otto saw his patron racked by a series of respectful jerks and spasms so violent that his genuflexion at the feet of his hosts might have been ascribed to the operation of cogs or pulleys secreted in his elbows and knees. The Prince of Saxe-Salza screwed a monocle into his eye and looked majestic. Addressing Otto over the head of the priest, who was still straightening up, he informed the young man that he would be starting his military training at the Wiener-Neustadt cadet school in a few days' time and advised him to make the most of it. 'One ill-learned lesson,' the prince declared with a booming laugh, 'and two years hence you'll stop a bullet in the chest.' An exceptionally tall man whose demeanour, though haughty, was less forbidding than his wife's, he had a fleshy but clear-skinned, intelligent face and a big bald dome of a head.

As for Duchess Clémence, it was a moment before she admitted to being aware of Otto's presence. Then, narrowing her eyes a little as if peering at him from a vast distance, she acknowledged his bow graciously enough, and told him, in the dry, clipped, brittle voice which Austrian ladies of quality had been perfecting for two seasons past, that she would sooner have seen him enter a veterinary corps than the cuirassiers. 'Austria has plenty of expert horsemen, whereas you, I'm told, are my dear friend Schwarzbrod's prize pupil. You would have served the monarchy better by mending our horses than by galloping astride them.'

At that she slowly turned her head as if Otto had wholly escaped her attention and allowed her languid gaze to rest on the courtiers pressing round her: fat and thin, florid and pallid, peruked, pomaded and crimped, their apricot or apple-blossom breeches set off by embroidery and trimmings, their chests adorned with the Maria Theresa Cross or other orders and decorations. Also on display was a contingent of officers, all very youthful and tall and all well nourished, with powdered hair and handsome, smiling, energetic faces. They were distinguishable only by the colour of their uniforms, which were blue or white depending on their membership of the prince's hussars or the duchess's cuirassiers.

War was their principal topic of conversation. Austria had changed a good deal in recent years. Gone were the days of carefree bonhomie and riotous pleasure. Panic, too, was a thing of the past. Today, with Bonaparte pursuing his oriental pipe-dream, the French fleet under Brueys sunk at Aboukir, the alliance with Russia and Britain resurrected, *de facto* if not formally, and Pitt and Grenville at last disbursing some of their gold, hopes were riding high. Austria was going to smite the barbarians from France just as she had not so long ago destroyed those savages from the East, the Turks. Vienna had became a barracks, the bastion of Western civilization and monarchical splendour. Its streets were alive with the comings and goings of British and Russian officers, with couriers galloping off to Italy, to the Kingdom of the Two Sicilies, to Germany or Graubünden. Dread captains of war sojourned in the shadow of St Stephan's Cathedral. Nelson and the great Suvorov had been sighted, and excitement was at fever pitch. Everyone itched to annihilate the barefoot armies that were scattering like frightened rabbits now that Bonaparte had made himself scarce . . .

The Prince of Saxe-Salza adjusted his monocle and announced, out of the blue, that the thrones of Europe were secure. Watched impassively by his wife, he enlarged on this theme.

'Let us never forget,' he said, 'that every throne is merely the outward manifestation of another, unseen throne. That, to my mind, is the true significance of the Dual Monarchy and its two-headed eagle: the partnership between God and emperor. Shall I tell you what I find striking – no, more than that: profoundly moving? When Suvorov leads his boyars and mujiks into a town, he replaces every so-called 'liberty tree' with a cross.'

A low murmur rose from the officers clustered round the princely pair. Their reactions varied in accordance with the colour of their uniforms, Otto noted. The white cuirassiers took their cue from Duchess Clémence's starchy expression, while Prince Ernst's blue hussars joined in his enthusiasm. They elaborated on the Suvorov anecdote, wondering how a soldier of such distinction could dress so poorly. It was quite an experience, they said, to see him walking the streets of Vienna escorted by elegant aides-de-camp, his grim face afflicted with a nervous tic, his squat little frame muffled up in a drab greatcoat or a sheepskin pelisse more appropriate to some old shepherd from the Caucasus or the Tirol. A young woman with a triangular face, her lace gown encircled just below the bosom by a broad band of tulle, had heard it from the Wallensteins themselves that Suvorov spurned the big four-poster in the sumptuous apartment they had placed at his disposal and slept on the floor, on a common soldier's palliasse. What was more, the scourge of the Turks disliked eating his meals off porcelain or silver plate; he favoured a mess-tin instead. The officers and their ladies greeted these revelations with mingled awe and distaste. Duchess Clémence's languor, on the other hand, made it hard to tell if she was listening at all.

A man in a powdered peruke, his pink knee-breeches and bottle-green frock coat underpinned by a pair of white silk hose, contributed another piece of tittle-tattle. In polished French this émigré, the Vicomte de Videmar, claimed that

Suvorov had a hatred of mirrors and would smash one, yelling like a lunatic, if ever he caught sight of his reflection in it. Warned of this in the nick of time by one of the Russian hero's aides, the Wallensteins had managed to preserve their mirrors from destruction by covering them.

The company dissolved into mirth. Prince Ernst removed his monocle and guffawed, throwing back his head for greater convenience. His booming laugh reduced those around him to respectful silence. A moment later, and without a glance in her husband's direction, Duchess Clémence spoke up.

'I fail to understand,' she said heatedly, 'why anyone should poke fun at a general of his calibre. He may seem uncouth in a ballroom, but he's a lion in battle. Smashing mirrors, substituting crosses for liberty trees – that's all very amusing but very, very foolish. Why try to make him out as nothing more than a pious old eccentric? The common folk of Vienna have more sense – they know very well that Suvorov possesses formidable powers.'

She paused. Otto stared at her in surprise.

'Do you know what they say, the people of Vienna? They know precisely why Suvorov dreads to look in a mirror. Why? Because, gentlemen, he would see *nothing*! Suvorov has no reflection: he has sold it to the Devil in exchange for gallantry and victory – that's what the grooms and chambermaids believe, and their notion of heroism may be nearer the mark than ours. They know that the Devil is among us, and that the Devil must be given his due. Even if I grant you that the Russians have replaced liberty trees with crosses, it would interest me greatly to know what colour those crosses will appear when reflected in the mirrors of time.'

The French bottle-green coat subsided hastily, the powdered face shrinking back under its peruke like the head of a frightened tortoise. The duchess's vehemence had withered even the diplomats and officers eager to curry favour with her. Gathering up the skirt of her gown in one hand, she progressed to another part of the drawing-room. Otto, although he would never have dared to take a hand in the argument, thought her obnoxious. She possessed more fire, more character and spirit than her admirers, true, but she was obnoxious none the less. Faintly bewildered, he drew Father Thaler aside and inquired if the prince and his wife got on well together. The vicar, indignant at such a question, threw up his hands.

The duchess had her peculiarities, to be sure. She was fond of voicing extravagant opinions, Thaler conceded, and not averse to flouting convention. The first few months of the marriage might also be said not to have gone altogether smoothly. But then Prince Ernst bowed to the duchess's insistence and purchased her a regiment of cuirassiers, so that they both possessed a regiment of their own. It was true that this was an unprecedented arrangement and that a certain rivalry could be detected between the prince and his wife, both of them being eager to command the more prestigious regiment, priding themselves on the exploits of the one, deriding the other's reverses, and comparing their respective tallies of dead and wounded. But for all that, Thaler pontificated, rivalry between regiments was a wholesome thing. It encouraged each man to do his best and all to fight like titans. And it was this delegated rivalry that enabled the princely pair to set a Christian example of unity and amity. Only the duchess's Austrian cuirassiers were now on active service, however. The Saxon hussars were at their barracks in Dresden, and since this precluded any fresh outbreak of vicarious hostilities between the couple, their face-to-face rivalry had been known to become, well, distressing, and productive of frightful altercations.

Otto asked if he still had time, not to abandon a military career, but to opt for the Saxon hussars instead of the Austrian cuirassiers.

'I don't see why not,' the priest told him. 'The couple own both regiments, so officers can be assigned to either, irrespective of whether they're Saxons or Austrians. They're the Saxe-Salzas' property, after all. You know young Ignaz Jungen? Vienna-born he may be, but he's now a cornet at Dresden in Saxony.'

'It's just that the prince seems less aggressive than the duchess, Father. Don't you agree?'

'But Otto, we've already settled on the Austrian cuirassiers. What's more, if you want my opinion, the war is about to flare up again – it's gaining in ferocity day by day – and in that case the Saxon hussars will not be required to take part. The honour of destroying the French armies will go to Her Excellency the Duchess Clémence's white cuirassiers. I'm sure you're eager to distinguish yourself in battle. Besides, think how people would view your request to be transferred to a non-combatant regiment. The malicious would construe it as cowardice. You'd be the talk of Vienna – indeed, our beloved patroness Duchess Gertrud would be the first to take it amiss.' Thaler laid a hand on Otto's sleeve. 'She insists on seeing you, by the way. Would you care to present your respects?'

They made their way to the other end of the room, where the old lady sat enthroned on a dark red sofa near a window draped in mauve velvet. Her peruke had grown still taller since her first interview with Otto, and the ringlets were dyed pink. All else – the pointed nose, the flabby but still powerful jawline, the bloodless, withered lips, the vermilion and white cheeks – was as it had been. Duchess Gertrud curtly dismissed her current companions, a gaggle of young *femmes du monde*, as soon as the vicar announced Otto's presence. She gave Otto her diminutive hand to kiss, then slapped him on the wrist with her reticule in a bizarre little invitation to sit down in the armchair facing her. No such invitation was extended to Father Thaler. Judging by her gaiety of manner, the duchess had either taken a definite fancy to Otto or was hatching some scheme. She jested and bantered, leant forward to whisper pleasantries in his ear, looked roguish, and generally behaved quite unlike the alarming creature of Otto's recollection.

'May I ask you to cast an eye outside, Herr Apfelgrun? Christine Kinsky has absented herself from Vienna for a few days, and I need to know how this evening's sunset is progressing. At my age a person is full of little fancies, but we have time, do we not?

'Can you guess what they were chattering about, those flibbertigibbets from whom you rescued me just now? Little Countess Pietranera was speaking of Bonaparte. Her ninny of a husband – her husband, or one of her numerous lovers – must have told her that Bonaparte was a French general and that he'd gone off to Egypt, or something of the kind. Bonaparte is not only done for, she told me, but *démodé*. I ask you, *démodé*!'

Gertrud shook with laughter, but hurriedly, as if she had no time to lose.

'At my age one hasn't enough years left to waste on laughter. A pity, because little Countess Pietranera would otherwise keep me supplied with the makings of a good laugh between love affairs.' She aimed another blow at Otto's wrist with her reticule. 'Bonaparte won't stay in the East indefinitely. What's more, who can claim to know what he's been up to there? It's obvious to a shrewd old body like me that Bonaparte always contrives to be where he isn't at all. He presents us with spectacles like the Battle of the Pyramids or the Aboukir disaster, but they're so much dust in our eyes. Did you note that Suez excursion he made with Monge and Berthelot three months after Aboukir? Christine Kinsky reads me the Paris gazettes. All such things are merely feints designed to hoodwink the foolish and leave him at liberty to weave a still more dangerous web. Do you know Bonaparte's strong point? Instead of hiding in the dark like our own gallant generals, he conceals himself in the light of day.' She raised a hand to her face and indicated her staring orbs. 'Ah, Apfelgrun, these eyes, these eyes of mine . . .'

Otto longed to say something, but he was too numb with nervousness to think of anything suitable. Gertrud turned to Father Thaler and briskly instructed him to go and find her niece, Duchess Clémence. The vicar obeyed with alacrity. It took him only a minute to thread his way through the guests, draining a glass of champagne as he went, and return with Clémence. Gertrud made the introductions.

'Your new cornet of cuirassiers, Clémence: Herr Otto Apfelgrun.'

Clémence extended her wrist for Otto to kiss, looking bored.

'Weren't you presented to me only minutes ago? I seem to have seen you before.'

'Capital, capital,' Gertrud broke in. 'This young man has been telling me how Nelson rescued the Neapolitan royal family in his ship and put them safely ashore at Palermo. Or was it I that told him the story? Or were we discussing something else? I'm well acquainted with Nelson, you know – he was a great friend of Lord Misrule's. I also adore Lady Hamilton for her warm heart and the way she braves public opinion. But do you know the striking thing about Nelson? His conceit, would you say? Hardly – he's only an Englishman, after all. No, what strikes you about him is something altogether different. You might think him a fool at first meeting – yes, a fool – and then, without warning, the fool unscrews like a Russian doll and inside you discover the most profound and prophetic man in the world. In short, Nelson needs unscrewing.'

Father Thaler laughed heartily.

'My dear Clémence,' Gertrud went on, 'I've had the honour of meeting several of your young cuirassiers, likewise some of Ernst's hussars, not to mention their wives. They're mere trinkets, musical-boxes that produce no music. I marvel at the sameness of them all. They're a flock of sheep, Clémence, however brave they may be. They must die to order – that's good, excellent – but they mustn't be too disobedient. Am I right? Tell me, Clémence, how can you tolerate officers who never disobey?'

Clémence smiled. She might have been a different person. She was a Russian doll like Nelson, thought Otto, and old Gertrud had unscrewed the sullen-looking person to reveal another altogether: mischievous, vivacious, even passionate.

'My dear Aunt,' Clémence said with great respect, 'my officers are trained to die without batting an eyelid. Everyone admires Suvorov, but do you know what constitutes his great strength and that of Russian soldiers in general? If one of them is hit, for instance while out on patrol, he falls

108

without a cry – without so much as a groan, however terrible the wound – rather than bring down fire on his comrades. No other army in the world displays such self-abnegation. Not even the French are capable of it.'

Gertrud gestured sharply as if brushing her niece's accumulation of words aside.

'Nelson lost an arm,' she said, 'his right arm, at Santa Cruz de Tenerife. Before that he lost an eye at Calvi. There was little left of him, but the one thing he did retain was his disobedience. Let me tell you a story I heard from that young scatterbrain, Beckford.

'When the British were faring badly at the battle of Copenhagen, Nelson's superior officer, Admiral Parker, signalled him to disengage. Nelson had other ideas. He proposed to fight on despite his predicament. His officers insisted that Parker was flying the signal to withdraw. Nelson called for his telescope and trained it on Parker's vessel. But Clémence, do you know what he did? Putting the glass to his blind eye, he studied Parker's rigging for a moment, then turned to his officers and growled, 'Devil take me if I can see that signal of yours. I've only one eye – I've a right to be blind sometimes. I really do not see the signal.' And fight on he did . . . No, Nelson isn't noted for his obedience.'

Otto had been covertly watching Clémence. She was indeed a woman capable of transformations. Her air of disdain, then pleasure, had now been succeeded by a look of eagle-eyed intensity. He felt flattered, yet for no good reason. He certainly wasn't vain enough to believe it was his presence that had kindled her emotions. It genuinely never occurred to him that he could stir the feelings of a woman of such quality. More at ease in the company of seamstresses and peasant girls, he was petrified by ladies of high degree and amazed that they should notice him at all.

The fact remained, however, that Duchess Clémence was clearly surprising even the other people nearby. Otto doubted if anyone had ever seen her looking so unaffectedly animated. Old Gertrud had wrought a miracle. She knew how to get her niece going – knew the workings of her mind.

Father Thaler had told him that Ducess Clémence relished strong emotions and enjoyed deriding absurdities. Her aunt spoiled her in that respect. The old lady had a mischievous streak and she could lie in her teeth, but she was younger in spirit than any minx in that crowded room. And Otto believed that she was also capable, from time to time, of affection.

Now Clémence was replying to her. She would suffer one of her cuirassiers to disobey his lieutenant-colonel's orders, she said, but only like Nelson: with style. Turning to Otto, she addressed him for the first time. 'You've been warned, Herr Apfelgrun,' she told him firmly. 'If you wish to disobey you must begin by losing an arm at Tenerife and an eye off Corsica, then buy yourself a telescope. It would put you to a great deal of trouble, in short, but it's the only price that will make disobedience pass for a virtue.'

She turned back to her aunt. Gertrud would have to excuse her; she must devote herself to her guests. The old lady kissed her and said that she, too, would strike camp as soon as Herr Apfelgrun had performed his first military duty, which was to inspect the sunset for her. 'But bear this in mind, Apfelgrun. Contrive to make the night a fine one. I want plenty of stars, do you hear?'

Otto made his way across the huge room, bemused by the babble of so many voices and closely scrutinized, after his lengthy conversation with Duchess Clémence, by a score of bewigged dandies. The grand staircase was still lit with flambeaux held by motionless, expressionless lackeys. He descended it almost at a run, then skirted the Kärntnertor mansion and entered the grounds beyond it. Occasional puffs of cooler air came wafting through the tepid twilight. Otto decided to disobey old Gertrud after all. He would tell her that Austria was cold as the grave this evening, and that the firs, yews and spruces were tinselled with hoar-frost. He would fabricate a landscape of his own. The notion made him laugh, all to himself. The situation was positively operatic.

It was more so than he knew. A few paces farther along the path, which was flanked by lawns, he caught sight of

Duchess Clémence. He hadn't heard her footsteps, so she seemed an instantaneous creation of the dusk. She stood like a statue, her dark blue hooded cloak revealing little of her face except her eyes, which studied Otto intently. Feeling even more awkward than usual, he prayed to heaven she wouldn't accost him. She had slipped outside for a little fresh air, nothing more, and their meeting was quite fortuitous. If she spoke to him he knew he would barely manage to stammer a reply. It never occurred to him that awkwardness could be endearing.

Clémence took a step towards him. Her expression was timid but resolute, a trifle wild-eyed. She was holding one of the strange canes Otto had seen earlier: the ones with knobs which contained secret messages carried by linkmen in Turkish costume. Her voice shook.

'Nelson must have experienced some supreme emotion when he put the glass to his blind eye, don't you think? A moment like that is worth a lifetime of glory, wouldn't you say?' Biting her lower lip, she commanded Otto to reply but gave him no time to do so. 'Do you believe,' she went on quickly, 'that a single second of real danger can contain more life than an entire lifetime?'

Otto was at sea. He said nothing.

'A person who raves has fever as a rule, but look, I'm cold as ice.' Very fleetingly, she put her hand on his. Then she unscrewed the gold knob of her long cane. Removing a scrap of paper folded in four, she handed it to him and vanished into the darkness. Otto made no attempt to follow her. He leant back against a tree trunk and closed his eyes.

A few minutes later he returned to the great drawing-room and presented his report to Duchess Gertrud. The old lady wasn't at all annoyed when he told her it was cold and frosty outside. She seemed genuinely contented. Rapping the floor with her stick, she told Father Thaler to summon the two lackeys whose task it was to convey her to and from the Palais Questenberg-Kaunitz. Otto then made his adieus to Prince Ernst and his wife Clémence, who distantly gave him her hand to kiss. Afterwards he spent a long time walking the streets, aimlessly and rather unsteadily because

111

of all the champagne he had drunk. It was four in the morning before he paused beneath a street lantern and summoned up the courage to open Duchess Clémence's note.

It bore no message of any kind: the paper was completely blank. He stowed it carefully in his fob.

9

That was the last social function of the winter. Otto spent the spring and summer of 1799 at the Wiener-Neustadt cadet school founded in 1751 by Maria Theresa, two hours' ride to the south of Vienna on the road from Baden to Leoben.

Officer cadets were quartered at the Burg and performed their arms drill in the castle yard, the Wappenwand, the walls of which were adorned with a hundred and seven coats of arms in relief. While loading his enormous musket, Otto looked for the Mahlberg arms. He learned how to bite the end off a cartridge, and also how to wield the cuirassier's long, heavy, straight-bladed sword. He carried out forced marches and mounted patrols by day and night, practised barking words of command in his naturally gentle voice, familiarized himself with explosives and bridge construction, memorized regulations and forms of procedure, learned how to read military maps, studied the tactics of Prince Eugène, Frederick II and the Prince de Ligne. His days were exhausting, but he was inwardly at peace. The Mahlbergs' armorial bearings were not in evidence on the walls of the Wappenwand. He occasionally unfolded the blank sheet of paper, his memento of that night at the Kärntnertor, and otherwise spent his evenings strolling with friends in the Gothic arcades of the Hauptplatz or on the city walls near St Peter's.

The pleasures of the cadet community were simple and reassuring. Perched astride a charger of playful, even skittish disposition, Otto traversed valleys carpeted with flowers and rode along the banks of mountain streams. He and his comrades performed their military evolutions across expanses of sunlit countryside, paused for refreshment at rustic inns, fished for trout, drank white wine, played bowls. Good at swapping badinage with quick-tongued maidservants, Otto was able to indulge in a few fleeting affairs. Country girls, in their blue or white aprons, appealed to him. They were agreeable creatures, and their utter lack of guile contrasted favourably with the vanity and artifice of society women. Otto, with his horror of hypocrisy, was popular with his fellow cadets. He did not find army life as alien as he'd expected, and wondered if the army ran in his blood. Many years ago his grandfather, a colonel, had presented him with some cardboard soldiers for Christmas. He and the old man had cut out hussars and grenadiers and equipped them with sabretaches, shakos and epaulettes prior to painting in the colours.

In October 1799 he received a posting. The Prince of Saxe-Salza had approved his temporary secondment to an infantry unit stationed in the heart of that sinister region known as the Military Frontier, the fortified strip of land between Austrian and Ottoman territory. The posting was a peculiar one. All his friends had been assigned to fashionable regiments stationed in Vienna, in Italy, or along the Bavarian border. Admittedly they had scored higher marks in training, but even so might it not be a clerical error? One of Otto's comrades, Konrad von Thieburg, reckoned that such a posting could have been decreed only by the Hofkriegsstadt or the General-Kriegskommandant, if not by the Chancellery itself. Had the Baden affair, the two-headed turkey, been resurrected once more? Otto, however, had a theory of his own – one he found pleasing but kept to himself: in the final analysis, regimental postings were the exclusive preserve of colonels proprietor, in this case, of Prince Ernst.

Otto made no attempt to have the decision revoked. He was far from distressed by the idea that his career should be governed by chance, by clerical error or bureaucratic inefficiency, still less by the whim of Prince Ernst: it suited his attitude, his vague sense of serene resignation, and his store of happiness remained intact. 'With a little dexterity,' he told Thieburg, 'you can extract a ton of happiness from the bottom of a thimble. Give me a Trappist cell and I'll transform it into an Aladdin's cave.' He was surprised when Thieburg accused him of self-righteous arrogance.

On the morrow of the passing-out parade that marked the end of their course, Otto hurried to Vienna to say goodbye to his parents. Lawyer Apfelgrun was as garrulous and sociable as ever, though his rambling remarks were hard to follow. But he recognized his son at once. He had compiled a little dictionary, a notebook in which he jotted down words that tended to elude him. His air of pride whenever he found one brought tears to Otto's eyes. The young man spent many hours at home in his father's company. He also lunched with Professor Schwarzbrod and his worthy wife, Greta. The professor volunteered to walk him home after the meal, hinting that he had something of importance to tell him. After beating about the bush for a time, he blurted out his surprise that Otto had been posted to the Military Frontier. Otto replied casually that the pen-pushers must have their reasons. 'I cut a less than commanding figure,' he said.

'I have my own ideas on the subject,' Schwarzbrod replied, 'but you must promise not to tell anyone.'

'You're thinking of Prince Ernst?'

'Of course, my boy. The prince is still in love with his wife – he's very suspicious of anyone who comes within a mile of her.'

Otto was perplexed. He didn't understand, he said. He'd never behaved toward Duchess Clémence in a presumptuous or unseemly manner.

'That's beside the point,' Schwarzbrod told him. 'The prince is no fool. Anyway, if you really want the truth, it was Christine Kinsky who engineered the whole thing. How do I come to know all this? I know, that's all. One more thing, Otto: Duchess Clémence will contrive to send letters to your outpost.'

He parted from Otto with an affectionate hug. 'I mustn't linger,' he said. 'Our daughter Marie-Josèphe is very poorly, you know, but we keep her at home with us. Poor Greta . . .'

That evening Otto talked of Duchess Clémence to his father. The lawyer listened uncomprehendingly, one hand cupped to his ear, while Otto described the Kärntnertor reception, the cane with the gold knob, the slip of paper folded in four. He confessed that the duchess was never out of his mind. Apfelgrun Senior smiled and nodded. It was all Otto could do not to weep, but to whom could he have confided such things, if not to this poor, deranged soul? Next day, October 13th, he and four troopers headed at full gallop for the Empire's eastern frontier. They reached the fortress of Vrenjac three saddle-sore days later.

The winter of 1799 came in like a lion at the beginning of November. All colour was obliterated overnight. The landscape, a series of yellow and grey undulations bounded in the distance by jagged crests and covered with hoar-frost, was suddenly deep in snow. It was Otto's task, as commander of the little fortress, to guard the southern plains and plot their topography. He performed his duties assiduously. The trumpet sent him leaping out of bed each morning into the dreadful chill that pervaded the ancient building, and his work was never done before nightfall. He visited guard posts, saw to it that the sentries made their rounds, sent out patrols, directed exercises, supervised his three junior officers, the kitchens and the quartermaster's stores.

The countryside was silent and desolate. Here and there in the barren waste, villages stood out like blackish blisters. Peasants muffled up in rags sat on the threshold of their hovels, heedless of the cold, smoking their pipes and casting lacklustre glances at passing patrols. The houses stank of urine and rancid butter, tannin and dead cockroaches. They were crudely constructed of undressed stone, their interiors so black with soot that anyone entering might have thought himself in a coal mine. Huddled round a central fireplace, the womenfolk wove garments of grey wool or put cooking pots filled with cabbages and potatoes on to simmer. To look down from the fortress battlements and see the villagers hacking away at the ground with their mattocks, one would have sworn that they had resolved to dig their own graves, but the frozen soil became harder and harder, and the exhausted men never succeeded in making holes large enough to contain a corpse. They trudged back to their cottages each night and emerged less and less often.

The wind never, never stopped moaning. It whistled along Vrenjac's maze of stone passages, drove the days and nights ahead of it like a flock of sheep, swapt away skies the colour of sulphur and autumn leaves and replaced them with skies of identical hue. Pale, wizened children were born in the cluster of hovels at the foot of the fortress walls. Their parents dressed them in rags like their own, pursued their bent-backed assault on the barren soil, begot more pale, wizened children, grew old, expired on their beds of rags, and the cycle was complete. History itself had grown old and senile on the frontier. No longer knowing what it did, it continually reproduced the same episode. The same desolate cry, the same language of destitution, had been heard here, as though in an echo chamber, for a thousand, two thousand years. Compared to this dung-beetle civilization, the realms of the West were a glittering arabesque on the face of the earth – fragile and illusory. Looking at this imperishable landscape, one felt that it was vain for Europe to carve her emblems in the niches of time, and that all her annals were but dust. For century after century her lookouts had peered at mauve horizons that periodically spewed forth hordes from the East – hordes like a mighty wind, like armies of lemmings or locusts: endless columns of warriors with high cheekbones and yellow faces glistening with mutton fat, streaming west-wards on absurd little horses and brandishing green, yellow or blue banners emblazoned with moons and stars. Hurling themselves at the ramparts of the West with elemental persistence, these spectral armies besieged strongholds and destroyed farms, crops and bridges, then melted away, leaving their ghostly dead strewn along river banks or heaped in front of castle gates.

From November onwards, mail began to arrive from Vienna. Weary horseman came galloping up to the fortress commander and handed him saddlebags stuffed with official correspondence. Most of these couriers departed post-haste, as though to reassure themselves that the passage of time still mattered in this province devoid of clock and calendar. The dispatches they brought were out of sequence and followed no pattern. They reported various developments, but who could interpret such happenings in ignorance of the events that had preceded them? The series of messages bristled with gaps and omissions, either because the Viennese bureaucrats had bungled their work, or, more probably, because some of the couriers had lost their way in the mountains and been killed by bandits, wild beasts, frightened peasants or Turkish soldiers as lost as themselves. Others, again, might simply have gone astray and circled in the vicinity of the fortress for months, or foolishly mistaken west for east or north for south and borne their dispatches off to Bohemia or Lombardy. Still others had fetched up in villages on the other side of the frontier and delivered their missives to Turkish peasants incapable of deciphering a single word – capable only of forwarding them to the authorities in Constantinople, who filed them away in the dusty, immemorial, never-consulted archives of the Sublime Porte.

Otto eagerly perused the correspondence in these bundles. It was seldom that he failed to find, tucked away between military orders and reports of the war in the West, an envelope addressed to himself. Each such envelope yielded a sheet of white paper of the same size as the Kärntnertor note and folded in similar fashion, the sole difference being that someone – Duchess Clémence? – had deigned to write the date in the top left-hand corner – the date, nothing more. Otto noted these dates, striving to recall what he himself had been doing at Vrenjac on the days when Clémence had dispatched her missives. The first to reach him was dated November 10th. Then the sequence went into reverse and a courier handed him one dated October 19th. Then back to November again. Then, not long before Christmas, he received a note sent on October 12th, the day before he had set off with his four troopers and thus the day when he had walked the streets near St Stephen's with Schwarzbrod and had later spoken of Duchess Clémence to his father.

It was Otto's habit each night to ascend the highest turret

in the fortress and scan the plain through its loopholes. He would have preferred to see lights and hear the silent countryside resound to battle-cries, the roll of drums and the thunder of artillery, but the power of the East had long been waning. Gone were the days of the Janizaries, gone the days of the suicidal Serdengechtiler and their blue banners of death, gone the days when khans built pyramids of their enemies' skulls – gone too, the victory at Kahlenberg on the eve of Vienna's Great Plague. The Eastern Empire was drained of energy. If it moved at all, it did so like a sleepwalker. Here on the Military Frontier the stirrings of the Sublime Porte were almost inaudible. Its old heart was beating ever more faintly, and down there in the metropolis beside the Bosphorus, the capital of catalepsy, minarets were crumbling and cupolas acquiring a film of verdigris. The city of the Janizaries had bolted its bronze gates. In the depths of dilapidated palaces, old men tottered amid mountains of parchment on which all traces of the Ottoman Empire's erstwhile vitality had been rendered indecipherable by the insects that were devouring its annals with an incessant crunching of tiny mandibles. Ah, yes, said Otto and his brother officers at the mess table – ah, yes, the ancient Empire might be comatose, yet its coma had endured for so long, and besides, the very splendour of the great seat of the Basileis at the height of its glory might have been another form of coma. When one came to think of it, mightn't that oriental land, tinged though it was with the pallor of death, be capable of producing a final spasm, of falling on Europe once more and rending it in pieces as a man *in extremis* convulsively seizes his father confessor by the throat?

And still the wind continued to blow, bearing off the days one by one. Otto was friendless. His three junior officers spent the whole time grumbling. The rank and file soldiers, most of them natives of the Banat, were tough and loyal. They resembled lumps of clay, gargoyles with lethargic, stony eyes. Trustful and tireless, they obeyed like well-trained dogs. One of them, Corporal Matthias, a battle-scarred veteran endowed with awesome physical strength, so delighted in doing Otto's bidding that his rugged face wore a perpetual smile of ecstasy. One day, Otto lost his temper and struck the big man – simply in a vain attempt to banish his unwarranted smile.

What with the sulphurous mists, the jackals and hyenas, the plaintive mewing of eagles, the howling of wolves and wild dogs, Otto was becoming edgy to the point of dementia. Back in Europe, his Wiener-Neustadt comrades – Thieburg, Dietrich, Lvov – had donned their pastel uniforms and were waging war in the sybaritic cities of Italy, the fragrant forests of Germany. The art of dying was one thing, but no one at cadet school had taught Otto how to contend with life in an outpost on the edge of the void. Duchess Clémence's blank missives continued to arrive in total disarray, and he vainly strove to regulate his days by her ruined calendar.

As winter wore on, every sound faded save the soughing of the wind. The sun lost its brilliance, and all forms of life shivered in the dirty snows of December, absorbed by those spongy expanses, those steppes, those barren wastes of rock, coarse grass and furze. As for the warriors of the Sublime Porte, given that some sultan, sheikh or padishah might have sent them forth once more to pillage the West, they too would have dwindled before ever reaching Otto's fortress. They would scarce have mustered the energy to mount a charge or sound a flourish or two on the drums. Their lances would have flashed on the horizon, but the nearer they drew the more apparent it would have become that theirs was merely a show of belligerence by a host of invalids and cripples, barely able to caw or croak or squeak – so much so that, after this approach, Vrenjac's garrison would only have had to lower the drawbridge and, without unsheathing a sword or firing a shot, send out a cart to gather up the corpses littering the glacis.

The nights crept by. Behind every blizzard loomed another. The mists, too, piled up on top of each other and stagnated. So did the passing days, which seemed to linger long after they were over. Was it really Vrenjac's function to guard the borders of the Dual Monarchy? The fortress had

120

transcended its geographical bonds. It was separated from Vienna less by leagues of plain and mountain, less by the waters of the Danube, Drava and Tisza, less by the forests of Transylvania, than by layers of cold. Otto was besieged by snow; not simply the snow he saw through his grimy fortress window, but all the snow that had fallen since November and all that would continue to fall until spring. How many days' ride would it have taken him to escape this boundless, trackless labyrinth, this indestructible land where festivals, anniversaries and genealogies were never celebrated? He tried to persuade himself that he had, after all, been sent to the Military Frontier by mistake, because it lay quite as much within the orbit of the Sublime Porte as it did within that of the Dual Monarchy.

Otto had begun by fulfilling his duties with care. He took great pains to preserve the crispness of his white tunic. Later, however, he adopted fatigue dress like his men and even neglected to remove his wolfskin pelisse at night. After quartering the countryside with his men in an attempt to map the Empire's outlying territories, he gave up. He ought to have produced new cartographic codes and unpublished sigla showing the location of villages no more visible than darns in a torn garment of trackless plains that ended nowhere. Could he really turn up at the Hofburg with a grey map destitute of all topographical detail? But at least he still ensured that scrupulous cleanliness and discipline prevailed throughout the fortress.

As courier succeeded courier, the war against France assumed an increasingly tangled, topsy-turvy appearance. It was reported, for instance, that Bonaparte had returned from Egypt to Fréjus in the frigate *Muiron* on 9 October 1799, shortly before Otto's posting to Vrenjac, but a few days later another dispatch announced that on May 19th, or almost two years previously, the Corsican had set sail from Toulon with three hundred ships and thirty-seven thousand men, bound for Alexandria by way of Malta. Other dispatches reported that he had seized power on the 18th Brumaire, which Austrians still called 19 November 1799, and that Masséna's troops had been stoned in the neighbourhood of Rome by peasants from Trastevere who, under the leadership of their priests, had massacred several Jews, crying 'Long live Christ! Long live the Blessed Virgin!' The Austrians' movements were reportedly no better coordinated. Archduke Charles had contrived to win and lose two battles on the same day, at Zurich and Mantua respectively, while the same dispatch revealed that General Dupuy had been murdered in Cairo by Moslem fanatics on 2 October 1798, an atrocity for which two thousand Egyptians had been beheaded and thrown into the Nile. Meanwhile, wearied and incensed by Austrian procrastination, Suvorov was reported as having decided, by agreement with Tsar Alexander, to take his troops home to Russia on 5 October 1799, although another, slower messenger who arrived next day brought word that Suvorov had defeated his old foe Joubert on August 15th of the same year, killing him and capturing Novara and Novi Ligure.

Otto reread these disjointed reports and arranged them in chronological order, but their sequence was so disrupted by each new arrival that the course of recent history began to resemble a palimpsest, one of those ancient manuscripts whose original text has been erased to enable a later scribe to superimpose new hieroglyphs on old. That was it, Otto reflected during his sleepless vigils at the top of the wind-swept watch-tower: events were like successive snowfalls, like crayfish lying higgledy-piggledy in a creel. The messengers who reported them merited neither praise nor blame: they were diligent and deferential servants of the decrepitude known as history. In the midst of his hardships, Otto clearly perceived that all of man's achievements, his wars and coronations and carnages, had already occurred; that all events were simultaneously begun and done with, mortal and incorruptible; that they wove an indecipherable tapestry – filled a lumber-room in which historians, chroniclers, annalists, ministers, monarchs and generals blindly rummaged like children plunging their hands into a mildewed trunk in the recesses of an attic and bringing out faded letters or lockets containing hair from unidentified and unidentifiable heads. Otto had had to attain these distant shores, this featureless, unrelieved land like the scarred retina of a blind man, before he began to suspect that time was in fact constructed like a ball of papier mâché kneaded by a thousand jaws, and that only men, in their stupidity, would persist in flattening it with their palms in the hope of transforming it into a sheet of smooth, white, virgin paper.

He was staggered one day to receive a communication that obeyed the dictates of the calendar. It arrived about half-way through the winter, and for once it concerned Otto himself. Having carefully examined the wax seal on the saddlebag and deciphered the date, which ended in '1800', he was dumbfounded to discover that a new century had taken advantage of his preoccupations to get under way without his knowledge. The Kriegskommandant further informed him that his time at Vrenjac was up, and that other duties would be assigned him by the lieutenant-colonel commanding the Saxe-Salza cuirassiers. He was to present himself at the Hofburg with all due speed, at latest by the beginning of February. Otto told Corporal Matthias to pack his belongings, strap up his bags, and see that his horse was properly shod. The old soldier eyed him so apprehensively – his smile had vanished for the first time ever – that Otto decided to take him along as his orderly. The smile reappeared at once.

10

Vienna was holding its breath. Spring and summer had gone the Allies' way. With Rastadt over and Bonaparte in the depths of the desert, they had nullified the conquests of the Army of Italy. Leoben and Campo Formio were consigned to oblivion. Jourdan yielded to Austrian pressure in Germany, Masséna in Graubünden and Vorarlberg. In March 1799 Archduke Charles gave the French a drubbing at Stockach and threatened the Rhine. Jourdan resigned his command. Rome, Naples and Northern Italy were reconquered. The following month saw the French thrown into confusion at Cassano. Suvorov and Kray's Austrians occupied Turin during May, and August 15th brought Joubert's death and the rout at Novi.

It was true that Bonaparte had landed at Fréjus on October 10th and returned to Paris seething with contempt – 'Everything was bound to go to pieces in my absence!' – but the scorn he poured on his lieutenants was unmerited, and by early autumn Jourdan's *levée en masse* had begun to turn the tide. Masséna disheartened old Suvorov by defeating Korsakov's Russians and Hotze's Austrians at Zurich on 26 December 1799. The Directory triumphed at Mons, reoccupied Holland in consequence, and compelled the Duke of York to reembark. All that remained in Austrian hands was Italy, with the exception of the Ligurian Republic, where Gouvion-Saint-Cyr preserved a foothold. Vienna grew anxious. Italy was the jewel in Bonaparte's crown, his mistress and the object of his desire. 'I want her naked,' he had muttered. If he leapt upon her, all Austria would be under fire.

'Never fear,' said Lawyer Gruhlpraser. 'Bonaparte seized power and gulped it down on the 18th Brumaire – your pardon, November 9th. He's sleeping like a snake with a sheep in its guts. A little rest will do him a lot of good. That's why I can see peace stealing up on us, so to speak, under cover of war. Careful, though – it's a fragile thing, this peace, so be gentle with it! No noise, I beg you: it's made of glass.' And he waggishly laid a finger on his lips as though tiptoeing into a convalescent's bedroom.

Gruhlpraser set great store by a letter which General Bonaparte had sent His Royal and Imperial Majesty Francis II at the turn of the year. Wasn't it bright with hopes for the future? 'All feelings of vainglory being foreign to me, my foremost desire is to prevent the bloodshed that will ensue . . . Your Majesty's well-known disposition leaves no doubt as to his own heart's desire.' A similar letter addressed to George III had rekindled the longstanding animosity between Pitt and his rivals, Sheridan and Fox. In Austria too, Bonaparte's appeal caused a division of opinion. Rector Ouarin twitted Gruhlpraser on his optimism and drew an analogy: 'The lion has sheathed its claws, I grant you. Is it because the sands of Egypt have worn them down, or because they're rectractile?' Foreign Minister Thugut tapped his cheek. A scoundrel's word was no guarantee, he said. Anyway, even if one accepted Bonaparte's sincerity, wasn't his letter a confession of weakness? Mightn't it be time to blow the mort over him? Gruhlpraser tut-tutted noisily at this.

Otto was interviewed on his return from the Banat by a peruked and powdered Hofburg official who toyed with the Maria Theresa Cross on his midnight-blue frock coat and didn't listen to a word the young man said. Otto also saw Schwarzbrod, who made vague allusions to Duchess Clémence, and was delighted to receive a summons from the Duchess of Mahlberg, being eager to give her a description of the Military Frontier's howling wolves, moribund peasants and sulphurous mists. 'She haunts that part of the world in her dreams,' he told himself.

Ushered into Gertrud's presence, Otto seated himself on a stool facing the Turkish cannon. The old lady promptly informed him that Christine Kinsky had been called away to Styria for a week to visit her mother, who was gravely ill. 'But I'm sure she won't return,' she added quaintly as she fondled Herr Feldmarschall's quivering snout. 'As for my niece, Duchess Clémence' . . .

Otto hung on every word.

. . . 'she's at Greinburg. Prince Ernst is with her, and can you guess what he says? The war has grown a trifle drowsy these days, he says, and it badly needs a dig in the ribs. I'm astonished. Our worthy Ernst, who always used to shower His Majesty with pacific advice, has now joined the firebrands. He changed sides overnight some months ago – on October 13th, if memory serves me. Now why October 13th, pray?' She broke off, convulsed with laughter.

'He's itching to cross swords with the French and put the fear of God into Bonaparte.'

There was another pause. Otto made no comment.

'The worthy prince has concocted quite a little scheme,' Gertrud went on. 'At the first hint of danger, Clémence's cuirassiers will be dispatched to Italy and hurled into the thick of the fighting.' At that moment a footman announced the arrival of an unexpected visitor, General Count Gustav Konig von Weitzau of the Aulic Council. The duchess irritably drained her coffee cup.

'He isn't an Aulic Councillor at all! He's eighty years old and a numskull, but one of our national treasures none the less. He saved Joseph II's life during the Belgrade fiasco in 'eighty-eight. You must excuse me, Herr Apfelgrun, I shall have to receive him. I can't offend a man of his rank, but stay awhile when we're rid of him. I seem to think I was about to tell you something.'

Otto had heard an account of the Belgrade affair some years before. Panic had set in during a river-crossing under Ottoman fire, gun carriages had been lost and horses drowned, and Austrian hussars had stupidly potted at Austrian infantrymen while Joseph II bellowed exhortations for his men to take heart. It was then that General von Weitzau, whose long career had hitherto been undistinguished to the point of invisibility, crossed the river camouflaged by foliage on a raft of birch logs, popped up in the middle of the Ottoman headquarters, and created such pandemonium that he saved his men from ignominious defeat. Vienna celebrated, Te Deums were sung, honours bestowed. Thereafter, the general had devoted himself to armchair strategy, criticizing the disposition of the Austrian armies and chuckling wryly whenever Archduke Charles, Wurmser, Melas, Kray or Mack lifted a finger. The memoranda with which he bombarded the Hofburg were not only unsolicited but remained unacknowledged.

Because his age now precluded him from bearing arms, General von Weitzau had turned to counterespionage. According to him, the streets of the capital teemed with spies 'as numerous as snails after rain', but he was busily exposing their wiles. He saw Vienna as a fantastic city inhabited by Janus-faced citizens. 'There you have the true significance of the "Dual" Monarchy,' he said firmly. 'It's a kingdom of masks, and I've chosen to explore what lies behind them!' He tirelessly combed the city in search of masquerading traitors. 'The first one I catch I shall turn inside out like a rabbit skin!' If he passed a carpenter with planks on his shoulder, he could tell at a glance that the man had graduated from the French artillery school at Brienne. Every shop assistant was in the pay of Schulmeister, alias Monsieur Charles, and Viennese notaries burning the midnight oil in their offices on the pretext of making up their accounts were really drafting reports for transmission to Paris by the first available courier. General von Weitzau was rather put out that the military authorities should pay no heed to these findings, but, being a man much given to self-sacrifice, he persevered with his mission. His principal assets were his advanced age and a jovial manner. He struck up conversations in coffee-houses and taverns, in the street – even in church. He was also shrewd enough to purchase innumerable bunches of roses and carnations and satisfy himself with an agile finger that they did not conceal pistols or daggers, vials of poison or scribbled notes. The air inside his town house was so laden with the musty smell of dead and wilting flowers that it gave him chronic asthma. 'General von Weitzau can see spies on the moon itself,' Dr Ulhue had remarked to Otto one day. 'Pray heaven he never catches sight of himself in a mirror. He'd stick himself in prison on the spot.'

It occurred to Otto that it would take a very big mirror indeed to accommodate the reflection of a man like Weitzau. The general was larger than life. Height, breadth, girth – all his dimensions were inordinate. His bald pate, which resembled a two-storeyed granite tower, presided over curly side-whiskers, heavy pink cheeks as pendulous as a pair of deflated bagpipes, and an off-white beard so ample that it obscured some of the decorations pinned to his scarlet coat. He jammed a cigar in his mouth as though intending to devour it whole and offered one to Otto.

'His Majesty Francis II,' he said slyly, 'expects us to conserve our peasants' resources by smoking Austrian cigars, and His Majesty is absolutely right.' He directed a jet of blue smoke at the ceiling. 'However,' he pursued in a playful tone, 'I am equally right to have my cigars sent from Tuscany, because they give off an aroma of gingerbread and brown sugar. They're the cigars Adam should have smoked in Paradise. Shall I tell you something, sir? If the Almighty had provided Adam with a stock of Tuscan cigars, I'll wager our forebear would have felt no compulsion to go and dally with Eve, the original sin would never have been committed, and we should still be in the Garden of Eden. Unfortunately, Tuscan cigars are in short supply at present. Eve's work, no doubt . . .'

The general almost laughed aloud but sternly checked himself. Long experience of hunting spies had schooled him in muscular control. Instead of laughing, he pulled a whole gallery of faces and inflated his cheeks a trifle – without, however, making any music.

'Joking apart, I see you hold a cornet's commission in the Duchess of Saxe-Salza's illustrious cuirassiers. My felicitations, sir. I would none the less ask you to note that my forthcoming conversation with Her Excellency the Duchess of Mahlberg must be conducted under the seal of military secrecy. The fate of the Dual Monarchy merits every precaution, sir, so farewell!'

Otto rose, but Duchess Gertrud frowned and dealt the general's knee a tap with her cane. 'Otto Apfelgrun will remain here,' she said curtly. 'More than that, my dear

128

General, Otto's presence is essential. He has just spent several months on the Military Frontier, in the heart of the Banat.'

'The Banat?'

'The Banat, General.'

'The Banat? Bravo! And what did he see there?'

Otto had seen nothing at all. It grieved him to say so, but he'd seen nothing apart from a handful of peasants who didn't even know whether they were Bosnians, Hercegovinans, Austrians, Albanians or Turks. Although he was distressed to have to admit to such a meagre tally, the general exultantly stroked his side-whiskers and cast a portentous glance at Duchess Gertrud.

'Quite right, my boy – very logical! The Turk never changes. The Turk is a subterranean beast, hence my memorandum to the Minister of War on the teaching of history at cadet schools. It bears out my theory that there's not an iota of difference between a soldier and a historian. Enough said!

'I knew your grandfather, Apfelgrun – a soldier to his fingertips. You, too, are a true soldier, I saw that at a glance. Which bears out my second theory: systems develop, inspiration remains constant. Your Mozarts will always produce the same music, even if you supply them with a few more notes, a few additional sharps and flats. As for the piece we're about to hear, it'll be music like the roar of the ocean deep, believe you me, not the trilling of nightingales!'

The general went on to claim that men were still fighting as they used to in the Stone Age. 'Man is a prehistoric creature: pre-his-tor-ic, know what I mean?' The flint axe might have been superseded by the Roman sword, the sword by the arquebus, and the arquebus by the cannon, but that signified nothing. In reality, the soldier spent his life carrying on the war waged by his parents, which was merely a continuation of the one waged by his grandparents. There was only one interminable, immutable war. Enough said!

'I know my Turks, believe me. I fought them myself in

'eighty-eight, my father would have defeated them given half a chance, and my father's father was aide-de-camp to Charles of Lorraine, and later to Starhemberg, during the campaign against Kara Mustapha in 1683. So you see, even if I do detect the beginnings of a smirk on Duchess Gertrud's face, I'm fully qualified to tell you this: the Turk in this year of grace, 1800, is the same Turk who besieged the Albanian fortress of Skruda in 1553–1443, I mean – and blew up the Albanians under Castriota or Scanderbeg, whichever you choose to call him. Enough said! No more yataghans these days, nor battle-axes, nor shields, nor maces, nor bows and arrows, but who cares? Who cares, as long as the Serdengechtiler of the Porte still beat out the same dirge on the same drums? Today as yesterday, the backbone of the Turkish army remains the Serdengechtiler, the berserkers, the regiments of the Blue Death, and do you know how a Serdengechti fights?'

Otto felt called on to reply. He confessed his ignorance, but he would have done better to remain silent. The general became heated. He sat up with a jerk, craned forward as if to inspect the toes of his boots, and stamped on the floor with each heel in turn. Gertrud gave a little shriek and begged him to spare her windows.

'Enough said! The Turk is a burrower, a mole, a subterranean soldier. You'll tell me the Porte possesses soldiers of stature too, but they're mere nothings, down-at-heel diversions who brandish scarecrows to simulate a vast host and wave their scraps of silk, their banners bearing verses from the Koran, at a safe distance. Eyewash, the whole thing! The real Turkish army is down below ground. The Porte has always operated like that, as witness Tursun Pasha's assault on Scanderbeg at Skruda in 1443 – or was it 1553? The Turk buries himself. He burrows, gnaws the earth and guzzles mud like a worm.

'What about the battle of Kahlenberg in 1683? The Turks had excavated a second, almost identical city beneath Vienna, complete with subterranean streets and squares corresponding to our own streets and squares. Galleries beneath every palace, tons of gunpowder in position – the capital would have been blown sky-high if Starhemberg hadn't found out in time. With whose help? You'll never guess: with the help of our bakers – our valiant Viennese bakers, God preserve them! But I assume you've sundry historical objections to raise, young man?'

Otto felt annoyed and ashamed. He couldn't think of the smallest objection. Being unequal to the Turks, he essayed a change of subject. 'There's only one question I'd venture to ask you, General. As things stand, doesn't the Turkish threat take second place to the French?'

'Excellent, I was waiting for that. Enough said! I've studied Bonaparte's career in detail, and believe me, my friend, it's a strange one. You think he was itching for battle as a junior captain? Far from it. He dragged his feet, left summonses from his superiors unanswered, took numerous spells of leave on the strength of imaginary illnesses. Well? Enough said! A man with Bonaparte's consuming thirst for action and glory must have had some reason for his idleness. Sure enough, I happened on a remarkable episode relating to the year 1793. That was when Bonaparte made strenuous efforts to enlist in a foreign army. Which one? The Turkish army!

'By God, sir, if you want the truth, ask us old ones! I was turning this matter over in my mind, baffled by its significance, when Duchess Gertrud put me on the right track by speaking of Egypt. The Pyramids, Jaffa, the siege of Acre, Mount Tabor, the plague, the two engagements at Aboukir, the Cairo revolt and the death of Dupuy – they all caused quite a stir. All very dramatic and sensational, yes, but all outward show, like a painting by Taunay or Bagetti – all dust in the eyes. When confronted by a treacherous beast, one must always try to fathom its secret intentions.' The general turned to Gertrud. 'My dear lady, I take the liberty of quoting your own phrase, which hit the nail on the head: "Everyone," you said, "plays hide-and-seek." The essence of Bonaparte's genius is that he hides in the light, not the dark. Bravo, and again bravo! The key to Bonaparte is his alliance with the Turks. Enough said!'

The duchess, looking like an indignant little eagle,

emitted a squawk of annoyance. Her lips moved soundlessly. Puce in the face, she aimed a third and more violent blow at the toe of the general's boot. At last she recovered her voice.

'I said nothing of the kind, you great ninny! What ever would have put such an idea into my head? Poor Gustav, you're nothing but an old fool. Would I really have spoken of collusion between Bonaparte and the Sublime Porte? Really, don't be so childish! Who are the Sublime Porte's allies against France? The Russians and the British. Well, my poor Gustav? Are you seriously telling me that St Petersburg and London are in league with Paris?'

The general resumed his seat. He displayed no hint of anger or resentment, just genuine distress at the discovery that a person of Gertrud's rank and intelligence could be so impervious to strategic niceties. He fixed his old friend, who had regained her composure, with a look of compassion.

'I reeled under the shock, I confess,' he said in the measured tones of one explaining a complex problem to a child. 'I wavered, I was almost unseated – to use a homely metaphor – but I'm still in the saddle and riding hell-for-leather!

'All that you say, my dear, dear Gertrud, is eminently logical, but go to Egypt and what do you see? A very peculiar Bonaparte indeed. Had you noticed that he always avows himself the foe of the Mameluke, never of the Turk or Egyptian? Interesting, no? Secondly, for whom does he never neglect an opportunity to express his respect? For Jesus Christ? No, for Mohammed and the Koran! He proclaims the sanctity of Islam rather as if St Dominic, instead of roasting heretics alive, had kissed them on the lips. But Bonaparte goes still farther. When in Egypt for the festival of Ramadhan, he plays the part of a pasha. Must I cite you more proof, such as his insistence on seizing Malta and wresting Corfu, Zante and Cephalonia from Venice, the Sublime Porte's enemy? Again, think how violently he assails those mortal foes of Islam, the Pope and the Knights of St John.

'I have a whole knapsackful of evidence. For example,

what was the date of Starhemberg's battle with the Turks at Vienna in 1653 – or 1683, as the case may be? July 14th! In other words, it celebrated – albeit in advance – the one hundred and sixth anniversary of the storming of the Bastille. To anyone who knows how to read it both ways, history is a weird and wonderful manuscript. More conclusive still: when Scanderbeg held the fortress of Skruda against Tursun Pasha in 1443, or 1553, whichever – what was the name of the sultan then reigning at Constantinople? Brace yourself, Gertrud: he styled himself, quite simply, Murat II! A coincidence, you say? Tut, tut, tut . . . Unroll the parchment of time in reverse, and all becomes clear. On the one hand we have Murat I, Napoleon's coxcomb of a general with his ostrich plumes; on the other his future successor in the past, Murat II, who will blow up the Albanian stronghold in 1443 – yes, that's it: 1543 – and unleash his Janizaries on Europe.' The general paused to stroke his beard with a look of triumph.

'My dear lady, my dear sir, a week ago I received a letter from one of my informants in Paris, so I can tell you how the Corsican was dressed when he prepared to overthrow the Directory. He wore a stovepipe hat – fair enough – and an olive-green frock coat – fair enough too – but now for the incongruous touch: his coat was gathered at the waist by a cashmere sash – cashmere, mark you! – and from it hung a Mameluke scimitar. Far be it from me to draw comparisons with Rustam. Tell me, Herr Apfelgrun, had you ever noted all these clues and put two and two together? Enough said!'

Otto, feeling that these two injunctions were incompatible, made no reply. Besides, Weitzau had the bit between his teeth.

'The Hofburg has been informed, thanks to me, but the Hofburg slumbers on. No one chooses to acknowledge that Bonaparte is only simulating a quarrel with the Turks in the hope that oriental glory will smooth his path to power – and all with the connivance of the Tatar. It wasn't Sieyès who engineered the 18th Brumaire, it was Suleiman II. Bonaparte is Suleiman's lackey, his puppet. He keeps us amused on the Rhine, in Lombardy and the Netherlands, to distract our attention and enable Christendom's one implacable foe, the Turk, to continue his work of demolition. Rest assured that, even as I speak, Suleiman is burrowing away beneath our feet. Tomorrow, as so often in the past, he will detonate his mines, rape our womenfolk and slaughter our children.'

The duchess was beside herself with irritation. The little dog, which shared its mistress's sentiments, bristled.

'Fiddlesticks, Gustav! The Turks have never raped the women of Vienna nor killed their children.'

'They did, my dear, in 1683 – or rather, to be strictly accurate, they could have done. What's more they'll do so again tomorrow. Why? Because those gentlemen of the court – including Archduke Charles, who would, incidentally, have done better not to run from Masséna in Switzerland – refuse to accept the obvious. And so?'

The general was quick to take his own cue.

'And so, I'm putting my last reserves of energy at the service of Christendom. Having very few men under my command – none, in fact – I've drawn up a list of all that the Turks have bequeathed us. Our chestnut trees – yes, they hail from Turkey, but there's nothing to be done about them. Nobody's going to chop down every chestnut tree in Vienna – let's be realistic! Then there's coffee. Do I recommend the imposition of a blockade on mocha? What foolishness! Be practical, logical and effective, that's my motto. I favour subtler tactics. In other words, I shall allay the Porte's suspicions by leaving the burghers of Vienna to sip their mochas at Steiner's. We now come to the Turks' third bequest to the Dual Monarchy: the croissant – a far more serious matter. It's thanks to the croissant that we shall flush out the Janizaries lurking beneath our feet at this very moment. Are you with me, Apfelgrun?'

Otto replied that he had grasped the gist of the general's remarks, albeit with some difficulty.

'No, no, Apfelgrun,' Weitzau said testily, 'I was inviting you to accompany me on a tour of the bakeries. Now's the time, when the ovens are cold, so come! Our respects, my dear Gertrud.'

The duchess insisted that she was temporarily confiscating Otto, but she would return him in due course. If the general withdrew to the anteroom, he and his young friend would be reunited before five minutes were up. The general clicked his heels and bowed low over the Turkish cannon. Gertrud, in a rare gesture of affection, patted the big man's bald, well-scented pate.

Her voice was so weary – frayed at the edges, as it were – that Otto had to come very close. She put her lips to his ear and whispered like a penitent in the confessional. A spy catching them unawares might have inferred that the old lady was imparting shameful confidences or betraying state secrets.

'You remember Lord Misrule? Yes, of course you do: the Englishman who used to visit me some years ago – the one who paid servants to weep, suffer, love and read in his place. Well, I'm no Misrule by nature, as you'll have guessed, but at my age, and with a useless pair of eyes, how am I to set about living a little while longer? I've tried to slow down my inner workings, but it's my heart that rebels. It makes my life a misery, this heart of mine. There's nothing to be done – it insists on throbbing with emotion, with anger and the like. It's an obstinate fool of a heart, and so, to my cost, I'm condemned to Lord Misrule's way of life. That's the truth of the matter.' For once, there was no mockery or irony, or even gaiety, in the old woman's tone.

'My niece Duchess Clémence has more native wit than her princely husband. By that I mean that her mind works in the opposite direction but arrives at identical conclusions. She shares her husband's overriding desire that the war will flare up again. War, she thinks, will provide a setting attuned to her emotions.'

Otto just sat there. If he understood anything at all, it was only that he felt extremely frightened.

'My niece is a good deal like me, Herr Apfelgrun, or rather, like all the Mahlberg womenfolk. We've no use for prudence. Only the biggest conflagration can warm us, only extremes of danger and disaster enable us to breathe easily – our hearts can only function at breaking point. No one can thwart the desires of a female Mahlberg, not even a man like

Prince Ernst. I sometimes wonder which is the wilder of the two, Christine or Clémence. Doubtless there's nothing to choose between them. They're beautiful carnivores, as that little priest of yours, Father Thaler, was saying to me only the other day, and once they've sunk their teeth in their prey they suck its blood for a long time to come. We Mahlbergs must always be in the seventh heaven or the bowels of hell.

'Prince Ernst knows this. He had you sent to the Banat, but I doubt if any man is a match for either of my nieces. We like nothing better than to evade the constraints of society, and believe me, we don't even shrink from gambling on the outcome of a war. I have faith in you, young man. I'll wager you won't disappoint me.'

Thoroughly bewildered, Otto took his leave and followed General von Weitzau outside. Certain technical aspects of the general's forthcoming operation were explained to him in the chill of the February night. Everything hinged on a historical fact which no one could dispute: that Vienna had been saved in 1683 by its bakers. The proof: Empress Maria Theresa, with her political and historical flair, had publicly commended the gallant bakers and licensed them in perpetuity to manufacture the little moon-shaped cakes introduced by the Turks and called croissants, or crescents, after the lagoon encircling Constantinople. Every Austrian was familiar with this glorious episode. On entering their ovens at dawn, the bakers had heard the thud of pickaxes. Promptly concluding that the Turks had mined the city and planned to blow it up, they alerted the authorities. Vienna and Christendom were saved. 'The Pope owes his survival to a croissant,' said the general, shaking with fiercely suppressed laughter.

Unfortunately, he went on, the bakers of 1800 weren't made of the same flour as those of 1683, so he himself had taken up the torch in their stead. He regularly toured the bakeries on the anodyne pretext of drafting a memorandum on the Austrian art of bread-making.

The bakers, who had finished their supper, were flattered by General von Weitzau's interest and each group of them gave him a warm welcome. They opened a bottle of plum brandy, then one of pear, complained of current hardships and lamented last autumn's excessive rainfall. After downing a glass or two, the general slyly suggested taking another look at the ovens. Otto visited a dozen bakehouses in the fat old gentleman's wake, but the operation drew a blank. Strain their ears as they might, no sound disturbed the surrounding subsoil. The general was not disheartened, even so. He even propounded a new theory to the effect that patience was as much a military necessity as a diplomatic virtue. If one conceded that sham and subterfuge were all that ever broke the continuity of war, and that Mars invariably rekindled his furnaces, be it an interval of months or centuries – why, then, who was going to quibble over one paltry year? Otto was chilled to the bone by the time they reached the general's house.

'Duchess Gertrud doesn't believe me,' said Weitzau, shuffling from foot to foot, 'His Majesty doesn't believe me, the Hofburg doesn't believe me, yet the sappers from Constantinople are toting away their sacks of soil as they did in 1683. It's an alarming thought!'

He seized Otto by the shoulders.

'But *you* believe me, don't you?'

He waddled swiftly off before he could receive an answer. Otto watched him push open the wrought-iron gate leading into his big, overgrown garden and disappear among the spindleberries and magnolias. His heart bled for the old man.

11

The lull was shattered. Hardly had Bonaparte become First Consul and restored the French Republic's discipline and morale, before he set his legions in motion. When Thugut suggested holding a general conference, he was simply ignored. The fraudulence of Bonaparte's sugary letters to Franz II and George III was now amply demonstrated: he was stoking his boilers hard. Not to be outdone, the Austrian General Staff resolved to carry the war to Provence, thereby compelling the French to denude their Rhine frontier. Switzerland would fall and Austria gain possession of the Rhône corridor. The one drawback to this plan was that Archduke Charles disapproved of it, so he was appointed governor of Bohemia and replaced on the Swabian front by General Kray. In this way a mediocre general came to be entrusted with Austria's future while Archduke Charles, the Dual Monarchy's finest military leader, was thrown on the scrap heap.

Vienna was unconcerned, however. The French, it was thought, would be deluded by this reckless squandering of talent. That was how the Comte de Baux had once saved his beleaguered Provençal town: when he threw its starving inhabitants' last remaining pig, fattened on their last grains of wheat, over the battlements, the attackers had been so impressed and disheartened that they lifted the siege. 'Archduke Charles is deputizing for the Comte de Baux's pig,' quipped Dr Ulhue, and added in a wry undertone, 'but he isn't a two-headed one . . .'

The High Command, who felt confident that the crucial confrontation would anyway take place in Italy and not in Germany, gave General Melas the task of capturing the last Italian stronghold in French hands, namely Genoa, which Masséna had heavily fortified. Genoa was keeping Austrian forces pinned down in Liguria and diverting them from Provence, so Genoa must be taken. The Saxe-Salzas'

138

white cuirassiers, who were to take part, would be assigned to General Ott's division.

Duchess Clémence reviewed her regiment in the Prater. It was a repetition of the scene at Baden, but with one tiny difference. No longer a member of Rector Ouarin's motley band of students, Otto now galloped past the reviewing stand on Lieutenant-Colonel Scherer's right, a white-uniformed figure astride a grey charger. The duchess was wearing the same scarlet uniform as before, her face half-hidden by the same black-visored shako, her expression similarly aloof. No progress in that respect, thought Otto as he spurred his horse along. He hadn't seen the duchess since the night of March 21st – not for a year, in other words. On returning from the Banat he had seen his mother, his lawyer father, Professor Schwarzbrod, Duchess Gertrud, and General von Weitzau, but he hadn't caught so much as a glimpse of Clémence. He had hunted Turks in the city's bakehouses without unearthing a single Turk, and now he was going to war in earnest. Sparks flew from the cobblestones as the cuirassiers paraded under the pale, silken gaze of the Gorgon-eyed duchess, swords clanking, hoofs clattering, voices raised in an intermittent chorus of hurrahs.

Old Gertrud had told Otto that his regiment was being dispatched to Italy, the war's focal point, at the instance of Prince Ernst, simply to keep her protége away from Vienna. Otto found it hard to understand such an elaborate precaution and almost as hard to understand his own feelings. He disliked war on principle, yet here he was, about to wage it – if only because of his outworn quip about the two-headed turkey – not only without regret or craven apprehension, but also, he had to admit, with a certain detached curiosity. Similarly, although he was enamoured of Duchess Clémence and she had mocked him, his feelings were so confused that he was indifferent to her mockery and devoid of shame and resentment. If it wasn't love he felt for her, it might have been a fanciful notion induced by the solitude of the Military Frontier. Time would tell, and anyway, he had other fish to fry at present. Otto held himself ramrod straight as he bounced along on his grey charger. He cut a fine figure, that much was certain, and he couldn't disavow a feeling of happiness. His heart was at peace.

He recalled a phrase from Hegel, several of whose works he had read at the fortress of Vrenjac, straining his eyes in the process because candles in such remote places were made of very poor tallow. 'The Alps exist,' Hegel had written on seeing them, and Otto was rather proud of subscribing to the same philosophy. Could one extend the application of that short phrase to 'Clémence exists', or 'The French exist, ragged but audacious', or 'New wine tastes sour', or 'I received some blank sheets of paper in the Banat'? Jesus Christ was alleged to have written something in the Judaean dust with his finger – the only text attributed to him, a rare edition, an incunabulum – but the wind was blowing that day, and no one ever read what the Son of God had written. Otto suspected that the whole thing had been arranged at the highest level, and that the wind was the breath of God, deliberately exhaled so as to obliterate Christ's inscription. How, after all, could God's grand design, and the mystery of life, and all the sound and fury of history to come, and the woes and joys of all mankind, have been miniaturized sufficiently to be explicated in the twenty-six letters of the alphabet, even if the Essenian alphabet did contain a few letters more? With the complicity of dust and wind, Christ had written a blank book, the only book voluminous enough to encompass all the images tucked away in the folds of the unseen future. The blank sheets of the Banat were governed by the same law. The fortunes of war, French bullets, Duchess Clémence's whims, Bonaparte's flashes of inspiration, horses and their quirks of temperament, the quality of powder and shot, the conformation of mountains, the pigheaded notions of His Royal and Imperial Majesty: such were the scribes that would, as the years went by, fill the sheet from which he, Otto, could at present extract no hint of meaning – not that he cared a jot about the text that would eventually take shape on its much-folded surface. He was indolent and easy-going by nature, he told himself. He liked everyone and everything, and accepted all the contradictions inherent in both, so there was no doubt that old Gertrud von Mahlberg, whose dreams were all of cuts and bruises, perils and indiscretions, daggers and infatuations, would sooner or later find herself disappointed in him.

After the parade Duchess Clémence received Lieutenant-Colonel Scherer and his officers in the great hall of the Arsenal. She delivered a stirring address and congratulated her regiment on its appearance. No one could wish for a more martial body of men, smarter uniforms, more conscientious officers. The cuirassiers were noted for their iron discipline and observance of tradition. The forthcoming campaign would not, however, be a display of horsemanship at the Spanish Riding School, and the sooner they realized it the better. The regiment was about to be hurled into the Italian furnace at Genoa, where it would come up against the forces commanded by Masséna, one of Bonaparte's most skilful tacticians. 'In a month's time, gentlemen, your colonel will be leading a very different body of men: their dazzling, glittering uniforms will be soiled with dried blood and pus.' The duchess's voice hardened a little. The revolution of 1789 and its Corsican perpetrator, she said, had subjected the armies of Europe to an influx of filth and lice. The elegant armies of the ancient monarchies, those enervated armies that dreaded to sully their gorgeous uniforms with the mud of the battlefield, had been sent to their graves by the clamorous captors of the Bastille, the ragged victors of Valmy, the villainous conquerors of Alexandria. The French had invented a different kind of war: a new age had dawned.

'Gentlemen,' she concluded brusquely, throwing back her head, 'it will be your privilege to confront the invincible. I am sending you to a far-off place: to the very antechambers of barbarism!'

The officers were taken aback. Lieutenant-Colonel Scherer's brief reply, though couched in respectful language, skilfully managed to convey reproof. Austria, he said, had for years endured French violence and the hatred of the soldiers of *l'An II*. She would continue to stand firm, whether in isolation or with the sporadic and meagre assistance – he gratified his officers by stressing the word 'meagre' – of other monarchies, precisely in order to stem the rise of barbarism and ensure that the soil of Christendom still radiated the glories of civilization. 'Excellency,' he wound up, 'we gladly accept your perilous mission. May history record that the beggar armies were subjugated at the Caudine Forks of elegance!'

Scherer's subtle retort was well received, but the duchess took the floor again. She spoke very briefly this time, fixing the younger officers with a stern eye. Otto felt that her concluding remarks were directed at him, though he might have been flattering himself.

'I demand absolute obedience from my men. Their methods must reflect the terrible, not the agreeable, for believe me, if civilization is indeed to triumph over bestiality, it must first adopt bestial ways. My officers will be as much in my hands as this lace handkerchief. You see? I either crumple it or inhale its fragrance. I bestow my favour or mete out my disfavour. I insist on total discipline. My soldiers must be so obedient to their superiors' commands that, if ordered to jump from the top of the ramparts, they will jump.'

The regiment set off that same afternoon. General Melas and his entire army headed for Italy. They crossed the Vienna Woods to Marienselz, then turned west along the upland valley of the Salza. Lieutenant-Colonel Scherer's cuirassiers straggled along rough roads cluttered with big, moss-covered rocks. The river gave off a smell of dank cellars and sludge. Several horses lost their footing and had to be shot, but the column soon reached Grossreifling where it could thread its way along the broad valley of the Enns, which was carpeted with soft, lush grass. They passed through Rastadt without drawing rein. Eager for the fray, the young officers rode with panache. They threw out their chests beneath their well-starched dolmans and looked ominous. Riding through villages pleased them most because their horses' hoofs made a sound like thunder on the cobblestones. The windows of the timber-built houses burst open and the villagers cheered lustily, but the regiment sped on like a tornado, without even a smile for the admiring throng.

Otto, possibly relieved to have left Vienna and the toils and wiles of Duchess Clémence, was in high good humour. He had been reunited with his friends from the Wiener-Neustadt cadet school, so his cup of joy was full. To him, as to many young men popular with women, nothing could surpass the company of his own sex, the candour, loyalty and affection of his male contemporaries. The cadet school graduates formed a band of inseparables. Konrad von Thieburg, tall, aristocratic and flaxen-haired, affected a sparse but exceedingly pointed beard in order to lend himself a martial air, and had also given his lips a permanently choleric expression by means of a waxed moustache. Having rather protuberant eyes, and being besotted with titles, armorial bearings and patents of nobility, he was teasingly nicknamed 'the Rampant Frog'. Otto preferred Siegfried Rottinstein – fat, mischievous, faithful, jovial, stammering Siegfried, explosive as a grain of gunpowder and for ever in pursuit of some woman – or Dietrich Feuchtagen, who had the face of a handsome monk, or, last but not least, Ulrich Lvov, his very best friend of all, a stocky young man with hair as dark as goats' dung and a generous but volatile temperament.

Corporal Matthias, Otto's orderly, resembled a giant goblin, with his red nose and enormous ears. Lurching along astride a nag as fat as a balloon, as the regiment wended its leisurely way along the foot of the russet hills, he hummed the songs of his native Banat from dawn to dusk. Although they were dirges and laments, he gave them the sprightly rhythm of a minuet. Matthias enjoyed trotting along these shady valleys, skirting fragrant, freshly-tilled fields and burgeoning clumps of birch or larch trees like rabbits' bellies coated with the downy fur of springtime. Sometimes, indeed, his horse frisked about, left the track and went galloping off across the springy turf of the grey or coppery end-of-winter meadows. Whenever Otto's troop passed a sheepcote and the lambs inside bleated, Matthias would answer them in his own similarly guttural dialect. Meanwhile larks rocketed skywards, soaring into the blue, and church bells sent greetings from valley to valley.

Matthias always rose before the trumpets sounded reveille. This was his own jealously-guarded moment. He went to work in the faintly sorcerous gloom of dawn, tiptoeing around with no more noise than a cat, setting his day in motion with the stealth of a bird-snarer. He polished his cornet's boots and restored the pristine brilliance of the leather accoutrements, harness and curb chains. He aired the greatcoats on a line suspended between two trees, groomed the horses, and was zealous enough even to polish their hoofs as well. Meanwhile, as the sun came up beyond the jagged mountain peaks, the mist lingered on in the valleys like a mischievous sprite, sketching in a clump of red willows, unveiling a bridge, severing a road. Matthias was a keen observer of its tactics.

Otto would emerge from his tent, also without a sound. The old soldier had won his affection, and he loved to catch him unawares. Matthias had shouldered an exalted responsibility: morning after morning he set the world's wheels turning and made sure that everything looked spruce. One might have imagined that he was polishing the pastures, testing the spring-water, inspecting the hills. There in the shifting chiaroscuro of daybreak, he seemed to be attending, not only to his cornet's knapsack and cartridge pouches, but to the destiny of pine forests, the whiteness of waterfalls, the arrangement of mossy boulders . . . And then, one day, the mist had gone: winter was truly over and Italy lay ahead, ripe for invasion.

All that marred Matthias's happiness now was his fear of getting lost. It was useless his questioning Otto about their route and eagerly consulting every map he could lay hands on: this part of the world eluded his comprehension. Italy was lovely to look at, he conceded, but how could anyone get his bearings in such a fairy-tale country? Otto gently chided him: he would never do well on campaign if he mistook one river for another. A soldier was simply a man who knew how to read maps. Look at Bonaparte, Otto added. Bonaparte never merely *looked* at his maps. He bedded down on them, rolled himself up in them, crumpled them – indeed, one would swear he ate them, devouring his areas of deployment in advance. Matthias accepted this and resolved to try harder. Otto went on to sing Italy's praises. A more legible landscape it would be hard to imagine. For two thousand years men had cultivated it, marked it out with low stone walls, cross-ruled it with rows of poplars, mulberry and chestnut trees. Why? So that uncouth soldiers from the Banat could find their way around in it, why else? He pointed out landmarks with his riding crop: the network of rivers and streams, the half-open fans of the wheat fields, the terraced squares of vines, the black cones of cypresses, the plump grey pompons of olive trees stretching away to the horizon, and, on every hand, villages whose tiled roofs were never the same shade of red. Men had even trimmed the hilltops to qualify them for an honourable place in the paintings of the Florentine masters, said Otto. And even though Matthias had never set foot in a Viennese picture gallery, listening abstractedly, he assured Otto that he had understood every word and would take his geography lesson to heart – only to turn mistakenly north at the very next fork in the road.

Otto's friend Dietrich Feuchtagen, meanwhile, was restive. He had gone to war to wield his sword, so why were they indulging in this protracted picnic? The languorous beauty of the Italian landscape was getting on his nerves. Otto reassured him: Dietrich would have his butchery soon enough. War was lying in ambush for them somewhere, beyond a peradventure, so it would cost them nothing to wait. One of these days it would fly at their faces unannounced, like a cat with every claw extended. Then, one evening, they glimpsed the roofs of Genoa in the distance. 'The houses of Genoa, set amid their rocks like diamonds in gold,' Otto recited, and Ulrich teased him for trying to sound poetic. 'You're wrong,' Otto told him, 'the poetry isn't mine, it's Don Quixote's.' Seagulls were wheeling lazily above the harbour, and the pigeons fluttering about in the city's terraced gardens, which were overflowing with red and violet blossom, seemed intent on love. With a jingle of curb chains, the cuirassiers halted on the brow of a hill. They looked startled for a moment – startled but perfectly ready to draw their swords and gallop into the sea.

General Ott was instructed to drive General Marbot's division out of Savona, thereby depriving Masséna's forces, which were bottled up in Genoa, of a possible escape route. Lieutenant-Colonel Scherer's cuirassiers were sent into action and inflicted heavy losses on the enemy. At the first exchange of shots, Matthias became separated from Otto and got lost. Being congenitally incapable of telling one uniform from another, he consulted some French artillery-men engaged in hauling their guns up a rocky knoll. One of them flew at his throat. Matthias, who was stronger than an ox, knocked the man senseless and sprinted smartly away. He waged war for two whole days, but all by himself. If ever he saw any soldiers, he was loath to fire at them because he never knew whether they were friends or foes. He staved off hunger by wringing the neck of a cockerel and roasting it in the depths of a cave.

Late on the second day he sighted Otto, whose troop was at grips with a patrol of Masséna's light infantrymen. Taking the French in the rear, he ran several of them through with his bayonet and put the rest to flight. There-after he was cock-a-hoop – filled with self-importance. Far from getting lost, he'd simply executed an encircling move-ment – a rather slow encircling movement, but never mind – so as to take the enemy in the rear and come to his cornet's assistance at the crucial moment. 'You're lucky I'm such a good sort,' Otto told him. 'Anyone else would have you clapped in irons.' Then, dryly: 'You get lost a sight too often, Matthias. Take my advice and always keep a spare uniform in your knapsack – a French lancer's tunic, let's say. That way you can change sides occasionally. Postilions change horses at every staging post; you'll be able to jump astride another war!'

Lieutenant-Colonel Scherer's officers spent the evening of Monte Corona in triumphant celebration, little guessing that next day, May 13th, the French would recapture the little fortress and take three thousand prisoners. For the moment they savoured their victory at an inn near the battlefield, an isolated building perched on a rocky eminence and smothered in clusters of blue wistaria blossom. The youngsters were full of braggadoccio. They assumed the air of old campaigners back from Thermopylae by way of Actium and Bouvines. They slammed their swords down amid the platters of cold meat on the tables and sauntered around with much jingling of spurs. No soldiery could have made a more brutal or licentious impression. Stammering Siegfried Rottinstein had manged to recruit some simpering peasant girls who wore their aprons very low on the hip to emphasize their waists. The youthful veterans quaffed chianti, exchanged congratulations, sang ballads from the Tirol and Vorarlberg. The wistaria was vandalized, the girls got kissed.

12

It was late – long past midnight – when Otto and his friend Ulrich staggered back to the presbytery where Matthias had rigged them up a bivouac. No sound came from the sea below them. They moved ponderously, awash with chianti. Ulrich was exultant. Their first engagement had been child's play. Without meaning to boast, he said, he'd charged the enemy like a stampeding buffalo. Otto concurred, but guardedly. He too had fought like a madman, but as for the sense of excitement, the celebrated thrill of danger so smugly described by their instructors at Wiener-Neustadt, he hadn't felt a thing . . .

'I can't fathom what you're doing in the army,' said Ulrich, who had already stripped to his socks and underpants and was stretched out on a palliasse, toying with his cavalry dirk. 'You're completely out of place in a war. There are only two things to do in a war, Otto: feel frightened and get an erection – pardon my vulgarity, but that's all there is. Personally, I have to keep my courage handy, but you – you seem to need none, or rather, you don't seem to know what to do with it. I saw you at Monte Corona. The bullets were flying thick and fast, but frankly, you looked more bored than anything else. Frankly, old man, I don't understand what prompted you to pick on a military career.'

Otto drained another glass of wine. He hadn't picked on anything at all; it was a military career that had picked on him. 'There's a subtle shade of difference there,' he said in a drunkenly didactic tone. He'd been dragooned into the army by the Hofburg or the Minister of Police, he wasn't sure which – but Ulrich must know that perfectly well after all those conversations in their room at Wiener-Neustadt.

In truth, they and their friends had revelled in boringly endless debate. They used to forgather at the day's end to expatiate on God, duty, death and women. They were pedantic, verbose and melodramatic, incoherent and vulnerable. They puffed at long, elegant cigars and sipped plum brandy while setting the world to rights. From time to time, as though ashamed of their own solemnity, they would inject a little cynicism into the proceedings by making some obscene, blasphemous or flippant remark.

'But for all that, Ulrich,' Otto continued in a rather unsteady voice, ' – for all that, I'm going to tell you an astonishing thing. The fact is, I'm delighted that fate has inserted me in an army officer's hide. I mean it, I really do! Thanks to His Royal and Imperial Majesty's policemen, I think I've found my vocation. Believe it or not, I'm in my element on campaign – I've never felt more at home. Mark you, I'd feel even more at home if Matthias's presbytery didn't give off such a stench of cattle dung and diseased pigeons.'

'You're deluding yourself,' said Ulrich. 'You were old Schwarzbrod's prize pupil. We all admired you. No one in Vienna doubted that you had a brilliant academic career ahead of you. You don't give a fig for politics, war, Napoleon, or Melas – you don't give a fig for anything but girls and butterflies – yet you expect me to believe that this war suits you!'

Otto chuckled dryly, mirthlessly. Seated on his palliasse with his back propped against the roughcast wall, he carefully filled his pipe. A mosquito sizzled in the candle flame. Soft, thick cobwebs floated in the corners of the room, sprinkled with fragments of hay. Crumbling a sprig of wistaria between his fingers, he laboriously strove to explain the advantages he discerned in a soldier's life. He'd always hated making decisions. Whenever he saw one coming, he took to his heels. Every time he made a choice he deprived himself of all the other things he'd failed to choose, and so was dogged by regret. Could Ulrich understand that, or was he being childish? Anyway, what about Ulrich himself? Didn't he sometimes reflect, on some dark and dismal evening, that he might have become the organist of St Stephen's, or a philologist at Marburg University, or a schoolmaster in some Carinthian hamlet with a brood of snotty-nosed brats to teach? At all events, said Otto, he himself was prone to such ideas. He was maimed by all he could have done but would never do, all he might have been but would never be – yes, maimed like an old soldier who feels pain in the foot he lost at Valmy eight years ago, or at the Catalaunian Fields thirteen centuries before that. That was how he saw things tonight. His head might be swimming with drink, but wasn't drink an aid to thought? He couldn't get over being what he was – or rather, he amended thickly, putting the little ball of crushed wistaria to his nose to counteract the presbytery's graveyard smell – or rather, he couldn't endure not being all that he wasn't. It was silly, but even as a boy he would spend whole afternoons in his room doing nothing, boring himself stiff yet refusing to go to a schoolfriend's party for fear of missing some other festivity. So he was grateful to the Minister of Police for having relieved him of a chore and chosen him a party – in other words, chained him to the keel of the galley. No more doubts or dilemmas for him! All he had to do now was either to pull on his oar in time to the galley-master's mallet or else receive a volley of blows from his bludgeon. But honestly, Ulrich, this stench of old pigeons was unbearable – no, they weren't pigeons at all, they were bats . . .

'And the relief I feel here is similar. In civilian life you're expected to favour either this thing or that. You have to adopt either one point of view or its contrary, sniff the scent either of wistaria or of magnolia, prefer Salzburg to Graz or vice versa, decide on a certain career, persuade yourself that one woman is more attractive than another, proclaim your love for some one person to yourself and the world at large, bestow your friendship on one particular man – for instance Dietrich Feuchtagen – or on another – for instance you, Ulrich Lvov – and so on and so forth. It's mentally exhausting. I'm lazy, but above all I'm baffled. How can I tell if I like one particular flower when there are flowers everywhere, or if I love one particular woman when the world is full of women?

'Do you understand? Am I making sense? Here in the army, thank God, it's different. No more choices, no more decisions. My friends and comrades are those whom the pen-pushers at the Hofburg have chosen for me – you, for instance, and Siegfried and Thieberg and Dietrich. We neither sought nor found each other, the five of us. We were simply dropped into the same box, placed in the same cage, by a directive from the Hofburg.'

The candle was burning low and had begun to smoke. Ulrich's face was invisible now.

'I see,' he said with feigned jocularity. 'So you don't even know for certain if you feel any friendship for me.'

'No – no, I don't. I only know we were commissioned in the same regiment, that's all.' That was what he liked about the army, Otto went on. It diluted your responsibilities, did your thinking for you. Officers and men alike were babes-in-arms – they were taken charge of. You were ordered to be heroic, to conquer or die, and so you *were* heroic, you conquered or died. The trumpet played a certain sequence of notes and you charged or retired. You were robbed of yourself – no, liberated from yourself. You obeyed, yielded, submitted. You drew your destiny from the quartermaster's store. No more initiative or volition, no more identity – it was absolute bliss. You were nothing any longer, just a particle of the whole. What a relief! You weren't even called Otto Apfelgrun or Ulrich Lvov. You didn't know where you'd been born, still less who you were. You left it all behind at the barrack gate, that little bag of trinkets and knick-knacks and delusions, that little collection of bits and pieces known in civilian life as – what *did* one call it in civilian life? A man, wasn't that it?

'May I remind you,' Ulrich said coldly, 'that one night six months ago, in Thieburg's room at Wiener-Neustadt, you maintained the diametrical opposite? I can recall your very words. Groups and communities were so abhorrent to you, you said, that you even found your own company too much of a crowd.'

'But that was six months ago,' Otto protested, somewhat taken aback. 'Surely you don't expect me to have said six months ago what I'd be saying six months thence – tonight, in other words? If so, what would all those months amount to: a puff of smoke, a mirage? In six months' time I'll be saying something else, but what? How can I tell at this stage? Be reasonable, Ulrich. It's tiresome enough having to think at all without always having to think the same thing.'

Ulrich tried to devalue his friend's eloquence, putting it down to too much wine or a touch of fever. He was sprawled on his lumpy palliasse, obliquely lit by a moon so full that its rays pierced even the dusty windows, and Otto seemed to smell his mounting anger like some noxious miasma.

'Believe me, Ulrich, because I'm in deadly earnest tonight. If what I say is nonsense, blame it on your filthy war, your idiotic army. The least it can do, all that garbage, is to make us think what we . . . what we don't think. You're on double rations tonight. Chianti is like war – one has to make the most of it. Shall I tell you something else? If I had my way, discipline would be even stricter. Regimental orders would extend to our private lives and innermost thoughts. We'd feel happy at the command of one bugle call and fall in love at the order of another. All our states of mind, so-called, would be dictated to us at morning muster by our captains and majors. "Cornet Apfelgrun," a general would say, "fall in love with that girl over there!" The bugler would sound four notes signifying passion, and off I'd go and fall in love as promptly as if I'd been ordered to pick up a tent peg. Don't argue, don't think, just charge the enemy and get yourself killed: that's the military ideal.'

'You are talking nonsense,' Ulrich suddenly bellowed. 'Sleep off your bellyful of wine. I tell you, you're besmirching everything, even the tenderest of emotions. How dare you claim that a man can feel passion to order!'

Otto mightn't have heard. 'You remember our discussions at Wiener-Neustadt with Dietrich and Konrad and Siegfried, and the time Konrad read to us from the modern German poets – Schlegel, Novalis, Hölderlin, et cetera? Their poems are very fine, I don't deny, but on the subject of death – pardon me, my friend, but on that subject they're a bunch of idiots. Their notion is that every man must have

152

a death of his own – one that he has reared, bottle-fed, cosseted and titivated so as to make it look nice. It has to be a product of volition, a known, predictable quantity. Well, that's not only meaningless – death couldn't care less what Herr Hölderlin thinks – it's hateful!'

Otto jumped up off his palliasse and stood there half naked in the middle of the little room.

'It's the opposite of what I want,' he shouted. 'I want my death to be no more mine than my birth, my loves, my inclinations and tastes. I want it to be the product of chance, and as unfair and stupid as possible. Lots would be drawn under the supervision of a notary so as to reduce death to the vile thing it is. I ask you, is there any death more squalid and fortuitous than the one we risk here? A Bavarian soldier loads his musket carelessly, and death passes you by. A French gunner makes a mistake in his elevation and your head, which he wasn't aiming at, is torn off, whereas your comrade's, which he *was* aiming at, remains on his shoulders for another half-century and indulges in another half-century's worth of thought, passion and folly. Capital, perfect! Absolute freedom! Remember Meister Eckart? "Be nothing if you wish to be everything." '

Ulrich, although seething with anger, made no reply. Silence fell, but the two young men tossed and turned for a long time in search of sleep, lulled only by the velvet fluttering of bats.

Very early next morning their squadron set off to occupy a small fort on a conical hill overlooking Genoa harbour. The character of the siege had changed. The French garrison, blockaded inside the port, now stood at bay. The Austrians attacked by land throughout the day, and at night the Allied fleet took over. British vessels commanded by Admiral Keith sailed in under cover of darkness and unleashed a savage bombardment.

'I don't care for this war,' said Ulrich, who had forgotten their previous night's altercation. 'We're like poachers smoking out a rabbit, poisoning it in the depths of its warren. Typhus is raging in Genoa. People are dying by the thousand – they're eating grass, roots, rats.'

'To tell the truth,' Otto replied, 'I don't like war to play the hypocrite. I prefer it to go about its business openly and advertise its ignominy. The sort of thing I abominate is Montenotte: a Virgilian landscape romantically strewn with the debris of battle.' He grinned. 'If I were the Almighty, Ulrich, or the commander in chief, I should institute certain measures. I should call a truce for as long as the sky remained blue. No wars in springtime – in fact no one would be entitled to fight except in sinister surroundings. Fighting in Italy would be banned altogether. Even in Austria war would be illegal except in the gorges of the Mur, where it's so dark and dismal, and in Vienna in Gedenstrasse, because that's where I went to school and had a very nasty mathematics teacher. Generally speaking, war would be restricted to the Military Frontier, and even there armies would have to wait until thunderstorms and cloudbursts had plastered the soldiers with mud and turned the countryside into a stinking morass.'

Ulrich, infected by his friend's gaiety, decided to tease him a little.

'Correct me if I'm wrong, Otto, but your ideal war sounds very much like the one Duchess Clémence rhapsodized about in the presence of our decorous, courteous Lieutenant-Colonel Scherer: a war fought by vagabonds and cripples – military excrement, in other words. Which reminds me: you often speak of our colonel proprietor, don't you?'

'I've never mentioned her name,' Otto protested.

'Precisely. You never mention her name but you speak of her constantly. Am I to infer that you're under orders from the Hofburg to conceive a passion for the lady?'

Otto shrugged. 'She's beautiful, no one would deny, but she's a woman of fashion, an affected creature. She's so conscious of her looks that no one's allowed to see her before her morning toilette is complete – no one, not even she herself, still less her maidservants. My informants at the Kärntnertor report that she can't bear to look at herself in a mirror before she has primped, berouged and bedecked herself. That poses a problem, for how can any woman adorn her person without looking in a mirror? I'll wager she makes her feminine preparations in the dark. That's why her powder, rouge, beauty spots and gold patches are never quite where they ought to be. It lends her a certain charm. True elegance, as the English would say, should be casual . . .'

Meanwhile, the war lay becalmed. Skies of infinite altitude looked down on Genoa. The sun climbed above the harbour, glided over the countryside, and, when evening came, doused its flames in the eternal sea off Cape Formion. The strong, fetid smells ascending from the harbour were infiltrated by a scent of honey and sun-warmed grass.

The French, maddened by their predicament, suffered outbursts of fury. At Monte Corona on May 13th they drove Melas's forces from the field, took three thousand Austrian prisoners, and killed a large number of officers and men. Lieutenant-Colonel Scherer sent for Otto.

'Our aides-de-camp have suffered heavy losses,' he said curtly. 'Replacements are needed, and General Ott has appointed you one for the duration of the siege of Genoa. Don't delude yourself. This is certainly a promotion, and an honourable and flattering assignment – but it's mortally dangerous none the less. It goes against the grain to send an officer on such a mission, I confess, but the decision rests with the general. If you want to know, he informs me that the order came directly from Her Excellency the Duchess of Saxe-Salza.'

Otto, standing at attention, received the news impassively. What had inspired this latest move on the duchess's part? Caprice, cruelty, jealousy? A wish to further his career? Or was she, like her cousin Christine in the sheepcote, merely gambling with life and death?

The Frenchman Masséna resorted to an atrocious expedient. He marooned the three thousand Austrians captured at Monte Corona aboard some dismasted hulks in the middle of Genoa harbour, well within range of his guns. That done, he informed General Ott that they would receive only half the ration of mouldy bread and scraps of horsemeat allotted to his own men, who were already starving, unless the Allies used Admiral Keith's ships to keep the Austrian prisoners supplied with food. Masséna's proposal was rejected, but he remained adamant. The Austrians expired on their hulks within sight and earshot of both armies. French and Austrian soldiers could hear their anguished cries and watch their death throes through field glasses. They gnawed their boots, their knapsacks and cartridge pouches, and fought among themselves. At night the survivors cannibalized their dead comrades.

Word came at the end of May that Bonaparte had left Paris on the 6th with Duroc and Bourrienne. Lannes crossed the Great St Bernard Pass during the night of the 14th. The march from Bourg-Saint-Pierre to Etroubles took ten hours. The guns were dismantled and hauled across on improvised sledges. Twenty grenadiers were harnessed to each piece of ordnance, but they slipped and slithered so badly on the mountain tracks that Lannes had to revive their flagging spirits with martial music. Austria's General Melas, who had been skirmishing with Suchet in the region of Nice, tried to fall back on Milan, but too late. Bonaparte reoccupied Lombardy's biggest city on June 2nd, and the inhabitants went wild with joy.

Genoa, meanwhile, was at its last gasp. Typhus had tightened its grip on the beleaguered port, and every injured horse had been slaughtered and eaten. As soon as he learned of Bonaparte's arrival in Italy and the capture of Milan, Masséna accepted the armistice which Keith and Ott had been offering him for the past month. Cornet Apfelgrun accompanied the Austrian delegation to the parley, which took place in the chapel in the middle of Conegliano Bridge, half-way between the Austrian and French positions.

Released at last from the siege of Genoa, General Ott's twenty thousand men were turned loose on Italy while Melas clung to Savona. Otto quickly discovered that, despite the prestige it carried, an aide-de-camp's status was thoroughly unenviable. He went galloping this way and that across an Italy rent asunder by ten warring, eddying advancing, retreating armies. He was seen at Piacenza and Alessandria, delivered dispatches to Zach, Hadik and

Melas. He brought word of the Austrian defeat at Montebello and of Desaix's return from Egypt. He also witnessed the dramatic turn of events at Marengo. Like everyone else including the French, he thought the Austrians had won. He saw Kellermann's cavalry repulsed. By ten o'clock that morning Lannes was giving ground, and even Victor was falling back in disarray. Three hours later Melas assembled his aides-de-camp and instructed them to announce to a startled world that Napoleon had been routed at Marengo.

Otto's orders from Melas were to ride post-haste to Vienna. He would be the harbinger of triumph, Melas told him – a latter-day messenger from Marathon. Matthias was delighted. He packed Otto's gear and rode to headquarters to collect Melas's formal announcement of victory. Otto, quietly awaiting his return, had almost completed his preparations for departure when a tornado of yellow dust came speeding along the road. From it emerged Matthias and his horse. The orderly dismounted and snapped to attention, puce in the face and trembling. Otto looked at him inquiringly.

'Beg leave to inform you, sir, but we haven't won the battle after all. We've lost.' Matthias went on to give details. Desaix had counterattacked at the head of the 9th Light Demi-Brigade. Desaix himself had been killed, but General Ott, hard pressed on all sides and driven back towards the Bormida bridges, had failed to save the Austrian army from disaster.

'We haven't won, we've lost,' Matthias repeated mechanically.

Otto, fed up with the whole mess, waited for Matthias's spirits to revive. He sat down beside him on the earthwork and smoked a pipe. To disguise his own dismay, he took refuge in flippancy.

'You see?' he said. 'If only you'd been quicker we'd already be on our way to Vienna with news of an Austrian victory. That's what comes of dawdling. Half an hour at most, and everything goes awry. We should be galloping along, bound for Vienna, and tomorrow all Austria would be exulting and Paris putting on mourning – and all that at the very moment when Bonaparte's Consular Guards would be setting off for Paris to deliver our regimental colours in triumph to the Invalides. It's true, when you come down to it – Scherer was right: aides-de-camp play a vital role in war. If we'd reached Vienna before Bonaparte's aides-de-camp reached Paris, victory would have been ours.'

Matthias, who had picked a long blade of grass and clamped it between his thumbs, was amusing himself by blowing funny little tunes. He periodically interrupted his recital for a bite of bread and sausage, but Otto said no, he wasn't hungry. The whole affair had spoilt his appetite.

13

In the course of its withdrawal to the north-east, Lieutenant-Colonel Scherer's regiment had to negotiate the Po marshes. The horses plodded in single file along the dikes and levees jutting from the waterlogged terrain, bowed heads nodding with the effort needed to breast the milky swathes of mist while laden with all their gear, not to mention the saddle-sore, battle-weary men astride them in their steaming greatcoats. Red sun after red sun glided through the poplars' leafless branches. Partisans occasionally sniped at stragglers without hitting them. Pallid, unshaven and soaked to the skin, the once dashing, gilded cavaliers of the Prater, of Genoa and Marengo, finally extricated themselves and their beasts from the marshes.

At Christmas they reached the wintry shores of Lake Garda. Supported by Bellegarde's Savoyards, they fought a ferocious hand-to-hand battle in the snow with General Brune's forces near Pozzolo. Early in the new year, after Ludwig von Cobenzl and Joseph Bonaparte had signed the Peace of Lunéville on February 9th, they withdrew to Austria. This treaty, which confirmed Austria's territorial concessions in Italy and Belgium and along the Rhine, reiterated the terms agreed at Leoben for the third time. By so doing it lent an unreal, repetitive, macabre appearance to all the foregoing battles. The young men of Austria and France had shed their blood merely to replace one armistice with another of similar character, and every cannon-shot had been the thunderous, fatuous echo of one that had preceded it. History was laughing up its sleeve.

Otto, who had rejoined Duchess Clémence's cuirassiers in the vicinity of Milan, was not displeased to be returning to Austria for a taste of garrison life. The regiment installed itself a few miles from Linz in an old monastry perched on the flanks of the Postlingberg, which afforded a distant view of the bluish ramparts of the Alps. Quite close at hand

and a thousand feet below lay Linz itself, together with the Nibelungen Bridge and the broad ribbon of the Danube. Bonaparte, playing king-of-the-castle on his numerous victories, signed treaties of peace with all and sundry. Spain's turn came at Aranjuez on March 21st. In England, Pitt's replacement by Addington paved the way for preliminary negotiations in London, which were concluded in October. Russia bowed out a week later, and in March 1802 Joseph Bonaparte and Cornwallis laid the Second Coalition to rest at Amiens. Peace and quiet reigned throughout Europe.

Linz being a long way from Vienna, Constanze Apfelgrun came to visit Otto with one of his sisters. Lawyer Apfelgrun, too, journeyed to Linz for the August 15th festivities. The old man was so touched by Matthias's kindness to him that he decided to mistake the corporal for his son. Orderly and lawyer went for daily promenades in the Mühlviertel highlands. Otto spotted them one day, seated side by side in the shade of a beechwood thicket. They'd been picking wild flowers, lovely blooms from the Bohemian Forest, glossy red foxgloves, martagon lilies, lady's-slippers, stems of wild raspberry, and an assortment of valerians. Matthias had opened a bottle of wine, dissected a cold chicken and a pie, and now, the meal over, he produced a handful of cigars from his knapsack. Otto watched discretely as the lawyer, with his waistcoat unbuttoned, amused himself by blowing smoke in the orderly's ever-joyous face, laughing uproariously. The ill-assorted pair regarded each other fondly. Matthias told stories in his unintelligible Banat dialect while the lawyer listened with extreme attention, cupping a hand to his ear. He nodded and smiled, looking shrewd and profound by turns. When Matthias laughed at one of his own anecdotes, the lawyer would join in so heartily that he had to get his breath back by patting his paunch.

Otto took his rare spells of extended leave in Vienna. Vienna had changed: so much had happened since he last saw his native city that a barrier had been created. The Kärntnertor mansion was shut up. Prince Ernst had decided to spend a few seasons at Dresden with his wife.

Saxony was the land of his birth, after all, and its royal court combined elegance with a congenial atmosphere and plenty of good music. The prince spent his days in the Erzgebirge, geologist's hammer in hand, adding to his collection of rock samples. In winter the couple repaired to Greinburg Castle, which stood not far from Linz on the road to Vienna, likewise overlooking the Danube. Although the duchess took advantage of this to inspect her regiment, she never came alone. Prince Ernst made a habit of escorting her on such occasions. Invariably courteous and charming, he often entertained Lieutenant-Colonel Scherer and his officers. Being a keen student of all the natural sciences, he valued Otto Apfelgrun's knowledge highly and was unstinting in his friendship for him. The melancholy which Otto felt at this period was bitter-sweet. Fate had sentenced him to spend years on the Postlingberg, but at least the scenery was beautiful and the place had a timeless quality. Innumerable winters and summers lay entombed in the splendour of the dormant November forests, the sparkling summers of Linz.

When Lieutenant-Colonel Scherer sent for him and Ulrich Lvov and somewhat pompously granted them two weeks' leave of absence to attend the Windiswraths' annual ball in Vienna, Otto's immediate impulse was to refuse. A few years earlier he would have been overjoyed, but he had lost his taste for dalliance and dissipation, and Duchess Clémence was just a distant dream. Scherer, swaggering about in his riding breeches, was clearly flattered that two of his subordinates should have been invited to the Dual Monarchy's most exalted social function. Every year towards the end of September, the Viennese *beau monde* focused its collective attention on the 'Hibernating Bear', a vast country house in the Weinviertel some leagues north of the capital. The ladies made a microscopic study of the guest list, which was the object of Machiavellian intrigues and constituted Austrian high society's roll of honour – even though kindly Countess von Windiswrath made a point of opening her portals to merit and talent as well as to noble birth. Otto was amazed to find himself on the

Windiswraths' list. It occurred to him that they were closely related to the Saxe-Salzas, but he promptly banished the thought. He couldn't be sure, and anyway, Ulrich Lvov had also been invited. Whatever had earned him the invitation, he grudgingly accepted it.

Scherer construed the whole affair as a tribute to his regiment's heroic conduct at Genoa and Marengo. If they had had to wait three years, he said, it was because protocol at the house of Windiswrath was finical in the extreme – rightly so – and quite as scrupulous and discriminating as that of the Habsburgs themselves. Its pace was so snail-like, the colonel pursued with a sly smile, that many a woman invited to the 'Hibernating Bear' for her beauty's sake did not receive the invitation until her complexion had already been ruined for years. Scherer rolled his eyes comically. On one occasion, he declared, a field-marshal had finally been received at the house on account of his exploits as a lieutenant in a battle already cited for instructional purposes by manuals of military history.

'No, gentlemen, what really surprises me is that the Windiswraths' *chef de protocol* should have acted with such speed and raised the portcullis for you in such short order. Believe me, this honour comes as a reward for our efforts in Italy. I've not forgotten, Herr Lvov, that you were decorated with the Order of the Golden Fleece on the morrow of Montenotte, and that you, Herr Apfelgrun, were aide-de-camp to Generals Ott and Melas.' Scherer pursed his lips in the semblance of a roguish smile. 'You even came within a hair's-breadth of announcing that we'd won the battle of Marengo, isn't that so?'

Smiling wryly, the colonel retired to his office to sign the two warrants. He sprinkled a pinch of sand on the blue ink, blew it off, handed the cornets their papers, and dismissed them.

'You know, of course, that domino cloaks and masks are *de rigueur*?'

★   ★   ★

162

Otto was intrigued by the mention of dominoes. He broached the subject to his friend von Thieburg, the Rampant Frog, who was loathe to enlighten him, doubtless because he resented not having received an invitation himself. However, he was so steeped in society lore that he couldn't maintain his sulky silence for long. The Windiswraths' ball was not a masked ball proper, he said, but an event at which women were requested to turn up with their faces bare while men had to come wearing masks and monk-like cloaks. The idea emanated from Paris, where it had proved immensely popular. Its originator was an Italian diplomat of the highest rank, Count Mareschali, who held many such functions at his house in the Champs-Elysées.

'At Count Mareschali's balls,' the Rampant Frog explained, 'the women wear all their finery – in fact they dress with a care verging on frenzy – but leave their faces unmasked, as I've already said. So why do the men wear masks? One doesn't have to be a great scholar to see the reason: Bonaparte and the rest – the Murats, Neys and Talleyrands – can amuse themselves in the comforting knowledge that they won't be recognized. The women, too, adore such entertainments. They can dally quite recklessly without fear of reprisals from their husbands, because any domino may conceal some all-powerful marshal or minister, if not Bonaparte himself. Two more points: married couples never turn up together, and it's the women, not the men, who ask their partners to dance.'

Otto was dumbfounded. How could a woman choose herself a gallant if every man's face was hidden?

'At random,' the Rampant Frog replied, ' – quite at random.'

'My dear Otto,' said Ulrich, seizing the opportunity to get in a dig at his friend, 'it seems to me that a ball of this kind is made to measure for your philosophy. At Genoa you bored me to death with your theories about chance. So observe how at Count Mareschali's it isn't death that advances blindly, as in war, but passion – pleasure, in short. The women take a lottery ticket and are given a package, and when they unwrap it they discover that it contains

Bonaparte, or Junot, or some fashionable young man-about-town, or even one of the policemen who are bound to infest such ballrooms and can do so only in disguise. That Italian diplomat is a genius. He guarantees the fair sex two of its favourite ingredients: immodesty and the unexpected.'

Dietrich von Thieburg stroked his flaxen beard and drew Otto's attention to a third ingredient, namely, danger. The women guests at Mareschali's balls became so exhilarated, behaved so brazenly and had their heads so thoroughly turned that they transgressed the bounds of propriety and risked incurring the direst vengeance. One Parisian lady, having danced the night away in the arms of a tall domino widely rumoured to have been Murat, was found in the gardens of the Champs-Elysées with her throat cut. The affair had been hushed up by the police, 'but believe me, I should be very surprised if the lining of certain domino cloaks or hoods at the Windiswrath's didn't conceal a few well-honed daggers and vials of poison – even a pistol or two. Signor Mareschali isn't a Venetian for nothing. Gold, blood and masks are his stock in trade. Being a diplomat, he's also a connoisseur of human nature. Provide a woman with danger, heroism and dreams, gentlemen, and that woman is yours!'

★ ★ ★

It was a magnificent structure. In the opinion of the *beau monde*, not even the residences of the Liechtensteins or the Saxe-Teschens, the Palais Lobkowitz in Prague or the Schwarzenbergs' mansion on the Rennberg in Vienna could hold a candle to this maze of baroque architecture set astride the summit of Hibernating Bear Hill. The park surrounding it had been designed by Italian landscape gardeners. In these fabulous grounds, where hare and fallow deer roamed free amid man-made waterfalls and rocaille-encrusted grottoes, the Windiswraths nurtured exotic varieties of plants. Some of the trees hailed from Ethiopia. 'They're the favourite trees of Prester John and

164

King Solomon, so the Queen of Sheba assured me only last year,' Countess von Windiswrath used to say with a modest smile. 'But don't venture too far into the woods: you may find yourself confronted by a dragon, a unicorn, or a werewolf!'

Approaching the terraced grounds by way of the drive, which was strewn with flowers and fresh herbs, elegant berlins and heavy, coronetted carriages drawn by teams of eight horses, their trappings bright with gold, pulled up at the very foot of the steps. Otto and Ulrich, who had hired a calash for the occasion, arrived at dusk after a laborious ascent through the twilit depths of an oak forest. As the sun went down behind Mount Runwolt, every window in the house lit up and set the dusk ablaze.

The two young men felt very ill at ease despite their cloaks and their swaggering gait. The farther they progressed through the glittering reception rooms, the more their self-assurance waned. Never had they seen such beautiful women. Mythical, fairy-tale creatures, satin-sheathed ice maidens, sirens clad in ermine or watered silk, they were surrounded by an austere assemblage of black, grey, or purple dominoes. It was a gathering composed half of cloistered monks and half of sorceresses, themselves bewitched. When one young woman laid her hand on the sleeve of a homespun habit, it was as if the domino-clad figure had become a leather-hooded falcon clinging to huntsman's wrist: one almost expected the savage girl to snatch off the mask and command it to kill – to bring her back a heart oozing gore.

Otto and Ulrich amused themselves by trying to guess the identity of various masked figures from their height and build, but with little success, their knowledge of fashionable society being so limited. Never having attended such a soirée before, they wished the Rampant Frog had come too. The Duchess of Mahlberg swayed past them, enthroned in a red velvet armchair borne aloft by four lackeys and preceded by two linkmen. Old Gertrud's maids had tricked her out in a profusion of enormous pink and green bows. Her sightless eyes stared blankly as she sat there chattering,

165

dispensing outrageous remarks and cackling with laughter. Otto finally caught sight of another figure that struck him as familiar. Tall, gangling and disjointed, it walked with giant strides on feet that would have graced a veteran grenadier. Could there really be two such anatomical curiosities? The neighing laugh that issued from behind the black mask dispelled any remaining doubt that Professor Schwarzbrod was one of the party. As soon as Otto made himself known, the professor folded him in a passionate embrace.

'Otto – Otto Apfelgrun! Expect no welcome from me, you faithless boy! Be off with you! You're erased from my tablets, finished and done with. Otto Apfelgrun is a thing of the past, a dead letter!'

Otto started to stammer some reply, but Schwarzbrod seized him fondly by the arm.

'My prize pupil,' he continued in an aggrieved tone, 'and he had to turn traitor – had to exchange the refined study of butterflies for the crude science of war. What possessed you, Otto? What induced you to go hunting Bonaparte with a popgun? Added to that, I hear you were unsuccessful – you came back empty-handed!

'Seriously, though, I miss you. Whom else did you expect me to vent my inanities on in that rabbit hutch, that hen-coop of a city? No one would understand them. Either that, or they'd perceive them as inanities, which is the saddest fate that can befall any inanity. I exclude Duchess Gertrud, needless to say. The duchess is our last remaining person of intelligence.'

Schwarzbrod unceremoniously towed Otto away from Ulrich and into a rotunda whose diamond panes had been painted in the yellow and black of the Dual Monarchy.

'You're doubtless aware that Duchess Gertrud has broken with Christine – you know: Christine Kinsky, whom she used to call "my eyes". Christine isn't even in Vienna these days, and her whereabouts are a secret. I believe you had a brush with that peculiar gentleman Herr Schulmeister – a red-haired fellow, rather short and endowed with a sizeable paunch. Redhead or no, he's one of Napoleon's most potent agents. Well, believe it or not,

Christine is with him. A Kinsky siding with the Jacobins, imagine! My God, those Mahlberg women . . .'

Unsophisticated Otto received enlightenment on a number of points. Although Schwarzbrod was a lone wolf, uncouth of manner and diffident by nature, he gratefully absorbed what little society gossip came his way. He told Otto that Archduke Charles was thought to have been spotted dancing a galop with little Countess Pietranera at last year's ball. It was also alleged that Thugut had been notified of his fall from grace on the same occasion, and tonight all the women were puffed up like hen pheasants at the thought that one of these black or grey penitents might be Cobenzl, Thugut's successor, or even Count Colloredo, Archduke Charles's aide-de-camp general. However, Schwarzbrod sniggered, nobody knew for sure, and much good it would do that lovebird Countess Pietranera to have circled the floor in the archduke's arms if neither she nor her friends could be certain that it was he.

Schwarzbrod clung to Otto's domino, kneading the sleeve between his fingers as if afraid that it might come unravelled. His tone changed.

'Marie-Josèphe is very ill. My daughter hardly eats a morsel, and the doctors have warned me to expect the worst. Her poor head, Otto . . . She'll be thirty in two months' time, and I seventy. All that my life has amounted to in essence, is a school break. You'll smile, I know, but I'm still in the school yard, playing ball, and it's all over. The janitor is crossing the playground with a big bunch of keys, about to signal the end of break by beating his drum, and that will be that . . .

'You were right to forsake the natural sciences, Otto. I sometimes tell myself I've been a fool. What do I know of the world? Butterflies' wings, pistils and stamens, yes, but everything else has passed me by. Still, I haven't done badly. Butterflies are the one subject I know a little about. If the Almighty hadn't strewn the earth with butterflies, my lad, what would I have been? A pauper patronizing the Wipplingerstrasse soup kitchen at a kreuzer a bowl, and I don't like cabbage or turnips. The Almighty doesn't exist,

167

Otto, but I can't deny that it was very decent of him to invent insects. Forgive me for rambling on like this. I so seldom get the opportunity – so very seldom . . .'

He gave Otto's shoulder a violent, almost aggressive squeeze and bade him au revoir. His ponderous, ungainly figure disappeared into the throng of dancers, thrusting dominoes aside with both arms extended.

★ ★ ★

Otto made his way into the ballroom and brazenly eyed the women from behind his mask. 'They're as good as naked,' he thought. 'All the men are grotesque, all the women obscene.' He decided to pay his respects to Duchess Gertrud, whom her maids-in-waiting had installed on a red velvet ottoman after gently tweaking her silk ribbons straight as though arranging a vase of flowers. Before he could reach the old lady and join her circle of courtiers, however, a hush descended on the vast room. The orchestra stopped short. The dancers froze, then completed their unfinished steps, but slowly, like people in a dream. The sputtering of candles and flambeaux was all that could be heard as Duchess Clémence made her entrance, radiant and majestic beyond belief in a white satin gown cut very low on the shoulder, gold ribbons at her throat and waist. The dominoes stepped aside to let her pass. Clémence gave them not a glance. Beckoning to one in particular, she took the floor with him. The couple danced all alone, without accompaniment, until the orchestra plucked up its courage again. The ensuing din, which was preceded by a crash of cymbals, suggested that all the unplayed notes were determined to make up for lost time.

Other couples took the floor. The musicians, camouflaged in loggias behind silver hangings embroidered with the Windiswrath cipher and the Hibernating Bear emblem, abandoned their staid old Austrian melodies in favour of livelier dances, polkas and mazurkas. Women and dominoes became a wild confusion of whirling arms and legs. It was as if a hundred marionettes had joined forces, got their strings entangled, and their puppeteers were now vainly striving to extricate them – striving to detach male puppets from female. Otto whirled and spun with the rest. He fancied that if the orchestra got its notes mixed up, or if it stopped playing at an inopportune moment, men and women would remain inextricably conjoined, arms mistake the shoulders to which they belonged, heads fail to rediscover their necks. Although his partners burned with curiosity, he stuck to the rules. His name would have meant nothing to them in any case.

He had lost track of Ulrich Lvov. While a quadrille was in progress he propped his elbows on a gaming table and asked a footman to bring him a lemon sorbet. For all he knew or cared in his present bemused state, the footman might have been Schulmeister or a policeman or the Minister of Police himself, the sorbet a poison concocted by the alchemists of the Medici. Countess Pietranera, her lovely face flushed with excitement, asked him a question. He answered her pleasantly enough, amused by her dainty, sparrowlike looks, but then he caught sight of Clémence. She was crossing the ballroom with her hands outstretched and her pale eyes staring. Although she had no means of penetrating his disguise, Otto knew beyond doubt that she was making for him.

Closely entwined, they glided across the dance floor. Clémence's head sagged, alternatively lolling backwards and tipping forwards onto the shoulder of Otto's domino. He might have been dancing with a sleepwalker. The music seemed to sparkle like gold dust in the torches' silky light. It was only when the orchestra stopped playing that Otto remembered where he was. There was a beautiful woman's body in his arms, and she was gazing at him imperiously.

'Will you permit me to say your name?' she asked.

He laid a finger on her lips.

'May I say your name?' she insisted fiercely.

'You think I'm Otto Apfelgrun?' he said at length.

'There's a honeysuckle bower on the other side of the waterfall. I shall be there at midnight. The honeysuckle bower at midnight – I'll be there.'

14

Otto didn't miss a single dizzy, oblivion-inducing dance from then on, nor did he miss many goblets of punch, even if he did dilute them with big glasses of iced water. He asked a girl if she was feeling merry. Not really merry, she said, but happy. Otto inquired if she was happy to be happy. Rather at a loss, the girl toyed nervously with a blue stone suspended from her neck, winding the thin gold chain around her fingers. Otto leant towards her and spoke in a confidential undertone. Since they didn't know each other and would never meet again, might he give her a piece of advice? He had a theory, he said. You uttered a few words without thinking, a collection of syllables arranged at random. They were almost meaningless, these syllables – you could have put them in a different order or even extracted them from other syllables – but the result was the same, young lady: the words had been spoken – those words and no others – and you'd crossed a divide, and nothing would ever be the same again, and you'd stepped across the threshold into . . . into the realm of infinite time . . .

In response the girl with the blue pendant begged Otto to bring her a dish of sorbet – one with lots of different-colored ices on it – but she'd sensibly disappeared by the time he'd battled his way to the buffet and returned with two such dishes. He put them down on a convenient mantelpiece. Just then a black and brown domino wearing a white silk mask inquired what he wanted with all that crockery. Was he setting up house? The voice was a woman's.

'Yes,' said the domino, 'I'm a woman. I'm breaking the Windiswraths' rule, I know, but the contrary could also be said, Herr . . . Herr Apfelgrun. It could be said that I'm even more of a woman than all these unmasked females. There are some who claim that women are always disguised, even when they aren't wearing the smallest dab of rouge, the smallest patch – even when they're naked. That means I'm disguised twice over. It's a way of revealing oneself, perhaps . . . You know how it is with two mirrors? One reflects your image in reverse, the other corrects it.'

Otto, who was loath to prolong this badinage, injected a note of boredom into his voice.

'You called me by my name,' he said casually. 'How do you come to know it?'

'I was eager to see you.'

'But how did you know I would be here? Only a week ago I should have laughed if anyone had told me I would be at this ball tonight.'

'How scathing you sound, Herr Apfelgrun. For someone reputed to be the nicest young man in Vienna, you're being most disagreeable. I'm not the Devil, look . . .'

She touched Otto's hand.

'My hand's real enough, isn't it? Not a piece of ice, nor an ember, nor a ghostly appendage. Just to set your mind at rest, I can't remove my cowl in front of all these people and betray my female condition. I'll help you, though. I'll give you a little more light – then, perhaps, you'll see me better.'

Swiftly, the unknown woman snatched a flambeau from its bracket on the wall and held the flame in front of her cowl. Otto could now see nothing at all: neither the white mask, nor the black and brown domino, nor the hand. He could only hear a rather tense voice issuing from the flame.

'Not such a great improvement,' said the woman. 'You can see me even less clearly than you did just now. Light is a better disguise than darkness.' She tossed the torch into the fireplace. A lanky domino approached them, hesitated for a moment, and returned to the dance floor. 'That may have been Colloredo or Archduke Charles himself – who knows? But we're wasting time on trifles, Herr Apfelgrun, and time presses. We've one or two little matters to discuss before midnight.'

'Before midnight? Before midnight, you said. Why?'

'Why midnight? Oh, simply because it marks the beginning of another day, that's all . . .' She made a sweeping gesture in the direction of the couples circling the ballroom. Her voice took on a menacing note. 'No, that's not all. I'm eager to know if you mean to keep your midnight assignation beneath the honeysuckle. Beneath the honeysuckle, sir.'

Otto clumsily raised a hand to his eyes to blot out the mask, exorcise the apparition.

'You know?' he heard himself say. 'You know of my appointment? But it's a secret!'

'A secret known to me.'

Two young women advanced on them with an air of interest, laughing shrilly. The taller of the two was wearing a gold belt inscribed with Kant's name, Potsdam fashion. The black and brown domino fell silent. The girls said their piece, then gave up and wandered away again.

'What if Duchess Clémence herself confided in me? That would crown everything, wouldn't it?'

'You know Duchess Clémence?'

'Know her? Heavens, not many people would flatter themselves on that score, as you yourself are better placed than most to judge. But I'm digressing – losing my thread. Are you aware that, after one of the Mareschalis' balls in 1796, a noted Parisian beauty was found in the gardens of the Champs-Elysées with her throat cut?'

Otto stared at the speaker through the slits in his mask, wondering if she could really be a living creature. The touch of her cool hand still lingered on his own. He pictured a woman's body under that black and brown simulacrum, the flesh as white as a wax candle.

'What a tangled web it all is,' sighed his unknown companion.

'Are you sure, madam, that it isn't you who are entangled, and that the web isn't of your own making?'

She laughed heartily.

'Oh yes, Herr Apfelgrun, I'm entangled – very much so. Not even a cat would find its kittens in my cat's cradle. Ariadne never lost her thread, but I, believe me, am not within a mile of extricating myself from the labyrinth. Truth to tell, I feel thoroughly at home there – I know it by heart. Besides, absurd as it may sound, as soon as I leave the labyrinth I lose my way.'

172

'You still haven't told me what you're doing here.'

She ignored the implied question. 'And pleasure, Herr Apfelgrun – what's your attitude to pleasure? I'm not too sure what lies at the bottom of it, but this much I do know: pleasure is a transitory thing, a matter of a few seconds, no more – a nothing, a mere nothing. Pleasure doesn't exist, and anything non-existent is well worth seeking. It's a delight . . .'

'My dear young lady, I can gladly dispense with delights of that kind. I like my pipe, my cat, the smell of cabbage soup in my mother's kitchen, playing backgammon, flirting with tavern wenches, but in other respects I'm not a candidate for pleasure. Danger holds no appeal for me. I'm sorry, but there it is: I'm not a romantic like you.'

The eyes behind the white silk mask flashed.

'Herr Apfelgrun, you shouldn't humiliate a girl you don't even know. I'm full of romantic notions, it's true. I know *The Sorrows of Young Werther* by heart, I record my thoughts nightly in a boarding-school exercise book, and I lace my bodice very tightly to suppress the stirrings of my soul, but as for all the young people who take their own lives after reading Herr Goethe's novel, I think them stupid. They deprive themselves of the best part.'

'The best part?'

'Yes: melancholy.'

'Why are you saying all these foolish things?'

'My God, you're right, forget I said them! How rash of me! You see how full I am of romantic whims, how much in love? What of my imposture tonight? Think for a moment: one can confess things masked that one would never dare to say openly. It's childish, I know, but you hold a girl's modesty cheap, and I, like any woman in my position, am setting my traps.'

'I'm doubtful,' Otto said coldly, 'if the methods you're using to entrap me, as you put it, are the best available.'

'Don't take me for a silly little goose, I beg you. The truth is, the methods I'm using are the very ones most likely to alienate you from me. Any child could see that, but I . . . I

173

do as best I can.' She seemed on the verge of tears, but only for a moment.

'Nevertheless,' she went on haughtily, 'you wouldn't wish me to angle for you like any romantic young girl – to primp and flirt and imprison my hair in a mesh of gold chains. Ugh! I abhor all those tawdry tricks. They're worthy only of the ninnies who roam the panelled halls of the Hibernating Bear . . .' While speaking, she had slipped her hand swiftly under her cowl and brought out the gold net that held her own hair in place.

'Take this, Herr Apfelgrun,' she said, proffering it, 'as a memento of tonight. It will prove to you that you weren't dreaming. Two people who have never seen each other can still have a memory in common, though of course, a passion shared and requited is better than a hopeless infatuation – don't I know it! However, I can't play both parts at the same time. I simply go my own way.

'It's true, don't you see? What I love is to love. That's more than enough for me – nothing else matters in the slightest. A woman finds it tiring enough to love without having to be loved as well. I doubt if I could endure it.'

The big ballroom clock chimed a minuet. The woman in the domino gave a start.

'You hear? It's nearly midnight. There are so many things in this world one doesn't know. For instance, can you tell me how many stars are revolving above this house tonight, every one of them a universe in itself? One really ought to read Messrs Newton and Tycho Brahe. But there are two more things of which I'm entirely ignorant. In the first place, I've no idea if you'll go to the honeysuckle bower, and for a very good reason: I'm sure you don't yet know yourself – after all, you did say you weren't in love with danger, didn't you? As for the second thing I don't know, I've forgotten it . . . Ah yes, I remember now. The second thing is, I'm quite as ignorant of what I'm going to do myself, and how I shall set about it. You hit the nail on the head just now, Herr Apfelgrun: I'm in a tangle, and what a tangle!'

Alone once more, Otto leant against one of the fluted

columns supporting the mezzanine. The girl with the blue pendant walked up to him and held out her hand for the ice she had asked him to get her a quarter of an hour before. Otto welcomed her reappearance. He went off to fetch her another dish but strode past the refreshment tables and out into the gardens.

The night was warm for the time of year. Dancing couples were shamelessly ravaging the lawns and flower-beds, trampling the daisies underfoot. Several dominoes whirled acrobatically, complete with glasses of champagne, and a lone woman was reeling around with a lighted candle in her hand. Otto, still clutching the gold hair-net, skirted an artifical lake and made for the waterfall at the far end. He found the honeysuckle maze with little difficulty.

*　*　*

Duchess Clémence was waiting for him. She had draped an otter-skin cape around her shoulders, and when Otto touched her neck she trembled. He asked if she was nervous, but she shook her head.

'No one knows we're here except Schwarzbrod, who pointed you out to me. He performed that chore at my request. I had no choice. I couldn't risk mistaking one domino for another and ending up in someone else's arms after so much effort, so many machinations. Besides, I might have taken a fancy to whoever it was, and what an imbroglio that would have been! No, thank you! I had trouble enough getting you on to Melanie Windiswrath's guest list, so someone had to tell me which cloak concealed you. Besides, Schwarzbrod would never betray me. I truly believe I respect him more than any other man on earth.'

'Did we come here to chatter about Schwarzbrod?' Otto said curtly.

She bit her lip and looked defiant.

'To this ball, you mean? It seemed too good an opportunity to miss. You would be in disguise, so I thought I might pluck up the courage to tell you what otherwise I don't have the courage to tell you. Needless to say, I was wrong.'

'Madam,' Otto broke in urgently, 'I have to inform you that there was a woman in the ballroom just now, a masked woman who knew that you had arranged an assignation with me at midnight, near the waterfall.'

'A woman? What woman?'

Very roughly, Otto seized Clémence by the shoulders. He threw back his cowl in one swift movement and glared at her.

'That woman, Clémence, was you!'

'Are you insane? Why should you say such a thing? Why should I have done such a thing?'

'How am I to know what goes on in your head? I've never fathomed your manoeuvres. You're nothing but coquetry, tricks and traps, fickleness and artifice. You're a woman like any other. You've led me by the nose – no, don't deny it! You were toying with me from the very first. How naive I was, and how you must have laughed at me! Those blank letters, my banishment to the Military Frontier, your coldness toward me, your absences, this ball, and now that charade of yours in a black and brown domino! I'm no match for a woman of your kind. Cruelty, perversity, deceit – no, Clémence, those aren't my strong suit. You're trying to send me mad, but I'm sorry, I'm not mad at all and I don't intend to become so.'

Clémence had shrunk back into the shadowy depths of the bower, eyes large in her horrified face. She let the otter-skin cape slip from her shoulders, then the top of her gown, and began to undo her bodice. Otto raised a restraining hand, but Clémence, as though mesmerized, was baring her breasts. She uttered a terrible cry, harsh as a rooster's. Otto caught her by the arm.

'Don't touch me,' she said fiercely. 'Do you believe me now? Have I exposed enough of myself for you to trust me? Have I demeaned myself enough for Cornet Apfelgrun? Am I sufficiently like the whores he consorts with? I've bared my breasts, but is that enough? You wish me to lift my skirts as well? You wish me to resemble those women of the streets, those serving wenches who please you so much? Don't defy me, Otto, don't defy me! No one has ever thwarted my wishes. Don't defy me, I implore you!'

Otto retrieved the cape and put it round her shoulders.

'I don't understand you, Clémence – I shall never understand you. Your machinations weary me. You want me to be clay in your hands – you want to feel satisfied that, if you ordered me to jump off a cliff, I should jump. I remember, Clémence. I know it was you just now, behind the mask. Or wasn't it? Either way, all is lost.'

'But why? Why should it have been me?'

Otto stepped back two paces and eyed her with revulsion.

'Why?' she repeated. 'Who was this woman?'

'It was you!'

'But why, Otto? Why me?'

'Because intrigue is the very air you breathe. Because you mean to destroy me, scatter my wits, subjugate me. Either that, or . . .'

'Or what?'

'Or you were putting me to the test – trying to discover if I would come here at the risk of my life. The Mahlberg women are like that, aren't they? Little girls who've read too many fairy tales and English novels. It's all very Byzantine. To be worthy of them a man has to walk through fire, and if they're charitable enough to give him their heart he has to accept the likelihood of being murdered. Poor Clémence, what a perverse young lady you are. I pity you.'

Clémence turned and ran from the bower, only to stop short beside the waterfall.

'What's the use of running away?' she cried. 'It's over. That woman has won, and even if it isn't over, *she* will be the one that determines everything from now on.'

'No, it was you that determined everything from the first. I'm a puppet, and I amuse you.'

'I'm frightened,' said Clémence, '– very frightened, but no matter. Fear was preordained. It has been my constant companion since the moment I first saw you at the Kärntnertor. I'm not afraid of fear – I would almost nestle in the

177

arms of terror, for how can anyone love without it? Are you frightened too, Otto?'

'Yes.'

'But you came here even so?'

'I wanted to see you,' said Otto, 'and I saw you.' His fingers sought the mesh of gold thread beneath his domino. 'And I shall never see you again,' he added.

Clémence raised her face to his. Her fingertips brushed his lips, which resembled black velvet in the gloom. It was an artless gesture.

'I wanted to see you too,' she whispered.

Fireworks time had come. The whole hill burst into a blaze. Scores of guests streamed out of the reception rooms and spilled across the lawns. Hurrahs and bravos rent the air. Clémence walked slowly back to the house. Rockets soared skywards and explored beyond the miniature lake formed by the waterfall. Otto eventually tracked down Ulrich, who had set his cap at a lady of handsome appearance but surly disposition. Ulrich insisted on taking a few more glasses of punch. Once in the cab, he fell asleep almost at once.

15

Duchess Gertrud died. She had found it cold at the Windis-wraths'. Whether on that account or because of her great age, the old machine had broken down. She rose cheerfully enough at about ten the next morning, but by the afternoon she was moaning and wheezing in her armchair beside the Turkish cannon captured at the battle of Kahlenberg. Vesicatories applied by Mlle des Trappes, her new French housekeeper, did nothing to alleviate the pains in her head. Dr Palfy, who was summoned without delay, pronounced her breathing shallow, her pulse poor and erratic: it pounded like a woodcutter felling a tree, then died away to nothing. Palfy prescribed English drops, three hundred and fifty of them in two doses, half in chicken broth and half in sherry. Between fits of coughing, the duchess informed her major-domo that, although heaven had given her no children, it had atoned by providing her with a string of ancestors, and since she was about to enter a realm devoid of time – and wombs, she added tartly – she was at liberty to regard her ancestors as her offspring. 'I'm the mother of that entire crew!' she declared, levelling a forefinger at the portrait gallery.

Very early the next day, she rang for Mlle des Trappes and announced that she was dead. She was tactful enough – 'These things happen, *ma chère!*' – to minimize the event. The housekeeper ran like a madwoman to the major-domo, who hurriedly donned his ceremonial black, complete with silver badge and gold chain, as though preparing to confront Death in person and raise his sonorous voice in a final cry of 'Her Excellency the Duchess Gertrud von Mahlberg!' Then, bending so low that his knuckles almost brushed the floor, he burst into the duchess's apartments.

The old lady was sitting up in her huge four-poster, comfortably ensconced among lace pillows embroidered with the Mahlberg cipher, while her maids daubed crimson powder on her cheeks and carried out adjustments to the tall peruke with the pink highlights. She scolded the major-domo, but without acerbity. 'No need to make a fuss, Alfred, we all have to go in due course. There's no special knack to dying – any fool can manage it.' It was unlike her to be so mild. Mortality had infused her fiery soul with gentleness. Her voice, as she acquainted Alfred with sundry items of information, was almost languid. Death had super-vened at five-twenty that morning. She had had sufficient sang-froid – an apt expression in the circumstances, she chuckled – to glance at the wall and note the exact time. It had been a tiring night, and she hadn't slept a wink.

The major-domo ventured a respectful interjection. He submitted that, because the duchess had told him she was dead, she could be nothing of the kind. Her proper course, he boldly suggested, would be to choose. 'Either one dies or one says one is dead, Excellency. One cannot do both at once.' Gertrud lost her temper at this. She caught Alfred a blow with her cane and reproved him sharply. Setting aside the impropriety of a major-domo's daring to contradict a female Mahlberg, she was better qualified than anyone to decide whether or not she was dead. Never having quaked at the prospect of death, she said, surely she could be accorded the privilege of knowing whether or not it had finally overtaken her?

Although her own time was already up, she did not propose to waste any of Alfred's on trifles. He would do better to take her word for it and make some preliminary arrangements. She issued numerous instructions, all un-doubtedly formulated well in advance. Her armchair was to be moved, not forgetting the cannon, to enable her to sit in state beneath the gaze of Gerhard 'Wolf-Jaw', founder of the Mahlberg line, the man with the jaw of which her own was a refined copy – refined or shrivelled, depending on one's point of view, she said archly. A historical résumé followed. Gerhard was the giant warrior who had com-manded the Teutonic Knights, whom she preferred to call the Knightly Swordbearers, at Tannenberg in 1410 against the army of Jagello, Grand Duke of Lithuania, and although it was true that the first of the Mahlbergs had voided his life-blood into the snow and been devoured by wolves, who cared? What mattered was that he had fought there and that, before his mangled remains rotted away in an East Prussian grave, he had injected his seed into that other grave, a woman's womb, which seed had been transmitted from womb to womb for four long centuries, losing a little of its vigour and virulence each time. It would also be proper, said Gertrud, to rehang the portrait painted of her by the Florentine artist Titoselli half a century earlier, when the deceased of 1804 was still in her blond, radiant, triumphant prime of life.

Her portrait was to be hung in the place it deserved, at the very farthest end of the gallery, because the direct Mahlberg line was now extinct. Theirs had been a long march through time indeed, a heroic, harrowing, resounding march across the four centuries it had taken for the Knightly Swordbearer's seed to evaporate, dissolve, and forsake all living flesh, even if the Saxe-Salzas did aspire to pick up the torch that had illumined Europe for so long, which was, in fact, no more than a charred twist of rag trailing in the dismal dust which that same Europe had become. But must she really occupy the very last place in the gallery, she mockingly, pedantically mused aloud, or shouldn't she eschew its walls because they were occupied by her ancestors, and she could hardly claim to be one of her own progenitors?

She reverted to her original train of thought. Having spent a lifetime deploring the fact that she was barren, she now congratulated herself on her infertility because there were only two exalted and coveted places in any family tree: those of the founder and of the ultimate scion, the first and last of the line, the pioneer and the liquidator. All the others – those who had passed the baton from hand to hand, womb to womb – were merely intermediaries and supernumeraries whose function it had been to transmit life to the person destined to ensure the demise of their line. Such was Gertrud's mission. She was in charge of the final reckoning. God had chosen her, Duchess Gertrud von Mahlberg, to be the woman with the defective womb, and had assigned to her the task of transforming this teeming, pullulating, chaotic family, obscene as any family or form of life, into something rounded and complete, self-contained and ripe for eternity, perfect and impersonal – something as smooth as a hen's egg or, better still, as that mythical serpent of which the freemasons so often spoke: the Uroboros, which knows neither beginning nor end, youth nor decrepitude, because it is for ever devouring its own tail.

The major-domo, who had listened unblinkingly to this impassioned dissertation, complied with all his mistress's wishes. Gertrud's instructions were followed to the letter. Attired in a black faille gown glittering with all the gold and diamonds amassed by the women of her line, four whole centuries of them, she was installed in her armchair with the Turkish cannon beside her and the first of the Mahlbergs facing her. The shutters and blinds were closed, and candles carried by footmen burned in every mirror. A platoon of lackeys was dispatched to the street to spread fresh straw on the cobblestones. The major-domo had rehung Gertrud's portrait, but his mistress had amended her plans yet again. She insisted that Titoselli's likeness of the radiant young woman of 1750 be hung, not at the farthest extremity of the portrait gallery, but precisely at its central point. 'Pooh,' she said, blowing on her fingertips like a schoolgirl, 'what does chronology matter now?'

Having discharged his painful funerary duties, the major-domo sought help from Father Thaler and the admirable Dr Palfy. He implored them to tackle the duchess and put an end to her masquerade. The two men turned up at the same time and were received together. Gertrud's manner toward Dr Palfy, a kindly and conscientious man with a delicate constitution, was courteous but uncompromising. The vicar of St Anne's she bombarded at point-blank range, heaping scorn on his head and seizing the opportunity to revile the Church for its pretensions to omniscience and omnipotence.

'If only you knew how ludicrous you look, you men of the cloth, when one watches you gabbling and genuflecting! I'd always suspected that you know nothing about the Almighty, Father, and now I have the proof. Death is your most valuable asset, but it doesn't happen the way you say – far from it. Death is the simplest of proceedings, as long as you confront it with your chin up. You've been deceived, Thaler – you've had your head filled with nonsense, but it's not your fault. These things are beyond you – they're beyond everyone. God himself is defeated by the concept of God. Have you noticed? He has never succeeded in furnishing you with the smallest proof of his existence. Poor God! He has failed, Father, lamentably failed to communicate any such proof, and God knows how hard he has tried! Well, if God's brain isn't up to it, how much less is a man's, let alone a priest's!'

'Excellency,' said Thaler, but that was as far as he got.

'He goes round in circles, this God of yours. He gropes his way along. He puts forward symbols, metaphors, analogies. He indulges in approximations, spreads rumours, whispers in people's ears. Jesus Christ is one such rumour, the god of the Koran another, and likewise those of the Brahmans, the Tupinamba and the Zoroastrians, but shall I tell you something, Father? Even if you mixed all those rumours together, they would still amount to nothing. Jesus Christ, Mohammed and Buddha are substitutes, façades, God's lieutenants – yes, like you yourself. They're vicars in the same way as each of us on earth is the vicar or deputy of everyone else. The finest rank in the army, I always say, is that of lieutenant. We get a little closer to God by skipping from the Bible to the Koran or the sacred books of the Hindus, that I grant you. We get a little warmer from time to time, like children playing hunt-the-thimble. We get warmer, but we never get within a thousand million leagues of our goal!

'God is our quarry, our eternal quarry, but he always eludes us. The most we can do, Thaler, is to pick up his trail – a trail as indistinct as the tracks of a hare on ice . . .'

The duchess sat there with her chin thrust out and her dislodged peruke wobbling precariously. She had raised her voice, but the result was a disappointment. Although her lips worked furiously, the sounds they emitted were no louder than the buzzing of a bluebottle.

Dr Palfy, who was subtler than Thaler and had learned from the latter's discomfiture, employed a different tactic. He held God to be so unknowable – he didn't shrink from saying this – that it was vain and sacrilegious to speak of him and more sacrilegious still to pray to him, worship him, or even believe in his existence. In short, only a man of very little faith could have faith. Father Thaler hissed like a cat at this assertion. Gertrud, who was highly delighted, nodded in agreement, but Palfy went on to say that at present they had other fish to fry, and that he, being a man of science as opposed to religion, could, if the duchess would graciously consent to an examination, demonstrate to her that she was not dead after all. Physiology, he said, could infallibly distinguish between the animate and inanimate states. He proposed to sound Her Excellency's chest and settle the question one way or the other.

'My dear Doctor,' said Gertrud, 'your religious reasoning is sound, but your advocacy of medicine is as futile as Thaler's of God. I wonder why you're so insistent. You should hear them all roaring with laughter!' The lace-gloved hand left the barrel of the cannon, rose into the air gesticulating like a tiny acrobat, or rather, like a wizened marmoset on the end of an invisible rope, and pointed a tremulous forefinger at the portrait gallery. The priest and the physician were completely floored. Gertrud gave her wig a sharp tap, and her face disappeared into it like a bird returning to its nest. She thereupon dozed off.

Thaler suggested to Palfy that it might be wiser not to cross the duchess because a tantrum might exhaust her remaining strength. The situation wouldn't last for ever – it was a temporary contretemps only – so why not simply acknowledge her to be dead? The physician objected. The duchess was a long-time patient of his. She'd died quite often in the past, and she never quibbled about his fee on such occasions. The only snag was, she refused to eat and drink. She'd remained dead for so long the last time that she almost did die, and disaster was averted by a whisker.

184

Having refused all food for five days, she'd been in a dangerously weakened condition. Palfy had pictured a time when there would be nothing left of her, not even 'the tracks of a hare on ice' – nothing at all save her wig, gown and petticoats, her frills and furbelows, her lace gloves: crumpled fabrics reminiscent of the chrysalises one finds in the country, which serve as humble monuments to the erstwhile existence of a living creature. 'But then,' Palfy added airily, 'do we human beings ever amount to more than an illusion, a residue, a burial-mound of uninhabited clothes?'

'Now you're being as lyrical as our duchess,' Thaler whispered spitefully.

'Forgive me,' said the admirable Palfy, tugging at his side-whiskers, 'but my present fear is that she's a trifle deader than usual. She's taking more trouble over her death and expending more energy and talent – applying more knowledge, too, for she's steadily gaining experience. On other occasions she has stirred and sat up after a few hours or days, like a gnarled old tree trunk – if I may venture an impertinence – that puts out new shoots after a hundred years of dormancy. Today, however, she refuses to surrender. She seems inflexibly determined, and since she's older and her organism is more decrepit than ever, if she insists on remaining dead for longer than two or three days without taking nourishment, I won't answer for the consequences. Not to put too fine a point on it, she may really die.'

'Couldn't she be fed by force – or in her sleep, perhaps?'

Palfy spread his hands despondently.

'But Doctor,' the vicar pursued, 'she's sleeping now. When she wakes, isn't it possible that she'll suffer a lapse of memory and forget she's dead?'

'Not a hope, Father. She has a flawless memory, and I wouldn't even count on her being asleep. I'm certain of nothing with her, though I can well believe she's genuinely blind, and I own I'd be astonished if someone told me she wasn't. Look at that beak of a nose and those staring eyes, wide open even in sleep. Don't they remind you of a lurking predator? Lying in wait for what? My God! As she herself

185

would say: lying in wait for God!'

The two men agreed on a plan of action. A maidservant would watch over the duchess with instructions to dispatch a footman in the event of a crisis, and advantage would be taken of the old lady's somnolent state to convene a conference to be attended by members of the family, eminent academics from the university, and one or two distinguished persons of sound judgement. The meeting, which took place at the Saxe-Salzas' late that morning, was chaired by Rector Ouarin. The Saxe-Salzas were present as a matter of course, together with Palfy and Thaler, several professors of medicine, a representative from the Hofburg, Professor Schwarzbrod in his capacity as biologist and intimate friend, and the coadjutor of St Stephan's Cathedral.

Rector Ouarin, having been acquainted by Father Thaler with the duchess's views on comparative religion, offered a suggestion. Why not beat her at her own Satanic game? The coadjutor feverishly demanded to know how. By following the example of the ancient Egyptians, who were always at pains to leave food in the mausoleums housing their dead. The coadjutor winced at Ouarin's heathenish proposal and nipped it in the bud.

'We have always been aware,' he said suavely, 'that our unfortunate duchess had an appetite for poisonous fruit. She was an avid reader of the blasphemous works of Voltaire, Diderot and Holbach. I also recall that she carried on a correspondence with no less a person than Mme du Châtelet, Voltaire's niece. God, in his infinite forbearance, has often endured her gibes at him – gibes uttered in the most select and right-minded sections of Viennese society. Well and good, my friends, may her soul rest in peace. But that Rector Ouarin, a noted and ardent champion of Rome, should follow in her footsteps and ridicule true religion – there I say: Hold, enough!'

Rector Ouarin, looking abashed, cited his conduct at Baden during the campaign against irreligion. He had merely thought –.

'Don't think too much,' the coadjutor broke in. 'Given our present predicament, why not send for Dr Mesmer?

186

He'll hypnotize her, make a few passes with his magnetic tubs and broken bottles, and that will be that: the duchess will recover. The question I would ask, however, is this: Have we the right to thwart the designs of Almighty God?'

After talking in circles with growing asperity, they found an unforeseen saviour in the person of the Hofburg official, of whom no one had expected much despite his impressive black side-whiskers. A tall, sallow, phlegmatic man, he nursed a passion for history because he felt that present actions should be enlightened by the exalted events of the past. The men of today were pygmies who, if given a chance to survey wider horizons, could perch on the shoulders of their giant predecessors. Foremost among those giants, in the Hofburg's estimation, were the courtiers of the Sun King as immortalized by Louis de Rouvroy, Duc de Saint-Simon. Never in the course of human history had there been a society more civilized, more rigid in its conception of propriety and more systematically ruled by etiquette than the court of Versailles, with its *petits levers* and *grands levers*, its squabbles over stools and chandeliers, wardrobes and headgear – a combination, the official gravely averred, of courtesy and severity. So saying, he carefully unfolded a closely-written sheet of paper.

'I propose to read you an anecdote recorded in his *Mémoires* by the Duc de Saint-Simon. It concerns the Prince de Conti,' he said, settling a pair of eyeglasses on his tapering nose. 'Saint-Simon describes him as being quite insane. In old age he suffered from attacks of fever and gout so severe that Finot, his physician, almost lost hope. With your permission, I shall now yield the floor to the Duc de Saint-Simon.' He proceeded to read aloud in French, with an accent as atrocious as his delivery was monotonous.

'What most perturbed Finot was that Monsieur le Prince declined to take any nourishment, arguing that he was dead, and that the dead ate nothing. Either he had to take some food, however, or he would really die. No one could ever persuade him that he was alive and that, in consequence, he should eat. In the end, Finot and another physician who regularly visited him in Finot's company ventured to tell him that there were dead men who ate. They offered to produce some for him, and did, in fact, bring him one or two trustworthy and well-rehearsed persons who were unknown to him, and who, although they feigned death like himself, ate. This artifice convinced him, though he refused to take his meals except with them and Finot. Subject to that proviso he ate exceedingly well, and persisted in this vagary for quite some time with an assiduity that drove Finot to despair, though he, Finot, used to die with laughter when telling us what went on and what was said at table by the otherworldly partakers of these repasts. The prince lived on for a long time thereafter.'

Saint-Simon's anecdote worked wonders. A buzz of satisfaction filled the Saxe-Salzas' drawing room. The Hofburg official preened himself as he polished his spectacles and slipped them into his waistcoat pocket. The only sour face in sight was that of the coadjutor, who disliked what he later termed 'this vile subterfuge'. He did not dare to oppose the Hofburg, however, and the plan was adopted by acclamation. All that remained was to secure the connivance of a few elderly, addle-brained folk in a poor state of health – preferably lame, gouty and covered with facial sores – and install them in Duchess Gertrud's apartments at the Palais Questenberg-Kaunitz. Father Thaler claimed that he would be able to persuade some of his parishioners to cooperate for Christian charity's sake. Prince Ernst shrugged, professed himself sceptical, and unexpectedly sided with the coadjutor against Saint-Simon, but it was Palfy who, with a touch of eloquence, carried the day.

'The duchess is unpredictable,' he began quietly. 'Her mind, though brilliant, is a lumber-room crammed with bits and pieces of every description. She scorns the notion of incompatibility. She's capable of stating, with absolute sincerity, that a thing is black and white at the same time. Contradictions roll off her like water off a duck's back. For example, I guarantee you that today she's not only convinced of her death but quite aware that she's still alive.

'She's capricious. She play-acts continuously, but mark this: the name of her play is fear. She mimes death in order

188

to evade it and mitigate its horror. Being provocative, childish and droll by nature, she may well lend herself to our little game, that's to say, contribute her own caricature of death: a caricature of the limbo we're preparing for her. In her case, distinctions become blurred and colours run and mingle. She sees nothing irreconcilable in life and death. I've more than once been told by her that she has thrown overboard – jettisoned, as she puts it – all concepts such as "here", "today", "tomorrow", et cetera, rather like the debris we describe as floating between two tides. That's why, even though my hopes are slender, I agree that we should play the "dead man's banquet" card. In any case, we've no alternative. It's our last remaining ace.'

The physician's little speech persuaded Prince Ernst and the coadjutor to give way. That afternoon, barouches deposited several antique Viennese personages on the steps of the Palais Questenberg-Kaunitz. Two ladies of advanced age and great distinction, having been recruited by Father Thaler, alighted with their rather shabby belongings. General Count Konig von Weitzau, alerted by Duchess Clémence, had volunteered at once. 'One last assault on the old enemy, Death?' he said, medals clinking. 'Well, I'm not without experience, and there's nothing I wouldn't do for my dearest Gertrud.' Lawyer Apfelgrun, who owed his nomination to Schwarzbrod, completed the party. What with his scattered wits and his incessant, birdlike twittering in a largely unintelligible private language, the unfortunate old man was tailor-made for the occasion.

Otto, conscripted by Father Thaler, accompanied his father to the Mahlberg mansion. The lawyer, who was delighted by this change of scene, had merely insisted on bringing his collection of goose quills along. General von Weitzau arrived a few minutes later. The floorboards protested under his immense weight as he lumbered through the antechambers and drawing-rooms, flanked by a pair of footmen bearing torches. Otto did not recognize him at first. Although his domed head was still as bald and his eyes were as round and prominent, the once off-white beard was as black as a raven's wing. 'Apfelgrun,' he barked, 'good to see you again. Enough said!' And he towed Otto into one corner of the great drawing-room.

'We've lost the battle of the bakeries, Apfelgrun, but is that any reason to abandon the struggle? The answer is no! Ergo, we must change our strategy. "The art of war is a simple one, and entirely practical." So says Bonaparte, but I would modify his formula as follows: "The art of war is a simple one, and entirely prophetical." Enough said! Why do our generals get themselves trounced? Because they're a war behind, whereas Bonaparte and the Ottoman Empire are a war ahead. Conclusion? Enough said! The Turks have won the underground battle, granted, so I shall cut my losses, bring up my bombards, and promptly apply my golden rule: "Never think you've won when you've lost." As for its converse, I apply that too, because it's even more pernicious to think you've lost when you've won. Our objective: to foil the enemy's plans for the next war.'

Such was the reason for the general's black beard. While studying the Arabs' epic history in Gibbon's *Decline and Fall*, he had been struck by one particular incident. This had occurred in the year 732, after the legions of Baghdad had completed their conquest of Spain under Mussa's command. Although Mussa was seventy-five years old, he had regarded the taking of Spain as a simple formality, a mere preliminary and springboard to greater things. In his view, the Arab Empire's real goal should be the northern territories of Germany, Scandinavia, and Russia.

'Being very old, however, Mussa was afraid that the northern campaign would be entrusted to a general younger than himself. So what do you think he did? He had his white beard dyed black so that the Sultan, impressed by his youthful appearance, would assign him the task of pushing northwards. His ruse didn't succeed, of course, but no matter: that's what I call the spirit of prophecy. I myself have followed the illustrious Mussa's example and had my beard dyed at Capellio's. I should add, Apfelgrun, that I'm also busy learning Arabic.'

The Hofburg official's plan went off without a hitch. Gertrud was delighted to receive visitors. She needed an

190

audience, and never more so than when playing for high stakes. The sound of Otto's voice took her aback, however – could he really, at his tender age, be one of the dead? Had he lost his life in some vile battle? Otto disabused her. He was simply escorting his dead father, Lawyer Apfelgrun, who paid his respects to the duchess in the manner of yore, with many a flourish of the arm and sweep of the leg. Gertrud liked to keep a tally of the living and the dead – not that she attached much importance to such a minor distinction since everyone would sooner or later sit down at the same table. Footmen came and went in the darkened rooms, their candles floating through the liquid, tremulous gloom.

Summoned by Schwarzbrod, with whom he had been on close terms since the affair of the Gravitsky caricature, the free-thinker Schulmeister turned up towards nine that night. The duchess welcomed him warmly. She had often heard him mentioned, she said, by her beloved niece Christine Kinsky.

'Christine is no longer in my service,' she went on. 'She's living in the Tirol, so I'm told. I miss the girl – I was very fond of her.'

Fräulein Kinsky was staying with friends in Salzburg, Schulmeister replied, but he'd just heard that she would be paying a visit to Vienna in two weeks' time. Gertrud swiftly counted off the days on her fingers.

'Two weeks from now, sir, I shall be in my tomb.'

Otto introduced himself to Schulmeister, who pretended not to recognize him.

'Is it long since Fräulein Kinsky was in Vienna?' he asked Schulmeister casually. 'News is so slow to reach our garrison at Linz. A friend assures me that he came across her here in this city, not two days ago.'

Schulmeister chuckled and buried one fat forefinger in Otto's waistcoat pocket. 'Some people will say anything, my dear fellow.'

Duchess Gertrud beckoned Schulmeister closer.

'Believe it or not, Herr Schulmeister, you've been known to me for a long time. I first heard tell of you from a friend of mine, an English eccentric who used to employ servants to

191

live instead of him. He valued you highly. No, no, don't protest! No false modesty, please, because I know it for a fact. You were the one appointed to mourn in his place when his son, poor William, was drowned at sea. Lord Misrule assured me that you were his best lieutenant, and more adept than anyone at worming your way into other people's feelings – almost into their very skin. Indeed, it wouldn't surprise me to learn that Misrule continues to employ you even in his tomb – for instance, that he instructed you to mourn my death on his behalf . . .'

The good Dr Palfy, with his greying hair, neatly trimmed beard and veiled expression, supervised the progress of the operation. Gertrud, very much at ease, chattered away in a sophisticated, scintillating, sarcastic, sepulchral vein. She sat enthroned with her guests facing her on a row of gilded white chairs, shoulder to shoulder. General von Weitzau came in for some barbed remarks.

'My poor Gustav, death has done you little good. You were a thoroughgoing fool in your lifetime, and you're still an ass now. A dead ass, but an ass none the less. I'm glad you came, even so. You were the most amusing general in the Royal and Imperial Army.'

Far from taking this amiss, Weitzau wellnigh burst with pride. He winked at Palfy, Otto, Lawyer Apfelgrun and Schulmeister as though to imply that the duchess was off her head but must be allowed to rave on because it would purge her blood.

'As for you, ladies,' Gertrud pursued, 'why so down in the mouth? There's nothing so extraordinary about dying a little. I ought to have died a long time ago, if the truth be told, but with all my obligations I never found the time. No one understands me, as usual. No one can conceive what my life became when I lost my sight. I lost it twice over, what's more, having been compelled to bid my beloved Christine farewell. I tried no less than ten other girls – ten ninnies, ten imbeciles! They told me nothing of note, just useless odds and ends, whereas with Christine it was a garden here, a river there, a cageful of songbirds some-where else . . .

192

'Without Christine's eyes, what was left me? Thaler advised me to concentrate on scents and perfumes. Every stretch of countryside has a smell of its own, true, but can you see me braving the rigours of a long journey in order to breathe the scent of Berlin's chestnut trees or Lake Garda's periwinkles, not to mention that of the ubiquitous Bonaparte, who must surely stink like the devil with all those unwashed soldiers around him? No Father, be serious. Lord Misrule would have understood me. Do you know what he used to do when he went to confession and was given a severe penance – when bidden to fast, for instance? He made his footmen go without food instead. Not that it lasted long, that phase. In latter years he stopped going to confession altogether, and his lackeys confessed his sins for him. Whenever he wanted to commit a sin, he had it perpetrated by one of his minions.'

The duchess's voice had gained strength. She raised no objection when her footmen served the company a snack of chicken broth and linzer torte with cherries. She simply requested the living to withdraw to another room and take their supper there. The meal progressed in silence and semi-darkness. All that could be heard was the scraping of forks on plates, the loathsome champing of toothless jaws, the sporadic clink as decaying stumps collided with crystal goblets. The footmen trod with care for fear of stumbling with their candles and spilling food over the dead. Lawyer Apfelgrun earned a rebuke for noisily gulping his broth but mistook it for a compliment and laughed, patting his waistcoat. Once tea had been served, gaiety returned. Gertrud, nestling in her armchair, retailed the latest gossip. Lawyer Apfelgrun listened avidly with one hand cupped to his ear, just as he had done at Linz when Matthias told him stories in unintelligible Banat dialect. The old gentleman was in his seventh heaven. He pulled indignant, even scandalized faces from time to time, but only at random and never for long. Turning to his immediate neighbour, who happened to be Schulmeister, he addressed him on the subject of goose quills.

'Just think,' he mused, 'If there weren't any geese,

writing would never have been invented – a chilling thought, don't you agree? I tell you, sir, the whole of human civilization depends on that chance phenomenon – or should I say, that miracle? – the humble goose!'

The ensuing days were less agreeable. The effect of that first night, with its candle-lit mirrors, its muttered conversations, its food and drink, its sounds of munching and swallowing, had been to stupefy the guests. Father Thaler's two female parishioners withstood the ordeal better than most. They took a pessimistic view of their fellow citizens, of the impurity that reigned in Austria, of the corruption and lechery rife among the men and women there. That being so, they declared, their temporary sojourn in limbo was a blessed relief. Lawyer Apfelgrun decided that he was bored and became fidgety. Dr Palfy watched his little band of therapists with growing unease as the days went by. Their strength was waning, their mood becoming more and more despondent. To purchase Duchess Gertrud's recovery at the expense of several innocent lives would be to exchange one evil for another, and what dutiful physican would countenance such a bargain?

In the course of a second conference at the Saxe-Salzas', it was proposed to set a time limit on the operation. Four days had elapsed and the old lady, though thriving, was still dead. In other words, argued some, the experiment had failed. Duchess Clémence, however, advocated perseverance, basing her hopes on the old lady's capricious temperament. Her aunt was quite capable of casting off her funeral garb from one minute to the next. Prince Ernst took the opposite view. Battle had been joined under adverse circumstances, he said, and should therefore be broken off at once.

'My dear Ernst,' Clémence told him briskly, 'old ladies aren't Saxon hussars.'

Two days later Clémence was congratulating herself. Gertrud had let it be known, out of the blue, that her death was at an end. She announced this happy event at the evening meal, or rather, she instructed her major-domo to kindle every flambeau and chandelier in the dining-room.

194

Her guests, now bathed in a sea of light, understood: the duchess had extricated herself from her self-imposed predicament. Champagne was dispensed, a drop or two only for the ladies from St Anne's, a brace of bottles for General von Weitzau.

'That's your privilege, Gustav,' Gertrud told him kindly. 'You can drink yourself silly and no one will notice. You always talk the same twaddle.'

The two maiden ladies from St Anne's, though glad that things had turned out for the best, dreaded their impending reimmersion in the debauchery of the capital, which was such an affront to womanly virtue. They would miss their days at the Mahlberg mansion. They had spent tranquil hours in the select and sober company of those who were mindful of spiritual joys, not of what they termed 'the vilenesses of the flesh'. They extracted a promise from Gertrud, who continued to bully them almost as much as before, that she would call on their services again in the event of another 'indisposition'. Everyone ate with gusto. From ten o'clock onwards, a succession of barouches drew up at the foot of the steps.

* * *

Otto started to gather up his father's goose quills, but Duchess Gertrud told him sharply that she needed him. The day wasn't over yet, she said, and asked him to read her a passage from *La Nouvelle Héloïse*. The drawing-room was less well lit now, and Otto had to enlist the aid of a nearby flambeau. He deciphered the French text with some difficulty, mispronouncing certain words. Gertrud, who seemed drowsy and distrait, barely listened. After half an hour or so, the major-domo came in to announce that the Duchess of Saxe-Salza had arrived.

'At last,' said Gertrud. 'Now I can take a nap.'

Otto made to withdraw.

'Don't go,' the old woman told him. 'Didn't I say I needed you? Stay here.'

Otto's father had stationed himself in front of a pedestal

table and was tidying his goose quills. The goose, he declared, was a shrewder creature than it looked.

'Believe me, Excellency, geese are only swans in disguise.'

He glanced around him impishly.

'The coadjutor's a goose, I say, and the vicar a swan.'

He was about to pat his paunch and laugh when Clémence made her entrance. Failing to notice Otto, who had shrunk back into a corner, she kissed her aunt, surprised to have been summoned at so late an hour, and the two women exchanged pleasantries on the subject of Father Thaler, General von Weitzau, Herr Schulmeister and the lady parishioners of St Anne's. Then Gertrud abruptly changed the subject.

'Come here, Herr Apfelgrun. I know you're skulking somewhere.'

Clémence looked dumbfounded.

'Closer, Herr Apfelgrun,' said Gertrud, ' – come closer, where I can hear you.'

When Otto was within reach of the big red armchair, right up against the Turkish cannon, Gertrud raised her head. Without warning, she shot out a clawlike hand, caught hold of his wrist, and tugged at it fiercely. Pulling his hand towards her, she placed it in that of her niece.

'There,' she sighed, 'there . . .'

Clémence, who had resisted at first, looked at Otto and gave up. Her hand closed on his like a vice. Otto didn't move. Her fingers seemed to burn into his flesh.

Lawyer Apfelgrun grew impatient. He circled the couple wide-eyed, for once without a saying a word. Gertrud nudged him gently.

'The old gentleman wants to go home,' she said. 'Very well, let him go.'

Clémence took her leave first. Otto lingered for a moment or two. He would have welcomed some remark from Gertrud, some explanation of what had happened, but the duchess, her thoughts elsewhere, said nothing. Her tremulous chin slowly subsided on to her lace ruff. Otto bade her farewell and left the house on foot accompanied by his father, who had brightened at the prospect of a nocturnal stroll.

The Bauernmarkt was almost deserted. Some tipsy students lurched into the yellowish cone of light cast by a street lantern, singing as they straggled across the width of the street. A two-horse waggon laden with barrels scattered the youngsters and sped off into the night with a metallic clatter. And then, quite suddenly, Otto found himself face to face with Clémence, a black-clad and almost invisible figure lurking in a doorway. Lawyer Apfelgrun, who was delighted to see her again, presented his respects with many a flourish. Titillated by the young duchess as only an inveterate but senile womanizer could be, he showered her with compliments. His gaze dwelt on her, and especially on her hair, which was gilded by the lanternlight, with undisguised admiration. It was a while before she spoke.

'Your leave is at an end?'

'Tomorrow,' Otto told her. 'Tomorrow I report back to Linz with my friend Ulrich. I take it you'll be returning to Greinburg, so we'll be travelling in the same direction. When do you leave?'

'In a few days' time,' said Clémence. 'I might as well retire to a convent, don't you think?'

Lawyer Apfelgrun pounced on this conversational opening. He was well acquainted with the Mother Superior of the convent at Klosterneuburg, a first cousin of his wife's, and would gladly effect an introduction for Her Excellency Duchess Clémence.

'Otto,' said Clémence, 'what if I sent for you? No! No, don't answer.'

'I should come.'

'Then I shall do so.'

'You will?'

'That ball the other night at the Windiswraths', that hateful ball – I was certain that . . .' She broke off. 'Without my Aunt Gertrud we should be lost . . . Yes, I was certain that the ball would enable me to tell you that I love you, but I couldn't say it.'

'Nor could I,' said Otto.

He was on the point of brushing her lips with his fingertips. He yearned to touch her face, throw himself at her feet, but he didn't move. Although his father wouldn't have understood or minded, he himself would have felt that he was deriding the old man – treating him like a stuffed dummy and taking advantage of his feeble-mindedness. Clémence hesitated, then proffered her hand in farewell to Lawyer Apfelgrun, who swooped on it with a host of mumbled valedictions. Otto took his arm, and the two men walked slowly off.

16

Otto and Ulrich rode a deafening post-chaise back to Linz, where a regimental berlin was awaiting them. Their arrival at Postlingberg late that afternoon was celebrated in style. Dietrich Feuchtagen was beside himself with joy. Being as fond of Otto as he was of good food, he could not have been more delighted. Spread with damask napery bearing Konrad von Thieburg's embroidered cipher and laden with Bohemian glass and silver plate, a sumptuous table had been made ready in the officers' dining hall, a former conservatory a hundred yards from the monastery itself. Dietrich, who had chosen the menu, enumerated its various items in the sonorous tones of a master of ceremonies: cold meats and sausages from the Tirol, trout *en papillotes*, hare stewed in its own juices with an accompaniment of dumplings, an apricot and almond tart. For wines, Müller-Thürgau, Dürnsteiner, and champagne. 'And the trout,' Dietrich added, digging Otto in the ribs, 'were guddled in the Mühlviert by your good Matthias!'

Also on the menu was gossip. Everyone wanted a full account of the Windiswrath's *bal masqué*, Vienna's latest intrigues, Schönbrunn's future plans. Ulrich preened himself and looked inscrutable. No, on his honour, he knew nothing. His friends would surely do him the favour of believing that Count Ludwig von Cobenzl and His Excellency Count Franz de Paula von Waldsee-Colloredo would never divulge their full intentions to a humble cornet of cuirassiers. Even though they had half unveiled them for his benefit, he was sworn to secrecy.

Otto devoted himself instead to society tittle-tattle. He told of Dr Ulhue's *faux pas*, Schwarzbrod's droll remarks, Father Thaler's genuflexions. 'Everyone is waiting eagerly for the vicar to be smitten with an attack of gout. Depending on when it catches him, he'll either remain permanently on his feet, but stiff as a post and unable to prostrate himself before Their Excellencies, or permanently on his knees, in which case, how will his housekeeper ever straighten him out sufficiently to put him to bed at night?' Two glasses of champagne later, conversation turned to more serious subjects, but only by fits and starts because they were broached by Siegfried Rottinstein, who stumbled over every other word.

'W-what news,' he inquired. ' – w-what news of little C-countess Pietranera's honeypot – I mean, her social c-commitments?'

'Countess Pietranera?' said Otto, casting his eyes up to heaven. He dipped two fingers in his fob pocket and consulted his watch like a doctor taking a pulse, then nodded gravely. 'My dear Siegfried,' he continued with every appearance of regret, 'I could, if I had to, tell you in whose bed Madame Pietranera was campaigning last night, but that would be stale news indeed – hours out of date. Like Napoleon, the countess wages a war of movement. "Love is a simple art, and wholly practical," that's her motto.'

Dietrich, whose mind ran on nothing but women, pressed Otto to reveal how he'd fared with them in Vienna. Otto said he'd met a flower girl in the Prater and invited her to Hugelmann's, and they'd attended a performance of *Agnes Bernauerin* at the An der Wien. Her name was Anna, Anna Lutgren, and her eyes were big and brown with a hint of yellow, and her voice was soft, so soft you could barely hear it, and she persisted in vanishing all the time. You took her for a stroll in the woods, and all at once she was far away among the elms and birches, and she called you, but there was no one to be seen among the trees, 'And believe me, you'd swear she'd been blown away like a puff of smoke, but the next day she'd be calmly waiting for you in the Prater.' Otto went on to say that the girl from the Prater looked not unlike a ripe cherry, and that he'd called her Nannerl, not Anna. She was a girl for the winter. Cold and frosty weather suited her well, and Otto solemnly informed his companions that he only liked flower girls, or goat girls or, at a pinch, women of the streets and tavern serving wenches – 'because they're kind and gentle and they always tremble a little,' he concluded, not that this bizarre piece of logic deterred anyone present from drinking a toast to the girl from the Prater.

Next came an argument about war. Ulrich spoke of it with fervour – almost, Siegfried said sarcastically, as if he wanted to captivate and bewitch it, compel it to show its pretty little face, its lace frills and petticoats.

'Their Excellencies are more interested in throwing parties at Schönbrunn than in burnishing the Dual Monarchy's sword,' said Konrad von Thieburg in perfect French.

Ulrich swore. He hated anyone to deprive him of his war, even in French as exquisite as the Rampant Frog's. Hostilities were about to be resumed, he said. Those who kept their ears open and were interested in something other than quarterings and bars sinister could detect strange rumblings behind the façade of this spurious peace.

'For instance?' Konrad demanded angrily.

For instance, said Ulrich, French spies were swarming all over Friuli, the Tirol and Upper Austria. They formed a redoubtable network controlled by Schulmeister. French agents disguised themselves as peasants, and those peasants hadn't come all the way from Brittany or Languedoc just to pick the Dual Monarchy's cherries. Konrad was mistaken – the war party was gaining ground at Vienna. The agreement signed with the Russians at the beginning of October spoke volumes in this respect. An uncle of Ulrich's, a law officer with excellent connections, knew all about it. If Napoleon violated the territory of Piedmont or the Kingdom of Naples, Austria – with Russian help – would fell him like an ox. Archduke Charles was busy reorganizing the Austrian army.

'No decree can transform a village idiot from the highlands of the Tirol into a soldier,' sneered Konrad. 'It'll take us an age to knock those yokels, those rustics, into shape.'

'One g-good spring c-campaign will change all that,' said Siegfried, toying with the remains of his apricot tart. 'W-wait and see. Those yokels will make brave f-fighting m-men.'

'A pathetic rabble, you mean!'

'Be that as it may,' Ulrich said in French, mimicking Konrad's refined accent, 'will little Countess Pietranera have managed to get her shift back on by the spring?'

In support of his contention that their men were a pathetic rabble, Konrad cited an incident the previous week. Some of them had been caught playing cat-and-goose. He explained this game to Otto, who had never heard of it before. It was simple in the extreme. You needed a cat, a goose, a river, and few imbeciles, preferably soldiers. Having tied the two creatures to opposite ends of a length of string, you threw them into the water and split your sides at the spectacle of fur and feathers flying as they fought each other, yowling and hissing. The game ended when they mortally injured each other and sank below the surface, to the uproarious amusement of all concerned. The worst of it was, this tasteful entertainment hadn't even been devised by the Austrian cuirassiers. It was a French invention much beloved of Masséna's hussars.

'My dear Konrad,' said Dietrich, 'that's the freemasonry of war for you. The men of the two armies communicate – they exchange everything. They share the cat-and-goose game, but they also share their morbid humours, their fleas, their crab lice. Think of it: a cohort of crab lice can shuttle back and forth, without benefit of a white flag, between the crotches of the Tsar's cossacks, Junot's lancers and Wellesley's hussars – even of Duchess Clémence's cuirassiers. That's war for you: millions of lice in action all over Europe, fighting to the death through the good offices of their human hosts. It isn't just a modern form of intercourse, either. Lice have united soldiers of every age. Pharaoh's warriors went hunting the same lice as the soldiers of King David. Have you forgotten your Thucydides? The messenger from Marathon scratched himself under his chlamys because he'd been bitten by an influx of crab lice from Persia!'

During the laughter that followed, Dietrich raised his champagne glass to the health of crab lice everywhere. 'Today as yesterday,' he proclaimed, 'the only neutral territory – or rather, no, it's the other way round: the only true battlefield – is a trooper's crotch!' Konrad grimaced disdainfully, but Dietrich rammed his advantage home. 'If the crab lice infesting Duchess Clémence's white cuirassiers would only crawl into the breeches of Prince Ernst's blue hussars, that at least would give the monarchy's handsomest couple something in common – a common preoccupation with lice, I mean.'

The Rampant Frog hurled his glass at the wall in a fury. He disliked hearing anyone poke fun at their colonel proprietor, even if she was a woman. Respect for hierarchies: that was what formed the cement of a monarchy the sovereign and dignitaries of which – the nobility, in other words – were God's vicars and procurators on earth. Did officers really have to be as trivial as their men?

'I *want* war!' Konrad bellowed. 'War is our mother, but I'm loath to wage it with this bunch of imbeciles known as the Austrian army. Napoleon's soldiers are scum, it's true. They're only uncouth oafs in life, but at least they're gentlemen in the face of death. They die with distinction, the scoundrels. Our men don't die, they're put down like animals.

'Personally, the only example I'm prepared to acknowledge is that of the Prussian army, which remains what it was when Frederick the Great routed poor Soubise at Rossbach in 1757. The Prussians don't shrink from administering corporal punishment. If General Count Konstantin spots a lapse of discipline in his corps he canes his colonel, who canes his squadron commander, and so on until the original thrashing lands with redoubled force on the rank and file. Do you know how to recognize one of Count Konstantin's officers? He'll be short of several teeth, and his men won't have a single stump left!'

'Bravo,' cried Ulrich, 'and the result is that this toothless army hasn't bitten a single enemy since the death of Frederick II. It specializes in defeat and desertion – desertion, Prussia's leading industry!'

'But it's an export industry,' Otto said nonchalantly. 'If Prussia deserts, the whole of Europe follows suit. Dietrich amused us all with his lice, but I can cite you another feature common to all armies. Deserters are a universal phenomenon. This continent is crawling with an army of beggars, vagabonds and thieves who practise one art only, and that's the art of running away. There are as many deserters as combatants.'

'You're f-forgetting another army,' fat Siegfried broke in, ' – an army of women, f-female sutlers, wives, p-prostitutes and regiments of b-brats. Every war puts a hundred thousand m-men under the sod, but the survivors, even the wounded, f-fornicate like mad to replace them. As soon as the battle's over, they set about making b-babies. Have you ever walked across a b-battlefield at night? You can't tell the moans of the d-dying from those of w-women in ecstasy, and nine months later it's the b-babies who are making all the n-noise . . . But tell us some more about l-little Pietranera . . .'

Konrad von Thieburg pushed back his chair and, in his best Rampant Frog voice, proposed a toast to the most beautiful, most noble Louise of Mecklenburg.

'To Her Majesty Queen Louise of Prussia, who fires on her deserters and has her cowards flayed alive!'

Dietrich refused to raise his glass. He admired the Amazon of Potsdam just as he revered Europe's other lady warrior, Duchess Clémence of Saxe-Salza, but he declined to drink a toast to Prussia, an ally even more deceitful and perfidious than England.

'Don't get so heated, gentlemen!' Otto called out above the general hubbub. 'Those deserters of yours aren't a total loss. Their company commanders keep their names on the rolls. That enables them to draw their pay and rations and thus line the pockets of their nankeen trousers for a while. Then, after the next engagement, they decently kill off their regiment's deserters by transferring them to the rolls of the glorious dead. Gentlemen, war is a sight less murderous than its reputation. Half the dead of Europe are alive . . . On the other hand, half the living may be dead.'

Such were the interminable, identical conversations, languid or impassioned, incoherent or disillusioned, with

204

their sincerities, their flights of fancy, their nonsensical absurdities, to which Duchess Clémence's young officers continually reverted while bivouacking, exercising, or resting up in one of the Mühlviertel inns where they liked to forgather during the summer of 1805. Otto was more taciturn than of old. He performed his duties conscientiously, his troop was considered a model of its kind, and his men respected him. Even so, he lacked drive. He was amiable, but remote and abstracted. To those who had known him in his student days at Vienna – the indiscriminate admirer of goat girls, the dandy of the Café Hugelmann, the charming, laughing, captivating young man of the Prater – the change was saddening. 'He resembles his own reflection in a mirror,' said his friend Ulrich. 'You'd think he was coated with – I don't know – ice, perhaps, or dust. An impalpable, invisible, luminous dust, but dust for all that.' Otto was given to strange spells of immobility and slow, sad smiles. He seemed to be searching for something. 'He has lost his nonchalance, his insouciance,' said Konrad, 'and, being a spoilt child, he's always waiting for someone to return them. I've looked everywhere, believe me, but I can't find them.' And Dietrich: 'His face hasn't changed. He hasn't aged, but he isn't a child any longer. He could be his own brother – his elder brother.'

At night Otto wrote long letters to his mother and read Shakespeare or Schiller, Goethe or his beloved Novalis, likewise Linnaeus and Commerson. He would receive some sign of life from Greinburg Castle, he felt sure, but none came. Two months had already gone by – two whole months, he kept telling himself during those July nights as he surveyed the black escarpments of the Alps – but he never lost faith in Clémence. On rest days he would make excursions into the forest, usually escorted by Matthias, who was more devoted to him than ever and had developed a craze for cupping his hands to his ears like Lawyer Apfelgrun. The big man's smile, the sunny smile that had so exasperated Otto during those miserable months in the Banat, was now like balm to his soul.

Matthias would feed their horses oats while Otto

gathered mushrooms. That black and brown domino at the Windiswraths' – could it have been Christine? 'How could I have treated Clémence like a suspicious, jealous, vindictive lover – I, who detest resentment and rancour?' In any case, even if it was Clémence who had indulged in that game of blind man's buff, why should he have insulted her? 'That martial, haughty exterior conceals the purest heart in the world. Having always loved everyone, men and women alike, I had only to fall in love to think myself surrounded by nothing but vileness and intrigue. I've little enough reason to feel proud of myself.' At other times he fancied that the two young women had conspired to ridicule him – that they were playing with him like a pet dog – but who cared, as long as Clémence favoured him with an occasional glance? Matthias smilingly cupped a hand to his outsize ear, understanding not a word, and Otto smiled back.

Otto's brother officers had noticed his withdrawal, his love of solitude, his disappearances. They inferred that, after several years in the army and two or three forays into the arena of war, their friend was missing the amusements of civilian life and hankering after his affairs of the heart or his entomological studies. Otto denied this without convincing either them or himself. 'It's true, Ulrich,' he once admitted in an unguarded moment, ' – it's true: there's no end in sight.'

Still awaiting a message, Otto hoped that it would never come – hoped that he would spend the rest of his days on the threshold of the land where his beloved lived, moved, and had her being. Then, one Saturday in mid-August, Professor Schwarzbrod burst into his room in the barracks at Postlingberg, grunting amiably and grinning like a carthorse, complete with his greenish overcoat and the cane with the detachable knob in which he collected not *billets doux* but seeds.

The professor was as wet as a water spaniel. Undressing without more ado, he slipped into a dressing gown of Otto's and proceeded to dry off in front of the fire like a sodden shirt. A thunderstorm had overtaken him on the road from Linz to Postlingberg, he said, a veritable Judgment Day cloudburst, and he would gladly have retraced his steps had he not been, so to speak, under orders. At this Otto, not wishing to betray his emotional turmoil, lit a cigar. Schwarzbrod chuckled. Yes, he'd come with a message from Duchess Clémence. 'I don't look much like Mercury,' he said, neighing with laughter, 'but Mercury was out of town and the duchess had no one else available. In default of Mercury, she told me, I would have to play Sosia . . . Poor Mercury!'

Did Otto realize that war was imminent? Prince Ernst of Saxe-Salza had been summoned to Vienna for a crucial meeting of the Imperial General Staff and would thus be absent from Greinburg Castle. Duchess Clémence would be expecting Otto there on Monday night. Schwarzbrod pretended to have qualms – 'Fancy abetting the plans of two equally harebrained lovers at my age!' – but invoked higher authority. His help had been solicited by Duchess Gertrud in person, and who would dare to thwart the last of the Mahlbergs? The professor had come bearing a map of the area, but unnecessarily: Otto knew the mountains like the back of his hand.

'To be frank,' Otto said, after a moment's hesitation, 'I've reconnoitred the terrain with Matthias – I could find my way to Greinburg blindfold. You chide Duchess Clémence for being headstrong, Professor, but I'm no better – I'm straight out of a novel by Herr Goethe. Even a man who has lost his heart can suffer from heartache. I didn't wait for the duchess's command, you see. I've already kept a number of nocturnal assignations beneath the crags of Greinburg. I waited there all on my own, gazing up at the castle like an utter fool. I was a little too early, that's all.'

'Yes, yes,' growled Schwarzbrod, 'one misses a host of things by turning up for appointments too early or too late . . .' And he went on to tell Otto that Duchess Clémence would confirm that she was alone by leaving a lantern in her window from midnight onwards.

Otto escorted Schwarzbrod back to Linz the same evening. The clouds had dispersed, but the storm had caused havoc. Road-menders, assisted by military engineers, were repairing the road and rolling the tornado's harvest of branches and tree trunks into the ditches on either side. At Linz the old scholar grunted warningly on noticing that the bridge over the Danube had been named after the Nibelungen. 'That's ominous, my boy. We're in the middle of a romance, a courtly romance, and you'd better mind you don't mistake your chapter. As you'll see on Monday night, there's another castle on a peak alongside Greinburg, immediately opposite the island of Wörth: Werfenstein Castle. Don't confuse it with Greinburg or we'll be done for – you will, I mean.'

'What have the Nibelungen to do with me?' Otto asked.

'Well, Werfenstein is an inauspicious place, a place of ill omen. It's where Ute lived, the mother of the celebrated Kriemhild. You know the story of the two eagles that were jealous of Kriemhild's lover, the raven, and deposited its remains on his body? Ugh! Just blood and gobbets of meat!'

Otto merely shrugged. He was no great believer in omens, and besides, he was delirious with happiness.

The following day crawled by. Matthias showed no surprise when Otto issued him with various mysterious instructions. If Otto had told him to desert, he would have deserted. He was his officer's shadow, and a shadow never questions its owner, just performs its shadowy duty. When Monday morning came, Matthias duly set to work. Folding them as neatly as a laundress, albeit a six-foot laundress with muscles like iron, he packed his cornet's gold-braided dolman, white trousers, shirt of fine batiste and short pelisse. He winked conspiratorially at Otto whenever they passed in the courtyard – they shared a secret, after all – and that night, when everyone in barracks was asleep, he made for their appointed rendezvous, a clump of oak trees, leading their two black chargers by the bridle.

Otto had decreed that they should travel by way of little-used mountain tracks. It was a longer route, and rendered somewhat hazardous by the recent storm, but it would have been more hazardous still to ride to Greinburg along the Danube valley. Although Upper Austria was not in a state of emergency, the Kriegskommandant knew that

Monsieur Charles's spies were about their furtive business, and the General Staff and the Minister of Police had redoubled their security measures. Patrols and guard posts watched the roads by day and night. Even though Duchess Gertrud had procured a travel warrant and sent it to Otto via Schwarzbrod, and he slipped this document inside his tunic before leaving, he had no wish to be stopped and interrogated.

The road was a lonely one. Also, being rough and precipitous, it seemed expressly designed for someone in the throes of a grand passion. The sky had been swept clean by the storm and Otto was able to spur his horse into a gallop because the huge moon picked out every pothole in his path. The mountains glistened as it played on the moisture still clinging to their forests, meadows and upland valleys. He could clearly distinguish villages curled round the peaks like slumbering snails, onion-domed churches recalling illustrations in *Contes de ma mère l'Oie*, proud castles with crenellated turrets and gingerbread architecture, wayside shrines capped with little triangular roofs, stone fountains gushing silver spray – all the appurtenances of an enchanted land. The mountains were alive with the sound of water because every torrent and stream was in spate.

Matthias, galloping along like a centaur, rode inelegantly with a certain native skill, whereas Otto expertly controlled his mount's every rise and fall, if not its every twitch of the flanks, with the unseen pressure of his knees. Their horses' hoofs made an alarming racket on the stony stretches, particularly when their route took them along the bottom of an echoing gorge, and Otto half fancied that the din would rouse not only the local villagers but the very mountains and the stars themselves. He felt that he and Matthias were interlopers in a world of primeval tranquillity. Eventually, however, they left the mountains, the roads turned to mud, and their hoofbeats made only a muffled sucking sound.

Matthias led the way, exhilarated by their headlong dash through the chiaroscuro of the imperishable night. Otto admired his orderly's skill: maladroit Matthias, who so often went astray in the lanes of Linz, even in broad daylight, could read the night like a well-remembered book. However it was that he contrived to find his bearings, whether by the stars, or puffs of wind, or the moss on tree trunks, or the direction of rivers, he was able to gallop madly up the granite escarpments. Otto waited for their chargers' breastbones to splinter on the rocks, but a path would open up as if by magic. The landscape disintegrated, rending itself asunder to let them pass. The bluish hills ahead of Matthias parted like a feather fan, then closed again to bar the path of any would-be pursuer.

They passed Perg towards midnight. Matthias skirted the village by urging his mount through the dozen or so small garden plots below it. But the low stone walls slowed their progress a little as, losing momentum, the horses jumped them like cats. The night sky began to cloud over. Just as they reached Arbing, the moon was obscured with such suddenness that they found themselves galloping on blindly, as if plummeting into a chasm. Matthias emitted a long, piercing cry. It must have been a sound intelligible to the two horses, because they pulled up two strides short of a sheer drop. Leaping from his saddle, the orderly fondled their muzzles and praised them in his Banat dialect. The two men gave their beasts a few minutes' rest, patting them meanwhile, before resuming their journey. There was no question of galloping now. After a slow climb on a loose rein, Matthias raised his arm and pointed. On the other side of a ravine loomed a castle with a speck of light visible at the base of its circular keep.

The bridge should not have been far, half an hour's ride at most, but there was no bridge left. The storm-shattered remains of its timber framework could just be discerned at the bottom of the gorge. The castle was less than a league away but quite inaccessible. The horses craned their necks and looked down, snuffing the air. It might at a pinch have been possible to descend the mountainside, but the river at its foot was a foaming torrent. Even dismounted, no one could have crossed it.

The two men withdrew. Looking around for an open space, Otto found a pocket handkerchief of a clearing enclosed by ash trees. He asked Matthias to take the lantern from his saddle-bag and light it. Matthias, puzzled, silently did as he was told. Otto took the lantern and held it at arm's length, then raised it high above his head and lowered it again, several times, like a priest wielding a censer at Eastertide. The light at the base of the keep went out. Instead of riding off, as Matthias expected, they continued their vigil.

Five minutes later the flickering light reappeared, this time at the very top of the tower. It moved up and down, up and down, just as Otto's had. He responded, and for a while the two lanterns followed each other's movements, passing a wordless message to and fro.

17

The morning of the following day was devoted to training a bunch of remounts which the Passau depot had delivered to Lieutenant-Colonel Scherer at the beginning of August. Eight-year-olds fresh from their Bavarian or Vorarlberg farms, they had never contended with anything more formidable than horseflies, hens and barking dogs. But they were heavy, sturdy beasts selected by the remount officers for their placid temperaments and their ability to carry a cuirassier and his mass of equipment with uncomplaining ease.

During their first few days, these equine recruits were subjected to a *sinfonia concertante* performed at their stable door with ladles and cooking pots. The troopers loved these cacophonous occasions. At a later stage, pistols were discharged near the mangers while a groom was doling out oats. Otto added a few refinements of his own. Once the horses were accustomed to noise, he tested their nerve still further by waving brightly-coloured guidons under their noses while the regimental drummers were doing their worst.

Ulrich had been intrigued to see that sometimes Otto would whisper in his horses' ears. Weeks earlier, even before the Windiswrath's ball, Otto had enlightened him. 'When they're fully trained,' he said, 'by which I mean that they could hear the Danube itself and the Mühlviertel mountains explode without twitching a nostril, I let them into a secret. I explain that it's all hogwash, this business, and that in battle they must do precisely the opposite of what we teach them here. At the first pistol-shot they're to take the bit between their teeth and turn tail, even if they wheel so sharply that they dump their riders in a ditch. Their best plan, I tell them, is to gallop straight back to their home farms, where the hens and horseflies are pining for them.'

That Monday, after his jaunt to the hillside opposite Greinburg, he and Ulrich repaired to the Rose Princess, their favourite inn at the approaches to the Nibelungen Bridge in Linz. The evening was cool, and the Danube's dark waters were ruffled by a breeze so absent-minded that it occasionally forgot to blow. The yellow branches of an old willow tree overhung their table on the vine-covered terrace, to which the mingled scents of fish, mud and vegetation ascended from the mighty river below. The menu comprised a mushroom omelette, some kind of chicken, and a fricassee of pigs' trotters. The two young men proceeded to get drunk on wine and words. Otto said anything that came to mind – anything at all, provided it passed the time and dulled his pangs of romantic disappointment.

Night was falling. The light faded, borne away on the fitful breeze that stirred the big, downy leaves of the vine and the supple tendrils of the weeping willow, almost as if it, the light, were an unseen, imperceptible river engaged in draining sky and scenery of the twilight's murky remnants. Now and then a waggon would rumble across the bridge, causing it to creak in every timber. Otto puffed voluptuously at a cigar with his blond head tilted back, looking more naively dandylike than ever as he rolled the amber tip from one corner of his mouth to the other. The two friends fell silent. They had congratulated the landlord on his pigs' trotters and were sipping a white wine lightly sprinkled with cinnamon at Otto's insistence. Ulrich was chasing fireflies with his square, stubby hand while Otto's hand, which was pale and freckled, sprinkled the red-tiled floor of the terrace with bluish cigar ash as it swung idly to and fro.

Finally, when Otto made some studiously casual reference to Duchess Clémence, his friend's expression changed. Ulrich leant forwards a little into the bright circle of lamplight, and scores of fireflies flitted around his curly black head like sparks that died as soon as they ignited.

'When it's Saxony's turn to enter the war,' he said, regarding Otto gravely, 'and Prince Ernst's Saxon hussars are also thrown into the hurly-burly, as we have been for so many years – when that day comes . . .' The night was so dense and dark by the time Ulrich made up his mind to continue that little could be seen of him but his bright, excited eyes. His tone was vehement, his voice so low as to be almost inaudible.

Otto must surely be aware, he said, that even if Prince Ernst and his wife didn't actually hate each other, they were undeniably at odds. That was the very *raison d'être* of their two regiments, the blue hussars of Saxony and the white cuirassiers of Austria, and it was just as well that the prince's regiment wasn't yet embroiled in the war, for then – then, Otto, who could tell what grim lengths they mightn't go to through the medium of their soldiers, those two conjugal competitors from the Carinthian Gate, in order to dispel their mutual loathing, their implacable, incurable sexual rivalry? Every domestic altercation would be simultaneously fuelled and resolved by crippling or killing a few hundred men whom the noble pair – the beautiful, bright-eyed duchess and her husband, that illustrious visitor to Postlingberg with his bald head and dignified bearing, urbane manner and admirable interest in entomology – would use as munitions in the squalid and degrading war which men and women have waged since time immemorial – time immemorial, Otto!

Ulrich, almost overcome by his own anger, continued in a vehement whisper.

Just as burghers or merchants entered their household expenses and tailors' bills in ledgers with black oilskin covers and drew up their balance sheets by candlelight, or as children playing with wooden soldiers broke their gunners' legs for greater realism's sake, so the prince and his spouse would devote the evening of each slaughter on the battlefields of Europe to doing their accounts. Those two gorgeous, vain, cruel, aristocratic owners of the Kärntnertor mansion would wrangle over the heroism or cowardice, victories or defeats of their regiments, the survivors, the deserters and the dead, until they had no further need to quarrel. Their battles would be fought out by persons other than themselves, namely, several hundred poor wretches

214

attired in blue or white uniforms who had been sacrificed to Napoleon's killers, or rather, presented as an offering to the enmity between man and woman; to the old, immutable, inviolable, concentrated enmity between all men and women; to the desire – how should he put it, Otto? Surely not the desire to kill? – yes, the same desire to kill as had motivated the ancient Mexicans to slit their children's throats on top of pyramids in order to appease the Aztec gods and slake their thirst for blood.

Similarly, on those sumptuous, sinister evenings at the Carinthian Gate, the groans and gore of innumerable soldiers would combine to form the exhausted, mutilated ghost of the couple's ineradicable hatred and purge them of their loathsome urge to destroy. Yes, Otto, that was it: once the prince had a few blue hussars to chew on like an Aztec god, to offset the welter of intestines spilling from his wife's white cuirassiers, all would be plain sailing. Once that happened, Otto, the Saxe-Salzas would become the most devoted couple in the Kingdom of Austria. How true it was, as Otto himself had said before the battle of Genoa – or was it at Savona? No, at Genoa, after dining at that inn smothered in rather faded wistaria – how very true it was that fate had sentenced all of them, in their several ways, to live, love and die by proxy!

Otto was speechless. Certainly he was used to Ulrich and his abrupt brand of friendship, his grumpy silences, his outbursts of affection and unpredictable fits of agitation, but even so he wondered if this extraordinary monologue should perhaps be interpreted as a covert warning. Had Ulrich simply been rambling on like a village idiot, albeit an inspired village idiot, or had he in reality been airing the secret that Otto imagined to be double-locked away in his own heart?

The terrace was quiet now. All the other patrons had gone, and the pretty serving-maid, having cleared the table, was waiting, twisting her apron in her chapped red hands with a reproachful air. The landlord, who had stationed himself at the rear of the terrace, was also eyeing them with resentment, but he would never have dared to hurry two officers from Postlingberg. Ulrich had ordered several liqueurs. He was rolling vintage brandy round his tongue with a look of feline contentment. After a while Otto tugged at a willow twig overhanging their table and released it with a jerk. Ulrich then called for the bill, and the two of them strode off through the chill night air to the clump of trees where their horses were patiently, noisily munching their oats. Ulrich gripped his friend by the shoulder.

'I'll warrant you we're done with Postlingberg for a long time to come. Let's hope the war doesn't separate us, Otto. Let's hope nothing does.'

'The Rose Princess,' mused Otto. 'A pretty name, but what does it signify?'

'A masonic lodge used to meet there in Joseph II's day. You know: rosebuds are emblematic of the Golden Number, or so the old books say.'

They rode off at a walking pace. Otto abandoned himself to his charger's swaying gait. As the roar of the Danube faded, so the metallic jingle of curb chains become audible.

*　　*　　*

On the day when Otto and Ulrich regaled themselves with a fricassee of pigs' trotters beneath the vine arbour at the Rose Princess, or possibly the day thereafter, Admiral Villeneuve bowed to his commander's insistence and set sail from the Spanish port of Ferrol, bound for Cape Finisterre, where he was to join forces with another squadron dispatched from Rochefort, his object being to give Napoleon two days' control of the Channel, time enough in which to invade England with the hundred thousand men who had been encamped at Boulogne for the past three years. One day later, however, while Otto was supervising a cavalry exercise at Postlingberg, the admiral committed a monumental blunder. Mistaking the French ships from Rochefort for a British squadron, he panicked and took refuge in the harbour at Cadiz.

On 21 October 1805, after idling there for two whole months, Villeneuve was trounced off Cadiz by Nelson, who won the battle of Trafalgar at the cost of his life almost at the very moment when General Mack was surrendering an Austrian army to Napoleon at Ulm in Bavaria. On August 26th, to revert to a week or so after Ulrich and Otto shared their fricassee of pigs' trotters beside the Nibelungen Bridge at Linz, Napoleon, who was still at Boulogne, anathematized the spineless Admiral Villeneuve, revised his plan of campaign, and issued new orders to Bernadotte, Davout, Soult, Marmont, Lannes, Ney, Augereau, Murat's twenty-two thousand cavalrymen and the horse guards. They were to navigate the land instead of the sea (on which he, Napoleon, had never felt truly at home): in other words, they were to make a headlong dash for the Rhine and invade Austria instead of England.

At Postlingberg, as the summer drew to a rain-sodden close, the remounts from the Passau depot continued to have guidons waved under their noses. Otto spent the evenings in his room poring over maps in search of a short cut between Linz and Greinburg Castle, but without much enthusiasm. He did so rather like a conscientious student revising the dates of the Babenberg or Hohenzollern monarchs, or like an insomniac brooding on the same ineffaceable memory, for the probability that he would never set foot in Greinburg was reinforced by each new order Lieutenant-Colonel Scherer issued for the quarter-master to increase the regimental baggage train's state of readiness. Emperor Francis having decided to launch his armies at that country in response to Napoleon's annexation of Genoa, the Saxe-Salza cuirassiers were preparing to set off for Bavaria.

One morning a few days after that decision was taken, therefore, those five inseparables, Konrad 'Rampant Frog' von Thieburg, Ulrich Lvov, Siegfried Rottinstein, Dietrich Feuchtagen and Otto Apfelgrun, fresh-baked lieutenants since August 10th, mounted up and bade their trumpeters sound the 'boot-and-saddle'. Then, some of them stroking their curled, pomaded moustaches and others verifying the excellence of their troopers' turn-out with a stern and inexorable eye, they gave the order: 'For-ward!'

Meanwhile, throughout France and soon in Germany too, with drums in the van and rear of each regiment, the conscripts and old soldiers of the Grande Armée, the veterans of Marengo, Montenotte and Lodi and the veterans-to-be of battles still unborn in the mountains and rivers of Europe, were converging on the Kingdom of Austria and the Duchy of Bavaria. Despite the equipment they carried on their backs, they travelled at a rate of one league per hour – more precisely, at a speed of four and nine-tenths kilometres – pausing only at midday for the *halte des pipes*, or pipe-smoking hour. That explained how the French troops – those rapscallions, as the Rampant Frog called them, angrily lifting his flaxen head as though hoping to glimpse the enemy's distant columns even through the green- and brown-swathed mountains of Upper Austria – contrived to descend like a swarm of rats on the heart of the continent from the Black Forest to Italy, and notably on Bavaria and the environs of Ulm. This was where Duchess Clémence's regiment, formally attached to Archduke Ferdinand's army but *de facto* under the command of Mack himself, a slim man with a golden sash around the waist of his scarlet breeches, had been assigned to bar Napoleon's path to Vienna until Austria's Russian allies could arrive from Galicia under their elderly commander, Mikhail Kutuzov. The marshal had lost an eye at the battle of Izmail some years earlier and was reputed to sleep the whole time, but was in fact, as cunning as a fox.

So the Passau remounts completed their apprenticeship during the cuirassiers' Arcadian ride from the cool, sunlit highlands of Upper Austria to the dark, dank foothills of the Bavarian Alps. None of this allayed Otto's romantic torment, even though his leisurely progress through the autumnal splendour of beech and hornbeam, mounted on the black charger that had carried him to Greinburg and closely escorted by his orderly, exultant at the prospect of battle, left him ample time to chat – with Matthias, who delightedly cupped both hands to his ears like Lawyer Apfelgrun rather than miss a single rustle from the surrounding forest, with Ulrich, Dietrich, fat Siegfried, or even with the

Rampant Frog, whom he fundamentally liked because he liked everyone without exception; ample time, too, during those evenings in the late autumn, with its slightly tarnished bronzes and golds – the autumn of an era, as the Frog used to say – to comment on the garbled reports that reached them fitfully, depending on the vagaries of the courier service.

While breaking their march at Burghausen, for example, the cuirassiers learned that Marshal Ney had received orders on 26 August 1805, less than a week after the fricassee of pigs' trotters at the Rose Princess, to leave Boulogne and make a dash for Saverne in Switzerland; that Ney, who was giving a ball at Montreuil, had compelled his officers to desert their partners in mid-polka and had hustled the braid-encrusted whippersnappers on to their horses; and that on September 6th, or a fortnight after the pigs' trotters, Napoleon had been present in person at Strasbourg, soaked to the skin but motionless and undaunted, when Oudinot's grenadiers forced the Kehl Bridge led by bearded sappers in white leather aprons.

But all these jests and rumours and reports and hours of idle chatter, which formed for the others a kind of verbal staging post between three tedious years at Postlingberg and the coming confrontation, with all its excitement and adventure, were no more to Otto than a membrane beneath which throbbed the anguish of love. He was nostalgically reminded of the frogs he had caught as a boy in the Wienerwald lakes, using a scrap of red rag as a lure; of watching their hearts and sinews quiver and palpitate beneath their tenuous skin; and even, on one occasion, of waiting till dusk to induce one of them to swallow a glow-worm so that, when the little creature went hopping off across the grass, it resembled a goblin's tiny lantern. Nostalgia was his favourite tactic when sick at heart. He delved into his memories of past follies in the not too sanguine hope of blinding himself to the wound in his heart – blinding him and helping him to forget the unforgettable face of Duchess Clémence who, quite unaware of him, was doubtless shutting up her country seat rather earlier in the autumn than usual, not for want of stags to hunt, but because Europe was again being trampled underfoot by a million soldiers, soldiers who had been as clean and shiny as new-minted coins at the end of August but who were slightly bedraggled now that October had come, and who were soon to be reduced to muddy scarecrows swathed in rags and torn old grain sacks.

Otto was in no doubt that, at a time of peril like the present, Prince Ernst and his duchess would be in attendance on the Emperor at Schönbrunn. Refusing therefore to remember whether Greinburg Castle had three storeys or four, he laughed, issued orders, sent messages to Lieutenant-Colonel Scherer via Matthias, ensured that billeting vouchers were honoured after a night's lodging at one of the big, four-square Bavarian farmhouses, dissuaded his men from pestering the Bavarian girls in their long, flower-embroidered dirndls, and saw to it that his troop was not ambushed on the march by any of the Bavarian irregulars who were undoubtedly armed and indoctrinated by agents of Monsieur Charles, alias Schulmeister, in whose company Christine Kinsky was said to be.

All this activity and vigilance should have blurred the distant image of Duchess Clémence, covered it with a mourning veil, as it were, but no: Lieutenant Apfelgrun dreamed on. Neither two million hobnailed but down-at-heel boots, nor two emperors waiting for others of their kind to join the fray, nor two million conscripted peasants, nor a whole host of slaughtered geese and rabbits, nor the rape of a hundred thousand peasant-women, could lay the ghost of Greinburg and dispel the vision of a woman who might or might not have raised and lowered a lantern at a window below the eaves of an old castle. Who was it who had been foolish or malicious enough to claim not long ago that Otto Apfelgrun was decent enough but shallow, glamorous but frivolous, a dandy among dandies but incapable of deep emotion? Even if that malicious fool had been himself, thought Otto as he lolloped along on his somnolent charger, it was nonsense none the less, and he managed at such introspective moments to emit something which, though nothing to brag about, resembled a laugh: a fossilized laugh, a shell emptied of the mirth that had once inhabited it, an archival laugh, a ruin of a laugh, a frail, crumbling memorial to the joys of long ago.

Kutuzov took his time; Napoleon made all possible speed. By covering sixty kilometres a day, his shabby, footsore soldiers enabled him to turn the key in the lock with which Mack had rashly thought to bar his advance through Bavaria: he bottled up Mack's army in the stronghold of Ulm, which seemed, said the Rampant Frog, fiercely tugging at his sparse flaxen beard, to have been expressly constructed with a military fiasco in mind. Ringing it were hills from which the French could survey every rooftop with a calm assurance rendered even calmer by the reports that Russian reinforcements were floundering about in the neighbourhood of Slazeneck, two miles from Braunau, making little attempt to hurry, rejoicing – no doubt – at the tribulations of their despised Austrian allies, and probably already casting glances in the direction of Moravia, where they were to appear a month later. As luck would have it, the Saxe-Salza Cuirassiers were not involved in the ignominy of General Mack's surrender at Ulm on October 20th, only twenty-four hours before Nelson's defeat of the incompetent Villeneuve at Trafalgar, because their commander Archduke Ferdinand had succeeded in escaping from Napoleon's steel-jawed trap. On October 14th, a week before Mack's shameful capitulation in the rain, Ferdinand overrode the general's angry protests and broke out of Ulm with a force of fifteen thousand men, mostly cavalry regiments of which Scherer's was one.

Once Ulm had fallen, Napoleon headed for Vienna and Archduke Ferdinand's corps, the result being that Scherer's cuirassiers had to ride hell-for-leather along the Danube to Passau, through Linz, and past Greinburg. This they did in broad daylight, so Matthias was able to direct a monumental wink at Otto and Otto to note that the castle had three storeys only, not counting the keep. He was repeating the trip he had made two months ago, but in the opposite direction, as if reabsorbing his own headlong gallop through the night like a spider reeling in its thread. But the passage of two months had wrought other changes. The cuirassiers' white uniforms were soiled and stained, their enthusiasm had waned, and the metallic sheen of the circling autumn sun had been superseded by glacial squalls of rain and sleet. As for the horses from the Passau depot, seasoned veterans now, after kicking up their heels briefly in the beauties of their native Bavaria, they were slithering back through the mire to their gloomy Austrian stables.

Instead of continuing eastwards along the Danube to Melk or Sankt Pölten, where Kutuzov's forces were preparing to inflict on the French their only defeat of the campaign by withdrawing across the Danube near Krems and worsting Mortier and Gazan's and Dupont's divisions near the castle where Richard Coeur de Lion had languished, Scherer's regiment abruptly veered north in the wake of Archduke Ferdinand and made for the town of Eger in north-west Bohemia. His cuirassiers lost a number of men and horses in the bloody engagements that followed. Dietrich Feuchtagen, who had expatiated on the ubiquity of crab lice two months earlier, sustained a bayonet-thrust in the shoulder and was packed off to hospital in Vienna. Eventually, however, the regiment came to rest in a safer area – safer, yes, but only for as long as Napoleon tarried in Vienna, which he had entered on November 13th, unopposed despite the fortifications that had repelled the Turks in 1683, and watched in awe by the townsfolk who thronged their windows for a glimpse of him.

On the eve of the French occupation of Vienna, Otto and his friends Konrad and Ulrich had been ordered to Brünn in Moravia, better known to the Czechs as Brno, where many officers and dignitaries of the Austrian imperial court had taken refuge. Meanwhile, the Usurper installed himself at Schönbrunn, the palace where his unborn son would spend the first few years of his brief but hectic existence: a son to be fathered by Napoleon on his imperial adversary's daughter, Marie Louise, whom he had yet to meet, and who had reportedly sought safety, not at Brünn like the rest of her father's court, but in Hungary.

222

*　　*　　*

Konrad, Ulrich and Otto had been sent on detachment to the Austrian headquarters, which had also withdrawn to Brünn, while their regiment, cut off from any orders it might have received from the Prince of Saxe-Salza or his wife, settled down in a remote spot north of Vienna to wait for the archdukes' spirits to revive after the drubbing Napoleon had given them.

Dominated by the dread shape of Spielberg Castle, the modest town of Brünn consisted, in these strange times, of several overlapping communities. The peacetime population had been swelled by an influx of survivors from all the lost battles of recent months, an army of defeated soldiers who broke into granaries and warehouses in search of food and shelter. This human detritus formed a second, mobile community, if such it could be called, equipped with enormous waggons, carts, sledges, coaches and gun batteries, all of them carelessly traversing the intricate lanes and byways of Old Brünn. The third community, so to speak, was that of the exiled Hofburg functionaries and their wives and families, together with a substantial number of Russian officers attached to Kutuzov's general staff. The three populations mingled, especially at night, and the streets, which were brightly lit and lined with elegant shops taking brisk advantage of this unexpected windfall, witnessed an incessant toing and froing of heavy draught horses, stalwart chargers ridden by dragoons or hussars, courtiers' handsome saddle horses, beggars, stragglers, prostitutes, officers, officers' wives and street urchins. Grinning troopers and motley bands of mendicant soldiers, bearded and apathetic, made way for carriages emblazoned with the imperial arms from which there alighted, on the steps of Brünn's palatial mansions, liveried footmen in spotless knee-breeches and silver-buckled shoes, ladies wearing sable coats over their muslin gowns, and dignitaries in court dress attended by dull-eyed, powdered and peruked old lackeys, their chests derisorily adorned with Austrian orders and decorations: a Maria Theresa Cross here, a Golden Fleece there.

Scherer's young lieutenants, less poor Dietrich and fat Siegfried, who had been seconded to a Hungarian unit, began by getting their uniforms refurbished. They then set off to explore the Dual Monarchy's provisional capital. Attracted by a garish inn sign depicting a tree in leaf, they made themselves at home in the big, noisy taproom. The next table was occupied by three young Russians, diplomats or aides-de-camp from their studiously aristocratic manner. These presumptuous gentlemen were loudly and provocatively deriding the luckless Mack's performance at Ulm and extolling the exploits of Kutuzov's army at Krems, on the left bank of the Danube, where the Russians had captured cannon, regimental standards and a brace of French generals.

Otto foresaw trouble. Konrad von Thieburg, while despising Mack for his mediocre generalship and his ignominious surrender at Ulm, could not permit an Austrian commander to be mocked by a bunch of St Petersburg fops. Drawing upon his inexhaustible store of anger, which had been amply replenished by their retreat from the Danube and the chaos prevailing in Bohemia, he swung round in his chair, the better to insult one of the Russian party. An ugly young man with a stiff and expressionless face, the Russian impassively studied Konrad through his quizzing glass as if the Austrian were some small and inanimate object, some piece of inferior taproom furniture. Konrad ran out of insults, whereupon the Russian lolled back in his chair, introduced himself as Prince Anatoly Kuragin, and added in conclusion, as though mentioning a minor detail, that Konrad was 'a contemptible little worm'.

Pandemonium ensued. Konrad slapped Kuragin's face and invited Otto to act as his second at a duel to be fought at dawn next day – pistols or sabres, the Russian could choose – but Otto, possibly influenced by several glasses of *Doppelkümmel*, threw off his usual placidity and rounded on both of them. Why should they manufacture a minor war in the midst of a major one? Thousands of Russian, Austrian and

French soldiers – yes, cried Otto, Frenchmen too – were dying like dogs in field, forest and hospital, either of their wounds or of the growing typhus epidemic. If God cared to amuse himself by inducing human ants to kill each other, it was up to the ants to foil his abject design. Otto, whom no one had ever heard raise his voice in anger, bellowed these words. Hands shaking, he proclaimed that he felt sickened by the stupidity of man, sickened by all the vain, frivolous dummies dressed up as officers, diplomats or courtiers, men who continued to pull faces at each other while whole nations were perishing.

He received unexpected support from one of the Russians. A little older than the other two and unmistakably an officer despite his plain civilian topcoat, he was a strikingly handsome man of medium height with clean-cut features and a sombre, weary look in his eyes. He seemed to possess an almost frightening ascendancy over his companions. Having introduced himself as Prince Andrei Volkhonsky, aide-de-camp to Marshal Kutuzov, he ordered Kuragin and Thieburg to shake hands. No one would have dreamed of disobeying him. Kuragin promptly apologized. The third Russian, whose merry little eyes endearingly compensated for his sallow, wrinkled complexion and the lone tuft of hair on his head, ordered a bottle of champagne.

'An excellent idea,' said Prince Andrei. 'Champagne is a great restorer of harmony. After all, gentlemen, you are officers and so are we. We pursue the same profession and share a common enemy, even if we don't fight under the same flag. What could be more fitting than to settle our differences?'

'Would you say the same if some of Augereau's or Oudinot's Prussian officers walked into this tavern?' asked Ulrich.

'They'll do that soon enough,' Prince Andrei replied calmly. 'Old Auersperg surrendered the Tabor Bridge at Vienna without a fight, in simple good faith, thanks to a vile subterfuge on the part of Murat, Ney and Bertrand, who were doubtless acting on the advice of that French spy – Schrumester, or whatever he calls himself.'

'Schulmeister,' Otto amended.

'That's it: Schulmeister.'

'It's a disgrace!' snapped Konrad. 'No officer in the service of a monarchy would have stooped to a lie, simply in order to capture a bridge from the enemy. Honesty between adversaries is a vital part of the dignity of war.'

'Of course, of course,' said the man with the sallow face, 'but Napoleon did give us fair warning. He has demonstrated, indeed, flaunted his duplicity so often in the past that Auersperg should surely have distrusted Murat's word? I'm sure Monsieur de La Fontaine illustrated the point in one of his fables, but poor old Auersperg can't have read it. Believe me, Prince, La Fontaine should be required reading for all commanders-in-chief.'

'Be that as it may,' said Prince Andrei, 'Murat, complete with pelisse and ostrich plumes and all his paraphernalia, is galloping along the road to Brünn at this very moment.'

Anatoly Kuragin, who had already forgotten his brush with Konrad, seized the prince by the arm and reverted to Ulrich's earlier question, but rather inarticulately.

'What if a Prussian officer walked in? The Berlin cabinet is incapable of expressing sympathy for our cause without – I mean, without expressing . . . as I phrased it in my latest memorandum . . . You follow me, I'm sure . . .'

The sallow man's eyes twinkled merrily.

'Ah, Demosthenes,' he said to Kuragin, 'I recognize you by the pebble in your mouth!' And his tuft of hair quivered with amusement.

'Napoleon's officers,' said Konrad von Thieburg, 'are the sons of blacksmiths, grocers, notaries' clerks, seamstresses, shopkeepers. How can they be expected to have a sense of honour or wage war like gentlemen? Prince Metternich contends that "man only truly begins at the title of baron". Personally, gentlemen, I find him too generous. I should have preferred him to draw the starting line at the title of count.'

'What does that make me?' Otto inquired jocularly.

Prince Andrei subjected the Rampant Frog to a long, enigmatic smile.

226

'Gentlemen.' He spoke in a mixture of French and German. 'I see from your insignia that you belong to the Saxe-Salza Cuirassiers. I've heard glowing reports of your prowess at Ulm, and Bagration has often spoken to me of his admiration for Duchess Clémence. Strange to relate, the errand on which Kutuzov sent me to Brünn – and but for which I shouldn't have entered this tavern tonight and made your acquaintance – was to apprise the Austrian General Staff of our victory over Mortier at Krems. Can you guess who received me at Ferdinand's headquarters just now? Prince Ernst of Saxe-Salza himself!'

Ulrich cast a covert glance at Otto when the name was mentioned, but Otto was listening impassively.

'Well,' Prince Andrei went on, 'your prince cold-shouldered me. If I expected any congratulations, I was sorely mistaken. Prince Ernst barely looked up when his aide-de-camp announced me. He was too busy tidying a stack of papers on his desk, a large table lit by two flambeaux which also lit his bowed head – a handsome head, bald though it is. When I informed him that Kutuzov had given Mortier a beating, do you think he was pleased? Not a bit of it. He frowned with annoyance. It was strange: I found myself confronted by an extremely intelligent face wearing a deliberately inane expression. Presumably the truth was that he couldn't bring himself to accept that Russian troops had won a victory at Krems when the Austrians had been defeated everywhere else. He did come to life, though only to rant and rave, when I mentioned that your Austrian general Schmidt had been killed in the battle.'

Konrad von Thieburg was crouching a little in his chair. He said nothing, but it didn't escape Otto that his friend's hands were trembling with fury. Fortunately, Anatoly Kuragin broke in, this time on a ribald note.

'I spotted Duchess Clémence's carriage outside the Palais Trakl,' he said. 'To every man his mate, if you know what I mean . . . But tell me, are there many such lovely creatures in Vienna? If so, I should love to have occupied the city if only . . . if only I hadn't been forestalled by that Corsican usurper, that surveyor of the desert sands . . .'

'My dear Kuragin,' said the sallow-cheeked man, 'does Duchess Clémence really compare in looks with your sister, the adorable Yelena Bezukhov?'

'There's a difference,' said Kuragin. 'My sister changes her lovers every fortnight, as you know, though it's true that her husband, the unfortunate Piotr Bezukhov. . . Need I say more? As for Duchess Clémence, my impression of her is that she's as passionate as, well – as a water ice!' He almost choked with laughter.

'Kuragin, my friend,' said Prince Andrei, 'champagne coarsens your wit. It's late, gentlemen, and we must soon go our separate ways – to my regret, for I fear that Murat will deny us any further opportunity to meet here in Brünn. But the court – both courts – are about to withdraw to Olmütz, where our armies are regrouping, so we may soon be reunited, S.D.L.V.'

Otto inquired the meaning of the four letters.

'*Si Dieu le veut*,' replied Prince Andrei.

*   *   *

Lieutenant-Colonel Scherer's officers returned in silence to their billet near the Dresden Gate. Otto and Ulrich were sharing a chamber so cluttered with armchairs and chests of drawers that it might have been a lumber room.

'Otto,' said Ulrich, running a nervous hand through his curly hair, 'did you know that the Saxe-Salzas were here?'

Otto shrugged his shoulders. How could he have known, in all this chaos? He eyed his friend without resentment.

'I hoped you'd understand,' he said. 'I've known the truth ever since that night at the Rose Princess. You judge me harshly, Ulrich, but what can I do? Someone's playing a three-card trick on me, and I never know where the right card is. In consequence anyone would think my words were dictated to me by a prompter . . .'

'Your story of the Nibelungen, Kriemhild and Ute?'

'Kriemhild? The raven and the eagles – jealousy and so on? Perhaps. I don't know, I've ceased to think about it.

There'll be time enough for that later. No. Do you know the story about Death? It's Persian, I seem to recall. Death was strolling through Baghdad market, looking for victims. Catching sight of a peasant, it gave a start of surprise. The peasant took fright. He mounted his nag without more ado and rode like the wind to Samarra to hide himself, but Death reappeared, walked up to him, and laid a hand on his shoulder. "Your time is up," Death told him. The peasant started to struggle. Why, he asked, had Death looked twice at him in Baghdad market that morning, only to strike him down at Samarra? "It's quite simple," Death replied. "I was surprised when I saw you in Baghdad this morning because I knew I had an appointment with you at Samarra this evening." '

Ulrich looked uneasy and vaguely aggressive.

'I dislike your stories,' he said. 'They always turn out badly. All that talk about God and ants . . .'

'God has to amuse himself somehow. Time passes slowly up there.'

'Well, *I* don't believe that's how he amuses himself.'

'Ah, but what if he isn't up there at all? What if he's in a dungeon somewhere? What if the Devil has defeated and imprisoned him? What if the Devil has put on God's clothes and made himself up to resemble his prisoner? What if he has disguised himself as we did at the Windiswraths'? What if God has never been more than the Devil's lieutenant? When you see all that carnage on the battlefield, you can well believe that God is an impostor, a demon who passes himself off as the Almighty, and that in churches all over Europe, with blood and corruption on every side, millions of imbeciles are in fact burning candles to the greater glory of Satan. That, Ulrich, is as true as what you told me at the Rose Princess in Linz, when you robbed me of the words that I myself had stolen from Duchess Gertrud: that we not only love and die but also pray by proxy . . .'

Ulrich abandoned the God of the ants and reverted to Baghdad.

'But at Greinburg, Otto, your appointment wasn't with death at all.'

'No, not with death, with a woman. But what if death had taken a leaf out of the Devil's book and disguised itself as a woman? Besides, what do I know of Greinburg? I saw no one, just a lantern being raised and lowered. Could I tell who was holding it? Do we ever know with whom we have an appointment? Do we ever know what body we make love to, Ulrich?'

'But there's no General Murat in your Persian fable, and Murat is heading for Brünn at a gallop even as we speak, so I hope he had an appointment at Baghdad. If we all have to quit Brünn in the next twelve hours, there won't be many appointments at Samarra.'

'Who knows? Reality may be more of a muddle than legend – it may be the legend of that genuine reality we call legend,' said Otto, staring out of the window at the overcast sky. Fires burning in various parts of the town had transformed it into a copper-coloured dome.

*   *   *

Prince Andrei had been well informed. Brünn started packing its traps at daybreak. The officers and notables of the court were preparing to leave for Olmütz in the north. The place was in turmoil. On the steps of patrician mansions – and of many middle-class homes also – major-domos sternly supervised hordes of servants as they stowed trunks, boxes and baskets into waggons or carriages drawn by oxen, such was the dearth of horses prevailing since the hecatombs in the Danube Valley. Otto, who had been feverishly busy all morning, now seemed surprisingly calm.

'I shall never understand you, Otto,' said Ulrich. 'Every minute counts, yet here you sit with me, unconcernedly twiddling your thumbs.'

'I'm like that: resigned by nature and prone to inertia. I never rush things, I let them make my mind up for me. You call that unconcern, but despair might be a better word.'

That afternoon, however, Otto made his way into town. The Palais Trakl, where Duchess Clémence once had been, was now deserted, its courtyard littered with filthy straw, and he could detect no signs of recent occupation. Ulrich was right, he told himself. He must have been out of his mind to imagine that Prince Ernst, one of His Imperial Majesty's chamberlains, would linger in Brünn with his wife when the entire court had already fled at Murat's approach. He paced up and down outside the house: it looked forlorn – in mourning, as it were. He lit a cigar. Sunlight gilded the blue smoke as it hung there, almost motionless, for the weather had turned fine again and Brünn was bathed in wintry radiance. Up and down, up and down he went his aimless and unhurried way, placidly, patiently, vainly pacing the courtyard of that sepulchral, sunlit house. He failed to see even a maidservant or footman who might at least have latched the doors and bolted the shutters to testify that once, in years gone by or that same morning, a woman had lodged there, and that the rooms still harboured the scent of her departed self, not mere emptiness. But no, only sparrows – the sole sign of life – were there, creating a commotion in the eaves of the slate roof.

And then the big front door opened and Clémence appeared on the steps with one of her women in attendance. She gave an almost imperceptible start and shook her head on catching sight of Otto, who thought he saw her turn pale – saw the blood drain from her cheeks. Gathering up the hem of her gown, a formal gown of emerald muslin, she almost ran to a side door leading out of the courtyard, still accompanied by her maid, and set off down the street as swiftly as if Murat's cavalrymen were galloping in pursuit. After some fifty paces she turned and retraced her steps. The maid, a penguinlike figure in black and white, returned too, but more slowly.

'Otto . . .' said Clémence. She was very close now, with her head resting on his shoulder. 'So this was the place, was it?' Weakly, she put a hand to her brow and frowned as though searching her memory for some recollection that they had arranged to meet in Brünn. 'Yes,' she said at length, with greater conviction, 'this was it.'

The woman in black and white walked up to them. She

231

laid a hand on her mistress's sleeve like someone trying to rouse a sleeper.

'So this was the place,' Clémence repeated. 'Have no fear, Fräulein von Wörth is as trustworthy as your Matthias. *Was* this the place?'

'It seems so, yes.'

'I leave for Olmütz tomorrow morning. Tonight you must take the path that runs along the right-hand side of the garden, between two rows of pear trees, to the orangery. The orangery, mark you, not a honeysuckle bower . . . No honeysuckle tonight, or you'll end up at the Windiswraths' and we'll lose each other yet again.' There was no gaiety in her laugh. 'My window is just above the orangery, so you'll have to play the acrobat. I shall expect you one hour after the stroke of midnight.'

*   *   *

The town through which Otto made his way that night was a city of the dead. The streets were strewn with smashed furniture, abandoned waggon wheels, broken axles, mounds of refuse. The shops, so brilliantly illuminated the previous night, were in darkness. Doors gaped open here and there. Other doors had been reduced to matchwood. Looters – deserters, stragglers, vagabonds of both sexes – scuttled off down passages whenever they heard the tramp of the patrols assigned to preserve what little public order remained as Brünn waited for occupation by the French. Seen under a clear night sky, the town resembled an expanse of ruins.

Otto pushed open the gate into the palace grounds. He knelt and kissed the path, just as he would have kissed the cobblestones of the Bauernmarkt in Vienna – the cobblestones trodden by Duchess Clémence – had his father's presence not restrained him. He scaled the orangery with ease. From the roof he was able to scramble into a walnut tree, one of whose main limbs passed within arm's length of Clémence's window. The casement opened without a sound.

Clémence lit a candle. She seemed intrigued – merely intrigued, not frightened or agitated in any way, though this might have been the effect of the candlelight, which blurred her features a little. She laid her hand on Otto's shoulder. Then, for no apparent reason, she withdrew to the farthest, darkest corner of the room. After a moment she returned. Slipping her hand under Otto's dolman, she ran her fingers over his chest. There was no tenderness or passion in the gesture: she was simply touching him. Minutes went by. Otto shivered. Clémence began to laugh, deep in her throat.

Otto took her in his arms. She said nothing as he undressed her where she stood. Her clothes slid to the floor. Otto tossed them into an armchair, and they disappeared into the gloom as if deprived of their existence for ever now that the man and the woman were one. Clémence looked very tall, very white, when naked. Otto stroked her cheek, and she wept. Then she sagged a little and rested her head on his shoulder, just as she had when they danced together at the Windiswraths'. She was gentle and yielding at first, then fierce and insatiable.

'What's to become of us?' she said at some stage, gazing at him trustfully. She also said, 'When you leave here, you'll be mistaken for one of those looters who are ransacking the houses of the rich.' The idea amused her. '*I'm* your loot,' she said. The bells of a nearby monastery began to toll. The monks were off to chapel, amply provided with food for prayer by all who were about to die. It was a long time before Otto echoed Clémence's original question. 'What's to become of us?' he said. He was a very poor looter indeed, he added, because he couldn't take his loot with him. 'I'm your night-time loot only,' said Clémence, 'and now it's morning.'

Otto opened the window, climbed into the walnut tree, and sat astride the branch. The first rays of dawn were stealing into Clémence's room. She was standing at the window, naked.

18

Duchess Gertrud had remained behind in Vienna. The courtiers of Schönbrunn were welcome to cluck like hens at Olmütz in the entourage of Emperor Francis, but nothing would have induced her to abandon the Palais Questenberg-Kaunitz, not even the fact that French troops were running amok in the capital. Although her health precluded her from touring the streets by carriage, Napoleon's soldiers excited her curiosity. She spoke of the war as if it were a game, rather more sanguinary than most – sillier, too, as she remarked to the visitors who called on her less and less often during these anxious days. However many steeples the marshals of France might knock down, she said, the old continued to hawk and spit and the young to play skittles.

As soon as Napoleon had occupied Vienna, old Gertrud proceeded to set up a sophisticated intelligence service. Determined not to miss a line of this latest play, she sent Mlle des Trappes to mingle with passers-by. She also enlisted the services of Constanze Apfelgrun's unpleasant footman, who carried his mistress's prayerbook with a devotion to duty that had grown in proportion to her son's exposure to the perils of war. The footman made an excellent agent. Adept at worming information out of everyone he met, he kept the duchess *au courant* with all the amusing incidents, all the acts of treason and treachery that were taking place in the occupied capital. Mlle des Trappes, on the other hand, was more of a scene-painter, someone who depicted broadly what went on in street and marketplace.

Gertrud learned that the fearsome French warriors who had scattered the Austrian armies like chaff were an unimpressive sight. A horde of bearded, stoot-stained, scrawny, indisciplined scoundrels attired in ragged breeches and peasant smocks, some of them even in the round hats of the French provinces, they did not sport dazzling pelisses or coats slashed with pockets *á la* Soubise, but went around

234

muffled up in tattered greatcoats half obscured by long strips of fat bacon, hunks of meat tied on with string, slaughtered ducks and geese, looted bottles of wine and loaves of bread. 'Never mind,' said Gertrud. 'Those walking larders so terrified our fine Austrian soldiers and gave their dandified officers such a dose of colic, they've already run as far as Austerlitz.' And she chuckled to herself.

It was an agreeable time. Gertrud was entranced by the spectacle of Napoleon's glorious rabble, such as she envisioned it in her murky drawing-room under the chill gaze of Gerhard 'Wolf-Jaw', the Teutonic Knight. Only one thing marred her pleasure: she had heard no news of her niece and Lieutenant Apfelgrun. Their assignation at Greinburg Castle, the details of which she herself had carefully worked out with Clémence, had never taken place – that much she knew from Professor Schwarzbrod, the romantic in her conjuring up a titillating mental picture of those two lanterns winking vainly at each other across a dark abyss. Since then, however, she had lost track of the young lovers. She did not even know if they had found an opportunity to meet in the turmoil of Austerlitz – but she was inclined, in her febrile heart of hearts, to put her faith in the romantic efficacy of war.

Some days after Napoleon's arrival in Vienna, the scenery was changed for the better. Gertrud's agents were among the spectators present at Schönbrunn for the parade which Napoleon held to correct the deplorable impression made on the ordinary folk of Austria by the muddy victors of Ulm and Sankt Pölten. Mlle des Trappes was bedazzled by the sight of him sitting his horse, waxen-faced and immobile as a statue, while the nine thousand grenadiers of his Imperial Guard marched past him through the grounds of the millennial Habsburg dynasty's royal palace: huge men in blue uniforms with scarlet turnbacks, bright red linings and lappets, white waistcoats and breeches, their stature rendered even more commanding by foot-high bearskin bonnets.

Gertrud reinforced her team of informants with an efficient new recuit. General Count Konig von Weitzau had also refused to leave his post. Defeat had been unacceptable to him ever since 1788, when he had saved Joseph II and Western civilization from the Turks. Fettered to the Austrian capital by a sense of duty, he felt unalloyed contempt for the officers and functionaries who had fled at the Corsican's approach, now that the Austrian army had been reduced to a flock of sparrows twittering in the countryside. He was still keeping a weather eye open, but the information he gleaned was so alarming that he hesitated to transmit it to Gertrud in the presence of a third party. Night after night, therefore, in the duchess's desolate drawing-room, the two old accomplices took stock of the situation. Although Gertrud realized that the general was talking nonsense, she gobbled it up as greedily as a little girl starved of sweetmeats, telling herself that ordinary definitions of the truth counted for little in the twilight of the Habsburg dynasty. The truth, which was enough of a puzzle to the living, was not only enigmatic to the dying but supremely unimportant.

General von Weitzau's perspicacity knew no bounds. Nothing escaped his notice. Napoleon, intoxicated by his victories, had lowered his guard. The wily Corsican – that master of Florentine or even Byzantine dissimulation, said the general, cocking an eyebrow – had been spoilt by his triumphs. He was losing his grip, that much was proved by his granting the world an insight into the evil designs which, till now, he had contrived to keep hidden. Had he not unveiled his Mamelukes, great booby that he was? It was popularly believed, no doubt, that the fantastically attired oriental horsemen who galloped at the head of the Grande Armée's parades were simply an adornment, a stage effect devised for the masses by a great theatrical producer. He had even gone to the lengths of tricking out his Mamelukes, not as genuine Mamelukes, but in a costume inspired by the manner in which French painters had been portraying such Arabs for a century past: a short embroidered waistcoat, baggy scarlet breeches girt with a gleaming silk sash, a turban of inordinate size, a curved sword, a short blunderbuss, and a regular ironmongery of daggers and pistols. But however much they might resemble stage soldiers, caricatures, or grand panjandrums à la Molière, those who were acquainted with history – and above all with the battle fought at Kahlenberg on 12 September 1613, which needed but one brisk puff of the bellows for its embers to glow afresh – knew that the clock of history surpassed all human dimensions, and that a century, as recorded on the dial of that mighty timepiece, advanced the minute hand no farther than a flea could jump.

It was clear, therefore, that the Turkish masquerade presaged tragedy. Now more than ever, reason demanded that Napoleon's every bat of an eyelash be interpreted in the light of his oriental aspirations. Having rashly put his Mamelukes on display, Napoleon was continuing to 'entertain the gallery' with mock battles and mirror effects such as those entitled Ulm and Brünn, which had attained their apotheosis in the so-called Battle of the Three Emperors at Austerlitz and its celebrated sunrise, with which the Grande Armée's bulletins had made great play – so Weitzau ventured to explain to Gertrud – simply to disguise its symbolic counterpart, the crescent moon of the Grand Turk, who was beyond a peradventure the real victor of Austerlitz. No one could deny that Austerlitz had been a magnificently murderous battle, fought as it was amid all those ice-bound meres, but it none the less remained a pure diversion, a feint designed to mask the Turks' stealthy advance on the Habsburg capital.

At this Gertrud dealt the general numerous blows with her cane and called him an old fool, but he greeted these rebuffs with an earnest smile, convinced that he had seen through her tactics. Gertrud, he felt, was keeping some trump cards up her sleeve – pretending to ridicule his theories even though she, too, had long since deciphered the turbulent manuscript of history. That was why the general accepted her scorn so manfully. He construed it as an oblique and mischievous manifestation of approval, and so, being an extremely good-natured man, he continued to address the duchess under a hail of blows and insults.

Because she was unable to keep track of his aberrations, Gertrud ended by wielding her cane at random. She soon ceased to listen to him altogether, and would give his pink pate an occasional tap with the ivory knob, out of a vague sense of duty. Her thoughts roamed elsewhere, and, since she insisted on voicing her own reveries aloud, the two old people took to speaking simultaneously. Gertrud's drawing-room thus became the *mise-en-scène* for a double soliloquy, more nightmarish than merely senile: twin effusions the phrases of which became monstrously entwined. The general continued to shuttle back and forth between Napoleon's mock campaigns and the Turks' surreptitious advance, while the duchess strove hard to construct some ultimate castle in Spain out of the romantic debris of her dreams.

The two monologues formed a kind of litany, for the towns and villages in which the general staged his thunderous verbal battles were the towns and villages haunted in Gertrud's imagination by Duchess Clémence and Otto Apfelgrun. Old Weitzau had only to recall the military disasters at Ulm or Brünn for Gertrud's thoughts to turn to her niece and the lieutenant. Her fierce heart had never drawn any clear distinction between the warlike and the erotic, and besides, as she reflected in the privacy of her darkened world, what were the funeral pyres of Austerlitz, which the general rekindled nightly during their tête-a-têtes at the Palais Questenberg-Kaunitz, if not the very furnace of ecstasy in which those two youthful bodies were consummating their passion?

* * *

Schulmeister, that elusive carrot-top who had travelled the length and breadth of Austria for so many years in Napoleon's pay, sometimes impersonating a vendor of lemons or hobnailed boots, sometimes in the guise of a workman or burgher, or even of a frock-coated dignitary, had cast off his motley at last. Two days after the French arrived in Vienna he emerged from his Mariahilf lair and paid a call on

General Savary, Napoleon's aide-de-camp, to whom he had been of considerable service during the battle of Ulm. He was given a hundred louis d'or to replenish his wardrobe and, pursuant to a decree promulgated at Schönbrunn on November 15th, was appointed to assist General Dupin as Commissioner-General of the French police in Vienna. The Viennese at large, unacquainted with his 'Brutus' pseudonym, or even with the name Schulmeister, referred to him in awe as Monsieur Charles or Monsieur Charles-Frédéric. Christine Kinsky accompanied him everywhere, brazenly flaunting the fact that she was his mistress. When Gertrud was told of this she burst out laughing and clapped her hands, delighted to discover that Christine possessed the same audacity and taste for heresy, the same arrogance and lack of decorum that had always, according to her, been the hallmark of the Mahlberg womenfolk. Schulmeister saw to it that order prevailed in the capital. Well-paid informers lurked in every coffee-house and theatre. At the same time, the French made an effort to woo the local population. General Bernadotte executed a grenadier who had snatched a flower-girl's earrings in the street. In December, to the huge satisfaction of the city's prostitutes, Napoleon awarded his rank and file a bonus equivalent to one year's pay, or sixty florins for an ordinary soldier and two hundred and forty for an imperial guardsman.

Such girls and women of good family as had not fled north coquetted with the French officers, and did so all the more ardently because Napoleon had showered his followers with gold. Murat was installed in the Saxe-Salzas' Kärntnertor mansion, where he kept open house and gave dinners for two hundred guests at a time. In private, however, the Viennese reviled these upstart generals for being as coarse as barley bread. They drew unfavourable comparisons between their gaudy uniforms and those of the Austrian officer corps, which were pastel-hued and almost femininely elegant. They scorned the ear-splitting drums, cymbals and trumpets of the French brass bands and missed their Austrian counterparts: the jingling Turkish crescents, the tinkling bells, the silver kettledrums stamped with the Emperor's initials and carried by waltzing white horses. The first night of *Fidelio* on November 20th, which was staged at the An der Wien under Beethoven's personal direction, became the talk of every drawing-room. The performance was boycotted by polite society, and Napoleon had turned up ten minutes late, a discourtesy of which Francis would never have been guilty. Heralded by a deafening roll of drums and escorted by his loutish marshals, the master of the world – that pint-sized Corsican general – had trotted in at a light infantryman's pace.

Far from lingering at Austerlitz after his victory, Napoleon had returned post-haste to Schönbrunn to supervise Talleyrand's negotiations with the Austrians. The Dual Monarchy had been deserted by everyone. The Tsar had returned to Russia. Prussia's diplomatic representative, Count Haugwitz, concluded the Treaty of Schönbrunn, which ceded Ansbach-Bayreuth and Neuchâtel to France in exchange for Hanover. Finally, on December 27th, Lieutenant Joseph Kaiser of the Civil Guard arrived hotfoot from Pressburg with the news that Emperor Francis and Napoleon had signed a peace treaty there – a humiliating document which stripped Austria of Venice, Friuli, Istria, Dalmatia, the Tirol and Vorarlberg, the last two provinces being ceded to Bavaria.

At seven o'clock on the evening of December 28th, having drained his cup of victory to the dregs, Napoleon set off back to France. Talleyrand followed a week later. By January 13th every last French soldier had departed. On January 15th a Te Deum was sung in St Stephan's Cathedral, to which the Emperor and his court rode in state through streets decorated with branches of pine and fir. Next morning the offices in the Hofburg, the censorship bureaux, the police jails – in short, all the cogs of the monarchy's machine – began to grind as if nothing had ever obstructed or interrupted their remorseless operation.

* * *

On their return from Olmütz, the Saxe-Salzas had to spend

several weeks redecorating their Kärntnertor residence, which Murat's rude soldiery had left in a filthy condition. Prince Ernst took advantage of this interlude to visit Dresden and inspect his regiment of hussars. Although Saxony had been spared the depredations of war and was at peace with France, he said, one never knew. Napoleon was a glutton whose digestion worked at lightning speed. No sooner had he gobbled up one country than he sank his teeth into another. It might be Prussia's turn next, thanks to the increasingly warlike ambitions fostered there by Queen Louise. If so, what then? Could Saxony stand idly by? Duchess Clémence pleaded that the rigours of Brünn and Olmütz had left her in need of rest. She would remain behind and supervise renovation work at the Carinthian Gate. She would also devote some time to her regiment. After being shuttled around from Ulm to Postlingberg and then to Hungary, Lieutenant-Colonel Scherer's cuirassiers were now stationed at Hinterhorf, only a few leagues east of Vienna. Although her husband did not disguise his annoyance, Clémence insisted on staying in Vienna.

To Clémence, the latter part of winter was sheer bliss. Acting at her request and under an assumed name, Professor Schwarzbrod had rented a charcoal-burner's cottage in Schleiblingstein Forest. She used to get to Schleiblingstein very early in the afternoon on certain prearranged days. Because her departure from Vienna by mail coach in broad daylight might have attracted unwelcome attention, she donned a dark cloak such as peasant women wore at this season and equipped herself with a wicker basket containing a live hen. At Untermauerbach one of her maids – the one who had been her confidante at Brünn – would be awaiting her with a horse. From there, without haste, she trotted along the frozen forest tracks to the cottage, which Schwarzbrod had sparsely furnished for her. Although Otto could never join her until midnight or thereabouts, Clémence relished the suspense.

Seated in an armchair in the little, smoke-blackened room, she stared into the flames on the hearth. She was happy, or so she told herself. The hen, still imprisoned in its basket, noisily flapped its wings from time to time. Clémence went and stood at the window. Before long, in another three or four hours, she would see her lover come trotting along the path through the snow-laden fir trees. Meanwhile she gazed at the snow in the glare of reflected sunlight, in the rosy glow of twilight, in the darkness of night. Time made no attempt to hurry her along, it revolved around her – patiently, smoothly, monotonously, like a big, silent wheel. The window was filled with stars, but she couldn't see them clearly through the condensation on the pane. Staring at those blurred pinpoints of light, she gave a start when the clock on the wall struck eleven. She went outside and walked a few yards in the direction of Hinterhorf. The keen air struck chill through her cloak as she listened intently to the crackle of ice, the clumsy fluttering of nightbirds' wings, the howling of wolves, the rustle as branches sprang erect when their burdens of snow became dislodged. The cold was bitter, but she revelled in it. A little while later she might hear hoofbeats. The next moment, Otto would appear. He would rein in, leap down from the saddle, and bear her frozen body away to the warmth of the fire in the charcoal-burner's cottage.

They would be as one. She would surrender her body to Otto for him to do with it as he pleased – as she pleased. Tirelessly, while the hen clucked and fussed in its basket, they writhed and wrestled together in the faint glow from the fireplace, rending each other and crying out like beasts bent on mutual destruction, dismembering each other as beasts are butchered in an abattoir. And then exhaustion would breed compassion, and Clémence would gaze into Otto's face and throw herself down before the fire once more in gratitude to everything on earth.

Otto had a recurrent fear. When he scrambled over the barrack wall at night, after the last trumpet call, and ran to the black charger which Matthias had tethered in a disused shed half a mile away, and headed for Schleiblingstein, he could never believe that Clémence would be waiting at the cottage. Inevitably he would get there just in time to glimpse, very briefly, the light of his departing mistress's lantern winking among the fir trees. That was why he crushed her in his arms, because he needed to feast his senses on her bones and flesh. Clémence was alarmed by these paroxysms of violence. He used to palpate rather than fondle her – palpate her breasts and shut his eyes and run his fingertips ungently over her cheeks, her lips, her genitals, then scrutinize them as if looking for traces of some magical dust: golden, silvery, or white. He might, Clémence told him in some dismay, have been an inspector of weights and measures, a magistrate or policeman examining a piece of evidence.

'I'm making sure you're here.'

'But I am!'

'Making sure you exist, I mean – making sure you're real. *Do* you exist?'

She took his hand and put it between her legs.

'I'm a woman. Leave your hand there – touch me and you'll know that I'm not content merely to exist. My ambitions go farther than that. I'm a woman as well.'

'I adore your lungs,' said Otto. 'You've the prettiest lungs in the world.'

'You say that only to please me. I've always yearned to have a pretty pair of lungs. Earlier on, while waiting for you out there in the cold, I saw a squirrel leaping about in the branches of a fir tree. Its fur was fair – just the colour of my hair, or so it seemed. Do *you* think I look like a squirrel?'

Otto gazed earnestly at her hair.

'It's true, you do resemble a squirrel, but a tigerlike squirrel.'

'I must be an odd-looking creature.'

'I've dreamt of being loved by a woman who resembled a squirrel ever since I was little, but only if the squirrel resembled a tiger. Squirrels of that kind are very rare.'

'Why are your eyes moist?'

'Because I'm close to you and afraid you don't exist, both at once.'

'Touch me again, Otto – there, on the nape of the neck. It

243

sends an icy shiver down my spine when you touch me there.'

'You see, you little show-off? You've a woman's back, not a squirrel's . . .'

'The first time I saw you, it was as if I'd gone mad. I didn't dare look at you because you were touching me with your eyes.'

'So you put on your Teutonic Knight's expression, and I, like a coward, retreated into my shell.'

'It was only because I didn't want to stay mad,' said Clémence. 'I wanted to be mad for a little while – yes, but I was afraid it would last. Now it's the other way round. My one desire is to *be* mad. Nowadays when I'm mad I'm calm and reasonable and all is well, but when I'm not mad I go mad . . . Touch me again, Otto. I want to feel that icy shiver down my spine.'

They made love again, and when she left a little before dawn Otto was sad. He feared that he was seeing her for the last time – that she was going to her death. He put his fingers to his nose and inhaled the smell of her flesh, a woman's flesh replete with bones and veins, intestines and blood. Their destinies would brush together like sheets of paper stirred by the wind, or like two ships greeting each other in the night and vanishing into separate worlds of darkness. And when her black charger plunged into the fir trees at the end of the charcoal-burner's clearing, Otto called in the hope that she would turn back – that he would see her just once more.

No one, absolutely no one, she said, would have the strength to part them. Besides, she was under her aunt's protection, and old Gertrud would mobilize every general and Knight Templar in her ancestral gallery to form a ring of fire around them which no one would be bold enough to penetrate.

'Even the Almighty watches his step with Aunt Gertrud,' said Clémence. 'We're in safe hands.'

Not even Prince Ernst could prevent them from loving each other, she said – not even the Hofburg, nor Napoleon, nor Christine Kinsky. Otto, however, was abstracted. He would spend minutes on end staring at his mistress's naked body with a seemingly vacant, moonstruck, idiotic look on his face. Clémence, who could be surprisingly coarse at times, used to laugh when her lover remarked on her choice of words.

'You've seen dogs mating, haven't you? Peasants can beat them to death with sticks, but nothing will detach the dog from the bitch till they're done with each other.'

'Which they never are, surely, if they're dead?'

'According to our gardener at the Kärntnertor, he witnessed an instance of that on his father's farm as a boy. A farm-hand thrashed two dogs till he killed them, but no one could separate them even then, so they were buried together, still attached. Can it be true, do you think?'

'*We* shall never be done with each other,' said Otto. 'But tell me, what made you mention Christine?'

'Christine is like the farm-hand. She's implacable – she goes on beating to the bitter end.'

'She's very fond of you.'

'As I am of her. We were brought up together. We've no need to speak, even, to share our secrets. Yes, she's fond of me, but what of it?'

Clémence had mounted her horse and set off down the track. The sky was beginning to pale, the rime- and snow-encrusted forest emerging from the shadows. Many years earlier, when Otto was a boy in Vienna, Lawyer Apfelgrun had taken him to see a friend of his, a retired judge who lived alone and had no interests other than his garden. Otto loved him dearly. The old gentleman used to talk to him about his flowers, but as time went by he showed signs of age and became increasingly muddle-headed. Lawyer Apfelgrun explained to Otto that their old friend was losing his memory and his wits, but Otto still visited him, still took his hand and stroked it fondly. One winter's morning, when the garden was bare of everything save frost and ice, he found the judge gazing at a desolate flower-bed sprinkled with parched grey grass. The old man's face was quite serene that frosty morning. Bending down, he went through the motions of cutting some flowers with scissors and carefully arranging them in a bunch. He stepped back and donned his spectacles as though admiring a profusion of roses and carnations, then straightened an imaginary leaf or two and put the non-existent bouquet to his nose. Otto went up and slipped his hand into the old man's. The cold was intense, and they were both shivering.

'You see?' said the judge. 'There aren't any flowers because it's winter-time and everything's frozen stiff. As for me, I'm a bored old man who knows he won't last till spring, and it saddens me because I should have liked to see my flowers once more – just once more – but alas, who ever saw a withered rose bloom twice? That's why I come here even so. I pretend it's already spring, you understand? I admire my roses and gather bunches of them, and, believe it or not, my garden has never been more fragrant than it is this year.'

Otto had told that story to Clémence.

19

Prince Ernst returned from Dresden early in the spring. According to him, no regiment in Europe could hold a candle to his blue hussars. Lieutenant-Colonel Scherer's cuirassiers had fought like lions at Montenotte and Pozzolo, he said smoothly – like lions, yes, but his giant Saxons would fight like automatons. It annoyed Duchess Clémence that her husband should brag about soldiers who hadn't seen action for years, and whose principal claims to fame were their stature and their smart blue dolmans. A year ago such a remark would have meant war, but today Clémence swallowed the insult without flinching. She had other worries. Although the change in her domestic circumstances had compelled her to renounce the charcoal-burner's cottage and her lover's body, she was unresigned to their loss.

She took several maidservants into her confidence. Whenever Otto was able to slip away from barracks for the night, he would don the frock coat, white hose and high cravat of a country gentleman and hurry to the Kärntnertor. Once across the wall and into the grounds, he concealed himself in a clump of spindleberries not far from the path where Clémence had handed him his first blank missive. There he would be met by one of her maids. If Clémence and her husband were entertaining that night, he was temporarily lodged in a gardener's hut filled with mattocks and rakes and overwintering lemon trees in tubs. Peering through the branches of the latter, he would see the big house lit up like a lantern – see dancing shadows and hear music drifting across the gardens. Then, when all the lights had been extinguished, the maid would reappear and lead him to a servants' entrance.

Otto was passed from hand to hand. He traversed pantries and cellars, lobbies and wood stores, tiptoed up staircases and along passages in a way that reminded him of childhood games with his mother and sisters. He was mystified by this labyrinth, for its topography seemed to change each time he entered it. He simply abandoned himself to the women who took him by the wrist without a word and delivered him, much as they would have delivered a package, to his mistress.

In cases of emergency he would be hidden in some lumber-room, laundry or disused drawing-room until the danger had passed. This could take a considerable time. There were nights when he had to lie low for several hours, only to be released and escorted back to the spindleberries at cockcrow without ever having reached Clémence's bedchamber, that one fixed point in a gloomy maze. It didn't displease him to be entrusted to her maids or to know that all of them were privy to his secret. Perhaps they poked fun at him during their scabrous conversations in the servants' hall, ridiculing his subservience to the duchess, his abject enslavement. Clémence might even have amused herself by discussing him with them; at all events, she never troubled to hide her nakedness when they thrust him into her bedchamber. He was nothing – he was self-abasement and genuflexion personified. He had no plan, no will of his own. Transported from room to room, he fulfilled his function and was then discarded. The maidservants disposed of him in the same way as they went about their morning tasks: sweeping floors, emptying slops, tipping last night's leftovers into the refuse pit. He was supremely happy. He likened himself to the deranged old crones who frequented Vienna's churches and prostrated themselves at the feet of Christ, asking only that the Son of God should deign to cast a downward glance at those who so gladly shared the humiliation, the dust and blood, of Golgotha.

He was at Clémence's mercy, bound hand and foot. He was necessary to her whims, her body, but only for the moment. No whim lasted for ever. She had only to give the order and every door would be closed to him. Or he would be locked up in a dungeon, brought an occasional hunk of bread and pitcher of water, and treated to his mistress's distant cries of ecstasy as she busied herself with a new paramour. Or Clémence would instruct one of her maids to show him into the prince's apartment instead of her own. Ernst's lackeys would seize him and discharge their pistols at his heart or cut his throat and toss him into the Danube, where his body would be found days later. Such were the perilous possibilities on which he brooded while waiting in laundry or lumber-room, but he never rebelled. Clémence wielded the power of life or death over him. Whatever it was that had prompted her to love him in the first place – danger, impropriety, or the sheer enjoyment of breaking him – he had made a compact with her and was resigned to its outcome.

Clémence's response was to laugh and tease him. He deserved a reward for making such rapid strides in the art of love, she said, and gave him a kiss. For a frivolous young man, he was making up for lost time with a vengeance. Then she reassured him. Couldn't he see that she, too, had burnt the last of her fog beacons and was sailing an uncharted ocean to the land of the lost? What of the risks she was running, the confidences she had shared with her maids, her declarations of desire? Didn't they prove her love for him?

Otto insisted that he was only her prey, her plaything. She could withdraw her favours at any time. She wasn't tied to him, and so much the better, because his love would shine in the darkness of rejection like a thousand suns. 'But you, too, could tire of my body,' said Clémence, 'or betray me, or ignore the messages you receive from the Kärntnertor. You could regale Viennese society with stories of my intemperate behaviour. Can you imagine how eagerly they would be exploited by Lawyer Gruhlpraser or Countess Pietranera?' Otto shrugged. 'No, it's the same for us both. Perhaps that's what passion is: uncertainty. A lover is his quarry's quarry. His exaltation stems from self-abasement – from submitting to subjection.' Clémence was ecstatic. 'You have the plague, Otto – we both have it. Each of your kisses reinfects me. My whole body is a disease!'

On other nights, when Otto's mood was less sombre, he would voice misgivings about her maidservants. What if one of them told Prince Ernst? Clémence had no such fears. All her women were devoted to her, she said, and besides, Otto was deluding himself. To them he was merely a man, a body which their mistress needed, and which they procured for her as routinely as they ironed her underwear or prepared her meals. Clémence's earnest tone belied her bantering words. Otto came and went in the dark of night, she continued. He was just a vague, dim, anonymous figure – so anonymous that he could have passed one of his guides in the street next day without being recognized. If she had told her maids to deposit Father Thaler outside her door, they would have done so with as little curiosity. 'Except that Father Thaler is always doubled over or down on his knees,' she pouted, 'so he wouldn't be much use to me.' Nothing would induce her servants to give her away, she added. 'No, we've nothing to fear. My maids are women like any others. One of them might hate me enough to betray me, but never to a man.'

Clémence was careful none the less. She suppressed the savage cries that had rung out so often in the charcoal-burner's cottage. She even refrained from keeping a lighted candle in her bedchamber. Otto saw his mistress only as a pale, almost unrecognizable form. He strove to reconstruct her face with his fingers and accustomed himself to a language of shadows and odours. The lovers took each other with a frenzy redoubled by the need for silence. Clémence was enraptured by this combination of a hushed house and two fiercely straining bodies intent on pleasure. The nights were her all, and happiness had wrought a change in her. Once so remote, she was now insatiable.

'I'm all joy,' she said, '– all joy.'

'There'll be war again. Napoleon won't stand for Prussia's provocations much longer.'

'But we're together, and my cup of joy is full. You're mine till morning.'

'And tomorrow?'

'It was war that brought us together at Brünn, Otto. Another war won't part us. Remember the two dogs – the ones they couldn't separate?'

A maid would come to fetch Otto well before daybreak, so their times together became progressively shorter as spring gave way to summer. Otto was eager to get the endless summer days behind him and wallow once more in the long winter nights, but autumn had barely begun when the inevitable happened.

By what devious means could Prince Ernst have learned about the lovers? Despite all their precautions, had a maidservant broken the feminine pact of which Clémence was so proud, or had some lackey been inveigled into betraying her secret by a few pieces of gold? Otto might even have suspected Christine Kinsky, but Christine had gone off with Schulmeister when the French troops withdrew. He knew from Schwarzbrod that the spy and his mistress were at Strasbourg. Napoleon had royally rewarded 'Monsieur Charles' with a large estate near Illkirch, and Christine had summoned the finest architects from Paris to build a château there.

It was Schwarzbrod who delivered Clémence's warning note to the barracks at Hinterhorf. They would be unable to see each other for the present, she wrote, but Otto was to keep calm. Keeping calm was one thing, he told himself; forgetting was inconceivable.

★   ★   ★

Prince Ernst behaved with dignity. He swallowed his anger and forebore to reproach his wife, but he was a man of iron resolve. His personal temperament, coupled with his upbringing as a boy at Dresden and long experience of a chamberlain's duties at the court of Schönbrunn, had endowed him with complete mastery over his emotions. Clémence would have preferred him to remonstrate and revile her, even to beat her.

The prince let it be known, at the end of a thoroughly convivial evening with the Liechtensteins, that he would welcome a talk with his wife the next morning. He received her in his study. When she entered, he was engaged in straightening a sheaf of documents with characteristic precision. His face betrayed no sign of dismay or distress. It was as handsome, serene and frigid as ever. Clémence could not but admire his composure as he idly spun the terrestrial globe that stood on his well-ordered desk, flanked by a pair of silver candlesticks. This, she supposed, was the manner he adopted when granting an audience to diplomats, judges, or ministers of the crown: capable and sincere, attentive and tolerant – even affable, not that this prevented him from making difficult, nay, ruthless decisions when he felt them to be prescribed by the Empire's welfare or the dictates of public or private morality. This morning, having sustained an emotional wound of terrible magnitude, he discussed his misfortune as urbanely as he would have discussed a tender for military equipment or negotiated a commercial contract.

'Here are my conclusions,' he said at length. 'That Lieutenant-Colonel Scherer's regiment belongs to you is beyond dispute. It must not, however, be forgotten that I, in my capacity as your husband, am colonel proprietor of your Austrian cuirassiers as well as that of my Saxon hussars. That being so, I am entitled to assign officers to either regiment. A custom had grown up between us that appointments to the cuirassiers be made by you. That breach of convention bore witness to the excellence of our personal relations, the strength of our personal ties, the extent of our mutual regard. The said custom has, however, been terminated by your misconduct, of whose vileness you must be aware even if you fail to appreciate the distress it has caused me. I shall now exercise my prerogative.'

'Lieutenant Apfelgrun is an Austrian.'

'What of it? You know as well as I that nationality is immaterial in such cases. There are Saxons among your cuirassiers – Lieutenant Konrad von Thieburg, for example. Conversely, Captain Granz, who commands one of my squadrons at Dresden, is a native of Salzburg. The brothers Kroll provide an even better illustration. On your advice, I assigned Hieronymus Kroll to Dresden on the strength of his fine appearance, and Konstantin to Vienna.'

252

'You mean to transfer Lieutenant Apfelgrun to Dresden – to the Saxons?'

The prince nodded, opened a drawer, and produced a reassignment order in Otto's name. He held it out.

'It isn't true – it can't be! You wouldn't do such a thing!'

'Yes, madam, I would and shall.'

'But you must be aware that war is flaring up again all over Europe. The Prussian armies mobilizing against Napoleon have already occupied the whole of Saxony, you know that better than anyone.'

'I do indeed.'

'Your Saxon hussars will be fighting the French within days, just when Austria is finally at peace.'

Prince Ernst spun the globe violently and threw up his hands.

'Prince,' Clémence cried, 'you could find yourself with a young man's death on your conscience!'

'What of the young man's conscience? Has he not been carrying on an affair with my wife?'

'I have had other affairs,' Clémence said desperately, 'just as your own fidelity to me has never been absolute. Any licence we enjoyed was enjoyed by mutual consent.'

The prince closed his eyes.

'This was an inordinate affair, a grand passion . . .'

'I implore you, Prince!'

'I have advised you of my decision. It is not open to negotiation, so the responsibility for a potential tragedy will be yours. You, Clémence, are the arbiter of Herr Apfelgrun's fate. You have only to say the word. His life is in your hands.'

Clémence looked at the man behind the desk: kindly but fearsome, powerful but – beyond all doubt – deeply afflicted.

'I love Lieutenant Apfelgrun,' she said.

'The love I still bear you, madam, and the affection you deigned to show me in the past, and the esteem you formerly deserved – all this inclines me to give Lieutenant Apfelgrun another chance. I take note that you . . . that you love this young man. Could you none the less bring yourself to save his life by losing him – more precisely, by undertaking never to see him again? This is a serious matter, so take your time. I shall expect your answer twenty-four hours from now. I would only urge you, yet again, to reflect that Herr Apfelgrun's life is in your hands.'

Clémence drew herself up to her full height. She failed to see that twenty-four hours would change anything, she said: he already had her answer. Prince Ernst clenched and unclenched his fists several times, so fiercely that the knuckles went white.

'I was convinced that your love for him would prompt you to sacrifice that love. Clearly, I was mistaken. To pursue this discussion further would be pointless. Lieutenant-Colonel Scherer will advise the lieutenant of his transfer tomorrow morning. I'm informed that Augereau and his corps have left Frankfurt for Gera. Herr Apfelgrun should just have time enough to reach Dresden before they invade Saxony. May I repeat my question one last time?'

Clémence turned and ran from the room. She took refuge in her bedchamber, racked with sobs. Was it in the nature of love to entail murder? Was love another name for despair? Only a year ago she would have been amenable to her husband's arguments. She would have acknowledged that reason and reflection can curb the most inordinate of passions. Since then she had learned that a woman in love is a madwoman, a demented creature who would send her lover to his death rather than give him up. A succession of mental images assailed her. She had often visited Vienna's central infirmary, where the wounded lay in serried rows after the massacres at Ulm and Austerlitz, and the recollection of those mutilated bodies conjured up a stench of gangrene and gore. She thought of the processions of flagellants on Good Friday, the wounds of Christ, the bloody sweat of the saints. Near to death in spirit, she closeted herself in her apartment for two whole days.

* * *

It was nightfall on the second day when Clémence saw her

husband again. He was surprised when his valet announced her. As he slipped a dressing-gown over his shirt it did not occur to him that she might have changed her mind. He knew that, beneath her carapace of self-control, she was capable of emotional, heroic decisions. One glance at her standing in the doorway, however, told him that he had different grounds for anxiety. Clémence declined to sit down. Her voice, when she spoke, was calm and steady.

'I waited until Lieutenant Apfelgrun had left for Dresden. Tomorrow you will receive a letter formally acquainting you with my decision for the future, just as you acquainted me with yours two days ago. You give me no choice.'

'You do indeed have a choice, Clémence. One word from you would have nipped this whole affair in the bud.'

'I repeat, you give me no choice. I hope to convince you that my decisions are as little negotiable as your own. You may threaten me or lock me up, but I shall never yield.'

The prince, guessing that she had come prepared with a lengthy speech, listened attentively.

'I intend to join my lover in Dresden. Should you try to prevent me, do not count on my survival – indeed, do not count on your own. The arrangements I have made are final and irreversible. I cannot tell how long I shall remain at Dresden. That will no more depend on me than any aspect of this imbroglio depends on me, or on you, or on Lieutenant Apfelgrun. It will depend on the duration of the war. You know how much I respect you, Ernst. I realize that your temperament ill equips you to sail the stormy seas of passion. I cannot fail to appreciate your distress, which troubles and saddens me even if I can do nothing to alleviate it.

'I also appreciate, however, that your distress is alloyed with fear of scandal. You are one of the court's most prominent figures. I can gauge how highly you value your reputation because I was equally jealous of my own until a short time ago. You have no wish to appear ridiculous, I'm sure, or to have your name held in derision and contempt by

Viennese society. I promise you, therefore, that I shall do nothing to advertise this affair.

'We do, after all, absent ourselves from the capital now and then. It's true that we generally leave together for the wolf-hunting season, but you did spend two months alone at Dresden earlier this year. You will also recall that three years ago I took myself off to Greinburg for several months' peace and quiet, and that you joined me there at weekly intervals. I shall therefore pretend to retire to Greinburg, having previously instructed the servants to reopen the castle and redouble the frequency of their comings and goings. But that's not all I shall do to safeguard your reputation.'

She paused before continuing in a wry, almost playful tone of voice.

'Fräulein Alma von Wörth will reside at Greinburg Castle for as long as the war detains me. You see how well the Almighty arranges things and how charitable he is to womankind? Not only are Fräulein Wörth and I of the same age and build, but she also possesses an abundance of fair hair and an air of refinement. In short, Fräulein Wörth will impersonate me. I have taken her into my confidence – she has, in fact, been my confidante since Brünn. I have also bequeathed her my wardrobe. She will seldom venture outside the castle, so the few tradesmen and peasants who visit it will be easily deceived. As for the servants, I've replaced them. None of them knows me except old Fabian, who would never dream of giving us away.'

The prince looked dumbfounded. More in surprise than anger, he slumped back in his chair. He had been prepared for almost anything, but this time Clémence had gone too far. He took the silver paper-knife with which he had been toying and put it on the wine table at his elbow. Then he rose, a tall, massive, elegant figure.

'What if I reject your underhand scheme, madam? What if I oppose it by every available means?'

'Do so and you'll have a scandal on your hands. My arrangements for leaking the truth are already made, as I told you. What's more, you'll have ample time to savour

256

their effect. The charges I've laid will be detonated one by one, in accordance with my instructions. Think how avidly your fellow courtiers at Schönbrunn will lap up each new revelation – think too how the Emperor himself will react. No, Ernst, you won't oppose me. Be sensible. When *you* told *me* of your decisions two days ago, I never even dreamed of trying to dissuade you.'

'You had no choice, you said.'

'No more have you. I tell you again: no one involved in this tangled web has the smallest choice, the slightest freedom of action.'

The prince shrugged. 'Very well,' he said.

'I would advise you to visit Greinburg from time to time. It's only fitting that a man should go to see his wife when she's resting in the country. It would seem odd if you didn't – people might talk. Fraülein von Wörth will welcome you as . . . as I myself would have done had I not been called away.' Clémence's laugh was quite unaffected and devoid of rancour.

'Do you recollect how Aunt Gertrud entertained us with her stories of Lord Misrule – you know, that elderly English eccentric who may or may not have existed? How we laughed! He had the notion that all human beings live at second hand – by proxy, as Gertrud put it – and that each of us is a puppet operated by the hands of another, or of many others, and vice versa. Surely you remember? Lord Misrule used to live out his emotions through his servants – he even had one who specialized in making love on his behalf. What a droll idea, you always used to say. Well, the droll thing today is that it's we, you and I, who . . .'

'Lord Misrule?' Prince Ernst was genuinely mystified. 'What has he to do with this affair?'

'Oh, nothing, and since he undoubtedly never existed, it's pointless to invoke his protection.'

'Why speak of him, then?'

'He doesn't exist, Ernst, I know. I believe him to be a figment of Gertrud's, but what she means is that Lord Misrule is far more the prince of this world than ever Satan was, and that he proliferates, and that each of us is the

Misrule of the other. Gertrud is Misrule because she lives at secondhand, of that there's no doubt. I too am Misrule, and the most extraordinary thing of all is that you, my dear Ernst, are likewise Lord Misrule. But I'm simultaneously one of Misrule's domestics – one of his maidservants – just as you also are in the service of the Misrule who is himself in yours. And as for Fraülein von Wörth, my friend, I'd stake my oath that she, too, has just entered his lordship's employ.'

★ ★ ★

Impatient to be off, Clémence did not linger in Vienna. War between France and Prussia, the latter towing Saxony to disaster in her wake, was imminent. Three days later, travel-weary after a long journey by mail coach, Clémence reached Dresden. She learned that Adegauer's blue hussars had already left their barracks to bar the path of Augereau's armies, which were advancing from the direction of Plauen and Gera. Although Clémence and her husband had often been entertained at the royal palace in years gone by, she was at pains to remain incognito, not for her own reputation's sake, but because of her promise to shield Prince Ernst from any breath of scandal.

With this in mind she put on a sober grey woollen gown and a plain fur coat, having first concealed her hair beneath a scarf wound like a turban. Thus attired she attended Sunday morning Mass, which was celebrated in the presence of Frederick Augustus III, Elector of Saxony, and watched him at his devotions from the anonymity of the crowded nave. The ritual was magnificent, the music sublime, the cathedral choir composed of Italian voices. Clémence was seeing the Saxon royal family as she had never seen them before. The Elector's wife, Marie-Amélie, whom she had not met for some years, was a handsome, majestic woman for her age, but seen from the nave she made a plump and discontented impression.

20

Summer had departed. The slow, golden river of autumn was submerging knolls crowned with fir trees, picture-book hamlets perched on the flanks of rocky gorges, hillsides on which vine-growers' villages rose in terraces. The sky was a secure infinity of crisp, pellucid blue, but the Saxon countryside, pretty as a plaything, was in jeopardy. Throughout the area bounded by the Elbe and the Saale, soldiers of both sides were on the move. At their respective headquarters, Napoleon, Augereau, Soult and Murat, and, in the opposing camp, General von Braunschweig, old Field-Marshal Möllendorf, Prince Hohenlohe, Frederick William III of Prussia, and even Louise of Mecklenburg, his queen, pored over the same maps, computed the distances between Jena and Merseburg or Gera and Dresden, and pencilled in the routes along which, in a few days' time, soldiers would trudge and gesticulate amid their waggons, caissons and pieces of ordnance like praying mantises – like vicious, ungainly, half-blind, semi-idiotic creatures encumbered by antennae, antlers, pincers, each trying vainly to extricate itself from the rest. It was the same whenever October came round. Autumn had acquired bad habits in recent years: it had developed a mania for producing not only bunches of grapes, brown leaves and the scent of mushrooms, but also, like some foul miasma expelled by the soil itself, a pullulating mass of soldiery.

Every horse-drawn vehicle had disappeared from Dresden the day Augereau set off from Frankfurt at the beginning of October. Napoleon, meanwhile, mounted on his sturdy little grey, headed fast for Würzburg. It was as if the coachmen of the Saxon capital were already taking orders from the French generals, not from their prince elector, in accordance with the well-known principle that every military commander issues instructions, not only to his own men, but to those of the enemy as well. This was exemplified

259

by what had happened at Austerlitz the year before. How could it be denied that Emperor Francis's Austrians and Tsar Alexander's Russians had formed themselves into columns and spurred their thousands of horses into a gallop at the behest of Napoleon, not of Francis and Alexander; or that they had unleashed volleys of musketry only after Napoleon, bedded down on the maps presented to him by Coulaincourt, had covered them with cryptic scribbles and decided to join battle; or that, in general, victory belongs to the commander capable of influencing the enemy's movements as well as his own? Similarly now, a year later, it was not until the grenadiers of Augereau's VIIIth Corps crossed the Main that every church bell in Dresden began to peal, and that every rattletrap cart and waggon in the Saxon capital was requisitioned by the army to transport men and supplies to the front. All the capital's private coaches and carriages, barouches and landaus, were snapped up by civilians and driven off along the roads of Saxony. Clémence, who had been in Dresden for two days, managed to hire a berlin. She paid in gold, congratulating herself on having secreted a dozen small diamonds in the hem of her gown to be sold as her needs prescribed.

The price demanded by the livery stable was high but not exorbitant, considering the hazards of the journey and the chaotic state of the country. Clémence's coachman was a feeble old man of kindly but nervous disposition. He was principally afraid for the horse that constituted his sole asset and object of affection, especially since he knew he could never have brought himself to destroy so beloved and loving a beast in the event of injury. Thus they crawled laboriously along in the safety of military convoys, obstructed inevitably by the host of parasites that accompanied every army on campaign. Hundreds of women added to the confusion. Some, like Clémence, were trying to reach the bivouacs where they hoped to find their husbands or lovers. Others, herding broods of children, were fleeing from the combat zone. Others still were camp followers: beggars and pickpockets, madwomen and whores, female sutlers perched on mules slung with twin casks of wine and basketfuls of live hens.

The coachman refused to venture beyond Eisenberg. The thunder of gunfire, which had been audible since morning, unnerved him. He flinched on his box at every detonation and whipped up his horse, which broke into a hysterical gallop. Clémence begged and pleaded and offered to double the agreed fare, but to no avail. The man had a family in Dresden and was too afraid that his precious horse would be hit by a stray bullet. He put her down at a crossroads, tossed her a hunk of bread, wheeled his conveyance around, and drove off.

Clémence picked up her bag and resumed the journey on foot with little idea of where to make for. No one could tell her, because the gunfire seemed to be coming from every direction at once and its source was unidentifiable. The officers whom she pestered for information knew nothing. It was reported that there had been a bloody engagement at Saalfeld, on the banks of the Saale, and that Louise of Mecklenburg, the Queen of Prussia herself, had been spitted on a French sergeant's bayonet. But the most exasperating thing, Clémence was informed by a Prussian cornet lolling against a haystack with his dolman unbuttoned to reveal a hairy chest, was that the senior officers hadn't even troubled to explain if they were advancing or retreating, with the result, he solemnly added, that no one could decide whether his men were heroes or runaways.

There were two battles involved, the first in the neighbourhood of Auerstedt, where Braunschweig's forty-eight thousand men were encircling a weak force under Soult, and the other at Jena, which Napoleon had reached the previous day. 'And the Prince of Saxe-Salza's blue hussars?' said Clémence. 'What of Lieutenant-Colonel Adegauer's hussars – do you know where they've been deployed?' But the Prussian cornet, looking exhausted now, merely spat tobacco juice into the hay and said, 'Be damned to the blue hussars!'

Clémence decided to head for Jena. She had been trudging along for several miles when a Prussian lieutenant of artillery charitably allowed her to ride on the limber of a heavy cannon drawn by half a dozen oxen, but another officer, a captain, drove her away with his riding crop and promised the lieutenant a hundred strokes of the cane. The riding crop scored her cheek and drew blood, but the wound seemed only superficial. She stole off to rest in a field pervaded by the smell of burning. The sun had set. In the west, towards Jena, a big red glow lit up the sky, so she took it that the battle had already begun. Setting off once more, she made her way into the outskirts of the city. All the houses were barred and shuttered. The battle had not yet begun, in fact, but half the city was ablaze with fires which its panic-stricken inhabitants had started by accident. Half-clothed women came running through the narrow streets with children clasped in their arms. Clémence passed the ducal palace and several churches with gilded onion domes. When a corpulent, well-dressed man accosted her, she asked if he had seen any Saxon hussars in blue uniforms. The fat man could not have been more charming. Yes indeed, he'd just passed a squadron of hussars in blue and would take her to their bivouac at once. They set off across some gardens, but suddenly, at the foot of a plum tree, the man stopped short. Seizing her gown by the collar, he ripped it open. He was grunting now, and his eyes had gone red. Clémence did not resist. The man threw her down in a cabbage patch and lifted her skirts, grunting more and more loudly. Clémence bided her time, then stunned him with a convenient piece of timber.

At five the next morning, October 14th, all hell broke loose again. The cannon fire was continuous, the stench of gunsmoke sickening. The source of the infernal din was the Landgrafenberg plateau overlooking the city of Jena, on which Clémence had once enjoyed a convivial picnic with Prince Ernst and Marie-Amélie, the Elector's plump wife, whom she had lately seen at Mass in Dresden. Today, however, the Landgrafenberg was enveloped in a dense white pall of mist. Towards ten o'clock the mist lifted like the curtain rising on the first act of a play; this particular play, however, had been wrecking its own scenery since before dawn. The sun shone down on a city in ruins. Clémence headed towards the sound of musket fire, slipping in pools of blood as she went. Corpses in uniforms of every hue lay sprawled in grotesque poses, soldiers stealthily hugged the walls.

There were no blue dolmans to be seen. When the sound of firing changed, drawing nearer, Clémence took refuge in an abandoned wash-house with mossy walls. Screened by some willow branches, she could survey a small arcaded square whose flower-bedecked houses had so far escaped the flames. A woman darted out of a nearby doorway, but a shot rang out and she pitched into the wash-house without so much as a cry: she was dead. Clémence shifted a little to make room for her. A lone horse careered madly across the square, lashing out in all directions with its hoofs.

By mid-afternoon the din had abated. Although isolated shots could still be heard, the battle was over and the gunfire had been replaced by other sounds: shouted words of command in French, hurrying footsteps, oaths, the clatter of hoofs, drunken singing, and everywhere, everywhere, moans and anguished cries. Clémence managed to push the dead woman's body aside and make her way out of the wash-house.

Now that Jena was in French hands, the Saxons and Prussians would doubtless be withdrawing to the north or west. Clémence decided to go west and reached the Weimar Gate without incident. There she scrambled on to a peasant's horse-drawn cart and joined the human flotsam receding in disorder from the city. After several miles, as she was passing through a large village she caught sight of blue uniforms. She could hardly believe her eyes: Lieutenant-Colonel Adegauer, whom she had often entertained to dinner in the past, was organizing a bivouac less than a hundred yards away. A tall, sickly-looking man, he was slouching in his saddle with a dirty bandage round his neck. Clémence jumped off the cart. She sat down wearily on a milestone. No one would have recognized her – with her torn clothes and gashed cheek, she might have been a beggarwoman or one of the whores that sold themselves to soldiers. Fortunately for her, the battle-weary soldiers were not on the lookout for women this evening. Clémence continued to sit there, a huddled, shivering figure. The hussars had lit camp fires. She could see their shadowy figures silhouetted against the flames, but it was impossible to tell if her lover was among them.

She sidled up to the bivouac. The sentries tried to shoo her away. She implored their compassion: she'd lost her children and hoped to beg a piece of bread. There was no sign of Otto, but that meant nothing because the regiment had probably become scattered. Other survivors of Prince Ernst's handsome band of Saxon giants must surely be around somewhere, either in nearby villages or away to the east of Jena. Still looking for Otto, Clémence noticed a trooper leading some horses to the water trough. She recognized him at once, having seen him the previous summer. It was Otto's pet orderly from the Banat, the odd fellow with the permanent smile. He wasn't smiling now, though: his face wore a lugubrious, lacklustre expression. Clémence ran after him and held out her hand as though begging. Matthias said he had nothing to give her. Clémence spoke to him urgently, in a low voice.

He heard her out, cupping his hand to his ear, then thrust her roughly aside, but not before he had contrived to mutter a few words of warning. The bivouac was too dangerous a place for a woman. At the far end of the village, opposite the wayside cross, a shrine to St Anne, she would see a farm. He would join her there as soon as he could get away. Clémence followed his instructions. She crept into an open barn beside the farmhouse and concealed herself among some agricultural implements. Time went by. She was just growing anxious when a big man in a peasant smock approached the barn. Matthias was clearly very proud of his disguise, which he had purloined from a villager's house. He told her he had decided to part company for the moment with Lieutenant-Colonel Adegauer's regiment. There was no danger, he said happily. The Prussian and Saxon armies had fallen into a thousand pieces, all of them hopelessly lost. In a few days' time, when Adegauer's officers drew up their lists of the dead, wounded and missing, Matthias's name would be among the latter. But as soon as he had found Lieutenant Apfelgrun, the two men would report to Adegauer, explaining that they had got lost, and with any luck the regimental commander would welcome Otto back with open arms. Clémence still had strength enough to smile at the notion that she was encouraging a member of her husband's precious regiment to go absent without leave.

It had been a hard-fought battle, Matthias told her. Adegauer's men had borne the brunt of Marshal Augereau's fierce assault, and, unlike the Prussians who had fled at the first French cavalry charge, the blue hussars had acquitted themselves like heroes. There had even been a possibility, around midday, that the Saxons would throw the French back. Lieutenant Apfelgrun had charged at the head of his troop under heavy French fire, only to be felled by a sabre-wielding Frenchman. Matthias, from a hundred yards off, had seen Otto's saddle slip until it was beneath his black charger's belly. He'd spurred his own horse towards the spot, but just then Murat's dragoons and mounted grenadiers, yelling wildly and flourishing their sabres, had counterattacked and routed the hussars.

Matthias had returned to the scene of the slaughter a little later. The field had been trampled by horses' hoofs and ploughed up by exploding shells, but he managed to ascertain that his lieutenant was not among the officers and troopers whose bodies carpeted it. That Otto had been wounded was certain. Less certain was the identity of those who had carried him off; possibly Prussians or Saxons but more probably the French, who had retained command both of the battlefield and of the entire city. Matthias took the duchess's hand. 'We'll find him, Excellency. We can't afford not to.' He continued to gaze around and cup his hand to his ear from time to time, apparently in the vain hope of hearing his lieutenant's cries for help. Clémence wept.

Duchess and orderly set off at daybreak. Thousands of corpses littered the outskirts of Jena, the Mühltal gorge, the banks of the Saale, the Iserstädt woods, the villages of

265

Cospoda, Vierzehn-Heiligen and Hermstädt. Sombrely clad women were sorting through the carnage with despairing cries, turning bodies over, questioning survivors. Stooping, they picked their way across the fields as though harvesting mangel-wurzels or potatoes. Come what might, Clémence reflected, women could never neglect their housewifely tasks. It was their job always to restore order, to dust, tidy, sweep, dispose of cobwebs, dead flies, dirt, corpses, scraps of intestine. If they were not restrained, they would tidy the very hills, launder the very rivers. The stench of flesh, charred or putrid, was suffocating. Clémence saw two old women tearing at each other's hair. Their bone of contention was a Prussian sergeant's mangled corpse, which each claimed to be her son. The older of the two seized her adversary by the throat and tried to throttle her. The other woman broke away, snatched up the sergeant's shako, and ran off with it. 'It's mine, mine!' she screeched triumphantly as she hopped away across the furrows like a magpie.

On the third day Clémence caught sight of a Frenchwoman whose face must once have been beautiful. She was dragging the body of a lieutenant, her fiancé, by the heels. She had been hauling him along since dawn, she said, and had already covered five miles or more. If she managed to reach Jena, she would have his body crated up and taken back to France.

'I'm the reason he's dead, you see. I'm the reason he chose to become a soldier.' She leant towards Clémence and spoke in an undertone, glaring vengefully around her all the while.

'Armand is a coward – *was* a coward, I mean. I never knew a less courageous man, though it should be said in fairness that his family had never battled with anything more formidable than their fields of wheat and potatoes. But my father is a colonel, so he refused to give Armand my hand unless he became a captain. That's why he enlisted in the Grande Armée, madame – for the love of me. He was so determined to become a captain that he hurled his men into battle at every opportunity – right into the thick of the

266

enemy fire. They died by the score, believe me!'

The woman's eyes glowed.

'You could say it was for my sake that he killed them, French and Prussians alike. His colonel told me that he'd never known a more intrepid man than my fiancé, yet he was really a coward, I do assure you. He loved me, madam, that's all. Mark you, I was a beauty once . . .'

She produced a little mirror and inspected her face, running the tip of her tongue over her lips.

Matthias took good care of Clémence. At night they would sneak into abandoned houses, most of them severely damaged by bombardment or fire, and he would improvise a palliasse for her and wait for her to fall asleep before sitting down beside her. If Clémence woke, tormented by some hellish nightmare, she would see his kindly face in the gloom and curl up in the reasssuring warmth of his arms.

The dead and wounded were still being retrieved six days after Jena, when Napoleon's forces had long since left the district and headed for Prussia. Half of the Grande Armée, led by Murat, Soult and Ney, marched on Stettin and Lübeck in the north. The other half, under Lannes and Davout, converged on Berlin and Potsdam, where Napoleon meant to avenge the defeat inflicted on Soubise by Frederick the Great and his legions at Rossbach half a century earlier. One morning Clémence saw some soldiers laboriously inserting a bulky corpse into a cask of brandy. It was General Morland, whom the French were sending home to his widow in the same manner as the mortal remains of Louis IX, Saint Louis, had been repatriated from Tunis in 1270. Clémence was so convinced by now that her lover was dead that her mind could frame no other thought: Otto's death excluded all else. Matthias seldom spoke any more. He scoured the countryside with grim determination, and Clémence joined him in raking over the corpse-infested ground.

Hoping against hope, they also toured the hospitals, the largest of which was housed in a church at Jena. Hundreds of hapless men lay there moaning while surgeons plied their trade in the ill-lit nave, French soldiers carried buckets of blood, and women tore up sheets to make bandages. The church reeked of ordure, urine, straw, blood, and pus; the vaulted ceiling resounded to a chorus of groans. A fatigue party was filling great baskets with the arms and legs which the surgeons had just amputated, using ordinary carpenters' saws. Matthias ran after them and asked permission to examine these severed limbs. He made a minute inspection of the feet, fingers and bluish elbows, knitting his honest brow as he tried to spot some minor peculiarity that might have identified one or more of them as Lieutenant Apfelgrun's.

They discovered two more hospitals, one in the Black Bear Inn and the other in the local lunatic asylum. On visiting the latter, the duchess and her companion were greeted by an exceedingly courteous gentleman wearing major's insignia. He delighted them by announcing that Otto Apfelgrun was indeed among his wounded patients, and that he could personally vouch for his speedy recovery. Clémence broke down and sobbed. Just at that moment, however, the major started clucking like a hen and scuttled off down the passage flapping his arms as though trying to take wing.

Their tour of the hospitals took them to neighbouring villages. Clémence and Matthias were guided by the wheeling flocks of crows, visible from far across the plain, that denoted where the French had set up makeshift infirmaries. That was how, on the outskirts of Apelda, they came upon an old farmhouse in which a score of wounded men were being tended and fed by the women of the village. There was no doctor, not even an officer in charge, so they had to visit each room in turn. Clémence was the first to discover Otto in an outhouse, lying on a heap of grimy straw. She cried out and Matthias came running. As soon as he saw who it was he started to laugh. Then he swept Clémence off her feet and broke into a dance from his native Banat, bellowing with delight. He clasped the duchess's head to his chest and smothered it with respectful little kisses. 'Excellency, Excellency!' he cried again and again. Clémence buried her face in his homespun smock.

Otto had been unconscious for several days. Now, convinced that the battle of Jena had taken place only the previous day, not a week ago, he asked where his charger had got to. He could recall his saddle slipping and was prepared to accept that he had been close to death, but now he felt better and was mystified to find Clémence there beside him with Matthias in attendance. Clémence recounted her adventures, her journey from Vienna to Jena via Dresden, her lengthy search of the battlefields and hospitals. Otto asked Matthias where Lieutenant-Colonel Adegauer's regiment was. They must rejoin it at once, but what was to become of Clémence? He kissed her and gave his orderly a hug.

Clémence brought him up to date. On the day following his victory at Jena, Napoleon had summoned Frederick III, Elector of Saxony, and congratulated him on the exemplary conduct of his troops. He had also rewarded several inhabitants of the city, notably a cathedral priest who had afforded him a decisive advantage over the Prussians and Saxons by helping French troops to scale the Landgrafenberg heights during the night of October 13th. But Clémence had a far more surprising item of news to impart. Napoleon had so cleverly succeeded in detaching the Saxons from their Prussians allies that now . . .

'Now?'

'The Elector of Saxony isn't an elector any longer, he's a king. He has changed his name overnight. He now styles himself Frederick I, not Frederick III. What's more, Saxon troops are no longer fighting on the Prussian side. They now form part of the French army.'

'Are you sure?' Otto asked.

'Positive, Otto. Prince Ernst's regiment is part of the Grande Armée, or will be from now on. Your blue hussars are preparing to advance on Potsdam, shoulder to shoulder with the French.'

'But the French are our enemies, Clémence. Besides, what of Konrad von Thieburg and Ulrich Lvov and fat Siegfried and all my other friends in the cuirassiers? They'll be expected to shoot me down, and I – I'll have to try to kill them in return. It's insane! And what of you, Clémence, with your Austrian cuirassiers on one side and your hussars on the other? No, really!'

'Austria isn't at war with France any more, Otto.'

'You know she'll go to war again, it's inevitable. And what of Matthias?'

'Matthias? He's with you. Matthias is another of Napoleon's new allies.'

'But he hails from the Military Frontier – from Austrian territory. You must be mad!'

'It's history that's mad, or Napoleon. But we're together, Otto – together! Isn't that miraculous? We're free for the first time ever, and Matthias is with us. You must rest, Otto. Try to sleep a little.'

Try to sleep . . . In his present condition, the words reminded Otto of his childhood. As a small boy he had been fascinated by a sampler of the kind young boarding-school girls were taught to sew, which hung on the wall near his mother's bed and was the work of her grandmother. He was particularly fond of this piece of embroidery: it depicted the letters of the alphabet enclosed by a border of multi-coloured flowers, but one of the letters – 'G' – was missing, and Otto could never look at the sampler without thinking of the shame and distress that must surely have afflicted a little girl in another century when, after toiling away with her needle for weeks on end, she saw what she had done. Remembering this, he fell asleep.

Very early next morning Matthias proceeded to get his lieutenant dressed. Otto's uniform was a terrible sight, slashed in several places and encrusted with mud, but it was a uniform none the less. He gazed at Clémence fondly, stroking her cheek and fondling her breasts, while Matthias shaved him.

'What a life it is,' he said lightly. 'You hurry off to Baden, partly for want of anything better to do and partly because you find the patriotic fervour of Rector Ouarin and his students grotesque, and you crack a foolish joke about the two-headed eagle, and you make the acquaintance of a priest who's always down on his knees, and you're introduced to a fanciful old duchess, and you abandon the study of botany in favour of a cuirassier's uniform, and you meet a young woman, and you're happier than you've ever been, and you're knocked senseless because your saddle slips, and Napoleon, the dirty hypocrite, takes advantage of your unconscious state to enrol your regiment in his Grande Armée, and now, sooner or later you'll have to do battle with your friends, with Austria, with the rivers and butter-flies of your native land. The fact is, Clémence, it has to be that aunt of yours, Aunt Gertrud, who's behind it all . . .'

He had reeled this off with scarcely a pause for breath.

'That's why I slept for so long,' he went on. 'I had no worries, Clémence. For one thing, I had no idea you'd left Vienna for Dresden – not that I underestimate you, believe me. I knew you were mad, but I didn't foresee this, and I also knew that old Matthias would always take care of you, Clémence – Clémence, my beloved one.'

He broke off, suddenly surprised.

'My beloved one? There, I've never brought myself to call you that before!' His throat tightened and his voice rose.

'It's a complicated business, getting to the point of telling a woman you love her. Napoleon has to abandon his plan to invade England, the Queen of Prussia says a lot of foolish things, you get a crack on the head with a sabre, a soldier from the Banat deserts, an Austrian duchess transforms herself into a Saxon beggar-woman and finds you in a stinking infirmary, and only then, not before, do you get the chance to tell her you love her . . .'

Matthias sat him up on his palliasse, then helped him to his feet. He took Otto by the arm and coaxed him to take a few steps, urging him on in Banat dialect. Meanwhile, Clémence unpicked the hem of her gown and extracted one of her diamonds, which proved sufficient, on their return to Jena, to purchase two horses and a barouche in fair condi-tion. Very early the following morning, Matthias cracked his whip.

'To Berlin!' Otto cried gaily.

21

Napoleon was laying about him. He had unleashed his professional killers on Germany, and Germany was in mortal agony. Augereau crossed the Elbe at Dessau. Erfurt, Torgau and Magdeburg fell. Hohenlohe and his sixteen thousand stalwarts surrendered to Murat. The French had Blücher bottled up in his Lübeck lair. Austrian peasants were going around in animal hides, wearing caps of wolf-skin or gory, uncured lambskin. The soldiers, too, were a squalid gang of clodhoppers. They wiped their reeking blades on their breeches, hunted wolves, warmed themselves by setting fire to churches. At night, in the desecrated palaces of princes and margraves, they feasted like murderous brigands with the women who catered to the weaknesses of their flesh.

Prussia's army fled like the wind before these maniacs from France. Gone were the days when lovely Queen Louise, wearing the uniform of the Anspach Hussars, had predicted that her cavalry would scatter the French 'cobblers' like chaff. Only the previous September, Berlin's arrogant, monocled officers, roses in their buttonholes, had sharpened their swords on the steps of the French embassy in Potsdam. Now they were fleeing in panic from the rabble commanded by Soult and Lannes, throwing themselves on its mercy, and kissing the 'cobblers' hands.

Queen Louise, who had hankered after war as a mistress desires her lover's body, was incensed. Some months before, on 3 November 1805, she had signed a treaty with the Tsar. That night, accompanied by Alexander and her husband Frederick William, she had walked through the palace grounds at Potsdam to the little garrison church. Fresh-faced and radiant in the torchlight, she had knelt before the bronze sarcophagi of the Great Elector of Brandenburg and Frederick II and had sworn to destroy the Usurper, Napoleon, whom she had nicknamed 'Noppel' or

– a humorous corruption – 'Moppel', meaning 'pug-dog'. Well, the pug-dog was now strutting down the Unter den Linden in Berlin. He, too, had visited the crypt of the garrison church to pay homage to Frederick the Great and thus to profane him, while Germany's greatest philosopher, Friedrich Hegel, on seeing Napoleon's horse beneath his windows at Jena, had actually likened its rider to history personified.

Prussian soldiers deserted in droves. They went to ground in the forests of Pomerania, and woe betide any Frenchmen or Saxons who strayed into their area. Spectral figures would burst from the trees, massacre the luckless men, and appropriate their sheepskin coats, weapons and cartridge pouches. Meanwhile, Clémence and her two companions also were camping out, sometimes in deserted houses, sometimes huddled together in the snow under a heap of straw and old sacks. They filled their bellies after a fashion, either by stealing like everyone else or by probing the soil for caches of food the farmers might have buried before taking flight. All three of them by now were quite as malodorous as the killers of the Grande Armée.

One night, when well beyond the Oder and approaching the French lines, they begged shelter at a monastery near Doppelmeskiter. The monks having fled, their premises had been taken over by an unfrocked French priest who had had enough of the war – this 'vomit', as he called it – and was harbouring a hundred-odd deserters from every army. A fearful-looking man with a nervous tic, he was much given to incoherent sermons invoking the Virgin Mary, the Seventh Seal and the Grim Reaper. Clémence, Otto and Matthias were invited to join his community. He received them in the chapter house, surrounded by villainous ex-soldiers and attired in a bishop's cope and mitre. At his feet lay a mound of books and manuscripts, ancient treatises on theological and historical subjects. While speaking he tore out pages and stuffed them into his mouth. Then, after chewing them thoroughly, he spat them out on the flagstones.

'We are the foes of history,' he bellowed. 'We shall be

consumers of books – we shall efface the very memory of that vile jest known as the past. Nationality, property, patrimony, ancestry, matrimony – see, this is all that will remain of them when every book has been devoured!' So saying, he hurled a wad of papier mâché at a Nativity on the far wall.

'Memory, begone! It is memory that has locked us out of the Garden of Delights, debarred us from the green pastures and innocent pleasures of bygone days. Out there the ultimate conflict is drawing to a close. Here we shall build the world afresh – a world of justice, love and happiness. We shall erect the New Jerusalem amid a revival of barbarism! I am the wrath, the love, of God!'

Each of these announcements added to the spittle that streaked his brown beard and was cheered to the echo.

'My lieutenant is a Saxon, my legions consist of Prussians, Russians, Frenchmen, Jews, Caucasians, Turks, Poles. We have torn down the pestilential edifice of Babel. We have signed a separate peace. Behold us, O Lord, with our frail tents pitched on the navel of the world. Our example will shatter the petrified princes and emperors of Europe. At the very midpoint of night, the fixed star of Justice looks down on this place. The Lord of the Flies has usurped the throne of the Almighty. We shall slay the impostor and reinvent love!'

The men who were chanting in the gloom did not look friendly in the least. All were armed with muskets, swords, cutlasses or butchers' knives. Otto had no intention of spurning the priest's hospitality, since any attempt to escape would clearly have spelt disaster. He and Matthias would have been murdered on the spot, leaving Clémence at the mercy of these filthy ruffians. Otto declared therefore that he and his companions shared their host's fraternal ideals and were likewise eager to sign a separate peace. That night they joined the community at supper in the refectory. The food was rich, the drink plentiful. The priest gorged himself, still finding time to chew a folio or two between courses. Once the wine had taken effect, his disciples began to recount their day's doings. They had killed three Mecklenburg peasants that morning and plundered a dozen farms. Another such expedition was planned for the morrow. Their favourite entertainment, it transpired, was to make their victims' eyes pop out by throttling them with lengths of rope.

The meal seemed interminable. Men and women staggered off into corners and sprawled there, higgledy-piggledy, in a drunken stupor. Snores and heavy breathing could be heard, punctuated by oaths and moans of delight. The priest, who had seized hold of Clémence, dragged her under the refectory pulpit and began to remove her clothes, only to doze off in mid-fumble. Otto and Matthias pretended to sleep. It was several hours before they dared to move. Then, light-footed as a cat, Matthias stole over to the pulpit and alerted Clémence. Still pinned beneath the priest's body, she had difficulty in extricating herself without waking him, but the trio eventually managed to make good their escape just as dawn was breaking.

They caught up with Lieutenant-Colonel Adegauer's regiment on the outskirts of Danzig, where several units of the Saxon army were fighting alongside the French. Adegauer congratulated Lieutenant Apfelgrun, and even his orderly, on having braved so many perils in order to rejoin their regiment. Otto, who had already endeared himself to his men, resumed command of them. Matthias bought Clémence another horse. He also stripped the corpse of a *cantinière*, so that the duchess, wearing a long, greenish cloak and an oval brass plaque inscribed with the regimental number, was able to mingle unobtrusively with the women accompanying the French army. She was soon befriended by a *vivandière* of great natural nobility, a majestic woman with ruggedly handsome features and the round, darting eyes of a hen. Mère Fromageot had been practising her trade for twenty years. She had embarked on her career at the age of fifteen, for love of an army drummer who had passed through her native village in Burgundy. After Valmy she had exchanged her drummer for a trumpeter. 'I stuck to musicians – in fact all my men put together could have made up a band on their own,' she told

Clémence, laughing heartily. 'I made a point of changing instruments from time to time. The fife's not bad, but a big bass drum isn't to be sneezed at either.' At Marengo in 1800 she gained a promotion that took her out of the bandsman class, having endeared herself to a captain of lancers whom she accompanied to Alessandria and Savona, but the captain of lancers sold her to a sergeant. The sergeant, a musketry instructor nicknamed 'Skullcracker' by his men, was a fearsome type. He, in turn, exchanged Mère Fromageot for a keg of brandy. Her new protector, a quartermaster, had beaten her black and blue.

Mère Fromageot was unattached these days. The whole army knew her and respected her, so she no longer needed male protection. She could not, however, dispense with war. To function properly, her lungs required an atmosphere compounded of gunsmoke and the scent of leather and horse dung. She roamed the battlefields with her horse and cart, bringing the soldiers creature comforts – kegs of brandy, strings of sausages, biscuits, loaves, and sides of ham. Above all, she peddled good humour, encouragement, and kindliness. Thanks to a rudimentary knowledge of medicine, she also could reduce a simple fracture. She knew some prayers and would teach them to soldiers who had forgotten how. 'For use in an emergency,' she told them with a smile, ' – just in case God turns out to exist.'

Clémence appointed herself Mère Fromageot's assistant. The troopers became accustomed to seeing the ill-assorted pair, one matronly and majestic, the other young and slender, escorted by their faithful companion, Fromageot's dog, a sturdy, long-suffering little griffon whose greatest joy was to lick the faces of the wounded. The *vivandière* had acquired it some years earlier, after the battle of Arcola. The dog had been doing its customary duty that day, but the bloodstained soldier whose face it was licking took fright and stabbed it with his bayonet. Fromageot had nursed the injured beast back to health and christened it Arcola. Clémence owned no dog, she said, but her aunt had one called Herr Feldmarschall because it was half paralysed

276

and trembled even in its sleep. Herr Feldmarschall had in fact died some months before, Clémence told her new friend, almost certainly of old age. They had found it stretched out beneath her aunt's chair, trembling no longer. Fromageot decided instead that it had died of love. When Clémence saw Otto next day, she asked if he had known of Herr Feldmarschall's death. No, said Otto, he hadn't, and something about the news made him want to weep.

'But dear Aunt Gertrud goes on talking to the dog and playing with it,' Clémence continued, 'just as if it were still alive. "You see," she told me, "that's the best of being blind: you can happily mix up people and animals, the living and the dead . . ."

One night, after an engagement on the outskirts of Oliwa, the two women and Arcola made their usual tour of the battlefield. Hundreds of men lay wounded, dead or dying in a spinney of ash and birch trees. Mère Fromageot and Clémence loaded the most likely survivors on to their cart and carried them to the nearest field hospital. That done, they returned to the scene of torment, two lone women in the midst of all those ruined young bodies. The night was very dark. Ponderously, Mère Fromageot stretched out beside a French soldier who was close to death and kept begging for a light, a candle. Clèmence saw her nestle against the dying youth, bare her breasts, and rest his head between them. Arcola licked his face for a while. When he stopped, Mère Fromageot rose, buttoned her blouse, shut the dead man's eyes, made a cursory sign of the cross, and went in search of another patient. Clémence could have kissed her.

'If they want,' Mère Fromageot told her a little later, 'I let them make love to me – it makes them feel better. Sometimes they die while they're at it . . .'

Clémence spent the whole of that night in Fromageot's company. She was such a kindly, intelligent soul. Eager to be worthy of her friendship, her saintliness, Clémence herself took to making love with the wounded. Arcola would sit down alongside, whimpering softly, until it was time to move on. Clémence took a mournful pleasure in her work.

Then came the night when a band of looters attacked Mère Fromageot for the sake of her cart and provisions. She fought them off with her whip and tried to urge her horse into a gallop, but one of them cut its hamstrings and another felled Mère Fromageot with the butt of his musket. Arcola started howling. Alerted by the sound, Clémence came running up and put her arms round the dying woman. 'No more music for me,' Fromageot muttered. 'Promise you'll take care of my little Arcola . . .'

*　　*　　*

The siege of Danzig, which opened early next spring, was a long and sanguinary business. General Lefebvre, a prudent tactician who husbanded the lives of his men, deployed his forces skilfully with the aid of his chief engineer, Chasseloup, and general of artillery, Lariboisière. Danzig's fortifications, though constructed only of timber, withstood the French bombardment surprisingly well. Napoleon, who had been at Finkenstein since April 1st, grew impatient and deluged Lefebvre with irate and contradictory orders. The Saxon troops conducted themselves with great gallantry. They stormed the Kalke-Schanze redoubt, and Danzig eventually fell on May 26th. The city, its shops still overflowing with English merchandise, resembled a gigantic warehouse. Women sold wine at the city gates for next to nothing, thirty-two sous the bottle, so the victors went on the spree. Adegauer's blue hussars had earned a little relaxation. Together with Clémence, Matthias and Arcola, Otto moved into a grain merchant's store in the Street of Clocks. There were sacks of wheat and rye all over the place, some slit open, their contents pleasantly scenting the air. Clémence and Otto made love often. They couldn't help laughing at Arcola, whose fur was so thick with flour that he looked like a snow dog. Clémence's body, too, was all white and silky with flour.

'Do you know what I shall do when the war's over?' Otto asked.

'Buy me a sack of wheat and a sack of maize?'

278

'No,' said Otto, 'when the war's over I shall love you. Will you love me too?'

'I, when the war's over, shall –'

'And then,' said Otto, not waiting for her answer, 'I shall take you to the fortress of Vrenjac in the Banat – in winter-time, so that you can hear the wind howl. It's an apt name, the Military Frontier. You'll be ashamed to remember all those blank letters you sent me.'

'I couldn't do otherwise, Otto – it was my only means of telling you everything. Otherwise, I should have had to write you a letter at least two leagues long, and it would have taken me five hundred years to write it, and you would never have received it . . .'

Colonel Adegauer entrusted Otto with a dispatch for headquarters at Osterode. Otto duly set off with Matthias, Clémence and the dog, but they found the Osterode cantonments deserted. Compelled to turn north by the bloody battle of Friedland, which took place on 14 June 1807, they entered Königsberg only two days after its capture by French troops under Marshal Soult. There they obtained rooms at a tolerably clean inn overlooking the cattle market. Savary had been appointed governor of Königsberg and the territory of Old Prussia, and lurking in Savary's shadow, as ever, was Schulmeister, alias Monsieur Charles, whose police instituted a reign of terror. The French being even more obsessed than usual with a fear of spies, the three newcomers were interrogated by a squad of policemen only one day after their arrival. They gave an account of their adventures, but the man in charge was unconvinced. He threw Otto and Matthias into jail and packed Clémence off to a hospice in Magisterstrasse on the right bank of the Pregel, an institution strictly administered by Visitandine nuns. He added that Lieutenant Apfelgrun would have to say his piece next day to 'Captain' Charles himself.

The former commissioner of the Viennese police received Otto in the burgomaster's office at the town hall. Sartorially he had made progress – his fine grey pleated frock coat sported black revers, his waistcoat was embroidered with flowers – but his hair was as carroty as ever. He pronounced himself delighted to see the lieutenant again and recalled the 'Hope Crowned' meeting at the sheepcote in the Vienna Woods. He also inquired after Duchess Gertrud and Otto's father, Lawyer Apfelgrun, whose acquaintance it had been his pleasure to make.

'Your father gave vent to some extremely profound observations on the subject of goose quills and their role in the civilizing process. But to revert to the sheepcote in the Vienna Woods. You came within an inch of death that night.' Monsieur Charles, who clearly relished this thought, patted his paunch and poured himself a glass of brandy. Then, as if he found his mayoral chair too formal for the occasion, he came and sat down on the hard bench beside Otto.

'Yes,' he pursued, slapping Otto's knee with a plump, benevolent hand, 'your life certainly trembled in the balance for a moment or two that night . . . but I rejoice that my leniency has enabled us to meet again under these singular circumstances. We're all the playthings of fate, are we not? You realize, of course, that ideology didn't enter into my calculations. For one thing, it was in your favour that you were a mere stripling. For another, I knew that you'd been imprisoned for stating that Austria boasted not only a two-headed eagle, but two-headed sheep, mice, fleas, and who knows what else besides.'

He guffawed at the recollection. Producing a watch from his fob pocket, he consulted it as though noting the time of his laugh, then poured himself another brandy. His tone became still friendlier.

'Professor Schwarzbrod had vouched for your loyalty to the revolutionary cause, and Schwarzbrod, I can now reveal, is one of us.'

Otto's jaw dropped.

'My dear Apfelgrun, were you really unaware that your worthy professor was a Jacobin? You were at Baden, I seem to recall. Very well, I'll tell you a surprising thing: Schwarzbrod was also at Baden – indeed, he got there on the eve of the battle in which you so "heroically" took part.'

'That's no news to me, Monsieur Schulmeister,'

Otto said calmly. 'I spent two hours with him in the Kurplatz.'

'My name isn't Schulmeister,' snapped his red-haired companion, 'it's Charles – *Captain* Charles. I hold a captaincy in the French army. I also command the military police in Königsberg and Old Prussia. That gives me very, very far-reaching powers. But to revert to our naturalist. What did he tell you at Baden?'

'Nothing of note. His presence there was completely fortuitous. Baden was one of his hunting grounds. He was looking for a specimen of the Typhoeus, a beetle he'd been after for forty years. Besides, it can't have escaped you that the professor is a very shy, absent-minded man.'

'Schwarzbrod shy? Absent-minded?'

Monsieur Charles burst out laughing. Could anyone conceive of a more artful front for an agent than that of a scatterbrained scholar with his butterfly nets and herbals, his diffident manner and exaggerated timidity? The policeman rose and walked to a window. Lifting a corner of the silk curtain, he looked down at the lawns in front of the town hall.

'Listen, Apfelgrun, I'm going to let you into a secret: Schwarzbrod is my equal in power and influence. I didn't even know that he was working for us. That surprises you, doesn't it? I ran into him by chance at Baden, where I myself happened to be at the time – on what business, you can guess – and I took him for a very retiring, rather eccentric scholar. Yes, it's true: I accepted him at face value. And there's more. Even when Schwarzbrod called on me to plead your cause – you know, in connection with Gravitsky's caricature – he didn't show his hand even then. The fact is, our friend was acting on orders from the very top, possibly from Savary himself. As for his shyness – my God, it's just a masquerade, a façade!' Monsieur Charles resumed his place behind the desk. He had a truly enormous neck, but there was something endearing about his face.

'I was about to say that I hadn't the least suspicion in regard to yourself. No, my friend, but shall I be completely frank? "*Cherchez la femme*," as we say in France. It was Christine Kinsky who introduced you to the "Hope Crowned" circle, don't forget, and Christine, as everyone now knows, was my mistress. She spoke of you to me after your visit to Duchess Gertrud – indeed, she spoke of you altogether too much. Oh, nothing suspicious! She said nothing compromising or objectionable about you, Apfelgrun, but that was just the trouble. What could have been more distressing and humiliating than to hear a woman with whom I was infatuated speak enthusiastically of a young man, and especially of a handsome young man renowned for his success with the fair sex? One has one's pride, after all! So you see, isn't it ironical, even after that night at the sheepcote, that fate should have led you here and placed you in my hands again, like a captive bird?'

Smiling, he flexed his pudgy fingers.

'I'm no great believer in the Almighty, Apfelgrun – I'm not even sure I believe in the Devil – but I do believe in coincidences, and of those there have been plenty. That's why it didn't surprise me to learn that two of Adegauer's blue hussars had turned up in Königsberg, claiming to have lost their way, when the truth was that they had expected to find the place occupied by Prussians, not French. That's desertion – no, worse than desertion: an attempt to quit the Grande Armée and rejoin the Austrians, who will soon be at war with us again.'

'Captain,' Otto said staunchily, 'I did not desert. I was aware that Soult had taken the town.'

'What of it? Your assertions are a matter of complete indifference to me. It isn't what *you* say that counts; it's what *I* say, and *I* say you're a deserter. I sympathize, mark you. In your place I'd have done the same. You're an Austrian, after all, not a Saxon, and that puts you in the Allied camp. I also know that your transfer to the Saxon hussars stemmed from a desire for revenge on the part of Prince Ernst of Saxe-Salza, whose wife, the delectable Duchess Clémence, is your mistress. A man gets to know things in the military police . . . That forges yet another bond between us, Apfelgrun: our mistresses are cousins.

We certainly have our trials and tribulations with women, don't we? You more than I, if the truth be told, because what with Christine and the duchess, you have two Mahlbergs to contend with, which is no laughing matter – or three, counting old Duchess Gertrud . . .'

'Monsieur,' Otto protested, 'I haven't set eyes on Christine Kinsky since that night at the sheepcote. If you won't accept my word as an officer, ask Fräulein Kinsky herself or consult your agents. They know everything – they'll tell you.'

The police chief sat back with an air of relief. His tone became more mellifluous still.

'I know perfectly well that you've never seen my mistress again, Apfelgrun. You think that exonerates you? You think that puts you out of danger? I find it surprising, nay, deplorable, that a man of your sensibility and discernment should be so obtuse. There's a flaw in your defence, you see. You aren't the person at issue here. That person is Christine Kinsky, who's romantic by nature like all the Mahlberg womenfolk. You disagree? You disclaim all responsibility, is that it? What a paltry, unimaginative argument! No, not only paltry but unscrupulous as well, because it seeks to lay the blame elsewhere, to wit, on my unhappy Christine, and that I rather resent. If I understand you aright, a woman should be censured for losing her heart? How unfair! Is it her fault she's in love? Love is a sufficient torment in itself. Must she be castigated as well? How contemptible of you, Lieutenant, and how discreditable!' The voice, though still urbane, had become fraught with menace and malice.

'As for you, you're not in the least enamoured of Christine, so you've no excuse – no extenuating circumstance, as we say in my profession. Your argument won't hold water. The responsibility is yours alone. Look at the matter from another angle. If you did not exist, Apfelgrun, would I be fretting now? Would I gaze at my mistress's face, night after night, trying to guess the nature of her dreams? The case against you is irrefutable! And don't go telling me that you don't exist – that you aren't a tall, rather wistful young man with an irresistible attraction for women, especially Mahl-berg women . . .

'I appeal to your better nature, Apfelgrun. Admit your guilt – admit that you haven't the least excuse, my friend, and your confession will be taken into account. You're far more responsible than if you'd loved Christine or actually courted her. In that case we'd have been dealing with a trivial, uninteresting little affair of the heart, a "psycho-logical drama", as they say in Vienna, a sentimental anec-dote for the Margots and Gretchens of this world to weep over in their cottages, a banal escapade – a "chambermaid's romance", as the French call it. But no, "psychology" has no bearing on this imbroglio. We're in far more hazardous waters . . .'

The policeman rose and circled Otto once before return-ing to his desk and ringing for an orderly. Lieutenant Apfelgrun, he said, was to be escorted to the gates of the town hall and handed over to the patrol that would take him back to prison.

*　　*　　*

Clémence was treated with the utmost consideration. Lodged in the dortour of the Visitandines, one of whom was detailed to guard her, she had been issued with a plain but spotless grey habit and a black headscarf. She was also allowed to keep Arcola. Being devout, she gladly joined the nuns at matins, vespers and Mass. She prayed with fervour and humility. Her conscience was clear. Separation from her lover scarcely troubled her, so absolute was her faith. Neither war nor policemen nor princes could lastingly deprive her of Otto. The Almighty himself would break his teeth on their union if he sought to destroy it. As for the Devil, just let him dare to show his evil face! Debased, degraded and sullied she might be, but she had never known such glory. Worldly dishonour only enhanced her love.

As she was returning from Mass with downcast eyes one day, engrossed in the worship of Jesus Christ, an orderly

284

officer handed her a letter from Christine. The sight of it roused her from her torpor. She ran upstairs to her cell and broke the seal. The letter was a long one.

'Dear Cousin,' she read, 'this letter will distress you, I fear. When we were girls together at Lürwath Castle, we shared all our joys. You would begin a piece of embroidery, I would complete it. Our teachers could never tell which of us had painted a particular watercolour. We sang the same songs. I was as fond of your little donkey, Green-Ears, as I was of my own poor Straw-Tail. As for the prayers we offered up in chapel, the Blessed Virgin herself could not have told whether they emanated from your soul or mine. Our nickname was "the Double-Eagle", do you remember?

'Today we are united once more, this time by a common affliction, and I doubt if the powers above will be able to determine whether I am acting on your behalf or you are framing my decisions for me. M. Charles, who functions as my lover (to use the phrase we customarily employed when telling each other of our romantic little interludes), has decided to release you forthwith. One of his subordinates will furnish you with the necessary safe-conducts. You will be conveyed by carriage to Vienna, where you will be safe, since Austria is not – or not for the moment – at war with France. You will have to travel the smouldering length of Germany, infested though it is with soldiers and brigands. I shall pray to St Anne that all perils and hardships be spared you.

'Otto will remain in the hands of the military police. M. Charles is convinced, or pretends to be convinced, that he planned to desert the Grande Armée and rejoin the Austrian forces. I have made no attempt to disabuse him, as you can guess. You must know how fiercely I yearn to part you from Otto Apfelgrun, Clémence, because it has always been our misfortune to love each other well enough to love the same things. Although my wish to separate you has now been granted, I have gained but little. I owe my success to pure chance, rather than to an Apfelgrun change of heart.

'You will return to your residence at the Carinthian Gate,

where Prince Ernst will welcome you with open arms. You will resume the life you led before you met Otto: a serene, luxurious, respectable existence spiced with the occasional amour. The informers whom M. Charles maintains in Vienna will advise us of your smallest deviation from that way of life. You will, I think, approve of these precautions. You used to say that we were she-wolves when it came to fulfilling our desires. And besides, didn't you yourself choose to dishonour your name and prostitute yourself, forget your dignity and shamelessly humiliate your husband in order to assuage your passion? Not, of course, that I blame you. I am just as well acquainted with the cruelty of desire, the torment and ecstasy of self-abasement.

'Otto will remain here, in the clutches of M. Charles, as a hostage. What does that signify, Cousin? It signifies that should your conduct in Vienna be imprudent, or should you flee from the Kärntnertor or Greinburg, or should Otto attempt to escape, the French military police will be given a free hand with him. I would not wish M. Charles to be driven to extremes, but we are all mere cogs in a divine machine whose workings defy our comprehension.

'You know that I have always been a realist, as this letter bears witness. Self-delusion is not my forte. By this I mean that you leave me devoid of consolation. If I were to enjoy your lover's body, it could only be by dint of subterfuge, by sneaking into his darkened cell and passing myself off as you in the same manner as Fräulein von Wörth has been concealing your depravity at Greinburg by dressing herself up in your finery. But would it give me pleasure? I strongly doubt it, even if I do believe that each of us is merely the impersonator – the deputy or lieutenant – of one or more of our fellow creatures. We shall see. But the problem goes even deeper. Whatever I do, I cannot undo the feelings you entertain for your lover. Worse still, I can only intensify them. Absence will inflame your passion for Otto, not diminish it, just as Otto himself will only love you the more. I was there when they transferred you to your present quarters. I watched you, hidden among my friends the Visitandine nuns. You have never looked more beautiful,

Clémence. I am envious of your fate, covetous of your misfortune.

'Passion is a great affliction, yes, but what joy it also bestows! It checks one's descent into limbo. I acknowledge that Otto will never be mine, and that his dreams will always be of you. Even were I to deceive him by my outward appearance, I should never change his dreams or haunt his nights. My sole reward in adopting such a strategem would be to enact your role and feel as close to you as possible. If you find my language extravagant, remember that my head, like yours, has always been filled with romantic notions. Your predicament, though distressing, is none the less agreeable: you are to be deprived of your lover, but he has dedicated his life to your body. My own predicament is hopeless. Only in that sense, and if it be true that passion dies of its own consummation, do I hold a few cards that you lack. But if it is indeed so, you must concede that your exile to Vienna, so far from your beloved, will preserve you from the perils of consummation. So here we are, Cousin, alike once more. I breathe through your lips; you speak through mine. I shall never have Otto except by way of deceit and imposture. You will not have him either, yet it is you that possess him.'

Clémence refolded the letter, trembling all over. She stared at the progression of upstrokes and downstrokes in violet ink, the disjointed phrases. Their meaning eluded her. Reason had deserted Christine, but no more so than it had deserted herself when she had made love to the wounded with poor Mère Fromageot. She threw herself down at the foot of her iron bedstead, prostrated herself before the crucifix on the cell wall, immersed herself in prayer, implored help and absolution, and ended by fainting clean away.

*   *   *

She set off next morning with the two Saxon troopers whom Monsieur Charles had detailed to escort her to Austria. The drive through Germany was beautiful. The fields were green again, and although some towns still displayed the stigmata of war – Jena, for instance, which Clémence traversed at a hasty gallop – traces of carnage had all but disappeared from the countryside. Crosses erected here and there – in field and forest, at the roadside, near rivers and, more especially, bridges – afforded the sole reminder that these mellow landscapes, these green and yellow hills, these poppies and periwinkles, were steeped in blood. Clémence rode the big black berlin in a dream, not knowing what she did or where she was. Her dreamlike state persisted even when some Prussian deserters attempted to ambush the carriage, though Arcola was beside himself and barked furiously. After being delayed at Regensburg for two days by stormy weather, they made their uneventful way through the sunlit hills flanking the Danube. At Passau the Saxon troopers headed back to Königsberg, as instructed, and Clémence boarded the Vienna mail coach. She broke her journey at Linz, wanting to see the Nibelungen Bridge of which Otto had spoken. She even dined at the Rose Princess and thought she recognized by her pretty face and chapped red hands the maid who had served Otto and Ulrich. Arcola was so much at ease that he might have been returning to familiar haunts. Clémence decided to call a halt at Greinburg instead of travelling straight on to Vienna. It would make her return to the Kärntnertor seem more natural if she rested awhile and put her wardrobe in order.

Even when seen by the light of the midday sun, the figure that greeted her on the steps of Greinburg Castle might have been her double. Alma von Wörth had played her part to perfection. Her muslin gown was adorned with colourful embroidery and Clémence's jewels, and she wore her fair hair low on her neck, just as Clémence herself was wont to do when residing in the country. Having welcomed her mistress with exclamations of surprise and much excited talk, she hurried upstairs to help Clémence unpack and move her own things out of the apartment she had occupied for the past nine months. After so long an absence, Clémence was eager for news of Vienna. Alma told her that Duchess Gertrud was quite her old self again. She no longer received Father Thaler, who had put on weight, but General von Weitzau still paid her regular visits. Professor Schwarzbrod, overcome with grief, was mourning the death of his beloved daughter, Marie-Josèphe. Lieutenant Feuchtagen had died of his wounds in Vienna's military hospital.

'And Countess Pietranera?' asked Clémence.

Alma burst out laughing. Countess Pietranera was still pursuing her biological studies but running short of suitable material for research. If the capital's more malicious tongues were to be believed, she had even been reduced to using the same lover twice.

Clémence, carried away by her own recollections, described the vicissitudes of the Prussian campaign. Alma listened enviously. To her, there was something sublime about her mistress's improprieties, her descent into destitution, the hardships and indignities she had endured at the side of the man she loved, the consolations she and Mère Fromageot had dispensed to the dying. Clémence spoke of the letter she had received from her cousin Christine Kinsky. 'I thought I should die at first, but my self-pride and anger have left me. All I feel for her now is compassion. Trusting as I do that God understands me, I pray and prostrate myself – I submit myself to his will. I cannot believe that he would strike down a woman as forlorn as I. At all events, I'm resigned. God will decide my fate, and I shall bow to his wishes. That's why, although my heart is filled with sorrow, I remain tranquil, and my memories of the past are so vivid that they seem to belong to the future.'

Clémence inquired if Prince Ernst had dispelled the suspicions of Viennese society by visiting Greinburg as agreed. Yes, Alma told her, the prince had kept his part of the bargain. What was more, she continued in a playful tone, she had quite enjoyed his company. He usually made a point of arriving at about five in the afternoon, so that the local villagers would notice his barouche driving up the road through the mulberry trees. In the evening she would dine alone with him – not like a mistress, she hastened to add, but in a wifely manner calculated to deceive the servants. These meals were enjoyable occasions. The prince, being a man of charm and refinement, had treated her with consideration. He brought her the latest news from the Hofburg, from Schönbrunn and the drawing-rooms of the capital. She hadn't always followed his words at first, because he addressed her as he would have addressed his wife and alluded to persons and events unknown to her. For example? Well, it had taken her quite a while to accept that Professor Schwarzbrod, with his retiring manner and puckish sense of humour, was really one of the most formidable agents employed by the imperial and royal police.

'Schwarzbrod?' Clémence exclaimed. 'What on earth do you mean? I've known the man for years. He's a scholar, a dreamer – he couldn't care less about politics. All he thinks of are his butterflies.'

'You're mistaken, Excellency. Schwarzbrod is His Majesty's agent-in-chief. Prince Ernst himself was dumbfounded when told so at the Hofburg. Did you know, for example, that Schwarzbrod was at Baden on the day of that famous battle, when the armistice was signed at Leoben?'

Clémence found the whole idea absurd.

'Of course I knew, Alma. He often goes to Baden, but only in search of specimens for his collection. In any case, my girl, how could you possibly think my old friend a policeman or a spy? He's the timidest man alive.'

Now it was Alma's turn to chuckle.

'Timid? Not according to the Hofburg. His timidity is a disguise. The professor is a resolute, redoubtable character. He has hidden behind his timidity for years, much as another might wear a false beard. Prince Ernst is convinced of it, believe me.'

'Well, well,' said Clémence, 'so the professor isn't what he seems. There are two Schwarzbrods, you mean?'

'Precisely, and this will make you laugh: he's referred to at the Hofburg by a pseudonym. They call him the Two-Headed Eagle!'

Clémence did not pursue the subject. She disliked the thought that her old friend should have deceived her for so long – and anyway, it could well be just another rumour. She plied Alma with questions. How had Prince Ernst behaved toward her? After dinner, said Alma, she and the prince would play a game or two of patience in the drawing-room. The prince would then spend some time in the smoking-room, perusing the gazettes, while she plied her needle in an attempt to finish off the large piece of embroidery – Mercury and Sosia in Hades – on which Clémence had embarked not long before the Prussian campaign. It was now on the verge of completion. 'And never fear, Excellency: no one would ever know that Mercury is your handiwork and Sosia mine. We have the same touch.' The prince and Alma would then retire to their apartments.

'It was all very disturbing, Excellency. I felt quite mad – emptied of myself and inhabited by another. The prince was so natural and unconstrained, I thought at first that he genuinely mistook me for you. My head was in a whirl. I didn't know who I was, Alma von Wörth or Clémence of Saxe-Salza, especially when . . .' Alma hesitated.

'Well?'

'When we made love.'

'You made love?'

'Yes, but in the strangest manner. We did so without passion, with great tenderness and restraint, more like husband and wife than lover and mistress. It only came to me that I wasn't you, or at least that the prince knew it and was simply carrying out the prearranged plan, when he asked me to moan with pleasure in a certain way . . .'

'I see. So you're familiar with all my . . . my little quirks, Alma.' Clémence smiled wryly. '*Vade retro, Satana,*' she mimicked, 'as Father Thaler would say.'

'Do you know what Schwarzbrod told Prince Ernst, Excellency? It seems there's a sinister old naturalist in the depths of Moravia who performs grafts on plants and trees – grafts designed to engender freakish new species. Well, the old man employs young virgins to do the work, but only after sodomizing them. Can that be true, do you think, or is

291

it just another of Schwarzbrod's jokes? According to him, it's a method prescribed by the alchemists of old. He says it comes from the *De natura rerum* of Paracelsus.'

'Otto told me that too. It doesn't surprise me unduly,' Clémence replied with a girlish laugh. 'Paracelsus certainly gives a formula for creating a mannikin out of spermatic fluid, as he puts it. What does seem true to me is that clearly, if men seek to redesign Nature – in other words, to usurp the place of God – they require the Devil's assistance. That, of course, presupposes that the God of our churches isn't "the Lord of the Flies", as Otto says, meaning the Devil disguised as God. If he is, all your old naturalist's tactics are in vain.'

But Alma had fallen into a reverie. 'It was just like the love between man and wife,' she mused. 'I felt quite carried away. They gave me so much pleasure, those nights . . .'

Clémence betrayed no surprise or resentment. She went on to say a number of things the meaning of which was largely lost on Alma. She claimed, among other matters, that this infection of one destiny by another – these exchanges of roles, these delegations of power, or love or hatred, these substitutions and 'proxifications', these dispossessions of one person's soul by that of another or by those of all others, no matter whose – impressed her as being the only proper remedy for the incurable loneliness of the human condition.

*　　*　　*

The Prince of Saxe-Salza accorded his wife a dignified welcome. He rejoiced that she had chosen to return to the capital after her long seclusion at Greinburg Castle. Clémence resumed her place in the Kärntnertor mansion as if time had suffered a fainting fit; as if nine whole months had fallen through a trapdoor or faded away like a mirage; as if no break had ever occurred, and she had been content to spend nine months in the country, visited weekly by her husband and devoting night after night to conjuring up the figures of Mercury and Sosia in Hades on her embroidery frame. And now, in their big, sleepy house near the Carinthian Gate, she completed gestures initiated nine months before: gestures suspended like the hands of a woman eternally combing her hair in a painting.

22

The Saxe-Salzas continued to entertain as before. Duchess
Gertrud, the Prince of Liechtenstein, Archbishop Hohen-
wart, Field-Marshall Karl von Steiniger, General Mayer
von Heldensfeld, the Silesian publicist Friedrich von
Gentz, the officers of the imperial court, Mme de Staël
herself – all the gilded, bloated, affected luminaries of
Viennese society, preceded by Hungarian attendants armed
with long silver canes – converged on the Carinthian Gate at
each change of season.

Little Dr Ulhue, who had taken only a few years to scale
the loftiest rungs of the social ladder, his simian agility
unimpaired by frequent attacks of gout, was vigorous in his
exploitation of historical themes. Several of his metaphors
and similes went down well in the Saxe-Salzas' circle. 'I
would liken the French Revolution and Napoleon to a St
Vitus's dance,' he declared, rearranging the furrows in his
prodigious, pallid brow. 'That's to say, a disorderly and
convulsive form of activity. How different from our monarchies! Austria dances the minuet, and the minuet is more
than just a terpsichorean legacy from the distant past. Being
a methodical dance, the steps of which recur with unfailing
regularity . . .' He shut his eyes, drew a deep breath, and
stressed each sonorous syllable. '. . . they recur, as though
inexorably obliterating the steps that precede them – as
though ceaselessly destroying their own destruction. It's
the Uroboros, the self-consuming serpent, all over
again . . .'

The Kärntnertor courtiers were the same as ever. One or
two defunct faces had been replaced as the seasons went by,
but the newcomers aped their vanished predecessors. They
seemed to loom up out of the depths of a mirror, cheeks
identically daubed with the cosmetics of death, formal
attire laden with the same medals, pectoral crosses, jewels.
Schwarzbrod, who frequented Vienna's drawing-rooms to

dull the pain of his bereavement, claimed that the Kärntnertor balls had taken advantage of Napoleon's antics in
Prussia to retrogress a few decades. In support of this
theory he cited the fact that Professor Ptask had had very
broad old-fashioned pockets sewn on his puce frock coat,
and that he had exchanged the daffodil-yellow plume in his
tricorn for a decidedly démodé aigrette of cloth. More-
over, he had for some months been wearing his hair clubbed. Dr Ulhue waxed enthusiastic about this archaism.
'Professor Ptask is right to describe Austria as the alpha and
omega of history,' he trumpeted. 'Excellently put, my dear
colleague, but will you permit me to complete your apoph-
thegm? The Habsburg dynasty, I would submit, is the
negation of that frivolity which the French and a certain
university lecturer at Jena – I refer to Friedrich Hegel – are
foolish enough to term history!' Poor Ptask was overwhelmed, never having dreamt that his clubbed hair would
attract such commendation. He took a pinch of snuff and
sneezed convulsively.

Schwarzbrod, who had been enjoying all this, murmured
into Duchess Gertrud's avid ear. 'Our worthy friend Ulhue
perfectly exemplifies his own philosophy of immutability.
He has talked the same balderdash ever since I've known
him.' Gertrud groped for the professor's shaggy head,
pulled it close to her lips, and offered a barbed remark of
her own. 'For my part, I consider Countess Pietranera an
even better illustration. Her behaviour never varies: she
removes her shift and resumes it *ad infinitum*.' Gertrud
cackled exultantly. 'And do you know what she gets up to in
all those beds? She plays the Uroboros!'

Austria had, for all that, undergone some innovations.
Archduke Charles of Lorraine-Habsburg, that competent,
phlegmatic and courageous man, was in charge of Affairs.
Count Johann Philipp von Stadion, who occupied the
Chancellery, was steadily arming the country for its future
trial of strength. Klemens Lothar, Count von Metternich,
Austria's envoy to France, was the darling of the Parisian
salons. Lover in turn of Caroline de Murat and Mme Junot,
he enjoyed the ear of Talleyrand. 'Tut, tut,' sighed Father

Thaler, who was going grey but had finally established himself as a regular visitor to the Kärntnertor, 'Herr von Metternich may well enjoy Talleyrand's ear, but the "Arch-Chancellor" possesses so many of them! I'm reliably informed that he sleeps wearing fourteen nightcaps. That makes twenty-eight ears in all . . .' The Prince of Saxe-Salza claimed that Metternich was none the less in favour of war, though without sabre-rattling. 'Are you absolutely positive?' queried Thaler, smacking his lips with a sound like a cupping-glass.

Prince Ernst was a *perpetuum immobile* as regular as the solstices and equinoxes. His handsome, fresh-complexioned face ('fresh as a soft-boiled egg,' to quote a jibe coined by Duchess Gertrud, who had always believed him a ninny and had loathed him ever since her niece fell in love with Otto Apfelgrun), his pink, powdered cheeks, his unfailing urbanity, the cryptic humour with which he leavened his gravitas, his bald pate – everything about the man was constant. Having debated whether to pardon his wife's depravity or rebuke her for it, he chose silence instead. It was a devilish device. Its intention was that, racked with remorse, Clémence would suffer, eat her heart out with shame, waste away.

The prince's calculations were only half correct. Clémence was transfixed with remorse, true, but she also derived great solace from it. Remorse became her accomplice, her secret source of ecstasy. She gloated over it and gorged herself on it, gulping it down in enormous quantities. If ever some distraction should dull her regrets, she swiftly whipped them back into life again, like a child whipping a top to hear it hum. Anything that recalled her infatuation and dishonour she considered a boon. Shame enabled her to relive the nights she had spent beside Otto's naked body. Far from wasting away with repentance, Clémence blossomed. She devoted herself to her grief, and her grief was blissful.

Her mood fluctuated. She could be silent and dejected or radiant, eager and imperious. Some weeks she spent in a kind of waking dream. This was when the running of the

enormous mansion claimed her attention. White and purple tablecloths and percale napkins were embroidered at
her behest with the Saxe-Salza cipher. The kitchen staff
made jams and preserves, and Clémence took a childish
pleasure in watching her stewardess arrange the pots on the
pantry shelves. What chiefly delighted her was the contrast
between the pointless tedium of her days and the tumult in
her breast. Her women made soap and stored it in a massive
cupboard, each shelf of which bore a label recording the
vast number of cakes already in stock. Clémence had
provisions enough to last for several years. She surveyed
them, ruefully shaking her head. So many years' supply of
soap, when the flames of hell might engulf her at any
moment . . .

She also spent melancholy hours at her desk, covering
octavo sheets with effusions in mauve ink and putting them
away in a chest of drawers between the folds of the white
satin gown she had worn at the Windiswraths'. 'I'm like a
girl on her wedding eve,' she used to tell herself, ' – all tears
and sighs and swoons . . .' She caressed a locket of her
lover's fair hair. 'Except that this girl is Otto Apfelgrun's
whore.' In the evenings she contrived to develop a touch of
fever. The blood throbbed in her temples, and she would
drink decoctions to cool her burning cheeks. Clémence
relished being inconsolable. She made up salves from re-
cipes taught her by her nurse: one part milk, one of
whipped goat's cream, one egg, one part crushed wheat,
plus some finely chopped watercress or more milk boiled
with a drop of lemon juice added. *The Sorrows of Young
Werther* reposed permanently on her bedside table. She
pictured willow-shaded meadows, wild woods haunted by
her lover.

Arcola seldom left her side. Alma found the limping
creature unattractive, but Clémence insisted that Arcola
was the handsomest griffon ever to grace the Carinthian
Gate.

'If you dream of a rose,' she said, 'and if, on waking in the
morning, you see a rose beside you on the pillow . . .'

'Good little Arcola,' said Alma, feigning approval.

'You're a rose, no less. Duchess Clémence had a dream. She dreamt she went to Danzig and met a fat woman who sold brandy and fell in love with a young man and took care of a poor, ownerless griffon, but in the morning the griffon was there beside her on the pillow, which meant that it wasn't a dream at all . . .'

'Quite so, Alma,' Clémence said gravely. 'That's why Arcola must never die.'

In the mornings, after drinking a big bowl of hot milk, Clémence would submit to her companion's ministrations. Alma brushed and braided her generous golden mane, then laced her into her corselet. The two young women were inseparable; they exchanged confidences, compared emotions, shared fits of giggles like a pair of schoolgirls. Clémence found fulfilment in Alma's company. It amused her that amorous sighs, languors, vapours, and the embroidering of ribbons with a lover's initials should at the same time disguise and divulge the ferment in her breast.

In warm weather they would go for leisurely strolls in the Viennese parks or make excursions into the country. But Clémence never revisited Schleiblingstein Forest. The thickets of firs and junipers, the charcoal-burner's dingy cottage in its mantle of snow, the hooting of owls and the scampering squirrels – with her lover gone, the Garden of Eden was a paradise lost. In winter she seldom left the Kärntnertor mansion except for divine service, which she attended regularly. She used to meditate in the side chapels of St Stephan's, looking like a young, fair-haired widow with her bowed head and black veil. Alma often saw tears of joy on her beautiful, ecstatic face. Clémence felt as if her body were on fire. She could have stretched out on the flagstones, arms in the cruciform position, hair dishevelled and breasts bared, and allowed the Lord Jesus Christ, lover of virtue and of suffering womankind, to trample her underfoot. At night she used to read Alma passages from St John of the Cross, St Angela of Foligno, or St Theresa of Avila.

'St Theresa,' she said, 'gives a better description of the pangs of desire than Messrs Schiller or Rousseau. Listen to

298

this, Alma: "Once in the throes of this torment, she would fain have endured it for the rest of her life." '

Alma was puzzled. It surprised her, she said, that the duchess could be so cheerful in the absence of her paramour.

'But that's just it,' Clémence told her, greedily sipping herb tea. 'I'm bewitched, my dear, by which I mean that I'm under the effect of some charm or philtre. I think I must have swallowed a goodly dose. I'm devoid of volition and almost bereft of desire. I *have* no desire, I *am* desire – yes, that's it: I and my joy are chained together. My dreams have become entwined with reality. This house, and Greinburg, and the Prater, and my carriages, and the grey horse I'm so fond of, and the cats in the pantries, and even you, my dear girl, and even I myself – all are inscribed in the ink of dreams. I'm neither in this world nor of it . . .'

Clémence smiled at her own folly. Alma, for her part, was alarmed. Her mistress's eyes were wide and staring like those of a madwoman. She delivered long speeches in a serene tone of voice, but the words meant nothing. She said she envied the Holy Women whose upturned faces glowed palely in the dim recesses of St Stephan's. She would gladly have kissed their emaciated, bloodless cheeks, their dead lips, their pallid, seemingly decaying eyelids, the sweat and blood of Christ's agony. She addressed litanies to God above.

'I don't see the passing days,' said Clémence. 'They flash past me like a cavalry charge, but a silent one. The horses gallop on yielding turf. Their hoofs make no sound – they're weightless and insubstantial. Lieutenant Apfelgrun will be restored to me by divine decree. See, here he comes in the leaf-green light of the birch and beech trees, wounded and melancholy. Where will our reunion take place? That's a secret, my girl, but let it be in heaven or hell, Dresden or Vienna, provided I can kiss him once more. And even if our nuptials are the nuptials of death . . .'

She ran to her desk and opened a slim volume of Novalis, her fingers trembling as they turned to the page she sought. 'A union formed with death in mind is a wedding that affords us a companion for the night. It is in death that love tastes sweetest. To lovers, death is a wedding night, the arcanum of a sweet mystery.'

Alma gave her an apprehensive look.

'No, Alma, I've no desire to die. It's simply that, in the realm I now inhabit, the distinction between life and death becomes blurred . . .'

'But Excellency – '

'I know, my dear Alma. You think me fanciful – you think me deranged, don't you?'

'Excellency – '

'Deranged or not, Alma, I know that somewhere in this world there exists an unknown place, and that there the celebration of our marriage is being prepared. What place is it? Ah no, Alma, that I have no wish to know. My one certainty is that the whole world is beautiful – every forest, every village, every mountain of it – because the smallest grove of cedars, the tiniest stream, may have been set aside for our reunion.'

*   *   *

Austria huffed and puffed. Whether in coffee-house or tavern or in the antechambers of the Hofburg, Spain was on everyone's lips. The Invincible was finding Iberia a hard nut to crack. Junot's grenadiers had burnt their fingers on the monks of Salamanca and Burgos; the giants of Austerlitz were being felled by the women of Castile. 'Isn't it providential,' whispered Father Thaler, 'that Christ and Our Lady, after weighing matters up, have finally reached a decision – a decision which I flatter myself I always foretold. Spain and Austria being the twin bastions of the Counter-Reformation, they were destined to lay the Antichrist low.' On 20 July 1808, even as Joseph Bonaparte entered Madrid in state under the eyes of its acquiescent officials and sorrowing citizens, General Dupont was encircled at Bailén, near Seville, and forced to surrender. 'General Dupont, the hero of Friedland, encircled,' said Ulhue, ' – encircled like a common or garden Mack at Ulm.'

Somewhat lamely, he essayed a play upon words in French. 'Dupont has been well and truly *"macké"*!'

Joseph, so recently named King of Spain by his imperial brother, had now withdrawn to the Ebro. Despite Pitt's death two years earlier, Britain sent men as well as money. Wellesley landed in Portugal with a force of fourteen thousand. In Vienna the war party snorted and pawed the ground. Empress Maria Ludovica, Francis's second wife, together with the Archdukes Maximilian and Ferdinand and Baron Stein, were triumphing over the advocates of entente, in other words, the friends of Archduke Charles. Gentz, the Silesian publicist, proclaimed that the trumpet of history was sounding the preliminary triads of reconquest.

Baron Joseph von Hormayr led the crusade. It spoke volumes that he, the most intrepid firebrand in Vienna, was Director of the State Archives and, as such, a man devoted to the past. Europe's intellectuals, having popped up and down so often since the fall of the Bastille, raised their heads once more. Germaine de Staël hurled prophecies and imprecations at the Corsican impostor. She found it deeply affecting to see hinds and stags graze peacefully in the Prater when Napoleon and the Great Elector of Saxony had jointly engaged in a loathsome massacre of deer at Dresden. 'Any gnat that took the air except by Napoleon's command,' Ulhue told her, 'would be a rebellious insect indeed. The tyrant crushes not only men but God's little creatures and the flowers of the Blessed Virgin.' At this the brothers Schlegel, lately arrived from Germany, roared fiercely in concert.

Clémence received news of her lover. Christine Kinsky wrote that Otto was no longer imprisoned at Königsberg. His acquaintance with various other jails had been dictated by the movements of the French army. After spending some time at Erfurt and Frankfurt, he was now in Dresden. Christine's letters struck a frantic note.

'Rest assured, my dear Cousin, that no woman was ever loved as you are loved. I offer up prayers to God in your name, and they take the form of benedictions. More devout than ever, I express my gratitude to Him and dedicate my days to praising heaven. God is moved by the intensity of my prayers, I feel sure, and I thank Him constantly. Need I complete this picture by portraying my own sorrows? There is no end, no limit to my wretchedness.

'I should be well advised to stop loving Herr Apfelgrun, of that there's no doubt, for although he treats me with consideration his heart belongs to you. The nights are long. I tell myself that he is more than just your quarry, your prey. To him you are the sun, the millennia, the future – all the gods and angels put together. What luxury, Cousin! What woman would not covet such riches? Compared to such a treasure, the diamonds of Golconda and the palaces of Babylon are but squalor.

'Yes, the most logical course would be to distance myself from a love that is draining my life-blood, if necessary with the aid of a little hatred, a little jealousy, but I lack the strength as well as the knowledge of how to go about it. Dear Clémence, you know that a woman cannot redirect the impulses of her heart. Besides, *I should not like simply to love a man who loves me in return. It pleases me to love a man who spurns me.* Can you understand that?

'I do not complain. My misfortune is my recompense. A woman neglected by her lover derives pleasures from love of which a woman fulfilled can have no inkling. Love is the tomb of love. Love, I submit, casts ashes on the corpse of love. Do not ascribe these words to jealousy. They are my way of proclaiming hope. I am climbing my Calvary. My lover's inattention and his all-consuming passion for you constitute my refuge. The effect of the chill, crystalline void in which my heart blazes is to fan the flames of my desire into white-hot incandescence.

'I am immodest enough to claim that my love for Otto is purer and loftier than yours, for the strange if not astounding reason that he loves me not at all, whereas you he reveres and pines for. Your love is for ever becoming coated in the obscuring dust of love returned, whereas my passion crackles and glows, fuelled by my love's disdain.

'Long ago we read John of the Cross together. I do not

consider it sacrilegious (though neither of us has ever been unduly fastidious in that respect) to suggest that the saint's barbaric poem – you surely recall it: "I am dying of not dying . . ." – might be rephrased: "My love comes of not being loved." Ah, Cousin, how sick a woman's heart grows when caught in the toils of enchantment. Unless one is Ariadne, how can one ever find a way out of the labyrinth? I now see quite clearly that Ariadne points the way to salvation for all save herself. And if one is, as I believe myself to be, Ariadne, the Minotaur and Daedalus all in one – what then? Don't think me bitter. I nestle loveless in love's embrace. No woman, I am convinced, can love without a sense of desolation.'

★ ★ ★

Clémence and her husband never mentioned the past. The prince spent his days in the service of the monarchy. At night the couple ate together in the mansion's formal dining-room at a long table resplendent with damask napery, cut glass and silver plate. The big room was brightly lit in accordance with Clémence's wishes, and a fire blazed in the hearth. The lofty windows stood open whenever weather permitted, the clumps of yews, elms and spindleberries outside in the grounds resembling black velvet. Conversation at dinner was studiously polite and anodyne, yet often quite amusing. Domestic peace reigned, imbued with a static, interminable quality by the ticking of the clock. Afterwards Clémence would retire to the music room to strum on the harp there or add a few stitches to her embroidery while the prince browsed through the day's newspapers in the smoking-room. At ten o'clock the two of them went upstairs to their respective apartments.

And although they shared the same bed every Saturday night, these reunions were expressive more of estrangement than affection. The Prussian campaign had brought them together, but only physically. The trap of indifference in which Clémence had thought to ensnare her husband was operating in reverse: its jaws had closed on her, not him. In having drawn no distinction between his wife and her maid-in-waiting, Prince Ernst revealed that he regarded any one woman much as any other. He made love with equal application to whatever body occupied his bed. The man Gertrud had called a ninny was proving to be disconcertingly shrewd.

Nine months ago Clémence had employed her companion to deputize for her at Greinburg. Now it was her turn to stand in for Alma. The two of them had exchanged costumes. Having acted as her mistress's puppet, Alma was now, without even knowing it, the puppeteer. At Greinburg she had been the duchess's substitute and deputy; now, in Vienna, she called the tune. It was apparent from the prince's strange, thin-lipped smiles that he found it not displeasing to upset his wife's calculations, to make her drink the potion with which she had intended to demoralize him. Perverse forms of amusement can be hazardous, and Clémence wondered if Aunt Gertrud had allowed for such ingenious transpositions in Lord Misrule's programme. She made a mental note to ask her if the elderly English eccentric had ever envisaged a similar reversal of roles. His servants had been richly rewarded for shouldering the burden of his sorrows, his tears, his love affairs. Had he ever, in his turn, wept on a servant's behalf and risked damnation for the sake of that servant's betrothed?

Clémence reconciled herself to the situation. She looked on destiny as a game of heads-or-tails and told herself that any masquerade was a risky business. What if Alma reassumed her old identity for a night? How would her husband react? She suspected that he would obey the conventions and betray no hint of surprise: clothes would make the woman as surely as manners made man. Calmly dissecting his fish, the prince would regale Alma with the latest court tittle-tattle in his dreary, official voice. Then, at ten o'clock, after a postprandial browse through the gazettes, he would emerge from the smoking-room and mount the stairs in Alma's company. Indeed, on the nights when he and Clémence played ombre, a three-handed card game, Alma would be invited to join them, and when the game ended,

Clémence half expected the other two to bid her a courteous good night and go upstairs together. If that ever happened, would she be expected to sleep in her successor's bed.

On one occasion the prince gave her news of Otto Apfelgrun. He did so in a very roundabout and seemingly inadvertent manner, on the pretext of retailing the latest gossip from Schönbrunn. Having knocked his generals' heads together in Spain, he said, Napoleon was now preparing to descend on Austria. Clémence must not be afraid, however: the Dual Monarchy was armed and ready.

'What a whimsical turn of events,' Prince Ernst said affably, even benevolently. 'Saxony has been France's ally since the Prussian campaign, so we must now contend with a combination of circumstances that would have been unthinkable only a few months ago: Saxony and Austria in opposing camps! This means that the regiments we jointly own, my Saxon hussars and your Austrian cuirassiers, will be pitted against each other. They may even cut each other to ribbons. Our national archives have never recorded a more bizarre situation.'

Clémence put a hand to her brow, on the verge of fainting. She controlled herself with an effort.

'All the more bizarre,' she said heavily, 'in that some of your Saxon officers are Austrians.'

'My God, Clémence, how can I forget it? I need hardly tell you how distressed I am that those hapless young men will so soon be riding into battle against their fellow countrymen. The workings of war are inscrutable, not to say ironic – we're utterly at their mercy. I spent today at headquarters, trying to secure the repatriation of all the Austrians in my Saxon hussars, but alas, I was too late. The armies are already deploying for battle, so our links with Dresden have been severed. We've no means of getting the youngsters back to Austria through the French lines – they're trapped. Any day now, Napoleon will launch them at Vienna, the capital of their native land. We must simply hope for the best . . .' Prince Ernst sighed, picking idly at his fish salad. When Clémence said nothing, he dealt her a still sharper blow, his bland tone belied by the cruelty in his eyes.

'Colonel Adegauer contrived to send me a last letter from Dresden, heaven alone knows how. He wanted to reassure me that the regiment would be faithful to its traditions. The blue hussars will join in the French assault on Austria with all their wonted gallantry. They're up to strength again, what's more, because Savary – or Monsieur Charles, he didn't say which – has pardoned Lieutenant Apfelgrun and released him from prison in time to resume command of his troop.'

'You mean,' Clémence said quietly, 'that he'll have to turn his sword against his own country and his former comrades – against Konrad and Ulrich and Lieutenant-Colonel Scherer?'

The prince shrugged, smiling ingenuously.

'My dear Clémence, it's a cruel situation, I grant you, but hardly unique. Similar instances abound. It was a French general who bravely resisted Augereau after his defeat of the unfortunate Mack at Ulm. Nordmann and d'Astres are Frenchmen too. Bellegarde is a Savoyard, even if he was careless enough to be born at Dresden, and he commands our premier regiment of cavalry. Field-Marshal Casteller-Courcelles, a Belgian, commands our VIIIth Corps. As for Lusignan, he may be an Austrian field-marshal and an imperial chamberlain, but he hails from Béarn.'

'All the men you mention are French émigrés,' said Clémence. 'Their circumstances are exceptional.'

'Macdonald is one of the Grande Armée's finest generals, but that doesn't prevent him from being a Scot. What of Prince Eugene, who repulsed the Turks at Kahlenberg in 1683 – was he an Austrian or a Savoyard? And who would care to define the nationality of our friend the Prince de Ligne? Is he Belgian or French? Or Scottish, since his mother was the granddaughter of Mary Stuart? Or Russian, perhaps, having been one of Catherine the Great's field-marshals?'

'Ligne is a law unto himself.'

'By the way,' said Prince Ernst, 'I'm still reading his memoirs. I doubt if anyone has described the French

306

Revolution better. "France has become ungovernable since she ceased to be frivolous." Prettily put, don't you think?'

'But Ernst,' Clémence said brightly, 'Ligne thinks of nothing but women. Do you know why he abominates the storming of the Bastille? Because it has marred men's chivalry and coarsened their manners.'

'Tonight,' Prince Ernst told her, 'I came across a curious phrase: "Beware of thawing out cold nations." What does it mean, I wonder? In my opinion, it's one of the French Revolution's stupidities to have made the nation absolute. Our ancient monarchies repose on firmer foundations, different rights and duties: the allegiance of every individual to one sovereign or another. That, at least, is how I see matters.'

'Where does that leave you, my friend?'

'Oh,' said the prince, 'I'm loyal to my sovereign, Francis of Austria. Honour demands it, even if my escutcheon is more heavily quartered than most. I may be a prince of Saxony, but I shall defend Vienna against the Saxons – worse still, against my own blue hussars.'

Clémence went to a window and opened it. 'Spring has scarcely begun,' she sighed, gazing out across the grounds, 'yet it's so warm, and what with that inferno you've got blazing in the fireplace . . . Don't you find it stifling too?'

After a few minutes she took refuge in the music room. There she compelled herself to finish off a motif on her embroidery frame, but the night that followed was sheer torment. Blood-soaked visions haunted her – visions of her lover lying mortally wounded. By flouting convention and spurning fidelity she had sought to set herself above the laws of man, but those laws were inexorable. She would not escape damnation. Her time of adversity had come. She thought of the Holy Women with their drowned faces. She prayed, but her heart was empty and her lips were dry. Alma was alarmed by her pallor next morning. She had left her bowl of milk untouched and was seated at her desk with a distracted air, writing in her diary.

* * *

Prince Ernst had not exaggerated. The idea of war was gaining ground in Vienna. Austria's diplomats fomented rebellion among her former Tirolean subjects, who were now under the tutelage of Napoleon's ally, Bavaria. Stadion mended Schönbrunn's relations with Potsdam and St Petersburg, thread by thread. The British fleet was cruising off Germany and the Low Countries. Sensing that a storm was imminent, the Emperor of the French returned post-haste from Spain to Paris. 'I shall send Austria back into limbo!' he proclaimed. Vienna responded in kind. On 6 April 1809, Francis addressed an appeal to the German nation: 'The freedom of Europe having taken refuge beneath our banners, our victories will burst the chains of our German brothers, who, though now in the alien ranks, are awaiting deliverance.'

The Austrian General Staff unleashed its legions. Archduke Charles launched a frontal assault across the Inn. Austrian troops entered Innsbruck. At Aich in the Tirol, General Bisson surrendered to twenty thousand peasants commanded by Andreas Hofer, the rebel leader, who rode a beribboned mule and loudly recited the rosary. The god of war was smiling on the Dual Monarchy. Unhappily, he redirected his smile as soon as Napoleon had bivouacked beside the Danube. Regensburg fell, and, despite stiff resistance on Hiller's part, the French forced the approaches to Austria.

The Viennese cut down trees in the Prater, those lovely, melancholy trees which Joseph II had planted for his subjects' delectation in happier days. Napoleon's orderlies were already preparing the royal apartments at Schönbrunn to receive him. On May 11th French pioneers threw a pontoon bridge across the river and the Prater was invaded. Bertrand's gunners set the city ablaze. Archduke Maximilian, who had been entrusted with its defence, could no longer communicate with Francis, who had decamped to Olmütz for the second time. Left to his own devices, he hoisted a white flag over the Burgtor. The formal surrender took place at Schönbrunn on May 13th. Napoleon played the merciful, magnanimous conqueror. 'Soldiers,' he declared, 'the people of Vienna, deserted, abandoned and forlorn, are to be treated with consideration. I am taking the inhabitants under my special protection. As for the unruly and vicious among you, I shall punish them with exemplary severity. Be kind to the poor peasants and to these good people who so thoroughly merit our solicitude. Let us not take undue pride in our successes. Rather, let us regard them as proof of the divine justice that punishes ingratitude and treachery.'

Prince Ernst of Saxe-Salza had remained in Vienna and was assisting General O'Reilly, to whom Maximilian had delegated his authority before joining Francis at Olmütz. He learned that Scherer's white cuirassiers were in position between Essling and Aspern with Field-Marshal the Prince of Liechtenstein's cavalry corps. Clémence, so distraught by now that she cast caution and propriety to the winds, asked if he had any news of Adegauer's blue hussars.

'Ah no, my dear, we know nothing of them. But they're bound to be somewhere between Sankt Pölten and Vienna, ready for Napoleon to toss them into the cauldron when the time comes. Have no fear, though, they'll acquit themselves gallantly.'

It was a peaceful, golden afternoon, and the couple were paying a visit to one of the greenhouses in the grounds. The prince pruned a sucker here, a wayward branch there. He picked off some faded blossoms and crushed them between his fingers.

'I passed Lawyer Apfelgrun in Fahnengasse,' he said, 'escorted by that disagreeable footman who used to carry Frau Apfelgrun's prayerbook – you remember how heartily we laughed at him once upon a time? I don't believe the poor old lawyer knows what has happened. He was smiling his usual rather idiotic smile. Curious, isn't it? All that's needed is some distemper of the blood, some noxious humour in the venules of the brain, and everything evaporates: anxiety, vanity, despair – everything. Lawyer Apfelgrun knows nothing of the war, so the war doesn't exist. He has abolished it and signed a separate peace. Lawyer Apfelgrun never suffers. Ah, Clémence, I would gladly write an encomium on senility.' The prince abruptly raised his head and looked at his wife with wide, sad, wistful eyes. He presented her with a minuscule rosebud.

'Yes,' he said, 'there are times when I envy Lawyer Apfelgrun.' He hesitated. 'You follow me, Clémence? I don't require happiness – that would be asking too much – but the absence of unhappiness . . .'

★　★　★

Clémence was unbearably restless. Every afternoon the coachman harnessed up his team and took her for a long drive. The city was teeming with French soldiers, and the duchess kept watch on the street from beneath the half-lowered blinds of her carriage. Now and then she would alight and take a turn in a park or garden or disappear into a church, hoping for a chance encounter with Christine Kinsky. There could be no doubt that Christine was somewhere in Vienna, because Count Andreossy, the French governor, had appointed Schulmeister, alias Captain Charles, prefect of the Austrian capital's police force – a post he had held there once before, in 1805. But Clémence never sighted her cousin. Even if their paths had crossed, she knew Christine would have either told her nothing or lied to her, but her emotional turmoil was such that it would have set her mind at rest to receive any news of Otto, however spurious.

Napoleon's firm intention was to cross the Danube just downstream from Vienna, deploy on the northern bank between Essling and Aspern, and crush Archduke Charles's forces in the plain below Wagram. On May 18th he occupied Lobau, a Danubian island roughly three miles long and four wide. At dusk on May 20th, after French sappers had thrown elaborate pontoon bridges across the river, which was swollen with melted snow, Lasalle's cavalry crossed them and set off northwards.

Archduke Charles attacked without delay, and by the following afternoon, Whit Sunday, Aspern was ablaze. Eighteen thousand Frenchmen and twenty-seven thousand Austrians died. Perched in a fir tree on Lobau Island with his telescope levelled, Napoleon watched the multicoloured soldiers perform their dance of death amid the green corn. The Viennese, too, looked down from their balconies as cannon balls swept away whole columns, horses died in droves, mist and gunsmoke billowed across the battlefield, and death claimed skirmishers and dragoons, cuirassiers and lancers, yelling infantrymen in blue, green and yellow, soldiers of every hue, soldiers rendered grey by distance. The Austrians intensified their pressure. The big bridge connecting Lobau with Vienna was carried away by the current, and nightfall found the French without means of retreat. They were trapped between the Austrians and the Danube.

Napoleon ordered a general withdrawal. During the warm, rainy night of May 22nd, all the French contingents that had ventured on to the north bank retired across the small pontoon bridge to Lobau Island. At three the next morning engineers dismantled the bridge between Lobau and the north bank, much as the defenders of a medieval castle would have raised their drawbridge, and the French were safe from pursuit. Their position was still precarious, however, crowded together as they were on a small island bounded by a river in spate.

Clémence, accompanied by Alma von Wörth, had gone upstairs at nightfall to watch the progress of the distant battle through a bull's-eye window in one of the mansion's attic rooms. The sky was overcast, and she could discern little on the other side of the Danube's gleaming grey ribbon apart from several huge fires. Objects were milling about in the light of these conflagrations – dark objects resembling insects or worms or ink blots that faded and dissolved into the flames like black sparks. Alma urged her mistress more than once to get some rest because nothing could be distinguished at this range, but Clémence paid no attention.

At three in the morning a triumphant yell went up from the Austrian army. The Usurper had been crushed and his forces routed. The plain lit up, but this time it was the windows of farmhouses throughout the Wagram basin that were ablaze. The bells of a thousand churches pealed forth, and the Viennese, who were destined not to sleep a wink that night, bayed like hounds at the kill. Morning found the Kärntnertor mansion seething with activity. Everyone turned up in self-congratulatory mood to inquire and impart the latest news. General Count Konig von Weitzau dispensed gems from his vast store of historical and military knowledge. He had it from a confidential but absolutely reliable source that fifty thousand French soldiers had bitten the dust, but that wasn't all: the dead included Augereau, d'Espagne, Oudinot and Lannes. Berthier had betrayed his master and gone over to Archduke Charles. Vienna was exultant, Germany even wilder with delight. 'Bonaparte has been vanquished!' read a proclamation on the walls of the town hall at Znaim, and at Bude: 'Bonaparte is dead, and the remnants of his forces, fleeing towards Italy, have been disarmed by Prince John.' Viennese balladeers likened Archduke Charles to St Michael and Napoleon to the dragon.

It was true that Lannes, whose knee had been shattered, was at death's door. It was also true that d'Espagne had succumbed, but everything else was a delusion. Safe on Lobau Island, the French built themselves a regular town there, well lit at night and amply provided with bivouacs, provision stores, streets, hospitals. Back at Schönbrunn, Napoleon inspected dazzling parades, granted audiences and attended entertainments. The Viennese, though disappointed, consoled themselves with the thought that the French had sustained heavy losses. Archduke John had left Italy and was marching to the aid of Archduke Charles. The Stephansplatz drawing-rooms buzzed with feverish talk: the French were wolves, locusts, jackals; the French surgeon Larrey was poisoning his Austrian prisoners to save medicaments. Burghers and artisans applied themselves to strategy in every Viennese coffee-house. They planted little flags on tavern menus and manoeuvred soldiers between Aspern and Lessing, Lobau and Deutsch-Wagram, Markgraf-Neusiedl and the Russbach. At the Café Hugelmann, the Dual Monarchy's cuirassiers and dragoons charged endlessly to and fro between cups of mocha, trout *à la crème* and currant pastries.

Meanwhile, closeted in her big house, Clémence brooded night and day on her lover's fate.

23

Five weeks went by – five weeks during which the war made no move. It lay doggo. Vienna grew weary of gossip because reality went its own sweet way, heedless of the dictates of reason. At the end of June, however, the armchair strategists were given a marvellous rumour to chew on: three distinguished military commanders – Bernadotte, Davout and Prince Eugène, Josephine's son – had been invited to dine with Napoleon at Schönbrunn on June 30th. Vienna's drawing-rooms seethed with excitement. The following morning, however, an Austrian court usher employed at Schönbrunn was 'indiscreetly' informed by the palace victualling officer that Napoleon had consulted his three guests solely on the comparative merits of Racine and Corneille. Bernadotte was all for Racine, but Napoleon had angrily settled the argument by declaring Corneille the winner. Vienna's society relapsed into lethargy. Strangely enough, however, the man in the street divined the French emperor's intentions with far greater accuracy. By some devious means or other the greengrocers, carters and wigmakers of Vienna were informed that once Napoleon's guests had departed, he himself had snatched a bare three hours' sleep before donning his grenadier guard's uniform and setting off back to Lobau Island.

In Vienna July 4th had been a wearisome day, with Austria sweltering in the grip of a heat-wave, but Prince Ernst was in fine fettle. After dinner he repaired to the smoking-room and, for once, invited his wife to join him there. Unrolling a big map on the floor, he crouched down and proceeded to stick red and white pins in it. At first Napoleon's red pins were concentrated on Lobau, but then the semi-recumbent prince, purple in the face and slightly out of breath, transferred some of them to the north bank of the Danube, facing the Wagram plateau, and arrayed them opposite the white pins representing the Austrian forces.

He then gave Clémence some technical information, especially about Archduke Charles's pins. Her white cuirassiers had been incorporated in Liechtenstein's force, more precisely in the Sigenthel brigade of the Hesse-Hamburg division, whose task it was to reinforce the six main corps, namely, those commanded by Hohenzollern, Kolowrat, Rosenberg, Reuss, Bellegarde and Klenau, not forgetting Nordmann's advance guard.

Prince Ernst now reverted to Napoleon's red pins. Military intelligence reports suggested that Masséna and Davout would form the right and left wings of the French attacking force, and that they would head for Wagram via Essling and Gross-Aspern as they had during their abortive foray in May. The second wave could consist of Marmont in the centre flanked on the right by Macdonald, now back from Italy, and on the left by Prince Eugène and Bernadotte. Lieutenant-Colonel Adegauer's blue hussars had been placed under Bernadotte's command.

'I have news of them, by the way. They left Saxony in May and came by way of the Upper Danube. They may even have ridden past our castle at Greinburg – an odd thought, no? Having bivouacked at Sankt Pölten on June 5th, they're heading for Lobau at this very moment.' Prince Ernst heaved himself off the floor with both hands and rose ponderously to his feet. The atmosphere in the room was stifling. He went to the window and opened it.

'Everything indicates that hostilities will commence tomorrow.'

'There's a storm brewing,' Clémence said casually. 'Won't that delay matters? The Danube is in spate. The bridges may well be swept away as they were two months ago.'

'The bridges have been rebuilt to Napoleon's specifications. He's a brilliant engineer, don't forget.'

'But the men's cartridges will be sodden.'

The prince who had been pacing nervously up and down, came to a sudden halt.

'That's the very reason Napoleon will attack. Why? Because all Archduke Charles's generals share your line of reasoning. Knowing Napoleon as I do, I'd stake my life on the opposite view. He'll join battle precisely because our cartridges are sodden. His, of course, are dry. That man is the Devil incarnate.'

The storm broke just before nine. The wind dropped, the creaking of weathercocks and inn signs died away. Then lightning rent the sky and every windowpane rattled. Rain descended on Austria in a solid mass. The roofs of Vienna glistened in the lightning's bluish glare. An hour later the rumble of thunder ceased, to be succeeded by an even more thunderous eruption of sound.

'The batteries of Lobau have opened fire,' said Prince Ernst. 'Napoleon is reputed to be a good geographer, and deservedly so, but I would call him a great meteorologist too. At Austerlitz he utilized the frost and the sun as well as his armies. Tonight he has clothed his men in thunder and lightning. I'm tempted to suggest that he wields his soldiers like a natural cataclysm.'

Clémence fanned her flushed face. Opening the neck of her gown an inch or two, she toyed with the gold cross suspended from her neck. The prince leant over her, took both her hands in his and held them fast.

'What does tomorrow hold in store, my dear? Will there be other such nights? By this time tomorrow, Austria may be no more – Austria or the Grande Armée, whichever . . . And what of us, Clémence? What of you and me?'

The storm, which was raging once more, lasted till daybreak. Towards four in the morning Clémence was awakened by a sudden lull. She looked down at her husband's head on the pillow, inert and waxen in the surrounding gloom, then rose and padded out on to the balcony in her bare feet. In the direction of the Alps, the pale midsummer sky was torn with phosphorescent, sulphurous rents and fissures. The bombardment began again: three hundred thousand men were about to engage in mutual slaughter. Every window in the house vibrated. Clémence went back to bed. Very gently, she put out her hand and touched the prince's face.

Shortly before noon the major-domo ordered a carriage to be harnessed up. The Saxe-Salzas were to lunch with the Prince de Ligne, whose celebrated country villa nestled in the hills above the Danube north of Vienna. No one could have devised a finer observatory than this high-lying residence, whose upper floor consisted of a terrace and winter garden in the Italian style.

The Saxe-Salzas' progress through Vienna was hampered by the prevailing turmoil. The French military police, assisted by gendarmes, had redoubled their security measures, and the hunt for spies was in full swing. For some weeks now, the French authorities had been tightening their grip on the city in response to its citizens' growing recalcitrance. Members of the Grande Armée had been jostled by the Hungarian butchers of Olchsengries on the left bank of the Wien. The university was in revolt. Dr Sedlitz of the medical faculty was becoming more and more bumptious. He had ceased to teach physiology and was giving practical courses in military medicine on the grounds that 'Monsieur Larrey, that self-styled surgeon, is sufficiently contemptuous of his Hippocratic oath to distinguish between Austrian femurs and French.' Count Andreossy and Captain Charles kept a close watch on Vienna's three hundred thousand inhabitants, every one of whom they regarded as a suspect. House-to-house searches were assiduously conducted, by night as well as day, in defiance of international law and of the old Germanic code. Letters were feloniously abstracted from the mails and opened. The decorative iron chains enclosing many of Vienna's streets had been cut so that squads of mounted policemen could charge freely at a moment's notice, wielding their sabres. A week earlier, four men named Wagner, Teller, Laurent and Riquel, who had wounded a French gendarme, were executed on the Esplanade by a firing squad.

The Saxe-Salzas' carriage threaded its way through a seething human warren. It was stopped on three separate occasions, each of which entailed a ritual interrogation accompanied by jeers and insults. Prince Ernst, beside himself with fury, was obliged to show his papers and safe-conducts to uncouth Poitevin or Breton peasants tricked out as gendarmes. Clémence was on the point of being searched by soldiers, but her blazing eyes deterred them. She joked about this afterwards to the prince. 'I really did fly into a rage, did I not? But then, mine is an antique rage, a rage matured over many centuries, a rage inaugurated in the twelfth century, if not earlier, perhaps by the Knightly Swordbearers whom Aunt Gertrud reveres so much. At all events, those Frenchmen will still be wondering what happened. Besides, I had Arcola beside me. Did you hear him growl?'

They resumed their slow progress through streets choked with waggons, soldiers and civilian bystanders. Whole families thronged the windows, and one or two houses flew banners bearing the two-headed eagle. The Saxe-Salza's conveyance, identifiable by its princely coat of arms, evoked enthusiastic cheers, much to the annoyance of Andreossy's gendarmes. Already on edge, they fired into the air, making the six English carriage horses rear and whinny, straining at their traces. It was early afternoon before the Saxe-Salzas reached their destination.

Charles Joseph de Ligne gave them a warm welcome. Clémence's glacial beauty had long captivated this elderly, bewigged Lothario, who was rumoured to keep assignations out of doors, even on the coldest of winter nights. He laughed when teased about this. 'I jeopardize my reputation, perhaps, but reputations are more easily lost on the battlefield than in young ladies' bedchambers. And you must admit that a man of my age is brave to risk pneumonia . . .'

The Prince de Ligne was indeed no longer young, having first seen the light of day at Brussels in 1735. Affable, frivolous and charming, endowed with a pretty wit and the cheek of the devil, he had indiscriminately sampled every side of human existence: blood, gold and danger, women's bodies, music, science, landscape gardening, painting, astronomy, literature. His career encompassed all the most irreconcilable desires, passions and effronteries of his age. A brilliant general who inspired adulation in his men, he had weathered the bloodiest of storms and survived the most terrible of times as nonchalantly as any gallant dancing a minuet in a painting by Watteau. The dour and virtuous Habsburg monarchy, incongruously housed in Europe's most licentious and hedonistic city, had gained a loyal, light-hearted subject in Ligne, though he had fallen into semi-disgrace since the death of Joseph II, the royal philosopher. But Ligne had also hired out his talents to Catherine the Great of Russia, endeared himself to Versailles beauties and women of the streets, consorted with the Encyclopedists, flattered Jean-Jacques Rousseau and preserved Beaumarchais from imprisonment. Freemason though he was, he abominated the French Revolution and the grim, dreary, morbid Republic that had done away with the charm and chivalry of the *ancien régime*. A lover of battles, he detested the modern world for its total preoccupation with war and for having substituted the laws of men for the enchanted dominion of womankind. Finally, though Austrian by adoption and distinction, he never concealed his fondness for the common people of France; and, unlike the bemedalled old fogies who commanded the armies of Austria, he admired Napoleon.

★　★　★

Ligne had converted his winter garden into an observatory well provided with optical devices, marine binoculars, telescopes and prismatic spyglasses. These handsome instruments of steel and brass shone like lethal weapons among the prince's fig trees, orchids and stretches of greensward. He solemnly conducted Clémence to a long, burnished cylinder mounted on a solid oak frame and equipped with several lenses.

'An astronomical telescope, dear lady. I was given it in my youth by Maupertuis himself. Just fancy, this is the very instrument he used in Lapland sixty years ago to determine the exact dimensions of the terrestrial sphere. It will now serve a different purpose. Tonight or tomorrow it will furnish us with the precise extent, not of the battle proper, but of its environs, its backgrounds, its periphery – in short, of all the constellations that preside over the carnage. Those constellations are indifferent to the discomforts or glories of the Habsburgs and Bonapartes, but they do afford us a scale of measurement. They miniaturize men almost to the point of extinction. They reduce them to the proportions of a swarm of bees. Tonight or tomorrow, therefore, my dear Clémence, although the course of human history may veer in one direction or another, it won't elicit so much as a mouse's squeak from the heavens above . . .'

Not long afterwards, Duchess Gertrud made one of her traditionally noisy entrances escorted by four lackeys in amaranthine jerkins and yellow gloves, a brace of black-clad, somewhat arthritic ladies-in-waiting, and Professor Schwarzbrod, whose company she often sought since deciding that Father Thaler possessed no more brains than a mushroom. The Duchess of Mahlberg was *en grande tiolette*. She had chosen to wear her pink peruke, in which her maids had entwined mauve ribbons studded with diamonds. Little countess Pietranera, dressed in daffodil yellow, did her best to be spiteful. Though not naturally malicious, she considered it good form to show her claws from time to time. Turning to the handsome young captain beside her, who had lost an arm, she confided behind her fan that the duchess's wigs were alive, and that their wisps and ramifications grew almost as fast as her face shrank. The captian chuckled into his remaining hand. Meanwhile, handling Gertrud as gingerly as an eggshell, the old lady's lackeys deposited her between two tubs of hydrangeas, facing Wagram and within reach of a telescope.

Gertrud fondled Arcola's thick coat, fondly and Germanically calling him her 'Herr Feldmarschall', then applied each of her eyes in turn to the telescope. Her lackeys trained the brass cylinder on Essling, and she sat motionless with one eye glued to the lens, almost as if she hoped that a spectacle of such magnitude would restore some of her sight. At length, with a gesture of disgust and resignation,

320

she sent the telescope spinning on its tripod, sat back in her chair, and resolutely crossed her little legs. Her feet, shod in black bootees bristling with mother-of-pearl buttons, dangled from her ankles like the feet of a doll in mourning. Tearfully, she captured Schwarzbrod's hand.

The Prince de Ligne, who had the greatest respect for Gertrud, bowed to her and welcomed her to his garden.

'Prince,' she said hoarsely, 'I propose to bivouac beside your telescope. Presently I shall try again – after all, one never knows. Meantime, you shall play the part of Christine Kinsky. That cannon I've been hearing all morning: tell me about it.'

Ligne described the terrain in which the armies were deploying.

'Vienna is behind us, Excellency. At our feet, the Danube. In the middle of the Danube and a little to our right, the celebrated island of Lobau. The cannon you can hear in the distance are firing from somewhere near Enzersdorf.'

According to Ligne, the coming drama would revolve around the village of Deutsch-Wagram, the rectangular grey walls of which could just be glimpsed six miles to the north. In front of Deutsch-Wagram lay the marshes, and flowing parallel with the Danube between Wagram and Markgraf-Neusiedl was the Russbach. This small river, which could only be crossed by means of bridges, formed the theatre's backcloth.

Gertrud swivelled the telescope – at random and without even putting her eye to it – as if following the thread of Ligne's remarks. She had recovered her caustic good humour.

'After all,' she said, 'my friend Horatio Nelson clapped a telescope to his blind eye rather than see the pennant flying from Parker's flagship at the battle of Copenhagen. I shall do likewise – in fact I'm better off than that hare-brained Englishman because I've no need to choose between one eye and the other. I shan't have to witness the discomfiture of the Austrian armies, which is all to the good. Proceed, Ligne.'

321

'The Danube is just below our vantage-point. Beyond it lies the plain, with Aspern, Essling, Enzersdorf – '

'Beethoven's deaf as a post,' Gertrud broke in, 'but that doesn't prevent him from composing symphonies and conducting them. Well? Am I not the equal of that thick-skulled German? It would be a sorry business not to watch a battle, simply on the grounds that my eyes are useless . . .' Her voice took on a fierce, rebellious note. 'Before long, Ligne, I shall have the advantage of you. Why? Because you'll be helpless when night falls, even with Maupertuis's telescope, whereas I'm an *habituée* of the night. It's my home – I stroll about in it as I would in a garden . . .'

The fighting was ferocious. In the ever-changing afternoon light, men scurried hither and thither through the fields of ripe golden wheat that bordered the Danube between Enzersdorf and Gross-Aspern. The colour of their uniforms was vaguely discernible.

'One can't be certain, though,' said Ligne, turning to Prince Ernst. 'Both armies comprise all the colours of the rainbow, so one would have to be able to distinguish their regimental insignia.' His eyes twinkled mischievously. 'Over there near Raasdorf, for example, I can make out a body of men in white, but who's to say whether they're your cuirassiers – Scherer's, I mean – or a regiment of Frenchmen similarly dressed in white? And what of those blue fellows? Are they Adegauer's Saxons or some Austrians in blue? Who knows?'

Prince Ernst flushed crimson. Malicious tongues had made much of the fact that his two regiments were on opposing sides. What could he say?

'Let us suppose,' Ligne pursued in a bantering tone, ' – let us suppose that the men themselves don't know which side they're on. What if they still think they're allies, as they were till last year? What if your Saxon hussars don't grasp that they've been auctioned off by the Great Elector of Dresden and snaffled by Napoleon, or if they and your cuirassiers prefer to remember that they still belong to the same colonel proprietor, despite everything, and refuse to fight each other? Or what if one regiment, still imagining

322

itself the ally of the other, comes forward to fraternize and gets cut to ribbons?' Ligne peered through the nearest telescope before continuing.

'My meaning is that colours become blurred when seen from afar. Every commander-in-chief suffers the same difficulty. If he hugs the fray in order to recognize his own men, he'll have his nose too close to the picture to be able to gauge its true extent and composition. If he keeps his distance he'll see its principal features to perfection, but he won't know which his men are. He must find the correct distance – in my opinion, rather like a landscape painter viewing his subject: from close at hand and far away, myopically and presbyopically at the same time. It's a great problem . . .'

Duchess Gertrud loudly announced that she could smell burning, part flesh, part wheat.

'Tell us, Ligne,' she said, 'how will Napoleon proceed this time? What sort of dance will he lead our poor Archduke Charles?'

In Ligne's view, Napoleon had already tricked Charles by carrying out a number of diversionary manoeuvres in the days preceding the battle.

'His intention was to persuade Archduke Charles that the French would duplicate the plan that so lamentably failed in May. He convinced Charles that he would hurl the bulk of his forces at Gross-Aspern and Essling from Lobau Island, so that's where Charles has massed his divisions – there, just in front of us. All well and good, but – hey presto! – Napoleon has emerged from his rat's nest by another hole. He has launched his spearhead at the Schengang-Enzersdorf axis, way over to our right – and what a spearhead! Masséna himself is in command of it, so . . .'

⋆   ⋆   ⋆

It was a chilly night. The guns thundered, the plain was a sea of flame. Now and then, from the direction of Aspern, ragged fusillades rang out with a sound which sounded to

Ligne like the ripping of cloth. Towards nine o'clock Lawyer Apfelgrun and his wife Constanze turned up with General Count Konig von Weitzau. The general, whose beard was its natural off-white again, had put on his full-dress uniform for the occasion. Constanze, looking around for Father Thaler, was vexed not to see him. Her devotion to religion had grown by leaps and bounds since her son's disappearance into the turmoil of the Prussian campaign. She wore funereal gowns of austere cut and consorted almost exclusively with Jesus Christ, the Blessed Virgin, SS. Anne and Brigit, and their earthly representatives. Having paid her respects to the Prince de Ligne, she made a beeline for the only cleric present, the coadjutor of St Stephan's.

Lawyer Apfelgrun on the other hand, in spite of his tremulous hands, pot-belly, and increasingly deficient vocabulary, had far from renounced his flirtatious habits: he simply carried them to less extreme lengths. Now as always, he delighted in the company of fragrant young women. Although it was some years since he had encountered Duchess Clémence in a Bauernmarkt doorway, her beauty had made such a deep impression on him that he recognized her instantly. After ascertaining that her husband had abandoned her for a court official, or someone of that sort, he sidled up to Clémence and bowed low. Forgetful as ever, he failed to remember the bow he had just performed and repeated it for safety's sake. Up and down he bobbed, ten times over, there seeming to be no reason why his obeisances should ever cease. Clémence, whose every thought was of Otto, watched the old man in anguished bewilderment, half fancying that he had taken it into his head to convey some coded message relating to her beloved. Arcola, meanwhile, had taken a liking to the lawyer and was rubbing against his breeches. At this point General von Weitzau lit up a big black cigar and came to Clémence's assistance – rather adroitly, in his own estimation – by loudly remarking that the battlefield was illumined by a majestic moon.

'Here we go again!' exclaimed Duchess Gertrud. 'Gustav

and his moon! It won't be long before it turns crescent-shaped . . . I know you, Gustav – you're about to trot out your Turks and Janizaries!'

The Prince de Ligne, who also was familiar with Weitzau's cock-eyed theories, roared with laughter. Weitzau, being a responsible man, never laughed. He announced that the Turks were no longer his concern, and that a danger far more dire was looming on the horizon. Now that he had read Edward Gibbon's *magnum opus* on the downfall of the Roman Empire, published in London twenty years before, the scales had fallen from his eyes.

'Honour behoves me to acknowledge my mistakes,' he said in a patient, self-important tone, stroking his bald head. 'I was on the right track, but I stopped short in midstream. To recapitulate: I discovered in the first place that Napoleon was merely a façade or feint on the part of some other agency, and I rather rashly plumped for the Sublime Porte. I was wrong. Once I'd made a detailed study of Jena and, more especially, Friedland, enlightenment dawned with the aid, I repeat, of Gibbon. One must render unto Caesar that which is Caesar's, and far be it from me to deck myself in borrowed plumes.'

'Gibbon's goose quills, you mean,' quipped Dr Ulhue.

Weitzau regarded him pityingly.

'If Napoleon is indeed the disguise of a second party, to wit, the Turks, that second party must in turn be the disguise, camouflage, or – if you will, ladies – the mask and domino of a third party, and it is that ultimate figure whose identity must be discovered. Enough said!'

Duchess Gertrud shuffled her feet in exasperation.

'One more effort, Gustav, and you'll end by knowing what you mean!'

'What I mean, Excellency, is this: if Napoleon is indeed the Ottomans' façade, deputy, or lieutenant, the Ottomans are themselves the façade of . . . Whose façade, pray? I give you a hundred guesses, a thousand. It all fits!'

A small group of guests had clustered round Weitzau. Constanze Apfelgrun was listening apprehensively, as if her son's fate hinged on the portly old general's words. Dr

Ulhue had cocked his head. Weitzau surveyed his listeners amiably, even tolerantly, before firing off the key to his conundrum at point-blank range.

'My theory is that history must be viewed from afar. Then, and only then, will it yield up its secrets.'

Lawyer Apfelgrun broke in. The general was right, he said. He himself saw objects better from a distance than close at hand. 'Except when I'm wearing my spectacles, General. Bear that in mind, won't you?'

Taking advantage of this diversionary remark, which he delivered with an air of inordinate cunning, he tiptoed swiftly to the back of the room and reinstalled himself beside the lovely Duchess Clémence without attracting the attention of his wife, who would not have minded anyway and had eyes for no one but the coadjutor. The old lawyer unceremoniously seized Clémence's limp and unresisting hand.

'You will agree, my dear Ligne,' Weitzau was saying, 'being a man of war like myself, that nations evolve in two interrelated ways. Short, staccato developments alternate with the high tides, the slow surges of history. For my part, I train my binoculars on the latter. If I wish to decipher the full picture, I must divest it of its anecdotal trappings, for instance, this battle, this stage on which supernumeraries – supernumeraries, mark you, not actors – are pitting themselves against each other.' Tilting his head, Weitzau projected a cloud of smoke at the ceiling and dispersed it with a vigorous expulsion of breath. 'There's your battle of Wagram: a few wisps of cigar smoke.'

'Bravo!' cried Lawyer Apfelgrun in the background, heedless of possible detection by his wife.

'And I contend,' Weitzau went on, 'that we are now witnessing the second act of the tragedy. The first unfolded in the fifth century, when Rome was sacked by tribes that came galloping out of the depths of Asia on their ponies – spirited little beasts, as Gibbon rightly points out. I refer to the Vandals, the Huns, the Visigoths, the Avars. Under their onslaught, a universe collapsed in ruins!

'Shall I make a confession? There are nights when I hear

326

the shrill, distant cry which St Jerome uttered in his cell at Bethlehem when Rome was reduced to rubble by Alaric's hordes. Listen to that cry, gentlemen: it is ringing out across the plain this very night!'

Weitzau put a finger to his lips and pointed at the darkness outside.

'It almost chokes me to have to remind you,' he continued in a strange little voice, 'but Rome, the city that had conquered the universe, had itself been conquered. Do you hear, gentlemen? Do you hear St Jerome? Enough said! The barbarian tribes moved on like a swarm of insects and bivouacked – if I may employ a military term, Prince – in our Finisterres. *Finis terrae* . . . And here we come to my discovery: they bivouacked, but that was all. They recovered their strength, grazed their horses, called a halt, pitched camp. They pitched camp, gentlemen, but not for a night – no, for a millennium! Enough said!

'Tonight the pendulum is swinging in the other direction, the tide has turned. Having a hatred of grandiloquence, as you all know, I shall put it very simply: we are witnessing the age of the Great Migrations, but in reverse. Time is rewinding itself. The hordes are galloping from west to east instead of east to west, you follow me? What has happened is this: the barbarians, after camping on our premises for ten long centuries, are going home. Those camp fires twinkling out there below our windows, on the banks of Central Europe's greatest river, are the beacons of Attila!'

To judge by the ensuing hubbub, the general had scored a notable success. Eyes wide and shining, he raised one hand to damp down the emotions he had kindled. Then, with startling suddenness, he drew his cavalry sabre and levelled it in the direction Deutsch-Wagram.

'Palimpsest!' he barked. 'A manuscript inscribed on parchment from which the original text had been erased. The palimpsest is the metaphorical womb of history, Prince, but I would go further. Is not the word palimpsest absolutely – ab-so-lute-ly – synonymous with the word history, with its never-ending cycle of which Heraclitus speaks? Just as Christ has never ceased to die on Golgotha, so there isn't a battle, a man, or a kiss that isn't haunted by the ghost of itself. I proclaim tonight that the battle of Wagram, like everything else in this vile, abject world, is unfolding in a . . . in a landscape from which its history has previously been erased!'

He seemed disconcerted by this flash of inspiration and strove to improve on it, but overpolishing can ruin the most felicitous remark.

'In a landscape cleansed of its history,' he amended lamely. 'By this I mean that all the skirmishes apparently taking place on the plain of Wagram – and you, Prince, will realize that Wagram is just a metaphor for Europe as a whole – are simply dream-battles enacted in a wheat-field purged of all the entrails that have fertilized it between the time of the Catalaunian Fields and the time, already past and yet to come, of Deutsch-Wagram, those two milestones of our civilization. Enough said! I state this because nothing has happened in the interval between the Catalaunian Fields and this night of damnation: between the years 451 and 1808–1809, I mean. The borborygmus that is history has obstinately repeated the same borborygmus!

'That being so, Ligne, you'll grant me that Napoleon is small beer. He's a wisp of smoke, your Napoleon, and his men are a shoal of jellyfish or herring. You'll even concede that the Grand Turk carries little weight. Attila, not Soliman, is bivouacking down there below our peristyles, back from the Catalaunian Fields. It isn't Soliman for whom the Corsican serves as a façade and lieutenant, it's Attila!'

Undeterred by Duchess Gertrud's uproarious laughter, Weitzau preened himself. Dr Ulhue tried to worm his way into the conversation but failed to find a point of entry. The Prince de Ligne was looking serious for once. He had always thought his old friend Weitzau a fool, but 'a fool touched with genius', as he had remarked to Professor Schwarzbrod some months previously. 'Yes, yes,' he'd said, 'Weitzau is stupid but perspicacious. I set store by imbecility – in fact I'm inclined to believe that every prophet is an imbecile by definition. Look at Ezekiel, or

Job, or Elijah: idiots for sure and solemn ones to boot, yet they're more lucid and intelligent and see farther than all the sages. They're God's duncers, Professor. They sit at the bottom of the class and make ink blots on their copybooks with their goose quills – yes, but dunces are almost alone in taking schoolmasters and education seriously, and it's through their mouths that God transmits his messages. They're so useless, so incapable of original thought, that God can rest assured that his message will receive no embellishment en route, no appoggiaturas or marginalia. Don't smile, Schwarzbrod, I mean it. Weitzau has furnished me with more food for thought than all the lecturers at Heidelberg put together. It's simply that one has to rearrange his ideas a trifle – straighten them out on the anvil with a few taps of the hammer. But believe me, my dear fellow, his eye is razor-sharp.'

Being no lover of melancholy, the Prince de Ligne now ordered supper. Weitzau's knot of listeners broke up and Ligne paid gentle court to Countess Pietranera. The one-armed captain saw his mistress stroll off into the garden with their host and disappear beyond an expanse of lawn. Countess Pietranera was charmed by Ligne's attentions. She cooed on principle when he admired her fan, ever eager to enhance the licentious reputation on which she prided herself. 'I got this fan from Paris,' she told him. 'It looks quite innocent when closed, does it not, Prince, but if I open it like this . . .' She did so. 'That surprises you, I'll be bound!' Ligne donned a pair of spectacles and drew in his breath sharply. The silken semicircle depicted scenes of unnatural copulation in which men and women were engaging in the most lubricious activities. The countess, who delighted in being shameless, contrived to blush.

'Dear Prince,' she said, hanging her head, 'it's a nasty thing, isn't it, and I'm truly ashamed of myself. You'll think me a naughty girl.'

Ligne had taken her hand with easy familiarity.

'You say these marvels come from Paris? That's good news indeed. So the butchers of 1792 have left some fruits of civilization untouched after all. You and your fan encourage me to hope that our men may yet win the battle of Wagram . . . But listen, our friend Weitzau has the bit between his teeth again.'

The general was rhapsodizing about fires. His encyclopedic knowledge of history enabled him to cite a whole series of conflagrations including those of Troy and Alexandria, Rome and Nalanda in India.

'Fire,' he boomed, 'is the Orient's favourite weapon, and the fire of the Orient, be it noted, attacks the written word. The Moslems have twice destroyed the world's past, once by burning the library at Alexandria, that corpus of classical antiquity, and again by annihilating the entire Buddhist corpus in the library at Nalanda in 1199. I would draw your attention to that date: 1199, the year preceding 1200 – yes, but add those four digits together and you get a round number, namely, twenty! Enough said! See Gibbon! Nor do I forget those other fires of oriental authorship, the blazing faggots of the Inquisition, which roasted books and men at the same time.'

'Not so, General!' cried the coadjutor. 'Not men, heretics!'

'Men!' Weitzau thundered. 'Men, I said, Monsignor, and tonight, even without recourse to Maupertuis's telescope, we're witnessing a conflagration that surpasses those of Seville, let alone Rome or Alexandria. We're watching Austria burn – nay more, gentlemen: we're watching Europe itself go up in flames! Store this moment in your memories. An entire civilization is turning to ashes on that plain where the fearless, useless soldiers of His Imperial and Royal Majesty are shedding their life-blood.

'But there's more to tonight than the combustion of Europe. What is, what was, Europe? An illusion, a spell! Europe has never existed, any more than the Alexandrian manuscripts which the Arabs reduced to dust were written by the trembling hands of the non-existent scribes of those non-existent places called Rome and Athens; and so, by burning Alexandria, the Arabs burnt no more than the detritus of nothingness, the mouldering dust of non-existence, you follow me? Ten centuries . . . No, I tell you,

330

not ten centuries . . . Spirals of reddish smoke above a seething river . . . A wilderness. A featureless, trackless, villageless universe devoid of written records . . . There never was a city named Vienna . . . And Europe, what is Europe? A tale told some day by old women to their grandchildren . . . And here are we, my friends, my dear friends, gathered together to keep vigil and hear the concluding words, the final snatches of that tale . . . *Has ultra metas requiescunt beatam spem expectantes . . .*'

The Prince de Ligne had listened respectfully to Weitzau's ravings. Not so Dr Ulhue, who inquired if Schwarzbrod had any vesicatories that might calm the general down. 'He'll have an apoplectic fit and die on us,' he said, but Schwarzbrod angrily turned his back. The din of battle was less continuous now, with long intervening lulls. Schwarzbrod had opened a window, and the night air smelt of hay and ashes. Duchess Clémence stood motionless at her husband's side, pale and numb. Audible between two prolonged fusillades were the croaking of frogs in the marshes bordering the Danube, the howling of dogs, the soughing of the dark wind, the stirrings of the exhausted but still unfinished night. Camp fires could be seen beyond the luminous river, and, clustered around each, a circle of flame-gilded silhouettes. Farther away the plain was in darkness except where more scattered fires seemed to burn in a void, like beacons at sea. From time to time a cornstook, or possibly a house, would burst into flames.

Conversation had been resumed, but in low, uneasy voices and halting little snippets. Schwarzbrod left his window and walked over to Duchess Clémence. Her obvious distress prompted him to try to console her in his clumsily sympathetic way, but she stared at him blankly. Dr Ulhue was amusing himself by idly pointing a telescope at the sky and the plain in turn, Countess Pietranera clinging to her handsome young captain's one remaining arm. Lawyer Apfelgrun had rejoined his wife, who was still conversing with the coadjutor of St Stephan's. He had cupped a hand to his ear and was nodding and smiling. General von Weitzau marched around with ursine tread and the air of a man in possession of horrific secrets. Duchess Gertrud had summoned the Prince de Ligne to sit beside her.

Ligne told Gertrud about a Greek Stoic who had bled himself to death in his bathtub – a favourite method of suicide in those days. Determined to make the most of the occasion, however, he had instructed a slave to open and close the veins in his wrist by turns, so as to savour the sensation of dying until the last possible moment.

Gertrud, a connoisseur of such matters, nodded approvingly. Ligne went on to say that Weitzau was a man inspired. They were indeed witnessing the death and burial of Europe, a spectacle imbued with funereal, voluptuous beauty. For himself, Ligne did not wish to survive the beloved society in which he had lived, luxuriated and waged war. They stood tonight on the threshold of a new society, and he had no desire to move into an abode so dirty, disorderly and uncongenial. Rather than pack his traps, he preferred to savour his era's lingering obsequies. Its final moments must not be marred by regrets. Weitzau had referred to the sacking of Rome by Alaric in the year 410. Perhaps this singular soirée overlooking the Danube was the echo, reflection or reverberation of another soirée, one held in the Eternal City fourteen centuries ago. Perhaps the patricians had forgathered in their villas to converse, drink and make love on the brink of the abyss, to watch the sun go down once more behind the Seven Hills while Asiatic hordes battered at the gates and Mongol horsemen were smashing the Coliseum's marble statues with sledgehammers. Ah yes, sighed the elderly charmer, how melancholy the moribund city must have been, and how sublime . . .

'I ask but one favour,' he told Gertrud in a confident, flippant tone, inclining his head towards her pink peruke, 'and that is to be granted sufficient composure to witness my own defeat – the downfall of a society that was, beyond doubt, the happiest of all societies . . .'

Gertrud asked him if the battle of Wagram was definitely lost. Ligne shrugged.

'One of my Parisian friends,' he said, 'a very dear friend,

the Comte de Brotteaux des Islettes, was sent to the guillotine in 1792. An eye-witness described his final moments to me. He alighted, a book in his hand, from the tumbrel in the Place de la Grève. They ripped his shirt open, cut off his hair, and bared his neck. He was then hustled towards the scaffold by one of those barefoot sansculottes, as they're so indelicately known. Brotteaux was quite unperturbed, it seems. The poor, illiterate imbecile jostled him even as he was mounting the steps, but he never stopped reading. His book landed in the bran tub at the same time as his head. It was an edition of Horace's *Odes* . . .'

The duchess gave a shrill, despairing laugh and repeated her question with a touch of annoyance. Was the battle lost?

'Who can tell?' Ligne replied at length. 'Defeat, victory – do they still have any meaning, those words? Both of them, defeat and victory, are lurking down there in the plain like lovers with their limbs entwined. Tomorrow one or other of them will stand revealed, Excellency, but that is unimportant. Our men may triumph or be routed, it will make no difference. The edifice is crumbling. We can delay its collapse for a year or two – a second or two in the light of eternity – but that's all. The ship's hold is ablaze, and we shall never reach the other shore. Napoleon and Charles are mere theatrical supernumeraries, my dear Gertrud. Their role consists in knocking on a door in the wings, only to be forbidden to enter by the real performers of the drama. We're survivors, you and I, and by "we" I mean our *salons*, our elegant ways, our bows and curtsies, our lechery, our literature. How can I put it? Our era has developed a hole, and pouring through it is a river of mud that will obliterate even the memory of bygone days. I ask you, what will remain of Mozart when the last note of *Don Giovanni* or *The Magic Flute* has been played?'

His voice became hushed.

'Ah, but how moving it is, that final note! It's the most precious note of all, and do you know why? Because it represents the threshold of silence. Beyond it lies the boundless realm of silence, and inherent in that final note are all the silences, the eternity of silences, to come . . .' He paused for a moment. 'Defeat, victory? Listen, Gertrud. We've experienced the Bastille, the Terror, *l'An II* and Valmy, then Bonaparte and Napoleon. Loathsome phenomena, perhaps, but merely tremors, dancing shadows, ripples of light on watered silk – nothing irremediable. All those terrible events took place on European soil, yet none of them put our civilization in jeopardy. No, believe me, there are other, less reversible phenomena.'

'Such as poor Louis's severed neck?' suggested Gertrud, sniggering behind her hand.

'His severed neck? A regrettable matter, certainly, but no more than that. Europe still has a whole warehouseful of monarchs to draw on, so it can't be called irreparable. No, the phenomenon I had in mind does not belong to the annals of history. In my view, what sounded the death-knell of our society was the introduction of the metric system in 1792, which also happened – *nota bene* – to be the year of the Terror. That was when the vile new age dawned. We now live in the world of the surveyor and measurer – in other words, of the race that will supersede humankind. The world has become susceptible of measurement, and so have freedom, happiness, even nothingness. The true demolishers of monarchy aren't Hoche or Napoleon, dear friend; they're the centimetre and the decalitre.'

'Really, Ligne!' snapped Gertrud. 'There are three hundred thousand soldiers asleep down there. They'll be beating their horrid drums like madmen in a few hours' time, yet all you can talk about is Mozart and the decalitre and a host of similar absurdities.'

'My dear Gertrud,' Ligne said quietly, 'that's precisely why I hate the French Revolution and the decimetre so much. I hate them for what they've made of war – for these butcheries, these . . . these mathematical massacres.'

'Did you know,' said the old lady, and her voice was trembling now, 'that Constanze Apfelgrun's son, Lieutenant Apfelgrun, is in the thick of that hurly-burly, and, to make matters worse, that he's serving in Napoleon's ranks?'

Ligne had heard so, yes. He wasn't personally acquainted with Lieutenant Apfelgrun, but yes, he knew.

'Are you thinking of your niece, the lovely Clémence?' he asked gently.

'Yes,' Gertrud mumbled, 'I am. She's much on my mind.'

*   *   *

Ligne insisted that his guests stay the night. The play wasn't over yet, he pointed out ironically, and it was bad form to leave a theatre during the interval. Nothing could be more humiliating to the cast. Besides, he said, the plot was shaping nicely, and everyone must be eager to know the dénouement. The coadjutor banished his ill humour long enough to tell an anecdote. He had once been summoned to Schönbrunn in the middle of the night to administer the last rites to an elderly courtier, Count Kohl. On entering the dying man's bedchamber, he'd thought he must be dreaming. Kohl was comfortably ensconced among his pillows with a book in his hand, namely, Mr Fielding's novel *Tom Jones*. After a few perfunctory words of welcome, Kohl had calmly read on.

'Your pardon, Monsignor,' he'd said. 'I appreciate your taking the trouble to give me extreme unction, but I don't have long to live. Kindly permit me to continue reading while you swing your censers. I'm anxious to know how *Tom Jones* turns out.'

Rooms had been prepared on Ligne's orders, and everyone, with the exception of Weitzau, retired for a few hours' sleep. The old general having dozed off in an armchair with a dead cigar in his fist, it was decided, because of his enormous weight, to leave him *in situ*. At four in the morning the guns began to thunder once more. Soon afterwards the sun rose in all its glory. Trumpets and bugles rang out, and the survivors of yesterday's carnage resumed their evolutions in the wheat-fields.

At ten or thereabouts, a messenger presented himself to the Prince de Ligne at the villa. A grain merchant from Baumersdorf, he had witnessed the capture of Deutsch-Wagram the day before. Bernadotte, at the head of his

Saxons, had passed through Raasdorf late in the afternoon and pushed on to Aderklaa. A deplorable incident had occurred on the banks of the Russbach, where a French regiment had mistaken Bernadotte's Saxons for Austrians. It was stupid of them, commented the grain merchant, since everyone knew that the Saxons now formed part of the Grande Armée, but it had to be conceded in fairness that the light was poor and the air thick with smoke.

Undeterred, Bernadotte had pressed on into Wagram, which was defended by Austrians – genuine Austrians this time. The grain merchant had hidden in the presbytery to watch. 'It was a massacre, Excellency,' he kept on repeating, 'a veritable massacre!' The Saxons, already decimated by their French allies, sustained a fierce Austrian counter-attack. The grain merchant had heard the two sides exchanging insults in German. The Austrian cuirassiers eventually yielded under the Saxon onslaught. 'They were blindly running each other through – spitting each other like quails. The village street was littered with corpses!' Then the Austrians launched a second counterattack and recaptured Wagram. 'The Saxons fled,' said the man, ' – or rather, what was left of them.'

Duchess Clémence had listened to this recital without a tremor. She continued to observe the course of the battle through binoculars, leaning on a windowsill at her husband's side. From time to time she would ask him to explain some point of detail. Towards the middle of the afternoon it became clear that the French left wing was giving ground under pressure from the Austrian right. Victory seemed imminent. An exultant roar shook the walls of Vienna. Thousands of handkerchiefs, parasols and hats were waved in the air, thousands of voices exhorted the monarchy's gallant soldiers to cut Napoleon's flanks to ribbons. Patriotic songs and paeans of triumph echoed and re-echoed from every rooftop. The Austrian victory was confirmed by the arrival of an orderly from O'Reilly: His Excellency the Prince of Saxe-Salza was requested to present himself without delay at the Hofburg, there to organize a fitting reception for the victors of Deutsch-Wagram. Prince Ernst departed with an air of self-importance.

After seeing him to his carriage, the Prince de Ligne rejoined his guests, who were celebrating with champagne. He helped himself to some, went to the window, and studied the course of the battle intently. Then he turned and raised his glass.

'Let us toast our victory at once, my friends, for another quarter of an hour will transform it into defeat. It's always wise to make the most of a fleeting victory. We've ample time for mourning, but only fifteen minutes in which to rejoice. Archduke Charles is as good as beaten. He has no reserves, whereas Napoleon . . . Look, the plain is swarming with Frenchmen.'

An hour later the merchant from Baumersdorf returned with another report. He confirmed Ligne's dire prognostications – the Austrians were in full retreat – and added a number of details. Bernadotte's Saxons, the remnants of Lieutenant-Colonel Adegauer's regiment, having recaptured Aderklaa in the small hours, had looted the abandoned houses, celebrated their success by drinking deep, and settled down in various farmyards for a nap. Soon afterwards a surprise attack by a squadron of Austrian cavalry had inflicted more heavy losses on them.

Other preposterous incidents had occurred. An Italian contingent, also mistaking the Saxons for enemies instead of allies, had opened fire on them at point-blank range. Then, as they had the night before, the Austrians had completed the massacre. 'Those poor Saxons seem fated,' said the merchant. 'They're always being mistaken for what they aren't, and everyone keeps laying into them.' Napoleon had finally routed the Austrians, however, and Archduke Charles's men were now fleeing towards the mountains of Bohemia.

Ligne's steward and butler served a makeshift supper. The prince offered a graceful apology for its shortcomings. The battle had run late, he explained. Napoleon was brisker as a rule. He normally wrapped up a victory within twelve hours, leaving no loose ends. Wagram had lasted three times as long and ended in gory confusion. The Emperor of

337

the French was clearly growing old – slowing down a little.

Eager to enliven the proceedings, Ligne ordered scores of candles to be lit and regaled the company with personal reminiscences. He recalled the Seven Years' War, the campaign he'd fought at Potemkin's side in 1788, his visits to Versailles. Countess Pietranera chaffed him on his chequered career. Was it true that he'd enjoyed the favours of the Marquise de Coigny? Ligne feigned annoyance. Flaring up into one of his 'straw fires', as he called his shortlived fits of temper, he protested that the Marquise de Coigny had allayed the suspicions of the Duc le Lauzun himself.

'Excellency,' he said, 'the Marquise de Coigny knew precisely what pace to set. She went so far and no farther. Even her motto played havoc with the ladies of Versailles and blighted their easy-going ways. "Never take a lover," she used to say, "for that is tantamount to surrender." '

'Heavens,' retorted Countess Pietranera, 'what a ninny the woman was! Personally, I employ the opposite tactic. Surrender is my path to conquest.'

Her handsome young captain preened himself. Schwarzbrod, who was still standing beside Duchess Clémence, neighed with laughter whenever Ligne produced a spicy, frivolous anecdote. Clémence, looking very pale, smiled and said nothing. Weitzau's silence might have been attributable either to the prostration of defeat or to the fact that he had exhausted his stock of ideas the previous night. Dr Ulhue made the best of things by coining a few reasonably adequate *bons mots*, but their quality went largely unappreciated on such a melancholy occasion. The warmth of the night delighted Countess Pietranera because it gave her an excuse to open her fan and shock the coadjutor.

It was close on midnight when the party broke up. Summoned to the door by footmen, a succession of carriages and barouches drove off with much jingling of harness bells and cracking of whips. The old prince stood at the foot of the steps with a lantern held high above his head. When the last conveyance had disappeared into the night, he extinguished the lantern and continued to stand there in the gloom.

Clémence's coachman, now wearing a bicorn with a red cockade, had returned from the Hofburg. When she told him to take the dirt road leading down to the Danube, he objected that it would be dangerous. French soldiers, snipers and marauders were bound to be lurking in the woods. Besides, he said, His Excellency Prince Ernst was expecting Her Excellency at the Kärntnertor. Clémence lost her temper. She would gladly have horsewhipped the man. He reluctantly obeyed, having to rein back with all his might while descending the uneven track, which was littered with loose stones. It petered out on the edge of a clump of oak trees, but Clémence could already hear frogs croaking and river water gurgling amid the furze and tall grass. She got out and walked off, with Arcola frisking along beside her despite his gammy leg.

Not caring that the Danube would presumably be guarded by French soldiers, she headed for the river bank and made her way along it. The sky began to pale. The greenish light and the mist on the water gave promise of a fine day to come. She heard isolated shots, muffled oaths, men hawking and spitting. A little while later the cocks started crowing. Arcola barked indignantly, other dogs howled in response, and the frogs continued their unending chorus.

Clémence sighted a French picket encamped around a brazier on the river bank and trudged towards them across the marshy ground, tearing her gown on brambles as she went. She told the sergeant in command that she was the wife of a Saxon officer and must get across the river at all costs, but the sergeant curtly informed her that, 'on orders from above', no one was allowed across. He shook his men awake, and they surrounded her, grim-faced. Pretending to retrace her steps in the direction of Vienna, she made her way along the towpath to a small jetty about half a mile downstream. The lone sentry guarding it seized her roughly by the arm. He had small, very close-set eyes and a ferocious expression on his sallow, sickly face. When Arcola growled at him, he swung his musket butt at the dog but missed.

339

Clémence shook him off with ease. She could easily have escaped, because he was not only encumbered by his equipment but also swaying with fatigue and brandy. Instead of running away, however, she confronted the man in silence. Her altercation with the soldiers who had proposed to search her on the way to Ligne's villa was still fresh in her mind, and she had no wish to lose her temper this time. The man made no attempt to recapture her. Whether or not it was a trick of the grey dawn light, he seemed frightened, with little flecks of foam on his lips. He backed away, muttering to himself as if terrified by the thought of being touched by this white-faced woman, and levelled his bayonet at her.

Clémence took hold of the blade and gently thrust it aside, then walked to the end of the jetty with Arcola at her heels. The sentry followed, shouting obscenities. Clémence told him to hold his tongue and untie for her a small green dinghy bobbing six feet from the jetty. Arcola, having watched this operation, declined to get in. The swirling water held no appeal for him, so Clémence bullied the soldier into carrying him aboard. But then, when they were in midstream, the man wavered. He let go of the oars and gripped the thwart as though half-inclined to jump overboard. The dinghy drifted off course and began to rotate, but Clémence berated the reluctant oarsman and he started rowing again.

When they got to the other bank she produced a gold coin from under her cloak. The man bit it, then swiftly stowed it away in his greatcoat pocket. Clémence chose a path at random and set off. She stumbled into shell holes and over ruts made by convoys of artillery and waggons belonging to the supply train. As it rose above the Carpathians the sun illuminated a horrific scene of devastation. Fire had left nothing untouched, and the ground was covered with a layer of ash. A white percheron lay on its side, pawing at the intestines spilling from its belly. The soldiers Clémence passed looked like charcoal-burners, with blackened faces and eyes of preternatural size and brilliance.

A murderous engagement had taken place here. Men

were groaning, stirring slowly, feebly, as if trapped in birdlime. Their bodies were incomplete, short of limbs, bereft of bits and pieces. They strove with infantile deliberation to relearn the art of walking, only to fall back into the ashes, the charred stems of wheat. Soldiers of the Grande Armée's medical corps were hard at work. They stooped, picked up corpses, and tossed them over the rails of open carts. Other waggons were already piled high with bodies in uniforms of every shade, all jumbled together, as if it were war's preposterous function to shuffle soldiers like cards and arrange them in multicoloured packs.

Clémence made her way through villages, across fields and gardens. Whenever she was stopped by enemy soldiers or gendarmes, she had only to look at them, showing no rancour, more pityingly than anything else, and they stood aside to let her pass. A French sergeant, bareheaded and musketless, walked ahead of her for a while. He was holding one mangled arm in the air to stem the blood that had formed a hard brown crust on the empty sleeve of his greatcoat. At some stage Clémence was assaulted by a burly peasant. She made no attempt to defend herself, just waited for him to finish. He did as best he could, ripping her gown and undergarments as if unwrapping a parcel or preparing to wash a corpse and lay it out. Not a word passed his lips. He performed his arduous, wearisome task with stolid perseverance while Arcola leapt repeatedly at his throat and even succeeded in lacerating it. Afterwards, Clémence walked on. She gazed up at the sun, observed its progress across the sky. Red as blood, it climbed to the zenith and began to sink. Its light was unreflected by the world beneath. Shine as it might, the fields remained as grey and black as ever.

Clémence put one foot before the other, clumsily but with extreme care, like an automaton in the Prater fairground. She gathered some carrots in a field and unearthed a solitary beetroot. If she sighted a corpse, or rather, since the men so often lay in heaps, a cluster of corpses, she would kneel to satisfy herself that her lover was not there. Sometimes a face would be obscured by the tatters of its owner's uniform, and she had to uncover it before continuing on her way. She discarded the carrots but kept the beetroot. When evening came, an elderly French sergeant-major took pity on her. He gave her a mess tin of hot turnip and potato soup, asked what she was doing in this hell-hole, and offered to escort her to a barn he had found near Aderklaa. She declined his invitation to sleep there and asked the way to Deutsch-Wagram.

It was still a fair distance, but the moon was bright and the sky resembled a mirror with tenuous wisps of smoke drifting across it. The bodies littering the fields were alternately steeped in Indian ink and quicksilver. When the moon disappeared behind a cloud and prevented Clémence from seeing faces clearly, she would run her hands over them and explore their contours with her fingertips. The houses of Deutsch-Wagram were now a mile or two away, she estimated. The grain merchant from Baumersdorf, a funny little man with a nervous manner, had spoken of the Saxons being routed at Aderklaa. He hadn't known if Adegauer's regiment was among them, but the Austrians had certainly given them a drubbing, after which the Italians had fired on them at point-black range. Worst of all, though, according to the grain merchant, had been the fighting at Deutsch-Wagram. Clémence still recalled his words to the Prince de Ligne: 'A mêlée, Excellency, a murderous mêlée! Those Saxons were spitted like quails . . .'

The moon vanished and the night became very dark. It occurred to Clémence that she had lost a shoe. She kept slipping, tripping over tree stumps and rocks, bumping into shattered gun carriages. She also stumbled over yielding objects. When that happened she knelt and touched a face or an arm or a dolman, but only fleetingly: otherwise she told herself, she would never get to Deutsch-Wagram in time. Arcola was exhausted by now. His old injury must have been paining him, because he could only keep up with Clémence by performing a series of ungainly little leaps. He licked her face when she fell over, then barked and pranced around as she struggled to her feet.

342

The lights of Deutsch-Wagram came into view. From the way they twinkled, Clémence guessed that the village lay beyond some trees, whose branches were stirring noiselessly in the gentle breeze. She tried to jump a small ravine, but her strength was failing. She landed short and tumbled to the bottom, hauled herself a little way up the side by clinging to shrubs and tufts of grass, let go and fell back again. Arcola had remained where he was. He craned over the edge and sniffed the empty air before climbing down, but his injured leg gave way and he tumbled to the bottom. Whimpering, he laboriously reascended the slope. He barked, but nobody came, so he scrambled down again. Clémence made another attempt to haul herself up by some brambles, only to sink to the ground in a dead faint. Arcola sat down beside her. After a while he laid one paw on her shoulder, yelping plaintively from time to time.

★   ★   ★

Deutsch-Wagram was less than a quarter of a mile away. A number of the villagers' charred, smoke-blackened stables and byres had been requisitioned as infirmaries by the surgeons of the Grande Armée. Otto, his chest torn open by a howitzer shell, was lying in a farmyard on some bales of hay. He had lost a great deal of blood. The same shell had wounded Matthias in the stomach. The old orderly had fallen at his lieutenant's side while defending a small bridge over the Russbach, but his wound had seemed less serious and his constitution was more robust. He had played dead and waited for the Austrians to withdraw before attending to Otto, who was still bleeding profusely. Half carrying, half dragging him, Matthias had covered the three or four long miles to the farmyard. Otto had groaned as his lolling head bounced across the stones in their path. It had been midday when their trek began. The battle had ended the previous night, and now another night had come – almost another dawn.

Matthias had a raging fever. He was holding his stomach with one hand because his wound, which he had plugged

343

with rags, was hurting him. His other arm encircled Otto. Although Otto's lips moved, he was past speaking. Nothing could be heard save the whisper of his breathing, which had been strong during the day but was now very faint. It seemed to come from far away. Matthias cupped a hand to his ear: 'My lieutenant,' he murmured, 'my little lieutenant . . .' Then: 'My dear little lieutenant . . .' He wasn't holding his stomach any longer. He had taken Otto in his arms and was rocking back and forth with the young man's head clasped to his broad chest.